MASTER OF ROME

JOHN STACK was born and lives in County Cork. He has always wanted to write but has done a variety of jobs ending up in IT. He is married with three children, and is the author of *The Sunday Times* bestselling MASTERS OF THE SEA series. His new novel ARMADA will be published in 2012.

Also by John Stack

Ship of Rome
Captain of Rome

JOHN STACK

Master of Rome

HARPER

Harper
HarperCollins*Publishers*
77–85 Fulham Palace Road,
Hammersmith, London W6 8JB

www.harpercollins.co.uk

This paperback edition 2011
2

First published in Great Britain
by HarperCollins*Publishers* 2011

A catalogue record for this book
is available from the British Library

ISBN: 978-0-00-742622-5

This novel is entirely a work of fiction.
The incidents and some of the characters portrayed in it
while based on real historical events and figures,
are the work of the author's imagination.

Set in Minion by Palimpsest Book Production,
Falkirk, Stirlingshire

Printed and bound in Great Britain by
Clays Ltd, St Ives plc

Find out more about HarperCollins and the environment at
www.harpercollins.co.uk/green

For Adrienne

ACKNOWLEDGEMENTS

Thanks to my agent, Bill Hamilton, who set me on the road, and all the team at A.M. Heath, in particular Jennifer Custer, Kate Rizzo Munson and Vickie Dillon, for all their hard work.

Thanks to HarperCollins*Publishers*; my editor, Susan Watt, for her support, insight and tenacious editing, and to Elizabeth Dawson and the team in Ireland: Moira Reilly and Tony Purdue.

Thanks to Ann Luttrell and Ben Cuddihy of the Triskel Arts Centre for all their local support in Cork.

Thanks to my Mum and Dad, Gerard and Catherine, whose enthusiasm always outstrips my own, and to my Mum- and Dad-in-law, John and Frances Moran, and also Aunty Pam Moran, for their support, not just of me, but of my family.

Thanks to the extended clan, Colm, Pam, Karen, Paul, Fiona and Doreen.

And finally thanks to Adrienne for all her support and love, who celebrates with me on the good days and commiserates with me on the bad, and thanks to my kids, Zoe, Andrew and Amy, who always point and shout loudly when they see my books in the shops.

TUNIS, NORTH AFRICA. 255 BC

The colossal animal surged forward against the crack of the bullwhip, its momentum increasing into an unstoppable charge as it bellowed in anger and terror, the scent of men fuelling its rage. It lifted its head and gazed ahead through hooded yellow eyes. The scene before it was a blur of movement, a dark horde that threw up a terrifying wall of sound; the hammering of ten thousand shields, the war cries of a multitude. The elephant bellowed once more, sweeping its scimitar-shaped tusks high into the air as the whip cracked against its hide.

The ground beneath the beast trembled and shook. Dust smothered its throat, the thirst maddening, while slowly the host before the creature drifted into focus, the mass into individual men. A sharp pain shot through the elephant's flank and it immediately turned its head to the site of injury, the blood stark against the grey hide. Every instinct called for flight, but years of brutal training demanded obedience and the bullwhip drove the creature on.

The elephant crashed headlong into a wall of shields and the war cries of men changed to screams of pain, the momentum of the creature's charge driving it deep into the Roman maniples. The legionaries struck out with shield and sword while overhead volleys of spears rained down to strike deep into exposed flesh, the unceasing pain driving the elephant into frenzied terror. The creature swept its tusks before it, scything through the massed ranks, cutting through flesh and armour. It raised its trunk, a spray of pink blood gushing forth from the fluid filling its punctured lungs, while its feet crashed down on the fallen, crushing bone and cartilage as the death cries of man and beast filled the air.

The Roman line buckled and caved before the momentum of the elephant charge was absorbed and then slowly repelled, the strength of twelve thousand legionaries pitted against the might of a hundred elephants. The front ranks shattered but fought on, the inescapable fight driving them to mindless courage, with men standing their ground against creatures that killed and maimed relentlessly until the burden of countless wounds drove them to their knees. Those who remained advanced against the Carthaginian phalanx that shadowed the elephant attack, but again the Romans were checked as cries of alarm swept across their lines.

The Carthaginian horse, four thousand strong, raced across the open ground, the routed Roman cavalry in their wake, the light-horsemen loosing spears at full gallop into the exposed Roman right flank. The maniples turned to engage. The centre became a confusion of commands and alarm as the enemy cavalry swept around the rear of the Roman formation. The legions ceased to advance, the fight on all sides. The order to 'steady the line' was given, a desperate command to stand fast, to take strength and fight against all odds.

The Carthaginians pressed inward, the cavalry driving their mounts ever on against upturned shields, the riders striking down with spear and sword. The maniples stepped back, the fallen trampled under hoof as legionaries struggled to wield their swords in the crush, the men to their rear unable to assist as the battle descended into butchery. In the centre, desperate commanders roared hopeless orders, the ever-tightening vice robbing them of the chance to break out while the battle line closed in from all sides, the Carthaginians advancing relentlessly, giving no quarter, their hatred for the Roman invader feeding their strength and determination as warriors pushed forward to fight in the front line, eager to bloody their swords, the pressure on the Roman lines never abating until the last man fell under Phoenician steel.

CHAPTER ONE

The searing wind swept through the streets of Aspis and beyond to the harbour, the parched air whipping the wave crests of the gentle swell into a fine spray, as if greedily clawing at the water after its five-hundred-mile trek across the arid Sahara. Atticus stepped out from the lee of a building into the flow of air and turned his face into the wind, breathing in deeply, sensing the enormity of the mysterious land in darkness before him, the hostile territory of the Carthaginians that pressed against the boundaries of the Roman-held port. He spotted the man he had searched for at the end of the street, and approached, the centurion turning to acknowledge him.

'Cursed wind,' he said.

Atticus nodded. 'The Sirocco,' he replied, remembering his grandfather's teaching, and how that same wind shrouded his home city of Locri on the south coast of Italy with oppressive humidity every spring. 'Any sign?' he asked.

'None,' Septimus replied, and the two men lapsed once more into silence as the predawn light began to illuminate the landscape before them.

The land along the coast was green and fertile, stretching east a thousand leagues to Egypt and west to the Pillars of Hercules. For forty generations it had been home to the Carthaginians, protected along its length by a mighty fleet that controlled the trading routes of the southern Mediterranean; until a year before, when the Romans humbled the Carthaginian navy at Cape Ecnomus, and thereafter invaded the once inviolate shores of North Africa. Now, not fifty miles to the west, the Roman army, fifteen thousand strong, were engaged with the Carthaginians near Tunis while the men at Aspis, Atticus and Septimus amongst them, waited impatiently for news.

Atticus looked to the eastern sky, watching slowly as the crimson skyline dissolved at the approach of the sun, the orb finally cresting the horizon with a spear of white light that flashed across the blue-grey sky. He looked over his shoulder and turned to walk back down the deserted street to the harbour. He paused at the water's edge, his gaze ranging over the forty galleys tugging gently on their anchor lines near the shore. As a *praefectus classis*, a prefect of the fleet, these ships were under his command, and his own galley, the quinquereme *Orcus*, was moored in the centre of the formation. Atticus studied the fleet with a practised eye, watching as men moved slowly on the decks without command, the routine of naval life dictating their actions, the only sound the howling wind that masked all others.

Atticus had come ashore an hour before, succumbing to a sudden compulsion to escape the confines of the *Orcus*, anxious to learn if any messenger had arrived during the night. It was an escape he had never sought from his previous ship, the *Aquila*, and he wondered if there would ever come a time when he would consider the *Orcus* as anything more than just another ship of the *Classis Romanus*, the fleet of Rome.

He turned once more to the figure standing at the end of the street, the centurion's tall stature imposing even from fifty yards. Septimus was motionless, standing resolutely in the face of the wind, his attention still fully drawn to the far southern horizon. Atticus began to walk back towards him. He glanced left and right down the narrow laneways as he walked, briefly spying individual or small groups of legionaries, the men emerging slowly from the homes that had been commandeered to house them, just ahead of the clarion call of the *vigilae*, the night guardsmen ending their watch by rousing the camp. He looked once more to Septimus and immediately noticed the tension in the centurion's shoulders, his body leaning forward at the waist. Atticus quickened his pace but, before he could cover the distance, Septimus swept his sword from his scabbard, the metallic sound caught and whipped away by the wind. The centurion turned, his eyes seeing beyond Atticus to the street behind.

'To arms!' he shouted. 'Sound the alarm!'

'What is it?' Atticus asked, and Septimus indicated over his shoulder to the horizon beyond.

'Drusus!' the centurion roared, searching amongst the soldiers that were appearing from every street. He spotted him within a second, the *optio* pushing his way through to the front of the gathering force, his ever-stern expression hiding his surprise at the sudden call to arms.

'Drusus, get to the officers' quarters. Inform the centurions I want them to form a battle line from this central point.'

The *optio* saluted, hammering his fist into his chest plate and turned to push his way back along the street. Septimus was fundamentally of the same rank as every other marine centurion of the fleet; but, given his experience and his position as centurion of the *Orcus*, the prefect's command ship, the other officers readily deferred to his orders. Within a minute the soldiers were forming on his position.

Septimus stood by Atticus as the prefect looked to the southern horizon.

'How many do you think there are?' Atticus asked.

7

'Hard to be sure,' Septimus replied. 'Over a thousand at least.'

Atticus nodded, concurring with the estimate. He turned and grabbed a legionary from the throng behind him. 'Get back to the *Orcus* and have my second-in-command report here,' he ordered and the soldier was away.

Septimus stepped out from the confines of the street on to the flat expanse of beaten earth at the rear of the town. The soldiers surged out behind him and began to form into disciplined maniples, the shouted commands of centurions and *optiones* filling the air as the ranks were formed and the battle line was drawn. The manoeuvre was repeated along the length of the town, the men keeping their helmet-covered heads slightly lowered in the face of the wind. The entire marine complement of the fleet was ashore, sixty men for each galley, legionaries all, and the line was dressed to form a shield wall over two thousand strong.

'Something's wrong,' Septimus muttered, his eyes focused on the approaching force. 'They're not formed into ranks.'

'I see it,' Atticus replied, noting the disorganized approach, so dissimilar to the serried ranks of the legionaries.

'Prefect,' Atticus heard, and he turned to see his second-in-command beside him. 'Baro,' Atticus began. 'Ready the squadron for battle and station two galleys in the outer harbour.'

'Yes, Prefect,' Baro replied, and took off at a run.

'Thermae,' Atticus said by way of explanation, and Septimus nodded, remembering the simultaneous land and sea attacks the Carthaginians had employed there.

The minutes drew out slowly as the approaching force wheeled towards Aspis, its formation still chaotic, the cloud of dust raised by their feet whipping towards the town on the constant wind.

'Two thousand,' Septimus muttered as the decreasing

8

distance increased his estimate, his eyes constantly checking the eastern and western approaches for additional forces, but finding none. He glanced down the line and saw many of the men inch forward, the anticipation of battle wrestling with ingrained discipline.

'Steady, boys,' he roared, and the shout was taken up by the other centurions, the legionaries redressing the line until it became firm once more.

Atticus glanced over his shoulder, seeing past the ranks and down the street to the sliver of harbour in view, watching as one galley then another passed through his field of vision, the wind robbing him of the sound of shouted orders only a hundred yards away. He looked to his front again, the approaching force now less than six hundred yards away, the horizon behind them clear. The sight puzzled Atticus, but he cast his questions aside, making ready to turn his back and return to the *Orcus*. The legionaries were more than a match for the disorganized men approaching and Atticus was anxious to return to his galley and take command of the fleet. He turned to the centurion.

'Septimus, I'm returning to the *Orcus*. I'll station two signal men on the shore to keep—'

'They're *velites*!' a shout went up, and the men began to mutter as they looked to confirm the report.

'Silence in the ranks!' Septimus roared. He held a hand out to the left side of his face to shield his eyes from the glare of the sun, trying to single out individual men.

'I don't believe . . .' he whispered after a moment. 'They are *velites*, light infantry. They're our own men.'

'This could be a trick,' Atticus said, the memory of Thermae still fresh.

Septimus nodded. 'Ready *pila*!' he shouted, and the *hastati*, the junior soldiers, raised their spears.

The men approaching were shouting, their voices borne on

the wind sweeping over the Roman line, their words interlaced into a confusion of sound, until one command carried above the rest, 'Hold! Do not loose,' and many of the *hastati* began to lower their spears.

'Stand ready!' Septimus roared, not daring to relinquish the advantage until he was sure, the sight of the Roman uniforms in conflict with his caution.

The men swept on but slowed as they narrowed the distance, wary of the inflexible line of shields facing them, the spear tips visible above the ranks, ready to strike forward. Eventually the advance petered out, the men forming into a ragged line a hundred yards short of the shield wall.

Atticus stepped forward from the Roman line. 'Who commands there?' he shouted across, and a soldier stepped forward, his hand held away from the hilt of his sword. His uniform was dust-stained and his face was creased with fatigue, but he held himself tall and he crossed the gap quickly to stand before Atticus and Septimus.

'I am Servius Salinator,' he said, 'commander of the Etruscan infantry.'

'Atticus Milonius Perennis, prefect of the fleet, and this is Septimus Laetonius Capito, centurion of the *Orcus*.'

The man saluted Atticus and nodded to Septimus.

'You are part of the proconsul's army,' Atticus said, and Salinator nodded, his expression strained. 'Then where are the legions?' Atticus continued. 'And why do you march out of formation?'

'The Sixth and Ninth legions are no more,' Salinator said, his voice laced with anger and shock. 'They have been defeated, near Tunis.'

'By the gods . . .' Septimus whispered, his thoughts immediately on the men of the Ninth, the legion he had served with for so many years.

Atticus stepped forward, his mind reeling as he grabbed Salinator's arm. 'Come with me,' he said, and he led him through the shield wall, leaving Septimus standing alone. The centurion gathered his wits and turned to his men. 'Stand down the line!' he shouted, and the order was repeated, prompting the Etruscans to move forward once more.

Septimus quickly followed Salinator as Atticus led him to the officers' quarters overlooking the harbour. The building was deserted and the three men stepped out of the warm breeze into the cool, dark interior, Atticus's eyes never leaving Salinator as they settled around a table. 'What happened?' he asked.

The Etruscan drew the back of his hand across his mouth. 'We met the enemy on a plain south of Tunis two days ago,' he began, his eyes, unseeing, fixed on the rough grain of the table. 'The Carthaginians attacked first, in the centre, with elephants, at least a hundred of the infernal beasts, charging in front of their infantry.' Salinator shook his head, 'The legions . . . they just stood their ground, to a man. It was the most . . .' He trailed off and Septimus straightened his back as he thought of the incredible courage.

'We were on the left flank, facing the enemy's mercenaries,' Salinator continued, his face showing the disdain he felt for the hired soldiers, 'and the cavalry was on the right. We broke through easily but the cavalry were routed. They were outnumbered, four, maybe five to one. They never stood a chance.'

'And the centre?' Atticus asked.

'After our horse fled, the Carthaginian cavalry attacked the right flank and swept around the rear. Some of the *hastati* broke through the elephant charge, but they were swallowed by the enemy infantry, and the bulk of the legions were trapped by the cavalry. We re-engaged on the right and the proconsul broke out with maybe five hundred men, but they were isolated and surrounded again and we were pushed back, so I ordered a fighting retreat.'

'You fled and left the legions trapped?' Septimus said, rising to his feet, his fists balled by his side.

'There was nothing we could do,' Salinator replied, standing to face down Septimus. 'If we'd stood our ground we would have been slaughtered like the legions.'

'So you ran,' Septimus said contemptuously, 'and saved your own skin.'

'Enough!' Atticus shouted, and stood to lean between the two soldiers. He turned to Salinator. 'Did you see the proconsul fall?' he asked.

The Etruscan tore his eyes from Septimus and looked to Atticus, the anger in his eyes never abating. 'No,' he replied after a moment. 'I think he was captured but I can't be sure.'

'What does it matter?' Septimus said, turning away from the table, concern for the Ninth overwhelming him.

'Were you pursued?' Atticus asked.

'I don't think so,' Salinator replied and, looking at Atticus, he spoke aloud a thought that had plagued him during his flight from the battle. 'But with the legions destroyed, nothing stands between Tunis and here.'

Atticus nodded and walked from the table. Salinator sat down again, his gaze moving to Septimus, his mouth creased in anger once more.

Suddenly a clarion call of alarm sounded, followed by another and then another, until they overlapped to form a continuous sound.

Salinator shot up once more, panic in his face. 'We were followed; the Carthaginians are attacking.'

'No,' Atticus said, his expression equally dread-filled, but for another reason. 'Those are naval horns.' He rushed to the door, pushing it open to run outside, his eyes blinking rapidly in the sunlight after the gloom of the interior. His gaze swept the seaward horizon. He felt Septimus come out to stand beside him, but his focus never left the fearsome sight that had prompted the sound of alarm from the galleys of the fleet. Atticus instinctively reached for the hilt of his sword.

'Poseidon protect us . . .' he whispered, and he broke into a run as he headed down to the shoreline, calling to the nearest galley to launch its skiff. In the distance, the dark-hulled Carthaginian galleys continued to deploy across the mouth of the harbour, their number already exceeding a hundred, the windblown waves dashing against their rams as their oars crashed endlessly into the restless sea.

Marcus Atilius Regulus straightened his back as he heard footsteps approaching the door, the proconsul drawing himself to his full height in the darkened, airless room. He stepped into one of the shafts of sunlight permitted by the shuttered window, feeling the sweat roll down his back in the infernal heat. He blinked a bead of moisture from his eye. Regulus was nearing fifty years old but his body was that of a younger man, the harsh campaigning of the previous twelve months having stripped his frame of the softness that had accumulated over many comfortable years in the Roman Senate.

He was thirsty, the meagre amphora of brackish water he had been given the night before long since gone, and he licked his lips to moisten them, conscious that his first words should not be spoken with a cracked voice. He watched the door shudder as a harsh metallic sound cut through the near silence; the room was flooded with harsh sunlight as the door was opened. Regulus squinted against the light but he resisted the urge to wipe the blindness from his eyes, instead staring directly ahead to the two figures facing him. They were both soldiers, but senior in rank, their bearing revealing the arrogance and confidence of command.

The younger man entered first. He was Carthaginian, his uniform of the style that Regulus had come to loathe over the previous months. He looked the proconsul in the eye, staring at him as if in fascination, studying him, and Regulus returned the gaze, suddenly conscious of the soiled, sweat-stained tunic he was wearing. The other man stepped in. He was taller than the Carthaginian, his skin a paler complexion, and his gaze wandered the room before settling on the Roman, a half-smile of disdain creasing the edge of his mouth.

'You are Regulus,' the Carthaginian said; more a statement than a question, but the proconsul nodded in reply regardless.

'I am Hamilcar Barca,' the Carthaginian continued. 'And this is Xanthippus.'

Regulus held his tongue, taking the moment of silence to study the men anew. He had heard their names many times over the course of the year-long campaign – from ally and captured foe alike. Hamilcar Barca was the overall commander of the Carthaginian forces, and Xanthippus, the Spartan mercenary, hired to command their army after their overwhelming defeat at Adys over a year ago, the man who had given the enemy victory only two days before at Tunis.

'What of my men?' Regulus asked, speaking for the first time, his voice low and hard in an effort to instil authority in his question.

'Sit down,' Hamilcar replied, indicating the single chair against the far wall.

Regulus glanced over his shoulder but remained standing. He stared into the Carthaginian's face, keeping his expression unreadable. Hamilcar stepped forward.

'Sit down,' he repeated menacingly. 'Or I will have my men come in and strap you to the chair.'

Regulus hesitated a second longer and then moved slowly to the far wall, sitting down in one fluid movement as if by choice.

Hamilcar smiled, although the gesture did not reach his eyes. 'For now your men are in the prison beneath this fortress,' he replied, his eyes never leaving those of the proconsul's. 'I have not yet decided their fate.'

'They are soldiers captured in battle,' Regulus said, leaning forward. 'Their lives must be spared.'

'They are Roman,' Hamilcar shot back. 'And their lives are forfeit to the whim of Carthage.'

Regulus made to retort but again he held his tongue, sensing that to antagonize the Carthaginian further was to risk the lives of the five hundred legionaries who had been captured with him. He repeated the number in his mind. Five hundred out of an army of twelve thousand. He whispered a prayer to Mars, the god of war, as he struggled to keep the burden of the terrible loss hidden from his enemy.

'You are defeated, Roman,' Hamilcar said, as if reading Regulus's thoughts. 'Your army is no more and your invasion is finished.'

'Is that why you have come here, Carthaginian?' Regulus retorted. 'To tell me this. To mock me?'

'No,' Hamilcar replied, stepping forward once more until he stood over Regulus. 'Your light infantry escaped our grasp at Tunis and have fled to Aspis. I have come here to demand you order those forces to surrender.'

'Surrender?' Regulus scoffed. 'The fleet at Aspis will already have evacuated them. There will be no surrender.'

'You are wrong, Roman,' Hamilcar replied, the arrogance of the proconsul stirring his anger. 'The port is blockaded and your fleet is trapped, and if you do not order those men to surrender, I will kill every last one of them.'

Regulus was stunned into silence, his mind racing to devise an alternative.

'You have until tomorrow to decide,' Hamilcar said, and he turned and left the room, Xanthippus following without a backward glance.

Regulus stood up as the door was closed, the room once more plunging into semi-darkness. He breathed in deeply, trying to clear his thoughts, but the warm air caught in his throat and he coughed violently. He reached out instinctively for the amphora and picked it up, remembering immediately that it was empty, and he threw it at the wall in anger, the clay shattering into a dozen pieces.

Over a year ago he had sailed south in triumph from Cape Ecnomus. He had met the Carthaginian army at Adys and swept them aside, had taken Tunis without a fight and had plundered the land around Carthage. The war was won, the enemy beaten on all fronts and, conscious that his consulship was nearing its end and that a successor could arrive any day from Rome to steal his victory, he had confidently sent envoys to Carthage with his terms for their surrender: abandon Sicily, disband the navy and admit total defeat.

Even now Regulus remembered the anger he had felt when the Carthaginians refused his terms. Thereafter he had spent every waking hour preparing his army for the moment the enemy would dare to step outside the city. They had emerged, a new leader at their head, and Regulus had marched on to the plains south of Tunis, ready to deliver the fatal blow that would finally subdue the Carthaginians.

But that victory had been snatched from him, replaced with ignominious defeat, and Regulus cursed Fortuna for the ruina- tion of his fate. He strode to the shuttered window and squinted through a crack in the timber to gaze at the city of Tunis spread out before him. In the distance, a dark pall of smoke rose from the plain, the funeral pyre of the battlefield, and Regulus whispered a prayer once more for the lives of twelve thousand men.

'We should attack now,' Xanthippus said as he followed Hamilcar across the battlements, 'before the enemy becomes entrenched.'

'No, I cannot risk the destruction of the Roman fleet. I need those galleys intact. We will wait,' Hamilcar replied, turning to look out from the heights of the fortress over the city of Tunis, the late evening sunlight reflecting off the taller buildings. His gaze settled on the pillar of smoke to the south, its tentacles reaching towards the city, borne on by the eternal wind, the *ghibli*. The fires had been burning since dawn the day before, when Hamilcar had witnessed the lighting of the pyres under the Carthaginian slain, their bodies ceremoniously committed to Mot, the god of death, while nearby the Roman carrion were put to the torch, a separate fire to which Hamilcar had added ten more bodies – those of the members of the council of Tunis who had opened the gates of the city to the Romans.

'You think this Roman will order his men to surrender?' Xanthippus asked, following the Carthaginian's gaze.

'Regulus will comply,' Hamilcar said with certainty. 'He knows their situation is hopeless.'

'Then surely those men know it too,' Xanthippus replied. 'Perhaps they have already surrendered.'

Hamilcar turned to the Spartan, a smile on his face. 'They have not surrendered,' he said. 'Nor will they under force of arms.'

'You are sure?' Xanthippus said.

Hamilcar nodded. 'I am sure,' he replied. 'For I know the resolve of the man who commands there.'

Over the previous year, Hamilcar had been determined to discover the identity of the lone captain who had frustrated his attack at Ecnomus. Learning that he had survived and had been promoted for his actions, Hamilcar had burned the man's name into his mind, searching for it in every spy's report that crossed his desk, tracking his movements during the course of the campaign, waiting for an opportunity to avenge his defeat at Ecnomus.

'Who is this Roman?' Xanthippus asked, seeing the expression of hostility on the Carthaginian's face.

'He is not Roman, he is Greek, like you,' Hamilcar said, the words spoken slowly as the strength of his conviction coursed through him. 'And when I have Regulus's order, I will deliver it to this man and accept his surrender personally.'

Hamilcar turned from Xanthippus and looked to the east, the horizon rapidly slipping into darkness as the sun fell away in the west. In his mind's eye he pictured the port of Aspis and the enemy within, his mouth forming the name of his foe. Perennis.

Atticus ran his hand along the forerail of the *Orcus* as he stared out across the thousand yards to the Carthaginian blockade, the two hundred dark-hulled quinqueremes slowly taking shape in the dawn light. He looked to the galleys of his command, each one with its bow facing the mouth of the harbour, the outgoing tide stretching their stern anchor lines behind them as if the ships themselves were eager to be let loose on the enemy after four days of silently watching the Carthaginian galleys.

'Dawn, at last,' Septimus said as he came up to the foredeck, his eyes red-rimmed from lack of sleep, his face darkened by stubble.

Atticus nodded, the tension in his stomach easing, feeling

18

the same relief at the sight of the rising sun. He had spent the night on deck, as had all his crew for the past four nights, ready for an attack that had never come, silently watching the Carthaginian running lights sweep slowly across the horizon under the star-filled, moonless sky, the enemy visibly holding station.

'Day five,' Atticus remarked, frustration in his voice.

'And still no advance,' Septimus said, finishing his friend's thought. 'You're still sure they'll attack at night?' he asked after a moment's pause.

'I would,' Atticus replied. 'The confines of the harbour protect our flanks and reduce their advantage in numbers. They could attack by day but it would be a costly victory. A surprise attack at night would be their best bet.'

Septimus nodded, knowing also of the terrifying confusion that would accompany a night attack, chaos that would be an ally to the aggressors. He looked to the rising sun and then to the enemy, their formation the same as it had been when he last saw it at dusk the evening before. He tightened his grip on the hilt of his sword and silently muttered a challenge to the Carthaginians, daring them to make their play.

The bireme moved quickly through the swarm of larger galleys, the helmsman giving way to the towering quinque-remes as he skilfully exploited the agility of the smaller ship. Hamilcar stood beside him at the tiller, watching the crewman at work, admiring the display of prowess, a skill Hamilcar suspected had been taught to the helmsman by his father or grandfather in the tradition of all Carthaginian naval families.

Hamilcar looked to the multitude of galleys surrounding him, noticing their clean lines and ordered formation, the efficiency of the crews clearly evident even after five days of monotonous duty. The bireme progressed smoothly and Hamilcar glanced to his right, catching glimpses of the inner harbour of Aspis between the moving galleys, the stationary Roman ships indistinguishable across a thousand yards of water. A shouted hail caught his attention and he looked to the fore once more, the familiar galley ahead a welcome sight.

The bireme moved swiftly alongside the *Alissar* and, as it nudged the hull, Hamilcar jumped on to the rope ladder and ascended to the main deck.

'Well met, Commander,' Himilco the captain said as he extended his hand.

Hamilcar took it. 'Report, Captain,' he said brusquely.

'As you predicted, Commander,' Himilco began. 'The Romans have made no move to surrender.'

Hamilcar smiled grimly and nodded, looking once more to the inner harbour, his view now unobstructed. The sight prompted him to reach into his tunic and he took out a brass cylinder, fingering it lightly as he turned once more to Himilco.

'Come about, Captain,' he ordered. 'Take us in to the harbour.'

'We are to attack?' Himilco asked.

'No, signal the fleet. Tell them to hold station: we go alone.'

Himilco saluted and within moments the *Alissar* broke formation and turned her bow to the inner harbour. Hamilcar looked to the cylinder in his hand, his expectation tightening his grip on the container. Within minutes he would finally be able to put a face to his enemy.

'Carthaginian galley approaching,' Corin called from the masthead, and Atticus looked to the outer harbour, the lone galley's oars falling and rising slowly, the formation of enemy ships behind her unchanged.

'An envoy?' Septimus suggested. Atticus nodded.

'But why now?' he asked, and turned to look for his second-in-command. 'Baro, get us under way. Signal the other galleys to make ready but to hold station.'

Baro nodded and the *Orcus* moved off at steerage speed before Gaius, the helmsman, brought her up to standard. Atticus and Septimus moved to the foredeck, the centurion ordering a *contubernia* of ten legionaries to accompany them, and both men lapsed into silence as they watched the opposing galley approach.

The two galleys approached each other warily, as if manoeuvring for position, the helmsmen testing each other's skill. The Carthaginian ship was first to slow its advance and her oars dropped neatly into the water, their combined drag bringing the quinquereme to a halt within a half-ship length before two oars re-engaged fore and aft to keep the galley steady in the gentle current. Atticus turned and nodded down the length of the galley. Gaius acknowledged the gesture and carried out the same manoeuvre with similar ease; as the two ships covered the remaining distance, in silence now that the drum beat had halted, Atticus stared across at the group of armed men standing on the enemy foredeck.

Two Carthaginians stepped forward and Atticus and Septimus responded in kind, moving to the starboard forerail as the galleys kissed with a heavy thud, the timber hulls grinding against each other, each moving independently in the swell as the oars maintained the connection. Atticus focused his attention on the taller of the two Carthaginians, noticing how the other deferred to him. He was of a similar age to Atticus but his bearing was that of an older man, his self-assurance clearly evident in his expression. He stood with his shoulders slightly stooped as if poised to charge. Atticus made to address him but the Carthaginian spoke first.

'You are Perennis?' he asked.

Atticus was taken aback. 'You have me at a disadvantage, Carthaginian,' he said, and waited for the officer to introduce himself.

The Carthaginian smiled, as if relishing a private joke. 'I am Hamilcar Barca,' he said, and again Atticus was stunned. 'You know of me,' Hamilcar said.

'I know of you, Barca,' Atticus replied coldly. 'You were the commander of the quinquereme that escaped Tyndaris.' The memory formed quickly in his mind and he felt Septimus shift restlessly beside him, the centurion's anger stirred at the discovery of whom they were addressing, remembering the desperate fight at Tyndaris that had cost him so many of his men.

'And you, Perennis, were the commander of the trireme that attacked this ship at Ecnomus,' Hamilcar replied, uttering the words to stoke the fire of his anger.

There was a moment's silence.

'What have you to say, Barca?' Atticus asked, an edge to his voice, keen to forestall any inconsequential talk and draw the line of battle between them.

'I have come here to offer you terms of surrender,' Hamilcar said, struggling to control his temper at the Greek's arrogant tone.

'There will be no surrender, Barca. Not at Aspis.'

'The Roman invasion of my country is finished, Perennis. Your pitiful force cannot stand alone.'

'It will stand as long as I am in command,' Atticus replied defiantly.

'But it is not you who commands here, Perennis,' Hamilcar smiled, and he tossed a brass cylinder across the gap between the galleys.

Atticus snapped it from the air and opened it, drawing out the scroll within. He broke the seal and quickly read the contents, immediately recognizing the handwriting from earlier dispatches. His mouth twisted in anger.

'What is it?' Septimus asked, noticing his friend's agitation. Atticus handed him the scroll without comment and Septimus glanced through it. 'An order to surrender?' he said in disbelief.

Atticus nodded. 'From the proconsul himself,' he spat, knowing now why the Carthaginians hadn't attacked over the previous days. He took the scroll from Septimus and read it through again in an effort to detect a subtext to the proconsul's order, some sign that the order was written under duress and his true intent was for the fleet to resist the Carthaginians. There was none. The order was explicit.

'Regulus knows of the blockade,' Hamilcar said to compound the order, to gain the Greek's surrender immediately by justifying the proconsul's decision. 'Given the odds, he has realized you can surrender with honour.'

Atticus looked up and stared at Hamilcar with an expression of disdain. 'With honour?' he said sarcastically. 'There's no honour in being chained to a galley oar.'

'Nevertheless,' Hamilcar said impatiently. 'You have your orders, written by your own commander. You must surrender now.'

Atticus looked to the blockade and then to Septimus, the centurion's defiant expression a reflection of his own conviction. He nodded slightly, and Septimus returned the gesture, in full agreement with his friend.

Atticus carefully placed the scroll back inside the cylinder and turned once more to Hamilcar. 'There will be no surrender,' he replied, and before Hamilcar could protest, Atticus dropped the cylinder over the side, the brass container striking the hull with a hollow clang before splashing into the water.

Hamilcar followed its fall, the gesture triggering a cacophony of conflicting voices in his mind. He looked up and focused once more on the Greek commander, his vision narrowing as the dispute inside him intensified. His pride called for immediate attack, to humble the insolent Greek and give his own men the victory their morale so desperately needed after the defeat at Ecnomus. But reason called for restraint, knowing he needed the forty Roman galleys to strengthen his depleted navy; to take them by force would cost him as many galleys as he would gain. He breathed deeply and forced his pride to yield, deciding to give the Greek one last chance, putting the needs of Carthage ahead of his own honour. He leaned forward over the forerail of the *Alissar*.

'Hear me, Perennis,' he said, suppressed hostility hardening his voice. 'I will give you twenty-four hours to reconsider your decision.'

Atticus made to retort, but Hamilcar raised his hand to forestall him, no longer trusting his own temper, knowing that further words from the Greek might cause him to abandon his restraint.

'Comply, Perennis, and you and your crews will live,' he said. 'Defy me and – I swear by my gods – you will all die.'

Hamilcar stepped back and turned, issuing orders for the *Alissar* to withdraw. Her oars were re-engaged, the ship turning neatly away.

Atticus watched the galley retreat, the Carthaginian's ultimatum weakening his previously unassailable defiance. With Barca in command, the odds against him were now greater than ever. He tried to suppress his uncertainty, knowing that Fortuna alone controlled his fate and he would rather die facing the enemy than live as a slave. He turned to order Baro to get the *Orcus* under way, but as he did the wind suddenly ebbed and slackened, allowing, for the first time, the drum beats of the Carthaginian blockade to be heard. It was a staccato beat, two hundred strong, like the sound of oncoming thunder, a presage of the storm that was poised to break over Aspis.

CHAPTER TWO

Marcus Aemilius Paullus strode purposefully across the main deck of the *Concordia*, ignoring the salutes of the soldiers he passed on his way to the side rail. He looked out over the fleet, the three hundred and fifty galleys of the *Classis Romanus* spread out in formation behind his flagship, and his heart swelled, the sight overwhelming him, the power of his command filling him with pride.

As senior consul, Paullus had rushed to Sicily six months before, taking residence in the walled city of Agrigentum on the southern coast. From there he had sought to take command of the war in Sicily, to carve out a victory that would rival his predecessor's triumph at Cape Ecnomus; but the enemy had withdrawn their naval forces south to Carthage and Paullus lacked the legionary army necessary to take the fight to the Carthaginians on land. He had led skirmishes to Panormus and Lilybaeum, the two main Carthaginian-held ports of Sicily, hoping to take the fight to the enemy, but his minor victories only served to deepen his frustration.

All eyes in Rome were on the conflict in Africa. There lay the glory, but Regulus had persistently evaded all efforts to recall him to Rome, his victories at Ecnomus and Adys giving him considerable support in the Senate, so he had maintained his position as commander of the expeditionary force. With defeat in Tunis, however, that command was no more, and Paullus couldn't suppress his rising anticipation. When news of Regulus's defeat had arrived from a supply ship that had escaped the harbour of Tunis, Paullus had immediately assembled the fleet to sail west, eager to take full advantage of his restored mandate.

Paullus made his way slowly to the aft-deck, surreptitiously watching the crew at work as he went, their frantic pace at odds with the consul's unhurried movements. The consul had never before been on a galley sailing to Sicily but, over the previous months, he had learned all that was necessary to command a fleet, his two victorious skirmishes against the enemy confirming his belief in his natural ability to lead.

Paullus turned to look out over the length of the *Concordia* as he reached the aft-deck. The mainsail was taut against the rigging and, beyond that, the *corvus* boarding ramp stood poised. He breathed in the warm crosswind and looked across the deck. The junior consul, Servius Fulvius Paetinus Nobilior, was standing by the tiller and he nodded at Paullus, the senior consul returning the gesture before turning once more to the sea ahead, his mind already focused on his plan of attack once he reached Aspis. Audacity was the key to victory, and Paullus smiled as he imagined the fear that would sweep across the sea-lanes as news of his arrival spread.

The horizon before the *Concordia* darkened, a shoreline came slowly into view, and the call of land sighted echoed across the fleet. Paullus moved quickly to the foredeck, giving himself an uninterrupted view of the seascape and the shoreline beyond. A flicker of colour caught his eye and he focused on the intermittent movement. The crosswind caused his eyes to water and he rubbed them irritably. He saw them again, flashes of vibrant colours, stark against the dark shoreline, and he suddenly understood what he was seeing, the vivid masthead banners whipping furiously in the wind, their number growing with each oar stroke the *Concordia* took to narrow the distance. An instant later the lookout's call confirmed his sighting.

'Enemy galleys, dead ahead!'

'Number and heading,' Hamilcar roared as he ran the length of the *Alissar*.

'At least three hundred,' the lookout called. 'Heading due west, directly for us.'

Hamilcar stopped as he came to the aft-deck and looked east to the approaching galleys. But for their masthead banners they could be Carthaginian ships, their design a copy of the galleys constructed by the master shipbuilders of Carthage, and Hamilcar cursed the sight. He looked over his shoulder to the inner harbour of Aspis and the forty Roman galleys that still faced him defiantly.

The deadline he had imposed was but hours away, and he reproached Tanit for her fickle nature. Many times during the preceding night he had been tempted to retract his proposal and order a full attack. He knew that tactically it would be a mistake, but his honour demanded a measure of retribution for the defeat inflicted on him and his men at Ecnomus. The *Alissar* had been his command ship on that day, the quinque-reme in the vanguard of the main attack, a position of honour that Hamilcar had assumed with pride but one which had become forever tainted with humiliation when he had ordered the *Alissar* to lead the retreat from Ecnomus.

Many of the galleys of the blockade had been in battle that day and, even a year later, the shock of defeat still lay heavy on the morale of the crews, another reason why Hamilcar had been tempted to attack Aspis. A fight in the inner harbour would be on the Romans' terms, and Hamilcar's gains would be negated by his losses, but success was nevertheless assured by numbers alone. Hamilcar knew his men needed a victory over the hated Roman fleet that many perceived to be indomitable.

He had been racked with indecision during the night, perhaps touched by the same lack of confidence that was endemic in his fleet. Now fortune had swung against him, punishing him for his hesitancy, and Hamilcar looked once more to the east and the approaching Roman galleys, a quiet determination stealing over him.

The proximity of combat cleared his mind of any further thoughts of what might have been. He was outnumbered, and the enemy was on two sides. He could not hope to hold his position at the mouth of the harbour. Defeat would be certain. Equally he couldn't order his fleet to disperse, knowing that fleeing before a blow had been struck would be the death knell of his command.

He would have to take the fight to the Romans, but first he needed to reduce the odds against him. He closed his eyes and pictured the surrounding coastline in his mind's eye, searching his store of local knowledge of the shores around his beloved Carthage. He opened his eyes and checked the height of the tide on the nearby shoreline. He looked to the north, his mouth hardening into a thin line, his previous hesitation forgotten, and he turned to the helmsman.

'Come about,' he ordered. 'Battle speed. Signal the fleet to form up on the *Alissar*. We sail for Cape Hermaeum.'

The helmsman nodded and sent a runner to signal the fleet as he put his weight behind the tiller, the quinquereme responding instantly to the rudder as the galley broke the formation of the blockade. Hamilcar leaned into the turn, his hand on the siderail as the drum beat intensified, the *Alissar* increasing speed to eight knots within a ship-length while all around him the galleys of his command responded in kind.

'Aspect change on the blockade!'

'All hands, make ready,' Atticus shouted at the lookout's call, quickly running to the foredeck to see the course change of the blockading galleys for himself. He stood poised to issue the order for battle stations, expecting to see the Carthaginians turning into attack, but instead their bows swung north, the blockade rapidly disintegrating.

'Galleys approaching from the east!'

Atticus heard the call and tried to see past the Carthaginian ships, their hulls blocking his view of the eastern horizon. He looked to Corin, the masthead lookout, the young man's gaze locked on the distant seascape.

'Identify, Corin,' Atticus shouted, his inadequate vantage point frustrating him. Was it another Carthaginian detachment? Maybe the blockading galleys were moving to redeploy for attack. Every passing minute counted, and Atticus had to fight the overwhelming urge to go aloft and see for himself. He focused on Corin's face, and saw the answer a second before the lookout responded.

'They're Roman, Prefect.'

Atticus turned to look for his second-in-command, seeing him on the main deck. 'Baro,' he called. 'Get us under way. Battle speed.'

Baro nodded and began shouting orders to the crew, their already frenzied pace increasing with the ferocity of his voice. Atticus moved quickly to the aft-deck as the *Orcus* lurched beneath him, her oars biting into the calm waters of the inner harbour, the galley increasing speed with every drum beat.

He suddenly thought of Lucius, his former second-in-command, and how the older man would have been on the foredeck with him, shadowing his every move. He had yet to achieve that same bond with Baro; he was a harsher man than Lucius, but effective in his own right, and Atticus knew he could trust the experienced seaman.

'Over three hundred galleys,' Corin called out in excitement. 'Heading west on a direct course to Aspis.'

Atticus heard the report and checked the line of his squadron, the other galleys getting under way. He nodded to Gaius as he reached the aft-deck, but the helmsman did not return the gesture, his attention as always locked on the task at hand, his hand playing lightly over the tiller as he made minute course adjustments to the one hundred and ten-ton galley. The weeks of inactivity while the squadron waited in Aspis had driven Gaius to near madness, the fact that the hull lay stationary beneath his feet was contrary to his every instinct. Now, although his face was expressionless, Atticus knew that Gaius was charged with anticipation.

'Your assessment,' Atticus said, and the helmsman looked to him for the first time.

'It looks as if the Carthaginians are running,' Gaius said after a moment's pause, his expression puzzled.

'But,' Atticus prompted, noticing the helmsman's hesitation. He too had noticed an anomaly in the Carthaginians' manoeuvre, but he wanted to draw out the helmsman's thoughts, knowing that Gaius's intimate knowledge of the capabilities of a galley, and his skill at attaining the best possible position in battle, made his opinion invaluable.

'They're staying in formation,' Gaius replied, after a moment. 'If they really wanted to flee then they would have broken formation and scattered, making our pursuit more difficult.'

Atticus nodded, looking to the rear of the Carthaginian formation a thousand yards ahead as the last of the galleys

31

disappeared around the northern headland protecting the port of Aspis. By the time the *Orcus* reached that point, Atticus knew the distance to the enemy rear would be even greater, his pursuit from dead-stop giving the Carthaginians the initial advantage.

'Maybe they're planning to fight,' Atticus said, doubting his own words even as he spoke them.

'They're too outnumbered,' Gaius remarked, glancing to the approaching Roman fleet.

Atticus nodded again and set his mind to the task. He moved to the side rail to get a better view of the sea ahead. 'Gaius, what's north of here?' he asked.

'The coastline runs north for ten leagues to a cape and then turns southwest for forty leagues into the bay of Carthage.'

They'll never get as far as Carthage, Atticus thought, but, as he looked to the approaching Roman fleet, waiting for them to change course to intercept the Carthaginian formation, a sliver of doubt remained in his mind. Barca had been beaten before, but never due to error, and Carthaginian seamanship still outmatched that of most Roman crews. If the enemy were staying in formation, then their true motive was yet to be revealed.

'They're running,' Nobilior shouted in elation.

Paullus turned to the junior consul and frowned, regarding the excessive display of emotion as undignified, although he too felt the satisfaction of seeing the enemy flee in the face of his command.

'Helmsman, change course to intercept,' Paullus ordered, and the *Concordia* turned two points to starboard, the fleet behind responding immediately.

The enemy fleet was still some five miles away, sailing parallel to the coastline, their galleys bunched together as if racing each other in a bid to escape. Paullus followed the line of their course, immediately seeing the land give way to the north as it turned a headland.

'Helmsman,' he said, 'increase speed. I want to reach that headland before the enemy has a chance of rounding it.'

The helmsman nodded, calling for battle speed, and Paullus nodded in satisfaction as he felt the pace of the *Concordia* increase. He looked to the main deck and the ordered ranks of the legionaries, sensing their expectation, allowing it to feed his own impatience, and he sneered in contempt as he thought of the enemy's futile attempt to escape his wrath.

'The Romans are turning to pursue,' the lookout called, and Hamilcar glanced over his starboard aft-quarter to confirm the course change of the enemy fleet before turning to look out over the aft-rail. The Roman galleys from Aspis were just breaching the harbour mouth, now more than two miles behind the last ship in his formation, and Hamilcar watched as they neatly formed behind the lead galley, beginning their pursuit in earnest.

Hamilcar turned to the sea ahead and the coastline to his left, silently naming the landmarks in sequence as the *Alissar* sped north, his intimate knowledge of the shoreline deepening his resolve to deny the Romans any part of his people's sacred land. To his right the Roman fleet was slowly closing the gap as they sailed diagonally towards him, revealing their simple plan to cut his course as he made to round Cape Hermaeum. Hamilcar thanked Tanit for the Romans' actions, forgetting her earlier duplicity.

His fleet was outnumbered, but Hamilcar knew he stood a reasonable chance of thwarting the Romans' attempt to trap him if he could level the odds or – better yet – turn them in his favour. Victory might yet be possible or, failing that, retreat with honour. Either way, Hamilcar needed to keep his fleet together, and Cape Hermaeum would give him that chance.

Atticus stayed at the side rail of the aft-deck as the *Orcus* settled on a northerly track, the galleys of his command slipping into the wake of the Carthaginian formation, using the enemy's course to avoid any hidden shallows along the coastline. He was joined there by Septimus, while the legionaries formed up behind Drusus on the main deck, the proximity of the enemy dictating every action on the quinquereme.

'The main fleet will reach the enemy first,' Atticus said, thinking aloud, judging the angles and speed of their attack.

'Pity,' Septimus replied, his hand kneading the hilt of his sword, the anger he felt at the loss of the Ninth increasing with every oar stroke, the fact that Hamilcar Barca was in command of the enemy fleet giving his aggression a keen edge.

Atticus looked to his friend and nodded, understanding his fury, his own battle lust rising within him. The Ninth was Septimus's former legion, but Atticus had formed his own bond with the legionaries over the previous years, understanding and accepting the symbiotic relationship between the two forces. He had put his ship and his crew in harm's way many times to protect the soldiers of Rome.

The *Orcus* sped on, her ram slicing cleanly through the calm water, the gentle swell separating cleanly across her cutwater to run down the length of her hull, her wake instantly sliced by the ships behind. The galley's crew settled into silence, the drum beat dominating; the trailing wind tugged at the furled sail, the creak of running rigging and the rhythmic splash of the oars replaced the shouted commands. The pursuit demanded nothing more of the crew than patience as each man waited for the battle to come.

Atticus rubbed his fingers on the side rail, his eyes constantly darting to the four points of his galley, checking and rechecking her trim, the unconscious routine of a man who had spent his life at sea. Septimus stood immobile beside him, his hand resting on the hilt of his sword, his eyes focused two miles ahead on the enemy galleys, watching with the endless patience of a career soldier.

'You'll target Barca's galley?' Septimus asked, glancing at Atticus, whose gaze was locked on the two convergent fleets.

'Don't worry, Septimus,' he replied, never taking his eyes off the waters ahead. 'We'll get him.'

The centurion nodded and looked to his men on the main deck. Once the battle was joined he would have no control over the course of the *Orcus*, depending entirely on Atticus to get him and his legionaries into the fight, the prefect deciding which galleys to target in the rush of battle. As a soldier, such reliance was second nature, but, as a commander in his own right, Septimus had developed a deep respect for Atticus's ability. When the fleets engaged, the battle would swiftly descend into a mêlée, and a centurion leading his men over a boarding ramp on to an enemy ship needed to know his line of retreat was secure. Over the years he had fought alongside Atticus, Septimus had never once looked over his shoulder.

'Barca is doing a bad job of trying to escape,' he remarked, looking to the headland beyond the Carthaginian galleys.

'I'm not convinced he is trying to escape,' Atticus said, giving voice to the doubt that refused to subside.

'The Carthaginians are no cowards,' Septimus replied sceptically, 'but they're no fools either. The odds against them are too high.'

'Then why haven't they increased speed or taken advantage of this tailwind and raised sail?' Atticus said. 'Only ships going into battle would keep their mainsails furled.'

Septimus shook his head, unable to answer. 'Either way,' he said, putting his helmet on for the first time, 'it looks like we're in for a fight.'

Atticus nodded and slapped his friend on the shoulder, knowing the centurion was eager to confront the enemy. Septimus turned and left the aft-deck, taking up his position at the front of his men on the main deck. Drusus saluted smartly before falling into the ranks; the *optio*, like all of Septimus's men, was ready for battle.

'Nabeul,' Hamilcar said to himself as the *Alissar* sped past the tiny fishing village, 'over halfway there.'

He looked to the Roman fleet, now two miles off his starboard beam, their course still convergent with his own, both fleets aiming for the headland ahead. We're moving too fast, Hamilcar thought, estimating that his own ships would reach the headland before the Romans and he immediately ordered the helmsman to drop to standard speed, the galleys behind the *Alissar* bunching up slightly as the pace dipped, before the crews brought their ships back into perfect formation.

Hamilcar relayed his orders to the squad commander at the rear of the fleet, keeping the command simple to avoid confusion or an error in signalling. The battle ahead was unavoidably going to be fought on two fronts, with the Carthaginians outnumbered on both. Only a quick result would achieve victory, a prolonged fight could only end in defeat.

Hamilcar's gaze fell across the deck of the *Alissar*, his men formed into loose ranks, many with their swords drawn as they prepared for battle. He spotted signs of nervousness amongst them – men moving restlessly; others with their gaze locked on the deck – and Hamilcar felt his anger rise anew. Before Ecnomus these same men would have stood resolute before battle, always with their eyes turned to the enemy, willing them on, eager for the fight. Now they were riddled with doubt and Hamilcar realized that his crews might easily panic should the tide of battle turn against them.

He looked to the sea ahead once more, the shoreline filling his vision on the left, the Roman fleet on the periphery on his right, and the headland dead ahead. For Hamilcar, his only hope was to get the larger Roman fleet to disengage and flee. He focused on the waters just beyond the headland, looking to the ally that could give him victory.

We have them, Paullus thought, slamming his fist on to the side rail in triumph. His galleys would reach the headland before the Carthaginians. He looked to the galleys flanking the *Concordia*, the earlier formation now ragged as ships competed to be first into battle, although none dared to over-take the flagship. The senior consul felt renewed pride in the overt display of confidence and aggression and he called for more speed, spurring his fleet to a greater pace, the thrill of battle surging through him.

The helmsman made minor adjustments to the *Concordia*'s course, steering the quinquereme to reach just beyond the headland to give the fleet room to turn into the fight and face the Carthaginians head on, allowing them to bring their deadly *corvi* to bear, the legionaries on every galley already moving forward to form up behind the boarding ramps, many of the soldiers whispering prayers to Mars, the god of war, to give them strength in the battle ahead. Paullus stood firm on the aft-deck, the junior consul beside him, a display of calm authority and steadfast courage in the face of battle. The headland was but a mile away and the enemy was now hopelessly trapped.

*

Something's wrong, Atticus thought, his intuition sensing the change before he could confirm it, his eyes turning to the gap between the *Orcus* and the Carthaginian formation ahead.

'Gaius,' he called, turning to the helmsman.

'I see it,' he replied, his own gaze locked on the sea ahead. 'We're gaining on them.'

The Carthaginians are slowing down, Atticus thought, his instincts screaming alarm, his eyes darting everywhere as he tried to determine the cause. He moved to the tiller, his mind registering the steady drum beat from below decks, the steady pace of battle speed unchanged.

'Baro, confirm our speed,' Atticus ordered, and the second-in-command acknowledged the command, calling for a marker to be made ready on the foredeck. He ran to the aft and signalled for the marker to be dropped, counting the seconds until it passed his position. He paused for a moment as he calculated.

'A shade over eight knots, Prefect,' Baro said. Battle speed.

'Something in the water ahead maybe, some hindrance?' Gaius suggested.

Atticus shook his head. The water was calm, the only disturbance caused by the wakes of the Carthaginian galleys.

'Barca wants our ships to reach the headland first,' Atticus said, speaking aloud the only conclusion he could draw.

'And our galleys will do exactly that,' Gaius replied, feeling the same sense of alarm as his commander.

'Baro,' Atticus said. 'We need to try and signal—'

'Aspect change in the Carthaginian formation,' Corin shouted from the masthead, and all eyes turned immediately to the fore. 'The rear-guard is turning to engage.'

A squad of twenty-five galleys turned neatly from the rear of the enemy force and away from the coastline, moving swiftly into open water. They were increasing speed, coming about at a terrifying pace, the galleys transformed within seconds from escaping prey to ferocious attackers. Precious seconds passed as Atticus watched the enemy rear-guard deploy.

'Your orders, Prefect,' Baro said, an edge to his voice as he waited for the command to deploy the squadron into line of battle to counter the threat.

Atticus ignored the demand, but looked instead to the main Carthaginian formation, their course unchanged, the vanguard of the Roman fleet now obscured by the enemy ships as they swept in before the Carthaginians' course.

'Will I order the squadron to deploy, Prefect?' Baro asked insistently, glancing briefly at Gaius, seeing the helmsman's body braced for the command to come, his knuckles white on the tiller.

Atticus glanced at the enemy ships sweeping down at an oblique angle, poised to slice into his galleys, their foredecks crowded with Carthaginian warriors, their war cries growing louder with every passing second. His experience called him to order his squadron to turn into the fight, but the words would not come, a deeper instinct staying his command. He looked to the headland where the two main fleets would clash, the place where the battle would be won or lost, the place Hamilcar Barca had chosen to make his stand.

Paullus stumbled forward as the *Concordia* lurched beneath him, the deck suddenly echoing with frantic commands and cries of alarm, the galley losing momentum as the rhythm of her two hundred and forty oars was fouled. Only moments before, the vanguard of the fleet had reached the headland, the Carthaginians still some two hundred yards short of the tip, while before the *Concordia* the sea stretched out far to the west, the coastline falling away around the sharp apex of the cape. The senior consul reached out and grabbed the side rail, looking to the galleys around him in shock as he watched their close formation disintegrate.

'What's happening?' he roared, spinning around, searching for the captain, finding him standing at the tiller, the commander shouting orders to his crew. He looked to the consul.

'A tidal stream,' he shouted in frustration. 'Rounding the cape. An ebb flow, at least four knots.'

The *Concordia* was now sailing in waters unprotected by the sweep of the headland. As the quinqucreme steadied beneath him, the captain pointed her cutwater directly into the current, her forward speed reduced by the ebb flow but the ship once more in control. Paullus looked to the enemy, the Carthaginian galleys closing fast on his left flank.

'Captain, come about. Order the fleet to turn into the enemy,' Paullus shouted.

'We can't,' the captain replied and, before Paullus could retort, a crashing sound ripped through the air as two Roman galleys collided, the first one having turned broadside into the current to face the enemy, the ebb flow pushing the galley out of position and into its neighbour.

'We cannot form up in this current,' the captain shouted in explanation, his own eyes darting to the approaching enemy galleys, the *Concordia* turned broadside to their rams, the swift current forcing the captain's hand.

Paullus stood speechless, the oncoming enemy galleys dominating his mind, the air around him filled with commands and counter-commands from the ships surrounding the *Concordia*, the thread of panic in every voice as crews sought to avoid collision while turning to face the enemy, the galleys becoming further entangled as all control was lost.

'Ramming speed,' Hamilcar roared, as the helmsman of the *Alissar* settled the quinquereme on her final course, her bow pointing slightly obliquely to a line amidships of a Roman galley, the enemy crew's hesitation in deciding between collision and the Carthaginian ram sealing their fate. The *Alissar* came up to fourteen knots, the six-foot-long blunt-nosed bronze ram sweeping cleanly under the surface of the water, the momentum of the galley keeping her hull down.

The helmsman made one final adjustment to her trim and Hamilcar watched with near awe at the display of seamanship, the sailor using the sudden onslaught of the current upon the *Alissar*'s hull as it cleared the lee of the headland to straighten the quinquereme's course, perfecting the angle of attack, making the elements work to his advantage while the Romans floundered in the same conditions.

Fifty yards became ten in the span of a breath, and Hamilcar braced himself for the impact, his whole body willing the *Alissar* on, putting the strength of his hostility behind the charge of his ship. The *Alissar* struck the Roman galley six inches below the water line, the ram splintering the seasoned oak with a single blow, the relentless momentum of the quinquereme driving the ram deep into the rowing deck, crushing bone and timber, the screams of dying men merging with the screech of tortured wood as sea water gushed through the shattered hull of the Roman ship, overwhelming the damned souls chained to their oars.

Hamilcar roared in triumph with his crew, his every battle instinct commanding him to send his men over the bow rail on to the Roman galley and annihilate her crew, but he suppressed the urge, knowing he had to keep the initiative if he was going to turn the Roman vanguard.

'Full reverse,' he ordered, and the rowers of the *Alissar* put their strength to the task, the ram withdrawing reluctantly against the hold of the splintered Roman hull. In the brief minutes of contact the *Alissar* had drifted with the current, but the helmsman again used its force to swing the bow around, drawing on skills that had been forged over generations, and the galley turned neatly away from the Roman line to withdraw into the lee of the headland before turning once more to re-engage, the *Alissar*'s rowers bringing the galley back up to attack speed as Hamilcar sought out further prey, his gaze sweeping over the attack.

The Roman vanguard was in chaos, unable to form a battle line in the hostile current, while Hamilcar's ships rammed them with near impunity. The Romans had only managed to deploy their boarding ramps on half a dozen careless galleys, their isolated resistance ineffective against the momentum of the Carthaginian attack.

Hamilcar quickly assessed his odds, looking to the four points of his ship. Beyond the Roman vanguard, the bulk of the enemy fleet had yet to engage, many of the ships still sailing in the lee of the headland, their formations intact in a coherent defence that the Carthaginian galleys could not challenge. For now, the main Roman fleet was stalled, the confusion of the vanguard robbing them of the sea room to advance to the battle line. Hamilcar knew the reprieve could not last and he turned his focus back to the battle at hand.

'Two points to starboard,' he commanded, and the *Alissar* moved deftly beneath him, the helmsman adjusting her course, compensating again for the current as he brought her ram to bear.

Hamilcar braced himself again, his heart hammering out the drum beats from the deck below, his gaze sweeping over the maelstrom of the battle in which over a hundred Roman galleys were fighting for survival. He looked to the enemy ship before him, her main deck crowded with legionaries, their shields raised, their voices raised in challenge and defiance. Hamilcar balled his fists, watching as the gap fell to fifty yards, and called for ramming speed. It was time to shatter their courage.

The sounds of battle carried clearly across the water, the crash of ramming galleys, screams of death mixed with cheers of success. The voices of command that called for greater slaughter as men fought for victory conflicted with calls for resistance as men fought for survival. Atticus watched the collapsing Roman vanguard in silence, the sounds washing over him and the crew of the *Orcus*, while his mind registered the approaching threat on his flank. Only Atticus's squadron remained unfettered, a liberty the Carthaginian rear-guard was poised to take, completing a strategy that would give the Carthaginians full control.

Atticus turned to his crew. 'Attack speed,' he ordered as he looked to Gaius. 'Hold your course.'

The helmsman nodded grimly in compliance, his eyes darting to the approaching Carthaginian galley three points off the starboard beam, and then to the headland ahead.

'But the rear-guard, Prefect,' Baro protested, the enemy ships now less than a hundred yards away. 'We must turn into their attack.'

'No,' Atticus replied angrily. 'We fight on our terms. We stay on this heading and follow the course set by the main Carthaginian fleet. Signal the right flank. Tell them they must only turn into a galley that targets them directly.'

Baro nodded and issued the orders, but he struggled to reconcile the decision with his own instincts, knowing that the inevitable losses the squadron would incur could be avoided if the entire command turned into the Carthaginian rear-guard. He made to protest again but he held his tongue. The Greek would not yield.

On a galley there were few secrets and Baro knew how the prefect had worked with Lucius, seeking the older man's advice but always making his own decisions. Despite his promotion, Baro had been unable to adopt the same role as his predecessor. In the past, Baro – and all the crew – had taken their orders from Lucius, the normal command structure of a galley shielding Baro from interaction with the Greek. Now Baro reported personally to the prefect. He despised the direct subservience to a non-Roman and, as he watched the squad of Carthaginian galleys descend upon their flank, he felt the serpent of hatred uncoil itself in his stomach.

A collective shout of aggression caused Atticus to glance over his shoulder; he watched with dread as the Carthaginian rear-guard accelerated to ramming speed. The *Orcus* and many of the leading galleys were already beyond their reach, the unexpected continuation of their course and increase to attack speed giving the Carthaginians little time and sea room to react, but for the bulk of Atticus's squadron there would be no reprieve.

The *Auster* was first to be threatened, her outermost position on the right flank drawing the rams of two galleys. She swung into the attack, her bow slamming obliquely into the first Carthaginian galley as the second turned sharply to strike her stern quarter, sweeping her oars, the ram gouging the strake timbers but failing to penetrate. The Carthaginian crew threw a flurry of grappling hooks to hold the Roman galley fast. The *Auster* deployed her *corvus* on to the first ship and the legionaries streamed across, but as they did the Carthaginians of the second boarded the aft-deck, sweeping the command crew aside before charging into the legionary rear-guard, the fate of the *Auster* already decided even as her crew fought on.

Eight other galleys were forced to follow the course of the *Auster*, two of them reacting too slowly as Carthaginian rams struck them cleanly below the water line, the enemy galleys withdrawing immediately, condemning all to the pitiless sea. Atticus felt the bile rise in his throat as anger and shame threatened to overwhelm him, seeing the same conflict in the eyes of his second-in-command, the urge to abandon their course and go to the aid of their comrades. He turned his back and focused on the waters ahead, his aggression narrowing to a fine point.

The main Carthaginian fleet were dead ahead, manoeuvring in the lee of the headland, while beyond, in the grip of the current, lay the chaotic remnants of the Roman vanguard, their flank still exposed to the deadly attack runs of the enemy.

'Ramming speed on my command,' Atticus said, his voice low and hard, his order almost unnecessary. Gaius made no reply, their attack from this point predetermined by the sea and the enemy. Atticus glanced around him to the remaining galleys of his squadron, their formation rapidly forming behind the lead galley, the *Orcus* becoming the thin edge of a war-hammer poised to strike the enemy's rear.

'We must withdraw,' Nobilior shouted above the din of battle, his eyes darting to every quarter, his face splattered with blood, a sword loose in his hand.

Paullus looked beyond the junior consul to the main deck of the *Concordia*. It was strewn with the fallen, enemy and Roman alike, their blood soaking the timbers; while only yards away the Carthaginian galley that had attacked the flagship was now fully ablaze, the screams of the rowers, trapped below decks, terrifying to hear.

Paullus closed his eyes, trying to focus his mind. Everything was happening too fast; the enemy swarming over his broken formation, his own galley narrowly avoiding the killing blow of a ram, the reprieve lasting mere seconds before the enemy boarded over the rails, the fight on the *Concordia*'s decks descending into a vicious brawl that was won at a terrible cost.

The battle line surrounding Paullus was chaotic, a tangle of shattered and sinking galleys. The water was filled with survivors clinging hopelessly to debris, their cries ignored by men still in the fight, while the clash of iron could be heard on every side as men fought for the decks beneath them, the Carthaginians boarding over the side, the Romans attacking across the *corvi*, their few successes lost in the tide of battle.

'We cannot hold,' Nobilior said, grabbing the senior consul by the arm, impatient for the commander to react. 'We must withdraw now.'

Paullus heard the words, each sound a blow to his honour. Beyond the battle line the bulk of his fleet was untouched, the colossal force unable to deploy in the current, the fate of the vanguard slowing their advance, while all around him the momentum of the Carthaginian attack continued unchecked, the Roman galleys unable to recover from the initial chaos that had engulfed them. Paullus realized the junior consul was right. With the Carthaginians holding the initiative, the vanguard could not stand.

The *Alissar* swept past the Roman galley at fourteen knots, the cutwater of her prow striking the extended oars of the enemy ship, snapping the three-inch diameter shafts, the shattered remnants of the oars swinging wildly on their mounts, killing and maiming the rowers below deck. Hamilcar immediately ordered the helmsman to steer away, the portside oars of the *Alissar* emerging once more as the quinquereme cleared the disabled Roman galley. Hamilcar looked over his shoulder at the carnage his galley had wrought.

The Roman galley had turned unexpectedly, a desperate attempt to avoid the *Alissar*'s ram, but the skilled crew of the Carthaginian galley had reacted instantly, changing their attack run to sweep the port side of the enemy ship, and Hamilcar smiled coldly as the helmsman brought the *Alissar* around without command, lining the galley up to make another ramming run.

Hamilcar could sense the instability of the Roman vanguard. The crew of the crippled galley in the *Alissar*'s sights was showing none of the defiance Hamilcar had previously witnessed, the Romans realizing they would be given no chance to fight back while, beyond the battle line, the as yet untouched enemy galleys were no longer moving to attack, their skittish manoeuvres testament to their hesitation.

Hamilcar looked to Himilco, seeing in his stance and expression the same sense of expectancy. He nodded to the captain, granting him the honour of giving the fatal command; Himilco returned the gesture in gratitude and turned to the helmsman.

'Ramming speed.'

The crew on the aft-deck cheered the order, the *Alissar* surging beneath them as if unleashed from a sea anchor. Hamilcar looked once more to the stricken enemy galley only fifty yards ahead, his eyes focusing on individual Romans, marking each one.

A sudden cry of alarm broke his trance and the masthead lookout's shout was quickly taken up by the Carthaginian galleys closest to the *Alissar*. Hamilcar spun around to face the headland on his left flank, immediately seeing the danger, his mouth opening in shock before twisting slowly into a snarl of anger.

*

The arrowhead formation behind the *Orcus* splayed as the distance to the battle line diminished, the ships clearing each other's wakes to give themselves sea room. Atticus stood at the tiller, constantly issuing orders to the signalmen who relayed his commands across the squad, the disciplined crews responding with alacrity as Gaius lined up the attack run of the *Orcus*.

Atticus watched the closest Carthaginian galleys react, the unengaged turning quickly into the attack, while those already committed to ramming runs remained on course to strike their prey. He looked to his flanks, conscious of the limited number of galleys under his command. A solid battle line favoured Roman tactics, the frontal assault giving them the best chance of deploying their *corvi*, whereas open water favoured the Carthaginians, affording them the sea room they needed for ramming. With the battle ahead in complete disorder, Atticus knew his line could not engage as one, and he could only hope his squad's initial attack would carry enough momentum to break the Carthaginians' stranglehold on the vanguard.

The *Orcus* swept across the water to the battle line, every oar stroke propelling her ram through the wave tops, her two hundred and seventy oars sweeping as one through the arc of recovery before striking the water together, the rowers pulling through the drive, the drum beat pounding in every mind, controlling every movement.

Atticus picked his target, Gaius nodding in agreement as signals were sent to the galleys immediately flanking the *Orcus*, every commander in the line taking this one opportunity to coordinate their attack, each knowing that after the initial blow turmoil would reign. Gaius shifted the tiller slightly, swinging the bow of the *Orcus* through two points, the Carthaginian galley ahead registering the course change, reacting swiftly to the challenge but forced to face the *Orcus* head on.

Atticus sent a runner forward to Septimus, watching as the crewman relayed his intentions, the centurion nodding, never turning from the enemy ahead. They were committed, and Atticus felt the weight of commanding his squad lift from his shoulders. In the fight ahead he would be a captain once more, the *Orcus* his only charge, and the outcome of the battle was now in the hands of the gods.

Septimus breathed deeply, the warm, dry air giving no relief from the heat of the day. He blinked a bead of sweat from his eye. He stood to the right of the raised *corvus*, the Carthaginian galley ahead filling his field of vision. Behind him his men stood silent; Septimus could almost feel their breath on his back, a hostile exhalation that spoke of their hunger for the fight.

The gap fell to fifty yards and Septimus braced his legs against the sway of the deck beneath him as the rival helmsmen competed for the best line of attack. An arrow struck the *corvus*, then another, the enemy archers finding the range, and Septimus turned his head to look over his shoulder.

'Shields up,' he ordered, his voice low and hard, the proximity of his men ensuring his command was heard in the rear ranks.

The legionaries raised their *scuta* shields to their chins seconds before the first flight of arrows struck the foredeck, the iron-tipped barbs striking deep into the leather and hide shields. Septimus felt the arrows thump against his shield, his taller stature and position at the front of his men making him an obvious target, and again he blinked the sweat from his eyes, marking the distance between the galleys, waiting for the moment to strike back, the killing urge rising slowly inside him. A legionary cried out in pain, the sound fuelling Septimus's fury, and he breathed deeply once more, his gaze never leaving the enemy, the sound of their war cries washing over the foredeck of the *Orcus*.

'Make ready,' he shouted, and the *hastati* swept their shields aside to change their stance, drawing their spears back, the tips trembling slightly with suppressed energy. Septimus held them there, waiting for the gap to fall to thirty yards.

'Loose!'

The *hastati* roared as one as they shot their spears towards the enemy, the deadly torrent sweeping up and out over the water, where it seemed to pause for a heartbeat before falling once more, the spears accelerating through the fall, striking the crowded foredeck of the Carthaginian galley, the unprotected archers bearing the brunt.

Septimus stepped back to stand behind the *corvus*. He drew his sword slowly, the blade withdrawing smoothly from the scabbard, and his men edged forward instinctively, the charge only seconds away, their disciplined silence a fallacious mask.

'Steady boys,' Septimus growled, and he glanced over his shoulder to his *optio*. 'Drusus, the Carthaginians are massed on the foredeck. Wedge formation.'

'Yes, Centurion,' Drusus replied, slamming his fist into his chest in salute. Septimus nodded, marking as always his *optio*'s inscrutable expression.

Septimus could no longer see the enemy's faces, but he could hear their ferocious battle cries. He leaned forward, ready to charge, the proximity of the enemy driving every thought from his mind save the lives of his men and the fight to come. The galleys collided with a tremendous crash, testing the balance of every legionary, and Septimus quickly called for grappling hooks, the crew of the *Orcus* sending a flurry of lines across the gap to the enemy deck.

'Release the *corvus*,' Septimus shouted, and his men roared a battle cry, their aggression finally given vent. They surged as one behind their commander, their feet on the boarding ramp even as it fell.

The *corvus* swept down like a hammer of Vulcan, striking the Carthaginian foredeck a furious blow, crushing the men under its fall, the three-foot-long iron spikes of the ramp slamming into the weathered timbers of the deck, locking the two galleys together. Septimus bunched his weight behind his shield and ran across the *corvus*'s length, his eyes seeing for the first time individual faces of his enemy, their expressions twisted in belligerence, their mouths open, screaming defiance.

The centurion led his men across without check, the momentum of their charge driving them deep into the enemy ranks, a wedge forming, with Septimus at the apex. The Carthaginians attempted to counter-surge, but legs made strong from countless marches held them fast and the line became solid behind overlapping shields.

'Give 'em iron,' Septimus roared, and his men acknowledged the command with a visceral cry, the Roman line surging forward a foot, the legionaries pushing out with their shields, feeding their swords through the emerging gaps in the shield wall, striking the flesh of men they could not see, their exhaustive training guiding their blades to the groin and stomach, killing blows that drenched the deck beneath their feet.

'Advance the flanks.'

Again the legionaries roared in affirmation and the Roman line began to straighten out, taking the enemy foredeck inch by bloody inch, the Romans giving no quarter, the Carthaginians asking for none.

The pressure against the shield wall grew as desperation crept into the Carthaginians' defence. Septimus responded in kind, the muscles in his sword arm burning from exertion, his left arm numb from the countless blows on his shield, the fury of the enemy defence reaching a crescendo as the Roman line neared the edge of the foredeck. Septimus glanced to his side, alarm flashing through his mind as he spotted that the shield wall was no longer straight, the unequal pressures testing the formation. He called for Drusus and the *optio* stepped out of the front line, quickly taking men from the rear ranks and feeding them into the weakest sections, dressing the line until it was straight once more.

Septimus continued to push ahead, his mind a blur of fury, the faces of men from the Ninth Legion flashing through his thoughts as he shot his sword forward. The blade found resistance but Septimus pushed it through, twisting it before withdrawing it once more, making ready for the next strike.

The Carthaginians broke, their courage finally giving way in the face of the inexorable advance of the Roman line. Septimus immediately shouted for his men to halt, knowing their instinct was to rush after the fleeing enemy. The Carthaginians were not beaten; they would regroup, almost certainly below deck, and if the legionaries followed in disorder they would be slaughtered. Septimus looked to the foredeck behind him, his battle lust slowly giving way to his other senses, the smell of blood and voided bowels assailing him, his mind unconsciously counting the slain.

He looked beyond to the *Orcus* and spotted Atticus on the aft-deck, the prefect signalling him, their prearranged gesture to withdraw. Septimus acted without hesitation, ordering his men to fire the deck of the Carthaginian galley, while others helped their wounded back across the *corvus*. Septimus was the last to leave, stepping across the foredeck that his men had so desperately fought for, the rising smoke from the fired main deck already masking the battle stench.

Septimus strode across the *corvus* and ordered it raised, standing motionless as the *Orcus* moved off, his eyes on the fire as it spread to the foredeck of the Carthaginian galley. The enemy crew had emerged once more on the main deck, their cries of panic echoing from the thick pall of smoke that engulfed them, but Septimus ignored the sound, watching in silence as the fire cremated the fallen of his command until the *Orcus* completed its turn into open water. Only then did he turn his back, his sword sliding once more into its scabbard as he made his way to the aft-deck.

The *Orcus* increased to ramming speed, Atticus ordering a minute course change as the next Carthaginian galley tried to turn away from a frontal assault, the enemy's confidence giving way as their rear was overwhelmed. Gaius leaned into the tiller, the hull of the *Orcus* speeding through the water, her power concentrated on the blunt nose of the ram.

The crew of the *Orcus* roared in spontaneous hostility, a vengeful demand for the loss of their comrades, retribution for the Carthaginian attack. Atticus let them roar, knowing his men needed their measure of revenge. The *corvus* was a weapon of the legionaries, a device that distanced the sailing crew from the fight, but the ram was theirs, and with it the crew of the *Orcus* would bring death to the Carthaginians.

Hamilcar roared in frustration as he watched the defence of his rear descend into rout, many of his galleys turning away from the fight by mindlessly fleeing east with the current, their course taking them directly into the main body of the Roman fleet, a net that would trap them all. He shouted orders to the signalmen, who relayed them to the fleet in an effort to stem the retreat, but only the galleys in the immediate vicinity of the *Alissar* took heed, their proximity to the command ship steadying their nerve.

Hamilcar ordered the helmsman to turn northwest to cut through the previous battle line. The *Alissar* was followed by no more than a handful of Carthaginian galleys, their passage unnoticed in the chaos of battle. Hamilcar moved to the port side, his hands kneading the rail in anger as he watched the destruction of his fleet, his earlier plan to bolster the fragile morale of his crews having ended in catastrophe.

A lone galley caught his attention and he suddenly ran back to the tiller, pushing the helmsman aside to take command of the rudder. He looked once more to the Roman galley, more than a half league away, its banners clearly visible, the enemy ship slowly withdrawing its ram from a stricken galley. A surge of energy shot down his arm and his grip tightened on the tiller, his arm trembling with muscle tension, his every instinct calling on him to turn, the conflict filling his head.

From the moment the rear of his fleet had been attacked, Hamilcar had known who was leading the assault, the direction of attack precluding all other alternatives. He had sent the rear-guard back to pin down the Greek's squadron, but Perennis had obviously refused the bait and sailed past them, a move that had cost Hamilcar the battle. During the frantic minutes when he had tried to rally his fleet, he had forgotten that realization, but now, with the Greek's ship in sight, he remembered.

He became conscious of the tiller beneath his hand, the force of his grip numbing his fingers. Half a league separated him from the Greek, the sea between them dominated by the advancing Romans. With a shout of anger he ripped his hand away, striding across the deck to stand at the side rail, frustration assailing him.

As he was heavily outnumbered, Hamilcar had never hoped to overcome the Roman fleet; but to turn their vanguard and withdraw his own fleet in good order would have been a victory in itself, a victory the Greek had taken from him. Now all that remained was ignominious retreat.

CHAPTER THREE

Atticus sat in the stern of the skiff as it meandered through the crowded harbour of Aspis, the heat of the day and the gentle swell adding to his sense of fatigue as he watched the oarsmen thread their way through the *Classis Romanus*. He had barely slept in the two days since the battle at Cape Hermaeum, the demands of his rank too numerous, and even now his mind refused to quiet, the unknown fate of two of his galleys gnawing at his thoughts.

Atticus recalled the names of the two ships, adding them to the bottom of the list in his mind, beneath the nine galleys of his command that were already confirmed lost in battle. Given the enormous size of the Roman fleet and the addition of over a hundred captured enemy galleys, there was still hope that some of the crews had somehow survived. As a fellow sailor, Atticus had nursed that hope, but as a commander he had already accepted that the galleys were lost with all hands.

The constant noise surrounding Atticus finally interrupted his thoughts. The air was filled with the sounds of preparation and repair, of hammers resounding against timber and iron, with the din occasionally cut through by the lash of a boatswain's command. Atticus sat straighter in the boat and dipped his hand over the side, cupping a handful of water and splashing it over his face, the salt smell filling his senses, refreshing him.

Ahead lay the inner harbour. Atticus scanned the rows of galleys. He saw the flagship almost immediately, standing apart from its neighbours, and he indicated his destination to the two oarsmen. As they changed direction, Atticus stood up and shuffled past them to stand in the bow, the skiff rocking gently beneath him as it moved into the shadow of the towering hull of the *Concordia*.

Atticus called up for permission to board and then clambered up the ladder to the main deck. A crewman was waiting for him and led him below to the main cabin, knocking on the door lightly before showing Atticus in. The room was cramped, with the normal spartan furnishing of a warship augmented by two couches in the centre of the cabin and an enormous strongbox against the stern wall. The two consuls were reclined on the couches and Atticus stepped forward, standing at attention and reciting his name.

'Ahh, Prefect Perennis,' Paullus said, swirling a goblet of wine in his hand, a wry smile on his face. He turned to the junior consul seated beside him. 'This is the man I was telling you about, Servius. The Greek captain Regulus promoted.'

Nobilior nodded slowly, looking at Atticus with a studious gaze.

'Your squadron fought well, Prefect,' Paullus said.

'Thank you, Consul.'

'In fact,' Paullus continued, his tone suddenly wary, 'I would go so far as to say that although our victory was assured, your squadron's arrival hastened our triumph.'

Atticus noted the inflection in the consul's words, the implicit demand for agreement, and he was immediately on his guard.

'Yes, Consul,' he replied, and Paullus nodded, satisfied the prefect knew his place. The senior consul had already drafted his report of the battle for the Senate, taking special care to ensure full credit for the victory would fall on his shoulders, while the report also spoke favourably of the junior consul. Beyond that, Paullus had no intention of sharing his triumph with any of his subordinates, and certainly not with a lowly Greek.

'Very good, Perennis,' he said, his expression genial once more. 'Report to the aft-deck and wait for me there with the other prefects.'

Atticus saluted, turned on his heel and left the room. Paullus watched him leave and then slowly raised himself from his couch, drinking the last of his wine as he crossed the cabin. He placed his goblet on a table, fingering the rim of it lightly as he glanced once more at the cabin door. Perennis had acquiesced without hesitation and Paullus was left with a sliver of doubt. The Greek was either very naive or very shrewd.

Atticus looked astern as he came back on deck. The aft-deck was covered by a canvas awning, a shade against the sunlight for the officers surrounding the chart table that had been set up in front of the tiller. The officers were legionaries and Atticus surmised they were all former tribunes, drafted from the army to serve as prefects in the expanding Roman fleet. As Atticus approached the table, one of them looked up.

'What is it, sailor?' he asked brusquely.

Atticus smiled. 'Prefect,' he replied, and he stood amongst them, looking down at the charts, conscious that every eye was on him.

'Who in Hades are you?' one of the officers asked, and Atticus looked up, the smile still on his face.

'Atticus Milonius Perennis,' Atticus replied, and he noticed the flash of recognition on the Roman's face.

'The Greek,' he said, and Atticus's smile evaporated, the Roman's derisive tone enraging him. He made to respond but the officer looked past Atticus and suddenly shot to attention, the others following suit.

'As you were, men,' Paullus said, and the officers stepped aside to make room for the two consuls at the table.

'We have won a great victory,' Paullus began. Many of the officers tapped the table top with clenched fists in approbation, the senior consul smiling magnanimously. He held up his hand for silence.

'But we cannot rest,' he continued, looking to each man in turn. 'We must strike while the enemy is weak. Without troops we cannot progress the campaign here in Africa; but Sicily remains the prize, and with this fleet I intend to take it.'

Paullus drew everyone's attention to the chart on the table, his finger drawing a line along the map. 'First we will return to Sicily. Then we will sail up the southwest coast of the island and use the might of this fleet to convince the cities of Heraclea Minoa and Selinus to defect to our cause. Then we will blockade Lilybaeum and force the surrender of the Carthaginian garrison there.'

The officers voiced their approval, the boldness of the plan inspiring their confidence. Paullus took a moment to listen to their praise for his strategy before he brought them to silence once more.

'Now return to your ships,' he said as the officers stood to attention. 'We sail on the morrow.'

The men saluted and were turning to leave when a voice stopped them short.

'We cannot leave so soon,' Atticus said. All eyes turned to him, an astonished silence descending over the group at the Greek's insubordination.

Paullus leaned in over the table and looked directly at

Atticus. 'You disapprove of my plan, Perennis?' he said, a hard edge to his voice.

'Your strategy is sound, Consul,' Atticus replied, his tone confident. 'But we cannot sail so soon. We must wait two weeks.'

'Two weeks,' Paullus scoffed. 'The Republic was not built on timidity, Perennis, as I am sure your people know. We must strike now while we have the initiative.'

Atticus swallowed the insult, knowing it was important to persuade Paullus. 'Orion has risen, Consul,' he began. 'We must wait for Sirius.'

'What are you talking about?' Paullus asked irritably.

'The weather, Consul. Between the rising of Orion and Sirius there is too great a risk of severe weather in those waters.'

This time Paullus laughed, a mocking tone that brought a smile of derision to the lips of many of the Roman officers. 'The weather cannot stop the will of Rome,' he said curtly. 'My order stands. We sail with the tide tomorrow.'

The officers saluted once more and walked away. Only Atticus did not move.

'You're dismissed, Perennis,' Paullus said angrily, the Greek's stubbornness irritating him.

'Consul, the southwest coast is hostile and there are no safe harbours north of Agrigentum,' Atticus continued, knowing his chance was slipping away. 'Ask any of the experienced sailors in the fleet. If we hit bad weather—'

'Enough,' Paullus snapped, his patience at an end. He stepped forward and leaned in until his face was inches from Atticus's.

'You fought well at Cape Hermaeum, Perennis,' he said coldly, 'and for that I will forgive this insubordination. But only this one time. Now get off my ship.'

Atticus stood back and saluted, his expression unreadable. Underneath, frustration consumed him.

*

Hamilcar looked up at the soaring height of the Byrsa citadel as he made his way towards the columned entrance to the Council chamber. He paused and traced the ancient walls from their base to the towering battlements, oblivious to the people stepping around him, many of them muttering curses of annoyance, the teeming streets having little tolerance for the unhurried.

The citadel was a sight that had never before failed to lift Hamilcar's spirits, but on this day it did not lighten his mood and, after a moment, he continued on, slipping into a current in the crowd that brought him quickly to his destination. He stepped into the cool interior, his eyes adjusting quickly to the gloom, and made his way across the marble floor, his footfalls mingling with the echoing sounds from the outer hall. He stopped at the antechamber door and knocked, entering as he heard a muffled summons from within. He closed the door behind him and looked to the two men in the room in turn. He was conscious of keeping a neutral expression, though, hiding his respect for the first man and his loathing for the second.

Hasdrubal smiled and stepped forward, his hand outstretched, and Hamilcar took it, matching the strength of the older man's grip, the brief contact invigorating him.

'It is good to see you, Father,' he said.

'And you, Hamilcar,' Hasdrubal replied, although his face showed his concern at how exhausted his son looked.

Hamilcar released his father's hand and turned to the other man, Hanno. He was a massive figure, broad in the chest and stomach, and Hamilcar nodded to him perfunctorily, his gesture ignored. He turned once more to his father.

'I came as soon as I got your message.'

Hasdrubal nodded. 'The meeting with the One Hundred and Four went well?'

'As well as I could have expected,' Hamilcar replied. 'On balance, the victory at Tunis outweighs the loss at Cape Hermaeum. The city is secure for now and I retain my command.'

'Congratulations, Hamilcar,' Hanno said sardonically, stepping forward, his movements slow and deliberate. 'I see your ability to delude those old men continues to save you.'

'My record alone speaks for me, Hanno,' Hamilcar replied scathingly. 'And the One Hundred and Four know my worth.'

Hanno smiled, as if conceding the point, although Hamilcar sensed the councillor could see through his confident tone.

The One Hundred and Four was a council of judges that oversaw all military matters in the empire, their number drawn from the retired commanders who had served Carthage with distinction. Hamilcar's mandate to command was based on their approval, with success being the main criterion; although Hamilcar had been victorious at Tunis, he had been forced to defend his actions at Cape Hermaeum, an argument that had fully tested the oratorical skills his father had taught him.

'The Supreme Council meets at noon,' Hasdrubal said, conscious of the time and impatient of the conflict between Hanno and his son. 'We need to reach a consensus on how best to proceed.'

Hanno grumbled in agreement and walked once more to the far side of the room. Over the previous years, two factions had emerged on the Supreme Council. One, led by Hanno, was opposed to the war in Sicily and believed that the empire should expand in Africa, and the other, led by Hasdrubal, supported the Sicilian campaign. Prior to the current alliance, the two factions had frequently hamstrung each other, with neither cause prevailing. Coupled with this, Hanno had shared command with Hamilcar in their defeat at Cape Ecnomus. It was only their agreed mutual support after the battle that had saved both their careers. Hanno despised his coalition with the Barcid clan, but for now it was in his best interest to maintain the union, his fate inexorably tied to each man. So before he turned back to face the father and son, he buried his animosity beneath a thin veneer of unity.

'Where is the Roman fleet now?'

'Our spies tell us the entire fleet sailed east for Sicily two days ago,' Hamilcar replied.

'Do we know their final destination?'

'No,' Hamilcar conceded. 'Although, given the time of year, I suspect they will make directly for the safety of their harbour in Agrigentum and wait there until Sirius has risen.'

'How long?' Hasdrubal asked.

'Less than two weeks. After that the weather will once more be in their favour.'

'Then you must be in Sicily when they move,' Hasdrubal said.

'I will sail for Lilybaeum,' Hamilcar said. 'The Romans will strike either there or Panormus.'

'What do you need?' his father asked.

Hamilcar didn't hesitate. 'The fleet stationed in Gadir.'

'Impossible,' Hanno scoffed, stepping forward to argue. 'It is the only fleet we have left in Iberia.'

'Nevertheless,' Hamilcar replied, 'I need those galleys if I am to protect the northwestern approaches to Sicily and continue the war there.'

Hasdrubal remained silent and looked to Hanno, knowing there was no point in trying to persuade his rival. The One Hundred and Four appointed commanders and approved strategy, but it was the Supreme Council that steered the direction of any conflict, and that included the disposition of the empire's forces. Hasdrubal wished only to know Hanno's counter-proposal, the price he would demand for supporting Hamilcar's request.

'What will it take for your support?' Hasdrubal asked of Hanno.

'I will agree to release the fleet at Gadir to Hamilcar's command,' Hanno said to Hasdrubal after a pause, 'on condition that his land forces now based in Tunis are given over to my command.'

'You still intend to continue the war against the Numidian kingdoms?' Hasdrubal asked incredulously, and Hanno simply nodded, not deigning to argue his position. Hamilcar made to interject, but his father shot him a look, warning him to hold his tongue. His son had no voice in negotiations at this level.

Hasdrubal held Hanno's gaze, but behind his eyes he was examining his rival's proposal. Throughout the conflict with the Romans, Hanno had also pursued a land war against the Numidians to the south. That campaign had only been suspended when the Romans invaded Africa, every resource having been recalled to defend Carthage. Now that the Roman threat had been eliminated, Hasdrubal was forced to concede there was no argument to prevent Hanno from restarting his campaign.

'Agreed,' he said.

'Good,' Hanno replied. 'I will take command of those forces by the end of the week.'

'And what of Xanthippus?' Hamilcar asked.

'The mercenary?' Hanno replied with disdain. 'That Spartan has served his purpose. Pay him off.'

Again Hamilcar made to speak but his father forestalled any further conversation. 'It will be done,' Hasdrubal said.

Hanno nodded curtly and left the room without another word.

Hamilcar waited until the councillor's footfalls receded before turning to his father.

'I needed those men in Sicily,' he said angrily. 'You conceded too much, too quickly.'

Hasdrubal's eyes narrowed. 'I agree the army at Tunis is a heavy coin to pay for a provincial fleet,' he said. 'But if we are to continue the war in Sicily, then Hanno must be appeased, now more than ever. He will be suffet this year, nothing can prevent that, and as leader of the Supreme Council he will have considerable influence on the uncommitted Council members, perhaps enough to permanently tip the balance in his favour.'

Hamilcar was silent, unable to see a way through the enemies ranged against him. Previously his thoughts had dwelt solely on overcoming the massive naval force of the Romans. But now he realized that the political threat to his flank, which he had believed neutralized, was re-emerging. He looked to his father, regretting his earlier criticism. He knew Hasdrubal's political instincts were far superior to his own.

Hasdrubal saw the uncertainty in his son's expression and he reached out, placing his hand on his shoulder. 'Look to Sicily, Hamilcar,' he said. 'Your enemy is there. Hanno is my responsibility.'

'But what of my men? I will need land forces if I am to defeat the Romans.'

'I will petition the Council to make mercenaries available when you need them. Until Hanno becomes suffet, I can garner enough support for such expenditure.'

Hamilcar nodded, his renewed trust in his father allowing him to focus his mind once more. Whatever the internal conflicts with the Council, Rome was the true enemy and Sicily the battleground. The northwest of the island was still firmly in Carthaginian hands, but it was only a matter of time before the Romans launched an attack.

Hamilcar clasped his father's hand in farewell and left the

antechamber, passing quickly out on to the busy streets. He paused and looked briefly up at the Byrsa citadel, the sight steeling his determination as he set off towards the harbour below.

The cutwater of the *Orcus* sliced cleanly through the crest of the wave, the galley sailing close-hauled, with the wind sweeping in over the starboard forequarter, catching the spray and whipping it away towards the Sicilian shoreline two miles away. The mainmast creaked against the press of the mainsail, the canvas whacking like a clap of thunder; Baro's shouted commands sent the crew racing to tighten the running rigging as Gaius dropped the galley off a touch.

Atticus stood at the tiller with the helmsman, his eyes on the southern horizon, the wind striking him directly in the face, pushing tears back from the corners of his eyes, his skin covered in a fine sheen of sea spray. He was silent, as was Gaius and many of the crew, their unease creating a tension that stifled every word. The sea around the *Orcus* was crammed with the galleys of the *Classis Romanus*, their formation loose and pliable, with each individual ship guarding its own sea room as the crews struggled against the adverse wind using a subtle mix of oar and sail power.

Septimus came up from below decks and made his way towards the aft-deck, shifting his balance with every step like a drunken man on solid ground, the centurion cursing softly with every pitch of the deck. He nodded to Gaius but the helmsman seemed not to see him. Septimus moved around to stand before Atticus, his friend's intense stare causing him to look over his shoulder.

The sky to the south was shrouded in iron-grey clouds, reaching from the distinct line of the horizon into the towering heavens, the anvil-head formations clawing ever upward, while beneath the cloudscape the sea was streaked with dark bruises as enormous shadows moved across the troubled surface. Septimus was mesmerized by the sight, his gaze locked on a cloud as it seemed to consume the remnants of the blue sky above it, unable to believe that when he had gone below deck an hour before the southern horizon had been all but clear. He turned to Atticus.

'This is the weather you warned Paullus about, isn't it?'

Atticus nodded, taking no pleasure in seeing his prediction fulfilled. Septimus turned back to the storm front, the wind flattening his tunic against his chest, the sea spray holding it there. 'Have you sailed through weather like this before?' he asked.

'Not with that thing on board,' Gaius answered, indicating the *corvus* with a scowl.

Atticus ignored the helmsman's reply, concentrating instead on the seascape. 'I sailed the *Aquila* through twenty-five-knot winds once,' Atticus said, 'but I had a lot of sea room. If that storm advances, we'll have the shoreline on our flank.'

'How far is Agrigentum?' Septimus asked.

Atticus looked to the coastline, not recognizing any feature that would indicate their position. An hour before, the fleet had been off the Carthaginian-held city of Selinus but, as the storm front developed, a general order had swept through the fleet to turn southeast and beat along the coast to Agrigentum, a forty-mile journey.

'Too far,' Atticus replied, and he looked once more to the southern horizon. 'Do you see there, where the line of the horizon is obscured, where the sky and sea are the same colour?'

Septimus followed Atticus's pointed finger and nodded. In places a curtain seemed to fall from the sky, a dark wall inter-spersed with shafts of sunlight from high overhead. It was moving across the horizon, the vertical lines expanding and receding, almost as if the storm were breathing.

'That's the squall line,' Atticus said, 'where the rain is falling in sheets. When that reaches us we'll be in the grip of the storm.'

Even as Septimus watched, the storm seemed to advance, the squall line surging forward with every gust, the sheer size of the front making it difficult to judge its distance. He felt sick, his stomach swooping with every pitch of the deck; despite the cold sea spray on his face, he felt hot and nauseous. And something else, something Septimus had never felt away from the battlefield: fear.

He heard his name being called above the howl of the wind and turned. Atticus was looking at him and pointing to the main deck. 'Septimus, I need your men to clear the deck. Get them below. We're going to seal the hatches.'

Septimus nodded and moved purposefully to the main deck, glad to have something to do. He ordered his men below and set Drusus the task of dispersing the legionaries throughout the lower deck. A hammering sound caught his attention and he turned to watch three crewmen fixing a cover to the forward hatch of the main deck, the men moving off quickly as the last dowel was hammered home, heading towards Septimus. He looked down the open hatchway below him into the darkened lower deck, the thought of being imprisoned and powerless abhorrent to him; he turned his back and moved once more to the aft-deck, the crewman slamming the hatch cover into place behind him.

A sudden roll of the deck caused Atticus to stagger, and Gaius shot out his hand to hold him upright, the helmsman never taking his eyes from the bow of the *Orcus*.

'The wind is shifting,' he said, and Atticus looked to the mainsail. A ripple shot across the canvas, followed by another and another.

'Can you hold it?' Atticus asked, but before Gaius could answer, the deck pitched violently beneath them, the bow striking deeply into the crest of a wave, the water sweeping across the foredeck.

Gaius leaned on the tiller and the mainsail tightened up, but a sudden gust defied his efforts and the sail flapped once more.

'We're too close to the squall line,' Gaius said in frustration. 'The wind won't hold steady.'

Atticus nodded but hesitated for a moment longer. If he dropped the sail the galley would have to rely solely on oar power, and the chances of reaching Agrigentum would fall away to none. He looked to the squall line again, estimating it to be less than three miles away. Even at that distance it was playing havoc with the mainsail, and Atticus knew if a sudden strong gust caught the *Orcus* broadside, the mainsail could have them over.

He sought out Baro on the main deck. 'Secure the mainsail,' Atticus shouted. Baro grabbed the sailors nearest to him and began barking orders, the crewmen responding as quickly as they could on the heaving deck.

Gaius dropped the bow off a point to take pressure off the mainsail, but the wind was becoming more unpredictable and the crew struggled to haul in the canvas sheet as the lifting yard was lowered. A sudden gust ripped the sail from their control and two men cried out as the running rigging slipped through their hands, the rough hemp rope ripping the flesh from their fingers. The men redoubled their efforts, but again they lost control and a rigging line parted, the lifting yard falling the remaining twenty feet to the deck, the men scattering beneath it, one man's scream of panic cut short as the yard collapsed on top of him.

Baro roared curses and the men hurled themselves on the

fallen yard and sail, smothering them as if they were felled quarry. The sail was quickly made secure, a new line of rigging attached, and the crew hauled the yard aloft once more to secure it to the mainmast. Baro ran to the fallen crewman, his screams of pain falling and rising with the surges of the wind.

Securing the mainsail had taken mere minutes, but in that time the squall line had advanced two miles, the wind that was driving the storm front increasing to twenty knots. Atticus looked to the shoreline two miles off the port stern quarter. Its features were almost obscured by the sea spray that filled the air, but Atticus could discern a solid white line that marked the breakers as they struck the rocky crags defining the shoreline in both directions. He scanned the galleys surrounding the *Orcus*, recognizing many of the nearest ones as ships of his own squadron.

He turned to face Septimus and Gaius. 'Options,' he said.

'Three,' Gaius replied. 'We run before the wind and try to make landfall immediately, or we reverse course and sail parallel to the shoreline, or we turn into the wind and try to ride it out.'

Septimus remained silent, knowing there was nothing he could add, his opinion counting for naught. He had caught most of Gaius's words, the wind taking the rest, and he looked from the helmsman to Atticus.

Atticus nodded, having reached the same conclusions as Gaius. He immediately discounted the first, running before the wind. The shoreline was treacherous. There would be no refuge there. The second option was fraught with risk. The galley would be sailing broad reach, the wind coming from behind at an angle. When the squall line overtook them, the wind speed would increase and the gusts would become more unpredictable. One mistake and the galley would be turned into running before the wind, sending the *Orcus* directly towards the jaws of the shoreline. Atticus realized that – of the three options – there was but one choice.

'Ready the helm. We're turning into the wind,' he said, and Gaius nodded. Atticus called for a runner. He sent him forward to bring Baro to the aft-deck so he could inform the second-in-command to ready the deck crew. He looked once more to the galleys immediately surrounding the *Orcus*. Each one was now locked in its own battle with the weather, their courses for the moment parallel with the *Orcus*, but soon each captain would make his own play to save his ship.

Atticus watched as one galley began to turn into the wind. He recognized the galley as the *Strenua*, one of his own, and he smiled as he thought of her captain, the man who had reached the same conclusion as Atticus, only faster. The *Strenua* turned slowly, the wind-driven waves slamming into her bow quarter, fighting the pressure of the rudder and the strength of two hundred and seventy men, but inexorably the galley made headway until her ram was pointing directly into the waves and the wind, the ship holding steady under oars.

Without warning, the pitch of the *Strenua* increased, and Atticus watched in horror as the swell overwhelmed the bow, sea water crashing over the foredeck as each wave tried to swallow the galley whole. She foundered with incredible speed, the waves consuming the bow of the ship, a deadly embrace that doomed all on board.

Atticus was stunned by the speed of the *Strenua*'s demise; as he turned to Gaius, he saw the helmsman's gaze already locked on the ship.

'The *corvus*,' he said. Atticus did not hear the words but read the helmsman's lips; both men instinctively turned to the boarding ramp on the foredeck of the *Orcus*.

'What is it?' Septimus shouted, the fear he saw in each man's face shocking him.

'The *corvus*,' Atticus replied. 'We're bow-heavy.'

Before Septimus could respond a wave of darkness fell over them, followed a heartbeat later by torrential rain that lashed against the timbers of the deck. The wind whipped past thirty knots and changed to a terrifying howl, the battle cry of Pluto who had come to claim his measure. The squall line was upon them.

The *Orcus* rolled sickeningly and every man was thrown to the deck, Gaius alone standing firm, never relinquishing his grip on the tiller. Sea water crashed over the starboard side, sweeping across the decks, taking two of the crew, and for a second the *Orcus* was poised to capsize before its buoyancy righted the hull. Atticus clambered to his feet, the deck giving little purchase, and spat at the storm, shouting a string of curses to Poseidon.

'We have to turn,' Gaius shouted, his face twisted in effort, the tiller trembling in his hands. 'The waves are pushing us broadside.'

'We turn into the wind now and we're dead men,' Atticus shouted back. 'Hold this position. I'm going to rid us of that cursed ramp.'

Atticus turned and grabbed Septimus by the forearm. 'Come with me,' he shouted, and they fought their way across the heaving deck, their heads down into the rain-laden wind. Atticus called to Baro and the second-in-command ran to get axes, gathering crewmen as he went; they made their way to the foredeck.

The *Orcus* rolled violently and again they were thrown off their feet, the deck tilting beneath them. They slid to the port-side rail, Atticus slamming into the barrier; the air was blown from his lungs as sea water washed over him. He struggled to breathe. A hand clawed at him and instinctively he reached out to grab it, but it slipped away and a cry of terror was lost in the deafening noise of the storm. He struggled to his feet and looked back to the aft-deck, signalling to Gaius to turn the bow a point further into the wind in a bid to find a balance between the threat of capsizing or foundering.

Atticus made the foredeck with Septimus, Baro and three other crewmen, and immediately they attacked the mounting pole of the *corvus* with their axes. Their blows were erratic, the pitch and roll of the deck robbing each man of the chance to find a rhythm, their feet slipping on the timbers. They fell in turn, coming to their feet each time with a string of curses.

With every passing second, the wind seemed to increase in intensity and the pitch of the *Orcus* deepened, her bow slamming into each roller. A wave of sea water erupted over the bow rail to sweep the foredeck, taking one of the crewmen, the sailor screaming as he fell into the water, his arms flailing, reaching out for the galley as he was carried further from the *Orcus*. Atticus stared at the crewman as he came back to his feet, feeling the weight of the axe in his hand, the haft wet with water, and he tightened his grip until his knuckles ached. He turned to the *corvus* and roared in anger, striking downwards, a splinter of oak spinning away as four other blades fell in succession.

Another wave crashed over the bow, carrying with it the body of a dead sailor. The corpse slid across the deck until it struck the side rail, but the next wave washed it overboard, the possessive sea claiming the sailor once more. A crack ripped across the base of the mounting pole and the men redoubled their efforts, striking at the point of weakness, the weight of the *corvus* now working to their advantage as the pole gave way under the strain. It separated without warning and the boarding ramp fell to the deck, the galley heeling over violently under the shift in weight.

'The guy ropes,' Atticus shouted, his words unheard in the

noise, but every man understood the order and they rushed to sever the lines attached to the mounting pole, each one cut with a single axe blow, the lines whipping away. Baro yelled in pain as a rope struck him on the face, knocking him to the deck, a crewman grabbing hold of him as sea water threatened to wash him over the side.

For a heartbeat the *corvus* remained defiantly on board but, as the galley rolled, it swept towards the port side and smashed through the side rail before crashing into the sea. The bow of the *Orcus* soared out of the water, suddenly free of the dead weight, and Atticus yelled at the men around him to hold on as Gaius completed the turn into the wind, bringing the bow around to slice cleanly into the oncoming waves, the cutwater separating each wave from trough to crest.

Atticus led Septimus and Baro back to the aft-deck, the second-in-command covering the side of his face with his opened hand, rain-streaked blood running down his arm. The wind pushed into their backs as they fought the pitch of the deck, their pace changing as the deck fell away or reared up before them.

As they reached the aft-deck, Gaius called Atticus to his side. 'We can't make headway,' he shouted, his voice laced with anger and frustration, and Atticus looked to the four points of his ship, trying to gauge the galley's progress.

The *Orcus* was pointed directly into the wind and the waves; the combined forces were driving the galley back towards the shoreline behind. Atticus ran to the side rail to see the oars, watching them intently as the *Orcus* broke over the crest of a wave. For several seconds the blades of the forward oars were free of the water and the rowers pulled their oars through air, the sudden release of pressure fouling their rhythm, until the galley fell over the crest and accelerated into the trough. The bow crashed below the surface, submerging the lower oar-holes and, as the bow resurfaced, Atticus saw sea water pour from them, knowing it was but a fraction of what the galley had consumed. He ran back to the tiller.

'Baro,' he shouted, leaning in, wiping the rain from his face. He outlined his plan, and the second-in-command stumbled away to the aft-rail. Atticus looked to the helm. 'Gaius, find a reference point on shore. We need to stand fast and ride out the storm in this position.'

The helmsman nodded. Atticus turned to Septimus and signalled to him to follow. They went to the main deck and Atticus ordered two crewmen to remove the aft hatch cover. He jumped down on to the steps the second the cover was away and clambered down, pausing at the bottom. The storm had transformed the rowing deck into a hellish place, the half-light filled with the sounds of wailing and the stench of sea sickness, while the waves hammered against the hull, the timbers groaning with each blow, the deck swooping beneath them with every pitch, the drum beat resounding in the enclosed space.

Drusus had the legionaries arranged along the central walkway that ran the length of the galley, the men crouched against the pitch of the deck, many of them stained with vomit, their faces drained of colour. Atticus ran to the centre of the galley, the sound of muffled screams guiding his feet, and he hauled up the trap door that led to the relief rowers in the lower hold. He looked down and dread struck him like a blow to his stomach. The men there were up to their chests in water, their faces upturned in abject terror; they fought each other to clamber up the ladder on to the walkway.

Septimus had followed Atticus and he called to the legionaries closest to him, the men drawing their swords to control the flood of relief rowers, stemming the threat of panic.

Atticus quickly ordered the oars on the lowest level to be shipped and withdrawn, along with all the oars in the fore-section, and he rearranged the men and the relief rowers until there were two on each remaining oar, giving each oar extra strength and control.

Atticus moved to the top of the steps of the open hatchway and signalled Baro to make ready. He took a minute to judge the pace of the oncoming wave before ordering the drum master to make standard speed. The *Orcus* surged forward with renewed strength and quickly began to make headway, the galley climbing up the slope of the wave. As the *Orcus* neared the crest, Atticus signalled to Baro to release a drogue, an open water barrel that was lashed to the stern.

The *Orcus* crested the wave and Atticus called for all stop, the rowers holding their stroke. The drogue slowed the galley's descent down the reverse slope, her bow biting into the trough but not as deeply as before, and Atticus immediately called for the oars to restart at battle speed, the rowers now fighting both the slope of the next wave and the drogue.

Atticus repeated the pattern a dozen times before he turned to Gaius. The helmsman was looking to a point off the starboard rail but, as he turned and caught Atticus's eye, he nodded. The *Orcus* was holding steady, neither advancing nor retreating.

Atticus put his hand up to shield his eyes against the driving wind and rain as he looked to the fore once more. He shouted his next command to the drum master without thinking, the routine already established, and he suddenly became aware of the numbness of his limbs, the bitter cold that had seeped into him as he sat motionless in the open hatchway. He closed his mind to the pain, knowing the storm could last for hours yet, and between commands he looked to the sea around the *Orcus*.

Atticus could see no more than two miles in any direction, the rain-laden air obscuring all else, but even in that narrow field the scenes of carnage were terrifying to behold. The shore-line had already claimed dozens of ships, the waves breaking over their shattered hulls, relentlessly pounding the galleys against the rocks in unceasing fury while other ships were drawn inexorably closer to their doom, the crews fighting hopelessly against the power of Poseidon, a desperate fight between mortal men and the son of titans.

In the open sea around the *Orcus* only a handful of galleys were still afloat, all of them sailing into the wind, but as Atticus watched, two more foundered, the *corvi* on their foredecks dragging their bows beneath the surface, the boarding ramp that had once saved the fleet of Rome now a terrible curse, while all around the sinking galleys the water was strewn with dead and dying men, the wind mercifully hiding their screams from the living.

Atticus looked to the fore once more and the solid wall of blackness that was the heart of the storm. Its strength was unbound, its oblivious butchery far from over, and the numb-ness Atticus felt in his limbs slowly crept into his heart, shielding him from the agony that was the loss of the *Classis Romanus*.

CHAPTER FOUR

Gaius Duilius sat motionless as the *princeps senatus*, the leader of the house, read the prepared statement, the senior senator's voice faltering with age and the gravity of the words he spoke. The three hundred-strong assembly of senators listened in near silence, with only sporadic exclamations of shock stirring the still air of the Curia Hostilia, the Senate house of Rome.

The galley dispatched by Paullus from Agrigentum over a week ago had arrived in Ostia twelve hours before, bearing the report that the vast majority of senators in the Curia were now only hearing for the first time; a report that outlined the destruction of the expeditionary army in a battle outside Tunis, and Paullus's resultant decision to sail to Africa. Duilius paid only scant attention to the leader's words, his attention instead focused on the reactions of others in the chamber. He had been aware of the full contents of the report within two hours of the galley's arrival, his network of spies and informants as always keeping him fully informed, and so now he was free to scan the faces of his fellow senators, specifically those amongst the ranks of his opponents

Duilius's task was made easier by the invisible yet explicit divide that existed in the Senate. On his side of the chamber, he was surrounded by men who daily challenged the established order of Rome, progressive senators, many of whom were *novi homines*, new men, the first of their family to be elected to the Senate. The other side of the chamber was dominated by members of the senior patrician families of the city, descendants of the men who had founded the Republic and whose strength depended on the status quo being maintained.

Duilius studied the expression of each man surreptitiously, discounting many out of hand, knowing them to be insignificant pawns or sycophants. Equally he disregarded those he knew for certain were within the inner coterie of the opposition, senior senators who were no doubt cognisant of the full details of the report but had the presence of mind to look surprised and alarmed. Instead Duilius focused on the remainder, searching for telltale signs of awareness, subtle indications of composure that would reveal their foreknowledge of the report and therefore their inclusion in the inner circle. He knew from experience that often the newest members of any coterie, many of them young senators, lacked the political sense to bury their awareness behind impassive expressions, and so this was a rare opportunity to advance his knowledge of the opposition's ranks.

Despite recognizing the brevity of his opportunity, Duilius froze as his gaze settled on one of the senators, Gnaeus Cornelius Scipio. He was an austere-looking man and his head was bowed slightly, as if to partially hide his expression, although Duilius knew that posture was unnecessary. Scipio was a skilled pretender and his self-discipline was matched only by his ruthlessness. He was the leader of the opposition, although few knew him as such, including those who were his closest allies, as Scipio's greatest talent lay in his ability to manipulate events *sub rosa*. For that reason alone,

Duilius knew him to be his worthiest and most dangerous adversary.

Duilius had learned a great deal from Scipio over the years since they had shared the consulship. That tenure had ended in ignominy for Scipio, his defeat and capture at Lipara earning him the cognomen *Asina*: 'donkey'. Yet he had survived politically, wielding his power behind the scenes, and already his machinations had led to the election of two senior consuls, Regulus and, in turn, Paullus. Duilius had fully adopted Scipio's approach, disguising the significant power he held during his tenure as censor to influence voting in the Senate, and the hatred and rivalry between the two men had deepened with every confrontation.

As if realizing he was being studied, Scipio glanced in Duilius's direction and their eyes met. He smiled coldly, a gesture that Duilius returned. Regulus's defeat in Africa would have repercussions, the balance of power in the Senate would be affected and careers could be advanced or impeded depending on how the aftermath was controlled. Neither Duilius nor Scipio were openly recognized as the leaders of the two factions fighting for supremacy in the Roman Senate, but with that one brief exchange across the crowded chamber, the two men had signalled the escalation of hostilities.

Hamilcar hesitated in the quiet of the entrance to the temple, the complete silence and his apparent solitude unsettling him. The afternoon sun was warm upon his back, raising drops of sweat at the base of his neck that ran down inside his tunic. The light framed his shadow as it reached into the interior of the vaulted inner chamber. He took a step forward and stopped again, hindered by a growing sense of unworthiness, a feeling that his gratitude would somehow sully the incredible feat accomplished by the deity that dwelt within the hallowed space before him.

The first rumours had arrived in Carthage the day before, the news sweeping the streets like a wildfire borne on the mighty *ghibli*. Hamilcar had immediately rushed to the port, anxious for more news from arriving ships, for confirmation that such a miracle had indeed occurred; but for the following twenty-four hours he was frustrated with further unsubstantiated rumours. Only that morning had a military galley arrived from Selinus and its captain had confirmed the report, prompting Hamilcar's flight to the temple of Yam.

Hamilcar stepped forward once more, moving through the unadorned porch and into the inner room, his gaze slowly sweeping over the engravings on the granite walls representing the untamed sea, the depictions sending a shiver of unearthly fear through his stomach. The statue of Yam was at the far end of the chamber. The shadows played across its form and Hamilcar held his breath as he looked upon it. In the war against the Romans, he had often called on the support of many of the gods, calling down their favour or the power of their wrath, but never before had he prayed to this minor deity, the overlord of violent tempests and the raging sea.

Hamilcar fell forward as if struck from behind, and the temple echoed with the crashing sound of his body hitting the floor. He spread out his arms and prostrated himself, pressing his forehead on to the marble slab as he began to whisper his thanks. The prayers came slowly at first, his humility robbing him of the words, but soon the strength of his gratitude overwhelmed him and he spoke without pausing for breath, humbling himself unashamedly in the quiet of the inner temple.

After a time, Hamilcar became silent. He raised himself up

and looked to the statue once more, wanting to remember every detail. Nodding, he turned to leave; as he left the inner chamber he saw a number of other people approaching, many of them carrying garlands and amphorae of wine, offerings for the previously ignored god. In time, as the news of the destruction of the Roman fleet spread, the temple would become inundated with grateful worshippers. Hamilcar was glad he had been given this time alone to express his gratitude.

He quickened his step as he made his way through the oncoming crowd, eager to return to the city and continue the development of his plan, born of the idea that had formed in his mind when he heard the first rumours of the storm. Soon he would sail for Sicily, but first he needed to plant the seed of his plan to take maximum advantage of the Roman fleet's destruction. The last of Hamilcar's doubts fell away as he walked towards the city. It was time to go on the attack, and with the gods on the side of Carthage, there was none who could stand against him.

Atticus stood with his face up to the sun, his eyes closed against the glare as he felt the heat infuse his body. The overlapping sounds of carpenters' tools filled the air, and Atticus's memory was stirred by the noise, his mind drifting back to that day in Aspis before the fleet sailed to Sicily, and the awe he had felt as he gazed at the assembled fleet. The thought made him open his eyes and he looked out over the eighty galleys anchored in the harbour of Agrigentum.

Many of the ships were listing badly, their hulls still partially flooded. Atticus noticed that some of the crews were using the new screw pump to drain the bilges, a curious-looking device recently invented by a young Syracusan. Of the remaining galleys, every one of them showed signs of storm damage, from splintered oars to severed mainmasts, and Atticus counted a half-dozen ships in the waters immediately surrounding the *Orcus* that would never be seaworthy again.

He moved to the side of the deck and rubbed his hand across the rail, his fingers finding and tracing the outline of a crack in the weathered pine. Eighty galleys saved. Over three hundred lost, amongst them the *Concordia*. Atticus scowled darkly as he observed that the majority of the surviving ships were Carthaginian galleys captured at Cape Hermaeum, the absence of a *corvus* giving them a vital advantage during those first chaotic minutes when the squall line overtook the fleet.

The storm had lasted for four long hours and, by the time it had finally ended, the sea had claimed close to a hundred thousand men. It was a staggering figure, and Atticus could not grasp the amount, a figure twenty times the population of his home city of Locri.

'We're ready to sail, Prefect,' Baro said, and Atticus turned and nodded his assent, his eye drawn to the open welt on Baro's face. As the second-in-command turned away, Atticus unconsciously fingered the scar on his jaw line, tracing the old wound as he had the crack on the side rail of the *Orcus*. His hand fell away as he saw Septimus approach.

'We're ready to go,' Atticus said.

The centurion nodded. 'Homeward bound,' he said, savouring the words, although there was little joy in his voice. 'How long will it take?'

'We have to take the long way around, past Syracuse,' Atticus said. 'A little over a week if the weather holds.'

'If the weather holds?' Septimus said icily. 'Surely the cursed gods have already taken enough?'

Atticus nodded, sharing his friend's anger at Poseidon's feckless slaughter, although his anger also ran deeply for another reason.

Gaius called for steerage speed and the *Orcus* got under way, her bow turning slowly in the inner harbour. Atticus glanced over the aft-rail to the temples overlooking the city. They were magnificent to behold, built when the city was under Greek control nearly two hundred years before, and he looked to each in turn, the temples of Zeus and Hercules, the ruins of the temple of Juno, burned by the Carthaginians when they sacked the city, and finally the temple of Concordia, the goddess of harmony.

Atticus stared at the last temple for a moment and then looked away in contempt. The storm had wiped out the *Classis Romanus*, but Atticus knew their fate had been sealed days before when Paullus had arrogantly dismissed his warnings. The Romans were a proud people. In some that pride had developed into a deep sense of honour – Atticus instinctively glanced at Septimus – but in others it had festered to become a deep-rooted conceit that fed their arrogance. It was this trait that Atticus had come to loathe, one he had encountered too many times in the men who commanded him.

The shout went up for standard speed as the *Orcus* cleared the lines of anchored ships and the galley sped towards the mouth of the harbour, the swell increasing as the protective headlands gave way to the open sea. Atticus looked to the four points of his ship, the sky clear on all horizons, and he ordered the course change, committing *Orcus* to the journey.

Ahead to the southeast lay the coast of Syracuse, and beyond, to the north, the Straits of Messina. Once clear of the channel they would sail with Italy on their flank and their destination dead ahead, a city built on the pride that defined its people and ruled by men who had chosen one or other of the roads from led from that virtue. Given the grave news that the *Orcus* was carrying, of the destruction of the fleet, Atticus knew, as the senior surviving officer, he would have to stand before the leaders of the Republic. With Regulus in Carthaginian hands and Paullus in Pluto's, he could not know who awaited him in Rome.

Scipio remained seated as the debate ended, and for a moment his view was obscured by the senators around him as they stood up and moved to the floor. They began to congregate in small groups, the junior members gravitating around the senior, nodding sagaciously as their mentors made obvious points regarding the loss of the army in Africa. Scipio leaned forward and watched Duilius leave the chamber alone, noting his rival's purposeful stride, the inherent determination and independence that set him apart from the verbose, inconsequential men of the Senate.

Scipio respected that characteristic in his opponent, for it was one he believed was central to his own survival and success; looking out over the floor of the Senate, he silently mocked the lesser men in the chamber, men who grouped together for mutual sponsorship and confidence. Scipio had long ago realized that the Roman Senate was essentially an assembly of individuals. There were no permanent party lines, and even the current factions would be transitory at best, alliances of convenience forged by members of the Senate to serve their own needs.

Scipio had no allies, only confederates, temporary accomplices he used to achieve his own personal agenda – and therein lay the true test of his ability to deceive. These men were never his equal, but if handled incorrectly former accomplices could become enemies, their hostility unleashed at the discovery that they had been used as the means for another's end. Regulus was one such man, a senator Scipio had raised from obscurity to senior consul, but in a moment of unguarded fury he had revealed his motives and Regulus had defied him.

On the day Scipio vowed to avenge Regulus's betrayal, he also swore to learn from his mistake, and his subsequent control of Paullus's nomination and election had been meticulous, the senior consul never realizing the true identity of his patron. Scipio's plan had been simple: to topple Regulus, remove him from command of the expeditionary army and replaced him with Paullus, but the proconsul enjoyed significant support in the Senate, his victory at Ecnomus trumpeted at every opportunity by his former junior consul, Longus, a pawn of Duilius. So Scipio's efforts in Rome had been thwarted.

He had thereafter engineered the vote to send Paullus to Sicily, hoping the new senior consul, free from the immediate restraints of the Senate, would forcefully wrestle the initiative from Regulus; but again he had been frustrated as Paullus continued to timidly defer to the Senate's will.

Now, however, Fortuna's wheel had turned. Scipio's impassive expression hid an inward smile as he observed the worried faces of his fellow senators, their anxiety creating a palpable tension in the Senate chamber that fed Scipio's satisfaction. They bemoaned the defeat of Regulus, but Scipio saw it only as a victory: Paullus had finally been granted the opportunity to intervene directly in Africa, to stamp his authority on the campaign. The senior consul had grabbed it with both hands in a belated display of courage and conviction.

For the first time in months, Scipio was confident that his underlying plan was moving forward once more. If Paullus could conclude his tenure with a victory over the Carthaginians, then the faction that bred him would be strengthened, and consequently Scipio would be a step closer to his ultimate goal.

He had chosen Paullus carefully, selecting a man with the right balance of ambition, arrogance and nescience and, although for a time Paullus's timidity had disappointed Scipio, it now seemed the senior consul was rising to his expectations.

CHAPTER FIVE

Atticus stood on the foredeck of the *Orcus* as the galley cut a path through the teeming waters of Ostia, his gaze ranging over the entire harbour. The sight never failed to overawe him, the multitude of ships competing for space, the sprawling docks consuming the cargo of each vessel as fast as it could be unloaded, the traders frantically trying to feed the insatiable appetite of the city twelve miles away.

The trading ships came from all corners of the Mediterranean, the origin of many of them easily distinguishable by the type of craft or the men who sailed them, while others were more anonymous, bireme galleys and sailing barges that were common to every port. Despite the war, the traders recognized few boundaries, and some of the ships that were docking in Ostia had sailed from ports in the Carthaginian Empire only days before, bringing untraceable cargoes that were swiftly exchanged for the faithless denarius. The Roman authorities had tried to stem this flow, banning vessels from the closest Carthaginian dominions of Sardinia, Malta and the Baliares, but the lure of profit had impelled the traders to disguise their activities, and the Roman merchants in Ostia were only too ready to aid the clandestine trade, their first loyalty given solely to the market.

The oar-powered vessels in the path of the *Orcus* gave way to the larger quinquereme, while Gaius manoeuvred neatly around the more unwieldy sailing barges until the *Orcus* reached the northern end of the port and the military barracks that was the home of the *Classis Romanus*. As always there were a number of galleys tethered to the docks, but most of them were triremes, smaller ships that were no longer considered worthy of the battle line and were used primarily for coastal patrol in the sea-lanes around Ostia.

Atticus studied the nearest trireme in detail. It was nearly identical to the *Aquila*, his first command, as were all the triremes in the Roman fleet, mass-produced copies of an original design that had served the coastal fleet for a generation. Atticus saw past the minor differences and smiled as he pictured his old ship, slower and less powerful than the *Orcus*, but nimbler and quicker to accelerate, an Arabian stallion to the quinquereme warhorse. The Roman fleet's switch to quinqueremes was unalterable, the changing face of warfare dictating the use of larger galleys, but Atticus still believed that the triremes had strengths disproportionate to their size.

Gaius called for steerage speed and then for the oars to be withdrawn as he steered the *Orcus* to a free berth. Atticus turned to leave the foredeck but he stopped as he saw a number of men running towards his galley. A mixture of sailors and legionaries, they were clearly agitated. Atticus spotted an officer at the head of the group, his head turning quickly as he swept the *Orcus* with his gaze.

'What ship?' the officer shouted as he neared the dockside.

'The *Orcus*,' Atticus called back.

The officer followed the voice and looked directly at Atticus. 'What fleet?' he called frantically.

'The consul's fleet, from Africa.'

For a second the officer seemed lost for words, as if Atticus's identification had somehow confirmed a terrible truth. 'Is it true?' he asked.

Atticus looked perplexed.

'The storm, the fleet,' the officer continued, his voice rising. 'Is it true? Has the fleet been destroyed?'

Atticus was stunned by the questions and he moved quickly to the main deck as mooring ropes were thrown and made secure. The officer mirrored his progress on the dock, his impatience increasing, and as the gangway crashed down he was standing directly before Atticus.

'Answer my questions, Captain,' he said angrily.

'Prefect,' Atticus corrected him as he disembarked. He noticed the officer wore the uniform of a tribune, and so their ranks were in effect the same, although Atticus doubted that the Roman would recognize the equality.

'All right . . . Prefect,' the tribune said derisively. 'Is it true, man?'

'What have you heard?' Atticus asked, wary of the larger crowd of soldiers standing behind the officer, not wishing to confirm any news before he had spoken to someone in authority.

'Just rumours, from traders arriving in Ostia in the last two days. They speak of a terrible storm off the southwest coast of Sicily that destroyed the consul's fleet. We heard there were survivors but there has been no confirmation from a military galley.'

'Who commands here?' Atticus asked, motioning to the barracks behind.

The tribune stated the name.

'Take me to him,' Atticus said, and he walked towards the barracks. The tribune hesitated for a second, overcome with frustration, but he followed, the men he had led from the barracks falling in behind.

*

Regulus shrugged on the fresh toga and stepped out of the bath, taking the proffered goblet of wine as he did so. He had not bathed in weeks and the simple cleansing ritual had gone some way to ease the constant feeling of foreboding he had lived with since his capture. He sniffed the wine and took a sip, savouring the taste before he followed his attendant slave to a shaded courtyard at the rear of the villa.

He had been brought to Carthage the evening before, escorted on horseback from Tunis with his hands tied like a common criminal. He had swallowed his protests, knowing that to utter them would invite ridicule, but the yoke of captivity was heavy and it was with difficulty that he kept his head high on the journey.

He had spent the night in another darkened room, but with the dawn came an incredible change in the nature of his captivity. The door of his room had been opened by a slave bearing towels, and as Regulus stepped out he immediately noticed the absence of guards, the villa in which he found himself quiet in the early morning sunlight. He had followed the slave to the bathhouse and, although the quality of the baths was by far inferior to his own in Rome, Regulus had rejoiced at the opportunity to cleanse himself. Now as he sat in the open courtyard, he wondered about the change in his condition. There was only one answer.

Regulus looked up as Hamilcar entered the courtyard. He stood without thinking and then cursed his carelessness, the change in his treatment softening his defences. He quickly recovered and squared his shoulders, adopting a look of superiority as Hamilcar crossed the open space.

Hamilcar smiled contemptuously, seeing through the Roman's charade. He had been watching Regulus surreptitiously for several minutes, noting how at ease the Roman was, justifying his decision to grant his enemy this simple boon, knowing that the Roman's compliance was vital if his plan was to proceed. He stepped closer to Regulus and stood before him, allowing a silence to lengthen.

'I know why you have brought me here, Barca,' Regulus said.

Hamilcar raised his eyebrows in question.

'My people have offered you a ransom for my return and you have accepted it.'

Hamilcar almost laughed out loud but he kept his derision in check, knowing his words would have a far greater effect.

'You are mistaken, Roman,' he replied. 'I have brought you here so I could deliver some news to you in person.' And Hamilcar proceeded to tell Regulus of the events during his captivity in Tunis. He began with the battle at Cape Hermaeum, leaving out the capture of many of his ships and, although Hamilcar did not speak of it as a defeat, he noticed a sly smile creep on to Regulus's face as he described the breakout of the galleys at Aspis to join the larger Roman fleet from Sicily.

Hamilcar paused, allowing Regulus to revel in the good news before he continued to describe the subsequent movements of the Roman fleet, their return to Sicily, their foolish disregard for the unpredictable weather before the rising of Sirius and the sudden storm that had destroyed them all. He continued unabated, even as he heard Regulus's wine goblet clatter to the ground, and as he finished he watched with cold triumph as Regulus stumbled back to sit once more on the low bench.

Hamilcar stayed silent, keeping his gaze firmly on Regulus, studying him, the Roman sitting with his head bowed. Hamilcar knew it would not last. Regulus would lift his head again. He would gather his strength and pride and accuse Hamilcar of deceit and fabrication. It would not matter.

In time he would persuade Regulus of the truth of his report and, although the proconsul would remain a prisoner, he would be treated reasonably, allowing Hamilcar to steadily gain his trust, so that Regulus would accept his proposal – one that he had, after all, already accepted in another form.

Atticus sped on horseback along the Via Aurelia, his chest close to his mount's crest. Septimus was on his left shoulder, while ahead the *contubernia* of ten mounted soldiers cleared a path with hurried shouts of warning to the human stream that travelled the great north road. Atticus's mind was on the task ahead, the rapid rhythm of hoof beats on the paving stones aiding his concentration.

The commander at the barracks in Ostia had confirmed the tribune's assertions. Ostia and Rome were awash with rumours of the fleet's destruction and two days of uncertainty had created a latent panic that was only kept in check by the absence of any firm proof, something Atticus was now going to deliver to the Senate.

The horsemen reached the Servian Wall and sped through the Porta Flumentana, their pace only slowing as they entered the narrow streets. The *insulae* soared above them on either side, while between them Atticus caught glances of the Palatine and Capitoline hills reaching up from the valley floor.

The streets were packed with people moving with intent, and Atticus's mount snorted anxiously as the crowd pressed in from all sides. Atticus spurred on his horse, ignoring the angry abuse of those he pushed aside. The pedestrians' temerity in the face of mounted armed men emphasized the confidence every Roman citizen felt in their safety within the walls of the city.

The narrow street soon gave way to the open space of the

Forum Magnum, the main Forum, and the horses increased to a canter as they crossed to the northwest corner and the Curia. Atticus and Septimus dismounted and walked quickly up the steps, their eyes raised to the columned entrance above. Atticus paused as he reached the top and looked over his shoulder to the city spread out before him. The air was filled with the constant hum of a bustling population, concealed within the myriad streets. Atticus recalled the last time he had stood on this spot, when those same people had crowded into the Forum below to celebrate the fleet's first victory at Mylae. He turned and saw Septimus waiting for him. He nodded and they went inside.

The noise of the outside world subsided with every step they took beyond the entrance to the Curia, to be replaced with the drone of voices raised in debate interspersed with calls of agreement and dissent. Atticus paused at the threshold, his gaze sweeping the tiered seating, searching for a familiar face to call attention to his arrival.

The chamber was no more than a third full, with many of the senators leaning into tight circles of private conversation, while others looked to the senator speaking at length at the near side of the room. He was reading from a parchment, his monotone delivery holding the attention of only those closest to him, whose enthusiasm for his words seemed lacklustre at best.

Atticus felt Septimus tap him on the arm, drawing his attention to the podium facing the tiered seating. An old senator was seated beside it, his back straight in the winged chair. His gaze was locked on the speaker. Atticus nodded and walked across the floor, his movement drawing the attention of some of the senators.

The *princeps senatus* looked towards Atticus as he heard the approaching footsteps. He stood up slowly, his expression a mixture of annoyance and curiosity and, as Atticus leaned in to whisper to him, a general murmur began to develop amongst the onlookers, quickly reaching a level that caused the speaker to pause in his oration and look towards the podium.

Atticus gave his message quickly and succinctly, leaving the *princeps senatus* little chance to respond, but the senators closest to the podium noticed the change in the leader's expression and their reaction fuelled further speculation that ended all other conversation in the chamber.

Atticus stood upright once more as he finished, and the *princeps senatus* stepped back, his hand reaching for the podium. He moved behind it and the chamber came to order unbidden.

'This man . . .' he began, pointing to Atticus and looking to him questioningly, having forgotten his name. After Atticus's whispered prompt, the older man continued: '. . . Prefect Perennis, of Consul Paullus's fleet, brings news of the gravest import.'

The mention of Paullus brought many of the senators to their feet. They had all heard the rumours and the *princeps senatus*'s demeanour was in itself confirmation. A barrage of questions swept across the chamber. The leader called for order but his frailty, compounded by shock, undermined his attempts, and his words were lost in the maelstrom.

'Citizens!'

Septimus's sudden strident call brought quiet to the chamber. Everyone looked to the centurion, his commanding stare holding their attention, drawing out the silence. He nodded to Atticus who turned to address the chamber.

'Senators, I have come here from Agrigentum to inform you of the destruction of the *Classis Romanus*,' Atticus began. He outlined the events of the storm, omitting his conversation with Paullus in Aspis but sparing no other detail, including the loss of the *Concordia* with all hands. The senators listened in complete silence, staggered by the disaster. The conclusion of his announcement was met by a deafening roar of questions and lamentations.

The dozens of discussions made individual debate impossible. Atticus remained at the podium, answering questions as they were asked, repeating details of the report a dozen times in as many minutes to senators at opposite ends of the room. Some men rushed from the chamber to seek out absent senators, feeding them the news as they led them back to the Senate. Each new arrival added to the confusion, the noise level growing as the numbers passed two hundred. Atticus could no longer isolate individual voices. The frustration of those who had not heard the report first-hand quickly turned to aggression as their questions were lost in the uproar.

Unnoticed by Atticus, Scipio entered the chamber, led by the junior senator who had sought him out. He stopped just feet inside the room and scanned the crowd, sneering disdainfully at the sight. He had seen this too often. The Senate of Rome, the leaders of the Republic, reduced to a panicked mob, lacking what Scipio always believed only he and a few others like him could bestow: the iron hand of leadership. He uttered a brief command to the junior senator at his side, and the younger man disappeared into the throng to search out the members of the conservative faction, drawing their attention to Scipio's presence. As a group they did not recognize him as their leader, but individually the majority of them had forged an alliance with Scipio, the junior senators acknowledging him as a patron, the senior members as a cohort; although each man believed his association to be unique, the web of secrecy that Scipio imposed concealing the breadth of his influence.

He stepped out into an open space in the floor and waited for the ripple effect of individual groups becoming quiet to cascade into a general silence as senators quickly turned in the direction indicated by others. Soon all were focused on the senior senator standing apart on the floor of the chamber.

Atticus, puzzled by the return to order, followed the gaze of the crowd. A wave of anger and dread swept over him as he recognized Scipio; his hands clenched the edges of the podium to steady his temper and nerve. Scipio was the manifestation of all that Atticus despised in Rome. He realized that the enmity he felt for the hydra-headed politician had not abated over the years since he had last seen him. It struck him now like a hammer blow to the stomach and he failed to keep his emotions in check. Anger twisted his mouth, accentuating the deep scar on his face.

Scipio turned to the podium and, seeing the Greek's expression, smiled coldly. The shock of the news the junior senator had brought had been tempered by the identity of the messenger. This was the Greek who had brought glory to his sworn enemy, Duilius, and compounded Scipio's downfall; the whoreson, who had somehow survived subsequent attempts to destroy him, always remained beyond Scipio's immediate reach. He turned his back on Atticus and looked around the room. It was nearly full and he motioned to the senators still standing on the floor to be seated, the men complying without hesitation. A hush fell over the vaulted chamber.

'Repeat your report in full,' Scipio said dismissively over his shoulder, and Atticus's voice filled the room once more. Scipio remained standing, adjusting his position until he seemed to become the conduit for Atticus's report, the senators instinctively shifting their gaze continuously from the podium to the lone senator on the floor. As Atticus's report ended for a second time, all eyes turned to Scipio.

'Can you confirm the loss of the *Concordia*?' he asked, keeping his back to Atticus.

'The surviving ships sailed to Agrigentum. The *Concordia* was not amongst them. I can confirm nothing beyond that,' Atticus replied, the identity of his interrogator giving his voice a hostile edge.

The tone was not lost on Scipio, and he quickly rearranged the sequence of questions in his mind. The senators were in shock, the loss of the fleet compounded by the almost certain loss of both consuls. In times of crisis, weak men often turn to the strong for guidance and reassurance, and Scipio was, for now, in a unique position. Duilius was not in the chamber – he had not yet arrived, and Scipio held the floor. The Senate was looking to him, but Scipio knew the spell of shock and uncertainty would soon be broken as other astute members of the Senate regained their wits. So he needed to act fast if he was to exploit the opportunity to the full. Paullus was undoubtedly dead, the Senate would soon need to elect a new leader, but there was also a chance to blacken the name of the Greek. He turned once more to Atticus and, needing to further antagonize him, adopted an expression of utter contempt.

'With the senior consul missing, you were the most senior officer to survive the storm?' he asked.

'Yes,' Atticus replied.

Scipio nodded and turned to face the senators once more. 'So you felt it was your responsibility to inform the Senate,' he said, gesturing to the house with a sweep of his hand.

'Yes,' Atticus said tersely.

'Your responsibility,' Scipio repeated, as if contemplating the word. He turned once more to Atticus. 'Are you familiar with the crime of *perduellio*?' he asked.

A dark murmur swept through the chamber, an undertone of surprise and outrage, and Scipio turned once more to the senators before Atticus could reply, conscious that he needed to control their anger at the loss of the fleet and that his approach needed to be cautious.

'Understand that I do not accuse the senior consul and the prefects of the fleet with this crime,' Scipio went on tactfully, 'but I do believe that such a loss demands a measure of responsibility. *Perduellio* is the crime of treason. Through the loss of the fleet, the security of Rome has been placed in grave danger. It is vital that we know where responsibility lies.'

Many of the senators nodded at this explanation. The loss of the fleet was catastrophic, and if it was due to negligence then perhaps there was a case for a charge of treason. They looked again to Atticus, many now unconsciously seeing him as a defendant rather than a messenger.

Atticus had never heard of *perduellio*, but he understood the implication of a charge of treason and his anger turned to caution. He sensed Septimus take a step closer to the podium and he drew strength from his presence, although his gaze never left Scipio.

The senator turned to Atticus once more. 'You've reported that Consul Paullus ordered the fleet to Sicily to threaten the ports held by Carthage on the southwestern shore.'

'Those were the consul's orders,' Atticus replied earnestly, conscious of Scipio's play on words, the subtle insinuation that Atticus was reporting a personal version of events that somehow concealed a hidden truth. He tried to anticipate Scipio's next question, knowing that this was the senator's arena and that Scipio held the advantage of experience.

'Your ship survived the storm,' Scipio said suspiciously. 'You are obviously an experienced sailor. Why then did you not anticipate such a terrible deterioration in the weather and warn the consul? You are a prefect and your first loyalty should be to the fleet.'

'I . . .' Atticus made to answer but he checked himself,

indecision staying his words. To protest that he did warn Paullus would surely look like a fabrication given Scipio's implied accusation, but to remain silent would equally condemn him.

Scipio was shocked by the hesitation, realizing suddenly that it was quite possible that Perennis had indeed predicted the storm and even warned Paullus of the danger. He quickly re-evaluated his attack. One of the central rules of debate was to ask only questions to which you already knew the answer, so you could not be taken by surprise. Scipio had believed the premise of his question was groundless, that it was impossible for anyone to predict the vicissitudes of the weather, but he had posed it regardless, content that any answer Perennis offered could not deflect the accusation of negligence. Although the Greek would never be convicted of *perduellio* on such inadequate grounds, the implied guilt would remain.

Now, however, there was every chance the Greek would implicate Paullus, and while Scipio cared little for the consul's reputation, many senators might be incensed by the attack. Scipio could lose his temporary control over the debate amid accusations of slander.

'Your responsibility was clear and you will be dealt with in due course,' Scipio said, determined to end his attack while he held the initiative. 'Until then you are dismissed.'

Atticus held his ground, still immobilized by uncertainty, until Scipio's will compelled him to move.

'Wait,' Septimus said, stepping up to the podium.

Scipio whipped around. 'Hold your tongue, Centurion,' he spat. 'You are both dismissed from the Curia. Get out.'

'Stand fast,' a voice shouted out, and the entire chamber turned to the senator standing at the entranceway.

Duilius strode to the centre of the floor, placing himself between Scipio and the podium. His expression was hard and determined and he stood silent for a minute as he regulated his breathing. His headlong rush on horseback from his estate beyond the city walls had taxed him, but it had also given him the chance to fully absorb the news borne by the messenger. He glanced over his shoulder to the podium; although his face remained impassive, he gave the two men standing there a subtle nod of alliance. He had heard the final moments of the confrontation between them and Scipio and immediately grasped his rival's intent. He turned once more to the Senate.

'Senators of Rome,' he began, 'this disaster demands that we stand united by loyalty, not divided by censure. The prefect is a messenger. He is not here to answer for the loss of the fleet.'

Duilius's dramatic arrival had broken the spell of Scipio's control over the debate, and the majority of the senators voiced their agreement, their attention turning once more to the heart of the crisis. Scipio marked the shift and he strode across the floor, his movement drawing attention.

'The loss of the fleet is a catastrophe that demands swift and decisive action,' he exhorted. 'We must confirm the loss of the consuls and act accordingly.'

Again voices were raised in agreement and Scipio stopped pacing to hold the attention of the Senate. Duilius took the opportunity to glance once more at Atticus, gesturing for him to leave. Atticus nodded, and he and Septimus quietly left the chamber.

Duilius watched them leave and turned his full attention back to his rival. The debate was now descending into a protracted discussion, with other senators standing in their seats in a bid to be heard. As Duilius looked on, the *princeps senatus* reasserted a level of control, calling out senators by name and permitting them to speak in turn. Scipio moved slowly to his seat, finally relinquishing the floor, aware that his moment had passed. Duilius shadowed his move, glancing surreptitiously at him as he sat down.

The political stakes had increased immeasurably with the loss of both the fleet and the consuls, and Duilius cursed the vital minutes that Scipio had held sway over the debate, knowing that many of the more fickle members of the Senate would remember that Scipio had stood before them when uncertainty reigned.

Septimus put his arm out and steadied Atticus, gripping his shoulder tightly as the two men stood at the top of the steps leading down from the Curia to the Forum.

'Thank Fortuna Duilius turned up when he did,' he muttered.

Atticus nodded in reply. 'That bastard Scipio,' he said, and glanced over his shoulder to the shadowed entrance behind him. The senator had totally outmatched him, backing him into a corner and then allowing no avenue of escape. He felt a fool, and was angry that he had not defended himself better. He turned abruptly and set off down the steps, Septimus following a pace behind.

The afternoon sun was warm on their backs and Septimus watched their shadows reach down the steps before them, seething at how his friend had been treated by the Senate, and in particular how Scipio had continued unchecked before Duilius arrived. He glanced at Atticus as they reached the bottom of the steps, noticing that his friend's attention was drawn to the southeastern corner of the Forum and the Viminal quarter beyond.

Thoughts of what had occurred in the Senate fled from Septimus's mind to be replaced with a forgotten anger. His sister, Hadria, lived at their aunt's house in the Viminal quarter, and it was obvious that Atticus was thinking of going there. Time had not diminished Septimus's resolve to prevent the affair between Atticus and his sister, but as he made to step forward and stand before his friend to bar his way, he hesitated.

He thought of how long it had been since either Atticus or he had set foot in Rome, how long it had been since he had seen his own family. He looked up at the Curia and remembered the danger Atticus had just faced and the many enemies he and his friend had faced together over the previous year. For an instant his pride reared up again and demanded he confront Atticus, but his friendship argued for a stay in his conviction.

'I'm going to the Caelian quarter to see my family,' Septimus said. 'I'll see you back at the ship?'

The question startled Atticus but he quickly recovered and nodded. Septimus slapped him once more on the shoulder and walked over to the *contubernia* of soldiers who had waited with their mounts. He took his horse and set off across the Forum. He did not look back.

Atticus stood still for a moment longer and then retrieved his horse, dismissing the soldiers as he did so. He mounted and looked to where Septimus had crossed the Forum but the centurion was lost from sight. Atticus spurred his horse and turned towards the Viminal quarter.

He reached the house with ease, recalling each corner of the familiar journey. As he tethered his horse outside Hadria's house, the intervening year fell away. His knock on the outer door was answered by a servant Atticus did not recognize, and he saw suspicion in the servant's eyes as he looked upon the tall stranger with a scarred face and intense green eyes. That suspicion was compounded when Atticus spoke, his unusual accent marking him as a non-native. The servant admitted him warily, leading Atticus to the open-roofed atrium that stood before the inner rooms of the house.

The servant asked him to wait. Atticus walked around the rainwater pool in the centre of the atrium. During his time away from Rome he had thought of Hadria almost every day, evoking her in his mind's eye, placing her within specific memories to capture the essence of her beauty, but trying always to keep his emotions in check, never knowing for sure when he would see her again, the great distance between them an abyss that only fate could cross. Now, that moment of reunion was but seconds away and his feelings for her swept over him.

Hadria appeared in a blur of movement, racing into the atrium, her head turning as she sought him out. Atticus looked at her intently, taking in every detail. She was different from the image that had sustained him over the previous year. Her brown hair was darker and shoulder length, framing her face to accentuate her sea-grey eyes. Her gaze possessed a steely determination, as if she was somehow more self-assured.

Hadria's face lit up as she saw Atticus across the tranquil pool, and she skirted around its edge to run into his opened arms. She breathed in the smell of him, letting it fill her memories, and when she broke his embrace to kiss him, the intensity of the contact drew blood from her lip that mingled with the taste of him. She had lived moments like this before, when he had returned from other campaigns, but each time felt like the first, the surge of emotion overwhelming her. She drew him ever closer, not daring to trust her senses and believe that he had returned once more.

Hours later, Atticus sat at the edge of Hadria's bed and looked out at the sun falling behind the Quirinal Hill. He felt a light touch on his lower back and he looked over his shoulder and smiled. Hadria was stretched across the bed, her hair cascading across her face, giving her a dishevelled look. He fell back into her arms. He kissed her tenderly, acutely aware of how fragile her naked body looked, but as she moved against him he felt the strength in her slender limbs.

'The messenger will be here soon,' he said, and she nodded. Septimus was home, which meant she would be summoned to see him. The anticipation of seeing her brother safe and well was coloured by having to leave Atticus.

'Can you wait until I return?' she asked.

'There's not enough time,' he replied. 'I will need to leave the city before they close the gates at sundown if I'm to return to Ostia.'

'You could stay here for the night,' she smiled.

'But your aunt, is she not here?'

'She is, but she knows of you,' Hadria replied casually.

Atticus was shocked by the revelation. He had thought that Hadria was striving to keep their relationship secret until she felt the time was right to tell her parents.

'I have been resisting my parents' efforts to have me re-married,' she explained. 'That raised my aunt's suspicions, and with so many servants in this house there are few secrets. She confronted me months ago and I revealed my love for you.'

'Has she told your parents?'

'No,' Hadria replied. 'She agreed to keep my secret as long as I agreed to tell my parents of our relationship when next you were in Rome.'

'Then I must accompany you tonight,' Atticus said.

Hadria shook her head. 'My father is away from Rome for another week,' she said. 'When he returns we will stand before him, together.'

She smiled in anticipation and Atticus embraced her once more, not wanting her to sense the doubt he felt in his own heart. Hadria's father, Antoninus, was a former centurion of the Ninth Legion, a Roman of the equestrian class. He had always treated Atticus with shifting levels of respect and contempt, his admiration of a fellow commander vying with his suspicion about Atticus's heritage. Now Atticus would stand before him as his daughter's suitor, and only Antoninus could decide which instinct would hold sway.

Scipio looked slowly around the candlelit walls of the dining room, studying the familiar murals, which told the story of Aeneas's heroic flight from Troy and the journey that took him to the shores of Italy, a simple thread of history that led, generations later, to the founding of Rome. Scipio smiled, remembering how – as a child – this private room had been forbidden to him by his father. He had defied that prohibition many times, sneaking in to view the legend that enthralled him; but even now, although his father was gone, Scipio still felt echoes of the fear that had marked each secret visit to the room.

The sound of approaching footsteps caused Scipio to stir and he looked to the doorway. A moment later, his wife, Fabiola, entered. She was wearing a simple woollen *stola* and the modesty of the garment strongly accentuated her classical beauty, her dark brown eyes reflecting the candlelight that flickered as she glided on to her own couch. She held out her hand and Scipio took it, his thumb stroking the back of her tapered fingers. She smiled demurely, nodding indulgently at his offer of wine.

Scipio called out to the doorway and immediately servants swept into the room bearing fresh fruit and cooked meats, each placing their platter in turn on the low square table between the couches. As they left Fabiola began to talk of inconsequential matters, keeping her tone light and sweet, pausing in her conversation only to refill her husband's wine goblet, her words carefully chosen to relax and amuse.

As Fabiola spoke she felt a keen sense of expectation rise within her. That Scipio had chosen to have dinner in the private dining room could only mean that he wished to seek her counsel, and she longed for her husband to put an end to her idle chatter and reveal his inner thoughts. In the past, their discussions within the house had been overheard by servants who had been paid spies of Duilius's, a betrayal that Fabiola had exposed. She remembered how he had had those spies brutally tortured and put to death. She paused for breath, and as she did so Scipio spoke.

'In response to the deaths of Paullus and Nobilior, the Senate has voted to hold emergency consular elections next week.'

Fabiola nodded in reply but remained silent.

'This may be my opportunity,' he mused, and he looked intently at his wife.

Fabiola took a moment to gather her thoughts. 'I agree there may never be a better time,' she said.

Scipio nodded. 'But I had not thought to run for the consulship for at least another two years,' he cautioned. 'If I strike now and fail, it will cost me any future chance.'

'Now or in the future, a protracted electoral campaign would be difficult.' *Given your past disgrace*, she almost said, but she continued seamlessly. 'The senators who are allied to you are weak men, subject to their passions. The loss of the fleet is a crisis that favours your oratorical skills. If you fan the flames of their fear and uncertainty, they will support you.'

Again Scipio nodded. He had surmised as much, but to hear Fabiola's endorsement strengthened his resolve. He gazed at her over the rim of his wine goblet, filtering her words through his own thoughts, and found no flaw in his plan, although it was fraught with risk. Duilius was sure to oppose him, perhaps with a 'new man' candidate of his own, and there was still a large block of undeclared senators between the two existing factions in the Senate. He looked at his options again, examining them from every angle, slowly spinning the goblet in his hand, creating a tiny vortex in the deep red wine.

Fabiola watched Scipio in silence, confident that her words had been of use to her husband, sensing that he was close to a decision. The struggle of the past year had been exhausting for both of them, the countless evenings entertaining political guests in the main dining room of the house, each banquet carefully orchestrated to persuade and cajole senators into Scipio's camp. Fabiola recalled how often she had fawned over men who were but a shadow of her husband in order to secure their support. That struggle had borne fruit in the partial resurrection of her husband's political strength, but it was insufficient compensation for Fabiola: she yearned for the time when Scipio would once more take his rightful place as the most powerful man in Rome.

CHAPTER SIX

Lentulus, the master shipbuilder, stroked the threadlike grey hairs of his beard as he listened intently to the debate raging around the table. He glanced at the Greek sailor at the head of the table, recalling the crucial elements of his report, and looked down at the notes he had made, at the brief scribbled words and crude diagrams that represented his initial thoughts.

He glanced at the sailor again, remembering when he had first met him years before. In many ways he was the same man; still tall and lean with an intense restlessness that often infected those around him – as it did Lentulus's apprentices now – but in other ways he had changed. The scar on his face was an obvious difference, but Lentulus noticed more subtle changes. His previous openness had been replaced by wariness, and his eyes now seemed to search beneath the skin of every man he looked at, as if trying to discern their inner thoughts.

'We have to try and rebalance the design,' an apprentice said, and Lentulus's thoughts returned to the conversation.

'We can't,' another said. 'If we counter-balance the weight of the *corvus* on the stern, then the draught of the ship will be compromised.'

'You're ignoring the increased ballast of the quinquereme,' the first said. 'The *corvus* was originally designed for a trireme. The larger ship can take the weight.'

'It can't,' Lentulus interjected, and he looked to the Greek sailor. 'Tell us again, Prefect, about the *Strenua* and how she foundered.'

Atticus restated what he had witnessed. As before, the four apprentices were enthralled by the report, particularly when Atticus described the speed at which the galley had been lost in the storm.

'It is not a question of weight,' Lentulus said in the silence that followed. 'It is one of balance.'

He stood up and began to pace one side of the room, his hands clasped lightly behind his back. He began to explain his conclusions, partly for the benefit of those in the room, but also to clarify his ideas by voicing them aloud.

'Neither the original trireme of the Roman coastal fleet,' he said, 'nor the Tyrian-styled quinquereme of the Carthaginian fleet, which we adopted, was ever designed with the *corvus* in mind. Each was built with a finely balanced hull; a balance the dead weight of the *corvus* corrupted.'

'But we addressed those concerns when we adopted the *corvus*,' one of the apprentices contested. 'It was built within the design tolerances of the galley. Perhaps the fault lies not with the ship but with the crews and their seamanship.'

Atticus's eyes darkened. 'So you believe the crews are to blame for their own deaths?' he growled.

The underlying violence inherent in Atticus's words was not lost on the apprentice, but he held his ground, not wanting to lose face in front of his master.

'I meant no disrespect, Prefect,' he said, a slight tremble in his voice. 'But the design cannot be wrong. It was rigorously tested.'

'Your designs were tested in the confines of coastal waters,' Atticus argued. 'They were never fully tested in open seas, or in battle, or in a storm. Those sailors you speak so ill of lost their lives proving that point.'

Chastened by Atticus's words and his conviction, the apprentice looked down at the table. Atticus continued to stare at him, his impulsive annoyance refusing to abate. The apprentice was a young man, no more than a boy, probably little older than Atticus himself had been when he'd joined the navy, and Atticus suddenly realized his anger was not directed at the apprentice but at himself. He remembered the day he had rushed to this very room with the seeds of the idea that would become the *corvus*. How he had stood before Lentulus and expounded on his plan for a boarding ramp, and how he had been filled with pride when that idea had become a reality and been proved in battle at Mylae. Although it seemed a lifetime ago, it was but a few years, and Atticus conceded that he had hidden that memory from himself to suppress his own culpability, knowing he had once been the greatest advocate of the *corvus*.

'The prefect is right,' Lentulus said, taking control of the meeting once more. 'In our haste and hubris we ignored the fundamental attributes of a galley, ballast and balance, and we failed to fully appreciate the effect the boarding ramp would have on those.'

The apprentices nodded in silent agreement and Lentulus dismissed them from the room with instructions to begin work on finding an answer to the problem.

'So you believe there is a solution?' Atticus asked.

Lentulus looked to the initial thoughts he had sketched out. 'No,' he replied after a pause, 'not if we need our galleys to compete with the speed and manoeuvrability of the Carthaginians.'

'We cannot fight the Punici on their terms, we need the

advantage the *corvus* gives us,' Atticus said, his defence of the boarding ramp sounding treacherous in his own mind.

'We may not have a choice, Prefect,' Lentulus said, pacing the room once more. 'Everyone in Fiumicino knows how and why the fleet was lost. Already crews are refusing to sail on any galley with a *corvus*, and with good cause. They will not, and we cannot, take the chance of such a loss occurring again.'

The conversation continued, but Atticus found it impossible to focus. He had been back in Rome over a week and this was not the first time he had had this argument, albeit with other men. That the master shipbuilder had asked for his report in person was evidence of the enormity of the problem the fleet now faced, trapped between the opposing forces of the Carthaginians and the weather, one threat calling for the retention of the *corvus*, the other for its rejection.

The meeting ended an hour later and Atticus left the barracks at Fiumicino to walk down to the shoreline to clear his head. The slips and scaffolding that dominated the beach were quiet in the noon heat, and he picked his way through them, the soft repetitive sound of waves crashing on the black sand allowing him to calm the voices of frustration. He turned his back on the beach and found his horse in the stables of the barracks, mounting it in one fluid movement as he set off for the city, his thoughts now focusing on the evening ahead, a smile creeping on to his face in anticipation. Hadria's father had returned to Rome and it was finally time for Atticus and Hadria's love to emerge from the shadows.

Regulus cursed as his foot caught a loose stone and he had to throw out his arms to regain his balance. The squad of soldiers escorting him did not check its pace, and Regulus was forced to trot for a half-dozen steps to regain his position in the centre of the formation. He looked up the hill to his left, to the citadel commanding the summit, comparing it to the descriptive reports he had read since he had first arrived in Africa. None of them had captured the essence of the fortress, its sheer brute size coupled with its daunting position, and Regulus was left to wonder how Carthage could fall with such strength at its core.

The squad led him to the quayside, and the traders and merchantmen crowding the docks opened their ranks to allow the soldiers through, the conversations continuing around the obstruction until it passed, voices raised in languages Regulus did not understand. He kept his eyes front, ignoring the baleful stares of the few who deduced his nationality, their incomprehensible curses lost in the clamour.

The commercial docks gave way to the military harbour, and again Regulus took the opportunity to observe it closely. The military harbour was circular in shape, with a raised island circumscribed by a lagoon at its centre and an outer perimeter quay. Boathouses covered every available space and, of the two hundred available berths, Regulus counted a dozen rams jutting out of occupied spaces, the extended claws of the beasts within.

At the far end of the harbour was a barracks house; the squad passed through the arched entranceway to a small courtyard inside. On three sides of the courtyard open doorways led to inner corridors and rooms, but on the side facing Regulus each door was heavily bolted, the metal turned green from exposure to the salt-laden air. The commander of the squad stepped forward alone to the middle door and wrenched back the bolt with a single pull. He turned to Regulus and motioned him forward.

'You have thirty minutes,' he said.

Regulus was puzzled but he stepped forward into the darkened room. The door closed behind him and the bolt was slammed home once more.

His eyes were immediately drawn to a small opening high on the opposing wall, which allowed in a pitiful shaft of white sunlight that barely penetrated the oppressive darkness. The opening was streaked with white excrement, and loose feathers fell through the beam of sunlight as birds, disturbed by the sound of the door, flew back to their perches once more.

'Proconsul?'

Regulus's gaze fell and he perceived four figures approaching him through the gloom. They wore tattered Roman uniforms and, as the sunlight fell across their gaunt faces, Regulus recognized each of them in turn. They were tribunes of his army, the command staff who had been with him in the breakout at Tunis. Regulus instinctively straightened his back, his officers following suit as they saluted him. He nodded in reply and then stepped forward, extending his hand. Each took it in a silent acknowledgement of comradeship.

'What news of the rest of the men?' Regulus asked.

'They have been enslaved, Proconsul,' one of the tribunes replied. 'We alone were brought here from Tunis five days ago.'

'Enslaved,' Regulus repeated, bowing his head. Over the previous week, Hamilcar had called on him three times at the villa. Each time Regulus had enquired after the fate of the five hundred men taken at Tunis, but the Carthaginian had refused to be drawn on the question, focusing instead on fresh evidence that confirmed his story of the Roman fleet's destruction. Regulus's suspicion and Hamilcar's obfuscation had made him accept that the fate of his legionaries was sealed the moment they were taken in battle.

'We have far worse news, Proconsul,' one of the other tribunes said, and he began to tell Regulus of the rumours they had heard of the storm. Regulus held his hand up to silence the tribune.

'Those rumours may be true,' he said, admitting out loud

for the first time his belief in what Hamilcar had told him. He explained what he knew in detail, and watched as their expressions displayed the terrible realization he had slowly faced over the past week.

Regulus studied them in the silence that followed. They were all young men, sons of senators and, in the case of two of them, sons of former consuls. The Africa campaign was their first, and Regulus remembered their infectious exuberance after the victories of Ecnomus and Adys, a boundless confidence fed by the naiveté of youth. Defeat and capture had shattered that brashness, but Regulus was proud to see that – in some at least – it had been replaced by maturity, a strength they would need in the months ahead.

The metallic grind of the door-bolt broke the silence and Regulus left the tribunes with assurances that he would soon return, already suspecting why they had been brought to Carthage, although unsure as to why he had been allowed to see them. The guard detail formed up around Regulus and they quickly left the courtyard, threading their way once more through the docks to retrace their steps to the villa. As they passed the base of the hill leading to the citadel, one of the soldiers followed a curt command and broke from the formation, striking out towards the fortress at a run.

When they returned to the villa, Regulus went immediately to the familiar surroundings of the inner courtyard. He called for wine and waited patiently in the shade, his thoughts on the tribunes and the wealth of their families in Rome. Approaching footsteps alerted him and he stood up to receive his expected visitor, an unconscious civility to echo the courtesy his enemy had shown him since his arrival in Carthage. Hamilcar entered the courtyard and nodded at Regulus.

'You have seen your men,' he said.

'I have, Barca,' Regulus replied, 'as your soldier reported.'

He sat down again and took a sip of his wine. 'So, you have spared my tribunes from enslavement for ransom.'

'Yes.'

'But why let me see them?'

'So you can confirm that they are safe and well,' Hamilcar said. 'I want you to travel to Rome to negotiate their ransom.'

'Me?' Regulus replied, astonished by the suggestion. 'You would release me?'

'On parole,' Hamilcar said.

Again Regulus was stunned. Parole was an agreement based on word of honour, one that Regulus would uphold because he held himself to be honourable. But the Carthaginian could not know that for sure, not from their brief acquaintance. 'It would be madness to release me, Barca,' he said, revealing his thoughts out loud. 'You cannot have faith in my honour, and the lives of four tribunes are too insignificant to guarantee my return.' His eyes narrowed warily. 'There's something else, something you're not telling me.'

Hamilcar nodded. 'There is something else,' he said. 'The ransom of the tribunes is merely a symbol of good faith.'

'Good faith?'

'For what I also want from you,' Hamilcar replied, and he walked over to stand before Regulus, slowly forming and re-forming the wording of his proposal in his mind, conscious of its importance. 'I want you to act as an ambassador,' he said, his tone wholly confident. 'And bring, to Rome, Carthage's terms for peace.'

Atticus balled his fists in anger. He was about to step forward but a desperate glance from Hadria made him stop. She was crying, the tears running freely down her face, and Atticus felt his rage build further. She looked away from him and he felt his restraint waver, every instinct telling him to cross the room to end the vicious flow of invective that was staining his honour and breaking Hadria's heart.

The room was full of voices and conflicting sounds: Hadria's trembling sobs, her mother's wailing cries, her father's continuous tirade, his fist slamming on to the table before him. Only Atticus and another were silent.

Borne on the back of Hadria's hope, Atticus's confidence had risen over the previous week as they waited for her father's return to Rome. They had continued to meet in secret, but she had begun to speak openly of her hopes for the future with a certainty that had allayed Atticus's doubts, a certainty he had carried with him when they'd entered the family house only minutes before, a certainty that had evaporated the second he saw her father's face.

Antoninus had understood immediately the significance of his daughter arriving with Atticus. 'How long have you been seeing this . . . this man?' he snarled.

Hadria told him, her breath catching in her throat.

'Does anyone know, has anyone seen you?' her mother, Salonina, said hastily, her face a mask of concern and horror.

'No,' Hadria answered, angered by her mother's repulsed tone.

'What were you thinking?' Salonina asked.

'I love him, Mother,' Hadria replied, and she looked to Atticus, her face a mask of sorrow.

'You cannot,' Antoninus shouted. 'He is *barbarus*, a foreigner.'

'He is of Rome,' Septimus interjected. He had never wanted Hadria and Atticus to be together, but he could no longer hold his peace, ashamed of his father's attack on Atticus, a man who had risked everything many times for Rome.

Antoninus turned to his son, seeing the defiance in his face, and he suddenly understood. 'You knew of this?' he hissed.

'I knew,' Septimus replied. 'And I tried to stop it.'

'You were in league with him, this Greek, against your own family?' Antoninus roared. 'By the gods, Septimus, you were a man of honour, an *optio* of the Ninth. This navy, this collection of *nothi* and *barbari*, has defiled you, defiled your honour . . .'

'Enough,' Atticus roared, and he fixed his gaze on Antoninus as the room went silent. The older man was burning with hostility, the scar running through his left eye giving him a maniacal expression, and Atticus felt his temper slip beyond his control. He had held his tongue in the forlorn hope that Hadria's parents would overcome their initial shock, knowing that anything he uttered would only refocus their anger, but now he had heard enough to know that their opposition was absolute.

'You have said enough, Antoninus,' he said.

'You have no voice here, Greek,' Antoninus replied, a hard edge to his voice. 'I fought your people at Beneventum and I will be damned if one of you will dictate to me in my own house.' He turned to Hadria. 'I forbid you to see this man again,' he ordered, and Hadria stumbled back as if struck, her shoulders falling in utter defeat. She looked to Atticus, her heart breaking, and she fled from the room.

'Now get out, Greek,' Antoninus snarled. 'And do not darken my door again.'

The utter contempt of Antoninus's words and the sight of Hadria's flight snapped Atticus's temper, and he stepped forward, his hand falling to the hilt of his dagger.

'Atticus,' Septimus shouted, and moved between him and his father, the unarmed centurion holding his hands out defensively. Atticus froze and looked to Septimus, then beyond him to the undaunted Antoninus, and for a second his anger drove him to the brink of attack. He stared again into Septimus's face, seeing the plea for restraint, and finally he shook his head and left the room.

Atticus strode through the atrium, his mind in turmoil as a flood of conflicting emotions swept over him. His pace slackened as he heard sobbing and he whispered Hadria's name. She stepped out from within a doorway and the conflict within him abated at the sight of her distress. He went to her and she fell into his arms, burying her face in the hollow of his shoulder.

'I couldn't let you leave,' she sobbed. 'Not without saying goodbye.'

'This isn't goodbye,' Atticus said soothingly. 'I'll come back for you. In time we'll be together.'

'No, we won't,' she whispered, the anguish of her words bringing fresh tears to her eyes. 'My father has forbidden it, I cannot defy him.'

'But we are in love,' Atticus said, confused by her submission.

'My father has the power of the *pater familias*, the head of this household,' she said. 'If I disobey him he will disavow me. I would be an outcast amongst my people.'

'It is no more than I am,' Atticus said, suddenly angry.

'Please understand, Atticus,' Hadria said, a desperate plea in her voice. 'Rome . . . my family; it is all I know, the whole world to me.'

'There is a world outside of Rome, Hadria,' Atticus said. 'We could be together there. Leave this city, come with me.'

'I can't,' she said, and seeing his face colour in anger she reached out for him. 'Please, Atticus. You cannot ask me to choose, not when I have no choice.'

Atticus heard her words and his anger increased, not against Hadria, but against the cursed city that kept her from him. He looked down to her upturned face and a wave of regret drove the fight from his body.

'So I'm not accepted in your world and you cannot live outside it,' he said, the words coming slowly. 'Then you were right, Hadria. We cannot be together.' And with a final brief kiss he swept past her out of the house.

Scipio rose to his feet to accept the nomination for consul, nodding to the senator who had put forward his name, his expression one of gratitude and mild surprise. A smattering of applause answered his acknowledgement, but it quickly died in the tense atmosphere of the chamber, and all eyes turned once more to the podium. The *princeps senatus* scanned the tiered seating, searching for further nominations, but none were forthcoming. He struck the podium with his gavel to bring the chamber to order.

'Senators of Rome,' he began, and Scipio took his eyes from the speaker to search the faces of the Senate members. The names of the five nominees were called out in turn. Two consuls would be elected from the five, with the senior position going to the senator with the most votes and the junior to the runner-up. Scipio dismissed the first three, knowing they had little or no support, their misdirected ambition matched only by their foolishness. They were no threat. The fourth name, however, was confirmation of what Scipio had suspected over the previous week.

He was Aulus Atilius Caiatinus, a young man who had served five years in the Senate. He was a patrician but, unlike his peers, he openly supported the progressive faction in the Senate. This placed him firmly in Duilius's camp and Scipio sought him out on the far side of the chamber, noting his position relative to Duilius, who sat in the back row. The final name was Scipio's, and again he nodded as many eyes turned at the mention of his voice.

With an announcement from the podium, the first of the nominees stood to make a speech in support of his candidacy. He was quickly followed by the second and the third. While

Scipio's expression remained inscrutable throughout the speeches, underneath he mocked the naiveté of the nominees. Over the previous week he had invested every shred of his political capital into the election for senior consul. He had called on every carefully nurtured alliance; where none existed, he had resorted to electoral bribery, combining the silver of his treasury with honeyed promises of post-election favours to guarantee votes from the unscrupulous.

As the third candidate sat, Caiatinus stood to speak. He began in a low, sonorous voice that lent gravity to his words, describing how he was the best candidate to lead the Republic in the perilous times ahead. His speech was carefully contrived and he subtly criticized Paullus's loss of the fleet, drawing attention to the dead consul's allegiance to the old order of Rome, an allegiance that had made him inflexible and unable to adapt to the conditions of the new war being raged on the sea against Carthage.

Caiatinus then spoke of his rival candidates, focusing on each one in turn. His attack on each character was ingeniously understated, providing Caiatinus with a false ethical superiority and, as he came to Scipio, he looked towards his chief rival, speaking his name in full, deliberately drawing out the pronunciation of his unofficial cognomen, *Asina*. Scipio bristled at the insult but kept his expression dismissive, careful not to reveal how deep the wound to his pride still ran.

The end of Caiatinus's speech was met with enthusiastic applause, and Scipio was given brief seconds to scan the chamber and ascertain who amongst the undecided had been influenced by the senator's words. In the silence that followed, Scipio stood and began the speech Fabiola and he had crafted.

Like Caiatinus, the tone of his voice commanded the attention of all in the chamber. Scipio was careful to personally address several senators he knew were uncommitted. These men were beyond his control, senior senators who were independently powerful and rarely allied themselves to any man or cause, and so Scipio had to rely solely on his oratorical skills and his ability to persuade men of his conviction.

Across the floor of the chamber, Duilius was similarly looking to the senators who were the focus of Scipio's attention. He watched as they were ensnared by Scipio's speech, the dramatic words probing their basest fears and uncertainties. It was a powerful oration, a worthy rebuttal to Caiatinus's speech, and Duilius realized the vote would be closer than he had hoped. Upon learning, days before, of Scipio's decision to run, Duilius had briefly thought to oppose him personally, but he ultimately conceded that the chances of success would be increased if the candidate for his faction was a patrician, considering the overwhelming majority of that class in the Senate. Moreover, Duilius now firmly believed he could wield his political strength to greater effect if he kept his influence hidden from the Senate at large, confident he could achieve more covertly than he ever could as a visible leader.

Scipio finished his speech with a tirade against the Carthaginians, a climax that roused the Senate. Many cheered as he spoke of the enemy's inevitable defeat and the might of the city that would humble them. As he sat down amidst tumultuous applause, he straightened his back and looked directly at the podium, casting a figure of absolute authority and bearing.

The *princeps senatus* brought the Senate to order and called for a show of hands for each candidate. The first three were piteously supported, but Scipio watched in consternation as the support was called for Caiatinus. Close to half the Senate raised their hands and Scipio struggled to count their number in the brief time their hands were held aloft. The final vote, for Scipio, was called. Again, innumerable hands were raised, and Scipio held his breath, knowing the count was too close to call.

The tension within the chamber rose as the *princeps senatus* duly eliminated the first three candidates. He called for a division of the house, a physical manifestation of the vote, where each senator would move to the side of the chamber of their chosen candidate. The senators moved quickly. The men on the flanks, for the most part, remained seated, while the centre dissolved to add weight to each faction. Immersed in the centre of his group, Scipio couldn't accurately guess the numbers on his own side, and he felt a bead of sweat snake down his back as he tried to count the numbers of the opposition. The chamber settled down once more as the last of the senators took a seat.

The *princeps senatus*, with an unrivalled viewpoint, looked to each side in turn. He nodded his head and Scipio leaned forward as the speaker looked once more to Caiatinus's side. The old man's lips moved as he silently counted Caiatinus's supporters, his head beginning to nod again as he neared the end of his count, as if his calculation was proof of his suspicion.

'Senators of Rome,' he announced, 'I hereby declare that the new senior consul of Rome is Gnaeus Cornelius Scipio.'

The chamber erupted, the members rising to their feet amidst cheers and calls of protest, even before the speaker reached the end of Scipio's name.

The victor remained seated, taking a moment to let the announcement soak through his consciousness. Eventually, he took a deep breath and stood up. Those around him immediately turned and spoke animatedly to his face, smiling and slapping him on the shoulder as he passed through them on to the floor of the chamber. He strode to the podium and stood purposefully behind it, his eyes staring straight ahead to a point above the heads of the three hundred senators facing him. The noise in the chamber was strident and Scipio held up his hand for silence. His gesture was quickly obeyed and the Senate came to order. Scipio paused in the silence that followed. He did not smile and his eyes remained cold. There was no feeling of joy, no spark of satisfaction, only an intense brooding sense of vindication, of a victory achieved that was fully deserved. He was once more the leader of Rome, and what would follow would be merely a reclamation of his full measure of pride and honour.

CHAPTER SEVEN

Regulus walked slowly across the main deck of the *Alissar*, his thoughts skipping from one subject to another, his concentration undermined by the inner voices of his conscience. He yearned for a way out of the predicament the Carthaginian commander had placed him in, or, failing that, a way to regain control of his fate. He longed for the counsel of a fellow Roman.

There was no hope. The campaign against the Carthaginians was in ruins. Two full legions had been lost in Africa, the fleet was totally destroyed; and whereas the Punici were now able to call on reserves, the Republic simply did not possess the ships to replace her losses. Sicily had been put beyond the grasp of Rome, and Regulus was forced to concede that the proposed terms for peace were fair and reasonable, merely a demand for a full withdrawal of all Roman forces from Sicily. Given that those remaining forces were negligible, the end result of the peace treaty would be the surrender of cities that would have inevitably fallen to the Carthaginians in due course.

And yet, despite the hopelessness of the Roman cause, Regulus could not bring himself to embrace the proposed peace treaty fully. Surrender, however reasonable, was anathema to the Roman spirit. The Republic had faced and suffered defeat in the past, but always it had fought on, never relenting until the fight was won. He looked at the ship around him and his mind skipped to another thought, one that had struck him the moment the *Alissar* had set sail from Carthage.

Regulus had never sailed on an enemy galley before, and he was stunned by how different it was to a Roman galley. The ships were identical in type and design, but the Carthaginian crew operated with a level of competence and skill that Regulus had never before witnessed. They seemed to work without supervision or command, as if each man not only knew his own task, but also that of the men around him, their overlapping experience creating a fluent efficiency that put the Roman crews to shame. Regulus now believed that the ability of the lowest Carthaginian crewman would easily match the seamanship of any Roman captain and, despite his own victory at Ecnomus, he couldn't assuage his growing conviction that eventually the Carthaginians would fully reclaim their rights to the sea, a dominion they had controlled for generations.

Hamilcar watched Regulus from the aft-deck and realized the Roman was still struggling with some internal conflict. The fleet from Gadir had arrived in Carthage only the day before and was currently restocking for the final leg to Lilybaeum in Sicily, while the transport fleet was also undergoing its final preparations. Hamilcar had persuaded Hanno to relinquish twenty elephants and five hundred mercenaries from the Numidian campaign, and had arranged for Regulus to witness their arrival in the military port, the sight of the colossal animals giving Regulus a harsh reminder of his defeat at Tunis and the vulnerability of the legions to their power. Even the departure of the *Alissar* had been carefully engineered, the flagship sailing slowly past the massed galleys of the Gadir fleet, and although Hamilcar would have preferred to sail with his fleet, he had hastened his departure to Sicily in order to impress upon Regulus the inevitability of his task, the step closer to Rome merely the first leg of a journey he would be honour bound to take.

Even in his own heart, Hamilcar knew that any peace treaty with Rome would be a charade. Only twenty-five years before, the two cities had been allies against Pyrrhus of Epirus, and a treaty had been signed wherein each city recognized the other's sphere of influence. That was before Rome blatantly ignored its terms and invaded Sicily, a Carthaginian domain, in a treacherous act that had precipitated the current conflict. By all that was right, and given their weakened state, Hamilcar believed he could impose a harsher treaty on Rome, but he had chosen his terms on the realization that a more lenient approach would lead to a swifter conclusion.

Carthage was fighting a war on two fronts against different enemies. This separation of its forces had already cost Hamilcar the army he had commanded at Tunis, a loss that would inevitably hamstring his efforts to finally defeat the Romans in Sicily, and one he had carefully hidden from Regulus. The key to the island was its cities, and while the most important of these were on the coast, they could not be taken from the seaward side alone. Any siege would have to include land-based forces, and so Hamilcar needed to buy time – time for Hanno to defeat the Numidians and release the army to his command.

The war between Rome and Carthage would continue but, in the meantime, the enemy would retreat from Sicily and Hamilcar would be granted a golden opportunity to fortify the island against their inevitable return. Carthage had been ill prepared when the Romans had first invaded Sicily and had lost Agrigentum as a consequence. That mistake would not be repeated.

Hamilcar left the aft-deck and strode over to Regulus, who greeted him with an irritated expression, as if Hamilcar had interrupted an important conversation, and he felt his annoyance rise once more.

'We will be in Lilybaeum tomorrow,' he said, in an effort to draw Regulus into a discussion that would finalize his trip to Rome.

'I will need more time to make my decision,' Regulus replied, his tone one of hollow determination.

Hamilcar kept his expression neutral and he nodded to show his understanding, while underneath he fought an almost overwhelming urge to throttle Regulus. What concept of defeat did the Roman not understand? They were beaten; the Roman fleet was no more. What thread of reason was Regulus grasping that prevented him from accepting the benevolence of Hamilcar's offer?

He decided to plant one last seed in Regulus's mind, one last piece of logic that might persuade the Roman to accept his proposal.

'It has been a long war,' he remarked, and Regulus nodded cautiously, surprised by Hamilcar's comment. 'I will welcome peace when it comes,' Hamilcar continued. 'If nothing else, it will allow my city to regain the strength this war has cost her.'

Regulus nodded in agreement and looked beyond Hamilcar as the idea began to form in his mind. The opportunity that the Carthaginian spoke of would be available to Rome too. It would cost them little, merely a couple of cities, cities that could be retaken when the time was right. Regulus unconsciously nodded as he carried the idea to its conclusion.

Hamilcar saw the gesture and he turned away, confident now that Regulus would do his bidding and carry his terms to his Senate. Thereafter, it was only a matter of time before Rome bowed to the will of Carthage.

'Hard to starboard, ramming speed!'

The *Orcus* banked into the sharp turn, her deck tilting precariously, and Atticus felt the muscles in his legs contract as he fought to keep his balance. He counted off the seconds until the bow swung through a full ninety degrees.

'Centre your helm,' he ordered, and Gaius put his weight behind the tiller.

The *Orcus* accelerated as the resistance of the rudder fell away. The drum beat began again, anticipating the surge that accompanied each pull of the oars through the calm water, and the crewmen on deck rocked back and forth on their haunches, many glancing to the formidable figure of the prefect standing motionless on the aft-deck, his eyes locked on some distant point beyond the bow.

Atticus cleared his mind and let the sound of the drum beat dominate his consciousness, allowing it to fuel his un-directed aggression. He breathed in the salty air, holding his breath to allow the taste to penetrate the back of his throat, and then exhaled slowly, pushing the last vestiges of air from his lungs in an effort to quell the bitter acid that clawed at his stomach.

'That's one minute, Prefect,' Gaius said behind him, and Atticus called for all stop, allowing the rowers to ship oars and rest.

'I make that turn two seconds faster,' Gaius said, his hand now resting lightly on the tiller as the *Orcus* rose and fell in the emptiness of the cove.

Atticus grunted in reply and moved to the side rail. He stood motionless once more, his eyes ranging over the coastline north of Fiumicino.

Paullus had taken nearly every available ship when he had sailed south weeks before, leaving the remnants to patrol the sea-lanes of Rome. The *Orcus* had been quickly drafted in to augment their ranks. It was tedious work, better suited to reserve crews and trainees, but the crew had welcomed the task, weary after many months in hostile waters. Only Atticus remained restless, unable to quash the uncertainties in his mind. Although on this day the *Orcus* had been scheduled for rest and repairs, he had ordered his galley north at dawn, taking advantage of the day's leave to further the training of his crew.

'Five minutes' rest then we go again,' he said over his shoulder, and Gaius acknowledged the order, shouting it forth to Baro on the main deck.

The *Orcus* descended into an uneasy quiet, the deck timbers creaking as the irregular surface of the water passed under the hull. Gaius stilled the sound of his own breathing and listened, almost sensing before finally hearing the sound of the rowers below deck. They were gasping for air, filling their lungs in an effort to regain their strength in the brief time allowed, their collective struggle making it seem as if the galley itself was breathing.

The helmsman looked to his commander, wondering how much further he would push the crew of the ship before calling an end to the day. They had been training relentlessly since dawn, honing their sailing skills, the absence of a *corvus* on the foredeck forcing them to concentrate their abilities on the little-used offensive tactic of ramming. Gaius did not know much of the greater plans of the fleet, but he had noticed, as had all the crew of the *Orcus*, that the new galleys being laid down in the shipyards at Fiumicino were all without the condemned boarding ramp.

For whatever reason, the prefect had been driving the crew remorselessly, and in the quiet of the interlude Gaius could only guess what demons the prefect was grappling with. He did not know his commander beyond their association on the aft-deck. In that arena they often thought with a unified mind, their expertise and abilities combining effortlessly, but outside it Gaius rarely spoke with him.

The aft-deck of a galley was a small space, and on many occasions Gaius had overheard conversations between the prefect and the two men he confided in, the centurion and the second-in-command; however, that useful source of information was no longer available. The centurion was not on board. He had not returned from Rome but had sent orders to his *optio* to disembark the legionaries at Fiumicino, their presence not required on the *Orcus* while in home waters. Moreover, the prefect did not confide in Baro to the same extent as in his predecessor, Lucius. This detachment was not all the prefect's doing, for Gaius had often heard Baro speak derisively of the commander before his promotion. Although Baro was now more discreet, it was obvious to Gaius that he was keeping his distance, and he realized that Baro's opinion had not changed.

He watched the prefect move from the side rail to stand once more in the centre of the aft-deck, his heading turning from side to side as he scanned the length of the ship. Gaius followed his commander's gaze. With the abandonment of the *corvus* came the unspoken command to all crews to fight the Carthaginians on their terms. Whatever else the prefect might have to worry about, Gaius knew this problem alone was enough to explain his dark mood.

The order was given for battle speed and the *Orcus* got under way, accelerating swiftly to eight knots. Gaius's hand tightened on the tiller; although he concentrated on anticipating the commands of the prefect, one part of his mind still dwelt on his previous reflections. He glanced at his commander and unconsciously kneaded the smooth, worn handle of the tiller. Whatever lay ahead, he would follow the prefect's every command.

The *Orcus* rounded the headland north of Fiumicino as the last light of the day was waning. She moved gracefully under sail, her oars raised and withdrawn, and the crew moved sedately across the decks. It had been a long day, and many of them turned to the welcome sight of port and the hot meal and cot that awaited them there. It was an uncommon luxury for the men. While on duty the crew ate and slept on the galley, normally on the open deck, but in Fiumicino, with the fleet temporarily stood down, the men enjoyed the comforts of an established military camp.

As the sea room diminished closer to shore, the sail was lowered and the oars extended. Again the action was slowed by fatigue and the beat was struck for steerage speed. Gaius nodded as Atticus pointed out a free berth and the galley was directed to the seaward end of a jetty. The *Orcus* answered all stop and lines were thrown to secure the galley fore and aft as the gangway was lowered. Baro assigned a deck watch and then dismissed the rest of the crew, the men moving with renewed energy down the length of the jetty towards the beach, while Atticus waited on the aft-deck, issuing final orders that would sustain his ship for the night before he too disembarked.

The hollow footfalls on the wooden jetty gave way to the sound of shifting sand underfoot. Atticus leaned forward into the slope of the beach, cresting the dune at its peak as the last sliver of the sun fell below the horizon, leaving only the reflected twilight from the high clouds. Much of the military camp at Fiumicino had been transformed into solid structures of wood and stone over the intervening years, but Atticus, as a temporary visitor, had been assigned a tent, albeit one befitting his rank.

Although his sense of direction on land was normally unreliable, he made his way unerringly through the maze of temporary streets. He walked as if in a trance, his mind preoccupied by a dozen different thoughts, each one fighting for supremacy. He favoured those that dwelt on the problems associated with the loss of the *corvus*, and tried to suppress the personal issues, but they struck him at unexpected intervals, invading his concentration with images of Septimus, Hadria, Scipio and Antoninus, each one destroying the carefully constructed serenity he craved, his temper rising and falling with each round of the struggle.

Atticus rounded the last corner and almost stumbled into his tent before noticing that a lamp was lit inside. He stepped backwards and his hand fell instinctively to the hilt of his dagger. He looked behind him, cursing his preoccupation and the failing sunlight that darkened the shadows on all sides. He moved warily to the entrance to his tent, drawing his dagger as he did so, the steel blade against the scabbard sounding unnaturally loud. He pulled back the flap of entrance and peered inside, his ears alert to any sound behind him as his eyes scanned the interior of his quarters.

A lone figure sat at the far end of the tent. Atticus recognized him immediately and visibly relaxed, sheathing his dagger as he crossed over to greet him.

'Senator Duilius,' he said. 'I didn't expect . . .'

Duilius stood up to greet Atticus and they shook hands.

'I prefer to keep my meetings private when I can,' Duilius replied, motioning for Atticus to sit on the low cot. 'It is good to see you, Atticus,' he said.

The two men fell quickly into conversation, each bringing the other up to date with events. Atticus spoke at length about the campaign in Africa, giving Duilius a level of detail not found in the formal reports issued to the Senate. They discussed the storm and Atticus spoke of his prediction and warning to Paullus.

'The man was always a fool, even before he left Rome,' Duilius replied. 'It is no surprise he remained one right up until the time of his death. Nevertheless, his recklessness has cost the Republic dearly.'

Duilius focused the conversation on the exposed weakness of the *corvus*, his questions incisive, revealing the level of knowledge he had retained since he commanded the fleet. Atticus ventured his own conclusion, supporting the abandonment of the device; he noticed that Duilius did not oppose his view, as if a consensus had already been reached, even at the senator's level.

'The Senate has authorized the construction of two hundred and twenty new galleys,' Duilius said in conclusion. 'And more than likely they will be built without *corvi*.'

Atticus had long grown accustomed to the enormous capabilities of Rome, but he was staggered by the number proposed, knowing that the construction schedule for these new ships would be punishing.

It was an aspect of Roman society that always amazed Atticus: the willingness to commit massive resources to every endeavour with a fierce belief that effort alone would give them victory in every conflict. Militarily, this attitude had worked well in the past, particularly on land where they were able to draw on a huge population base. They had employed the same attitude at sea, constructing massive fleets at incredible speed to counter the enemy. Only against the power of nature were their efforts thwarted – and yet, this latest resolution of the Senate proved that their belief was unshaken.

Thoughts of the Senate brought Scipio to mind, but Atticus contained his anger and instead thanked Duilius for his intervention when Scipio had effectively accused him of treason.

'You have heard of his victory in the consular elections?' Duilius asked.

Atticus nodded. News travelled swiftly between Rome and Fiumicino.

'His success was unforeseen, and it complicates matters further,' Duilius said, lapsing into silence as the topic brought to the surface problems within his own mind. He glanced at Atticus and saw the concern in his expression, knowing its origin. 'For the moment you are safe from Scipio,' Duilius said. 'Your rank protects you and you have influential friends, me amongst them.'

Atticus nodded in thanks but Duilius frowned. 'But he will exploit any mistake, real or perceived, that you make, Atticus. If you can, stay beyond his immediate reach.'

'Will you not seek to remove him from office?' Atticus asked, frustrated by Scipio's return to power. 'We have both witnessed the consequences of his pride and recklessness.'

Again Duilius was silent and Atticus cursed the rashness of his question, sensing that he had overstepped a boundary and presumed a confidence that Duilius could not extend. Duilius looked at him intently, as if weighing the consequences of his reply. 'For now, Scipio is acting in the best interest of the Republic. He retains the full support of the Senate.'

Atticus nodded, trying to determine how much to read into Duilius's reply.

'Atticus,' Duilius continued, 'with the loss of so many of our skilled crews in the storm, and now the loss of the use of the *corvus*, the fate of the Republic is at risk. And you are right, with Scipio in charge that risk is increased. But for now we can only work within the system. I can try to curb his excesses in the Senate, and you must do the same at an operational level, in the fleet.'

'How? My rank is nothing to Scipio. I cannot influence him.'

'But you can influence the experienced men of the fleet. They respect you, I suspect more than you realize, and many of them will look to you when their faith in Scipio fails.'

Atticus looked beyond Duilius to the ephemeral shapes that the flickering lamp created on the wall of the tent. He tried to focus on them, to clear his mind and to sift through his confused thoughts. When Duilius mentioned the precarious fate of the Republic, Atticus had instinctively scoffed at the warning. What did he care for Rome and its fate? It was a hollow, soulless entity that had never accepted him. And yet when Duilius spoke of it, the senator's conviction deeply affected him, and Atticus was forced to concede that – for the briefest of moments – he shared that conviction. He stood as Duilius took his leave and shook the senator's hand again, a simple gesture that marked them as equals. In Duilius he had an ally, and Atticus was left to contemplate how men like the senator constantly challenged his opinion of Rome.

The rider approached the Servian Wall at full gallop, conscious of the dying sun off his right shoulder, the shadow of his flight already reaching far out into the fields beside him. A half-mile ahead, at the Porta Flumentana, he could see a group of legionaries standing to the side of the gate, allowing the last of the stragglers to enter the city before closing the gate at sundown. He spurred his mount to greater speed, its iron-shod hooves striking chips from the cobbled road. The rider pumped the reins as he leaned in to the curve of the horse's withers.

He shouted to the legionaries as he saw them move to

close the gate but they ignored him, the soldiers talking amongst themselves, indifferent to the approaching horseman. The order to close the gate came as inexorably as the falling sun that triggered the command. The rider yelled again, but this time in warning as he aimed his mount at the closing gates. The thundering sound of hooves alerted the legionaries and they jumped back at the last second as the rider shot between their ranks and through the half-closed gate.

The soldiers shouted in anger and many went to draw their swords, but the rider had already disappeared into the warren of narrow streets beyond the wall. He slowed his mount, the animal breathing hard as it cantered towards the centre of the city. The sun had fallen, but the sky still clung to the remnants of its light and the open windows of houses radiated shafts of yellow that ricocheted off the whitewashed walls, extending the twilight to illuminate the rider's path.

He reached the hollow gloom of the Forum and scanned the temples that looked over it, watching as the disciples of each deity lit the blazing torches that marked the entrances. He turned to the northeast corner, spurring his mount once more, conscious of the need to find his destination before the blackness of night engulfed the streets.

He knew Rome well, but he only had an unconfirmed street name as a direction, ascertained through snippets of information gathered over the previous two weeks. He cursed the lateness of the hour, wishing he had more time, conscious that he was now effectively a prisoner of the city, and if he didn't find the man he was looking for he would be forced to seek refuge in a tavern. He would have to spend the night in the city and dawn's light would reveal his absence from his post, a dereliction the man he despised would surely exploit.

The streets on the northern side of the Capitoline Hill were wide and well swept, and behind the boundary walls the rider could see the soaring roofs of the expansive houses silhouetted against the sky. He searched the nameplates beside each entrance, glancing occasionally over his shoulder to the sky above; within minutes he could no longer see both sides of the street from the centre of the road. He moved to his left, halving the effectiveness of his search, but he reasoned the wealth and importance of the man he hoped to see would place his house on the higher side of the street.

With relief he found the house. He dismounted and hammered on the wooden door. A bolt slammed back and the door opened. Two soldiers stepped into the opening. They were household guards and their impassive expressions changed to ones of annoyance when they noticed the obvious unimportance of the man facing them. They were about to dismiss him, but his request caused them to hesitate, the sheer temerity of it transfixing the soldiers, caught between mockery and caution. The rider persisted, emphasizing his rank and posting, insisting that the master of the house would see him if he were informed.

He was led into the courtyard. One of the soldiers marched into the house while the other bolted the outer door shut. The rider waited in the silence that followed, handing the reins without comment to a stable lad who appeared to take his mount. A moment of doubt assailed him but he swallowed his uncertainty, committing himself once more to his course. The soldier reappeared and beckoned the rider to follow him into the house. He exhaled in relief, his doubt falling further away.

Scipio remained seated as the soldier of his household guard led the stranger into the room. He searched the man's demeanour for traces of overt anxiety, the type of signs a man might display in the midst of enemies, but the stranger seemed remarkably confident. Scipio dismissed the soldier and indicated to the man to stand before him, albeit at a distance; he allowed a silence to develop as the footfalls of his guard receded.

'I am honoured that you agreed to see me, Consul,' the man said.

Scipio's face darkened in anger. 'You will speak only when spoken to,' he snarled, and again the silence was reasserted.

Within a minute, Scipio noticed that the man's previous confidence was waning and he smiled inwardly, preferring any lesser man who addressed him to be cowed in his presence. 'Why have you come here?' he asked eventually.

'I wish to serve you, Consul.'

'I have servants enough,' Scipio said dismissively, although he was intrigued by the man's unexpected appearance, given his rank and position. 'In any case,' he proceeded cautiously, 'why would you wish to serve me?'

'Because we share a hatred for one man,' the stranger said without hesitation.

'Really,' Scipio said warily. 'Which man?'

'The Greek, Perennis.'

Scipio was thrown by the unexpected declaration, but his face remained impassive. He searched for signs of duplicity but found none. 'You claim to be his second-in-command,' he said.

'I am,' Baro replied. 'I have been for over a year now.'

Scipio nodded, suppressing his growing sense of anticipation in favour of further caution. He chose his next question carefully, focusing all his attention on Baro's expression. 'Why do you hate Perennis?' he asked.

Baro's face reddened and he took an instinctive half-step forward, compelled by a sudden surge of aggression. 'Because of what he is and because I am forced to serve under him,' he spat.

'You are a Roman citizen?' Scipio asked, shocked by the intensity of Baro's animosity.

'Yes, Consul,' Baro replied. 'The son of a freedman from the Aventine quarter. It blackens my honour that I should take orders from a non-Roman.'

Scipio did not comment on Baro's motives, believing them to be less important than the strength of the hatred itself. Therein lay the depth of Baro's sincerity, however irrational his enmity might appear to another man, and Scipio was satisfied that Baro's hatred ran deep. Only one other question remained.

'How do you know of my hostility towards Perennis?' he asked.

'There are few secrets on a galley, Consul,' Baro explained. 'The deck is small; the bulkheads are thin. Over time I have heard enough to know the Greek considers you an enemy.'

Again Scipio nodded, convinced of Baro's legitimacy. 'So you believe we should form some kind of alliance?' he said sceptically. 'The senior consul and a lowly deck hand.'

Baro bristled at the dismissive tone but he held tightly to his conviction, knowing that now he had revealed his disaffection he had to stay the course.

'I can be your eyes and ears on board the *Orcus*, Consul. Sooner or later the Greek will be vulnerable and, fully informed, you could exploit that weakness.'

Scipio unconsciously sat straighter in his chair as he absorbed Baro's words, his own conclusions already forming unbidden beyond the scope of Baro's basic premise. Baro's idea had merit, and Scipio deepened his concentration as he questioned him once more on his motives and his relationship with the Greek. He became more incisive, probing each facet of Baro's answers, and before long he invited Baro to sit at the far end of the table.

Two hours later, Scipio called for his guards to escort Baro back to the Porta Flumentana. He handed one of his men a scroll marked with the seal of the senior consul, the only pass that would allow for the gate to be opened during the hours of night. He dismissed Baro curtly, telling him he would let him know of his decision in due course, although his mind was already made up. Scipio knew many men of Baro's calibre: determined, even ruthless, but lacking the intelligence to properly formulate an attack on an enemy. Baro was merely a weapon; a spear, cold and mindless. What he lacked, the consul would provide. Scipio would become the spearman and already, in his mind's eye, he was taking aim on the heart of his enemy.

Atticus pushed back the flap of his tent as the first rays of the dawn sun clipped the canvas apex of his quarters. He felt optimistic as he recalled parts of his conversation with Duilius the evening before, focusing on the explicit assertions of support that the senator had given him. He spotted Baro emerging from his own tent not twenty feet away and he called him over, his second-in-command responding with alacrity.

'Assemble the men on the beach, Baro. I want to be away within the half-hour.'

'Yes, Prefect,' Baro replied, and he moved off towards the mess tents to gather the crew.

Atticus watched him leave, his mind shifting seamlessly to the day ahead. His opinion on the *corvus* had been supported by Duilius and he was pleased that the persistent training he had employed over the previous weeks would not be in vain. He turned towards the mess tents, eager to begin his day, and he allowed the sound of gathered voices to guide his steps. In the legions each *contubernia* of ten soldiers cooked and ate together, a long-established routine that ensured efficiency, but with new men arriving daily to crew the new galleys, communal mess tents had been erected. This was a luxury that the crew of the *Orcus* had exploited ruthlessly, and one Atticus was sure his men would sorely miss when the *Orcus* turned south once more.

As he rounded the last corner, he stopped dead. Septimus was standing in the middle of the roadway, his eyes scanning the approaches, and as he turned towards Atticus he too froze. Memories of the last time he had seen Septimus flooded back to Atticus and his mouth formed into a tight line as he resumed his approach. The centurion also moved to close the gap, his hand as always on the hilt of his sword.

'You're back in Fiumicino,' Atticus said dismissively, surprised by the sudden enmity he felt.

'I never left,' Septimus replied. 'I'm billeted at the landward side of the camp, along with the rest of the legionaries.'

Atticus nodded and a silence drew out between them.

'I came here to find you,' Septimus said, his words coming slowly, tension in his voice.

'You're reporting back to the *Orcus*?'

'No, I . . .' Septimus hesitated. 'About Hadria, Atticus,' he resumed. 'My father does not speak for the family.'

'He only said what you've thought for a long time, that I'm not worthy of Hadria,' Atticus said, his voice trembling with suppressed anger, the thoughts that had festered in his mind surging to the surface, threatening to overwhelm him. 'Your father spoke for you and every other Roman who believes in your cursed superiority.'

The colour of anger rushed to Septimus's face and his grip tightened instinctively on the hilt of his sword. He had not wanted a confrontation, given what he had decided, but Atticus's words could not be ignored.

'I defended you, Atticus,' he said. 'I tried to explain to my father that you were Roman, if not in name then in deed.'

'Therein lies your arrogance,' Atticus replied aggressively. 'My honour, my deeds, do not make me Roman. They make me the man I am – and that should be enough.'

Septimus stepped back, fury coursing through him. He had witnessed this side of Atticus before, this aggression towards Rome, but never had it affected Septimus so keenly. For Atticus to find insult in being described as Roman was an affront to every Roman, one that cut Septimus deeply, and he realized that the decision he had made was the only restraint keeping his sword arm in check. The conflict over Hadria had driven a wedge between them, one that could not be removed.

'I did not seek you out to fight this fight,' he said, wishing to end the conversation and be away.

'Then why have you come?' Atticus asked cynically.

'The Ninth is reforming and my request for a transfer has been accepted.'

'A transfer?' Atticus asked, his anger abating with shock.

'I am to command the IV maniple, my old unit.'

Atticus hesitated, his mind flooded once more by conflicting emotions. They cleared quickly as a sense of betrayal overcame all. 'Then the *Orcus* will fight on without you,' he said.

'You and I both know we cannot share command, not now,' Septimus said angrily, not willing to accept a full measure of blame for the fates that had shattered their friendship. 'Your relationship with Hadria has seen to that.'

'No,' Atticus said wearily, 'Rome has seen to that.'

Septimus snorted in reply and turned to leave. He stopped short and looked once more to Atticus, trying to see past the aggressive expression to the friend he once had. He could not, and he walked away without another word.

Atticus stood silent in the middle of the roadway, the noise of the camp around him increasing with every minute of the new day. Baro and the crew appeared from the mess tents, their mood light and jovial, and Baro nodded to his commander as he passed, leading the men off towards the beach. Atticus fell in behind them. His previous optimism had fled. There was no place for that sentiment; his mood darkened with every step he took towards the *Orcus*.

CHAPTER EIGHT

The quinquereme moved steadily through the crowded sea-lane, its course never deviating, and the trading vessels gave way before its imposing bow. Many of the traders cursed its passage, angered by the ship's disregard for the ancient rule that oar-powered vessels should give way to sail, but their irate shouts died as they realized the masthead banners were not Roman but Carthaginian, and they gave the quinquereme a wider berth, almost colliding in their haste, as if the galley was flying the warning flags of a plague ship. From ship to ship, the warning cries of the galley's approach swept along the teeming sea-lane and, like the searing wind that precedes a bush fire, the forewarning opened a passage in the lane. The Carthaginians took immediate advantage, anxious to complete their mission, and the quinquereme accelerated, each oar stroke taking them closer to Ostia.

The *Orcus* moved steadily under sail, her pace matching those of the canvas-driven trading boats that surrounded her. The crew exchanged banter over the rails to the nearby craft, marking time as the *Orcus* sailed through the arc of its patrol route. Atticus paced slowly across the aft-deck, checking the line of the helm intermittently. He glanced at the shoreline a mile away, vaguely familiar with its outline.

'Quinquereme dead ahead, one mile and closing.'

Atticus looked to Corin and then the bow. The galley was on the exact back bearing of the *Orcus*, clearly visible through the separating line of the sea-lane.

'One of ours,' Atticus thought, although he couldn't imagine from which port it might have sailed. The survivors of the storm were still based in Agrigentum, and he was unaware of any quinqueremes based in any other Roman ports. He turned as Baro ran on to the aft-deck.

'She's Carthaginian, Prefect,' he blurted. 'That's why the lane is separating; the traders are sending warnings forward.'

'All hands, battle stations,' Atticus shouted, and the mainsail was quickly lowered as the *Orcus* accelerated to battle speed, Gaius cursing the crowded waters as he tried to keep the helm straight. Atticus looked to the empty main deck. Patrol duty in the sea-lanes of Ostia was, at best, procedural, given that the city's only seaborne enemy was supposed to be in Sicilian waters, and the *Orcus* was devoid of its usual contingent of legionaries. Atticus let his hand fall to the hilt of his sword, kneading it with his palm. He looked to Gaius and noticed the frustration and worry in his face. With so many trading ships, the available sea room would be minimal, and bringing the ram to bear would be extremely difficult.

'Gaius,' Atticus ordered. 'Come right on the starboard beam. We'll draw them out of the lane.'

The helmsman nodded and swung the bow through ninety degrees, cutting across the course of a dozen trading ships, their crews giving way before the unyielding galley, conscious of the impending skirmish. Atticus kept his eye on the enemy ship, glancing occasionally to Corin at the masthead, his brow creased with doubt.

'They're not turning,' Atticus said, but he quickly shook off his uncertainty, knowing that to overreact and second-guess an opponent could be fatal. It was better to fight on your own terms. He held the course of the *Orcus* for a moment longer, judging the angles.

'Gaius, come about. Attack speed. Bring the ram to bear amidships.'

The *Orcus* turned neatly through the open water and headed back towards the sea-lane, the Carthaginian galley bow dead ahead but now broadside to the *Orcus*'s attack. The gap fell to three hundred yards. Then two hundred.

'Still no reaction,' Atticus thought, perplexed, although he could see the enemy crew lining the side rail, many of them pointing to the *Orcus*, others waving their hands. The enemy was in sight, there for the taking, and every fibre of Atticus's experience called on him to order ramming speed. Suddenly he spotted one of the Carthaginian crew holding a shield over his head, a gesture of truce, and the order came instinctively to his lips.

'All stop.'

The order was repeated without hesitation and the *Orcus* came to a stop as the oars were dipped.

'Your orders, Prefect,' Gaius said warily, the *Orcus* falling rapidly out of position as the Carthaginian galley continued its course.

'Standard speed, fall into their wake and then lay along-side,' Atticus said. He called to the main deck, 'Baro, have the men make ready in case it's a trap of some kind.'

The second-in-command confirmed the order and Atticus focused once more on the Carthaginian galley.

The *Orcus* was swiftly in position, coming at the Carthaginian galley from its most vulnerable side. Her bow came within a half-ship length of the enemy stern, the Carthaginian coming to a full stop, shipping its oars to allow the *Orcus* to come alongside. Gaius deftly completed the manoeuvre and Atticus moved to the main deck, conscious of the silence that had enveloped both crews as they stared across at each other.

The Carthaginians lining the rail on the main deck parted, and Atticus stepped back in shock as he recognized the Roman stepping into the space with a measured stride, his arm extended slightly to hold the folds of his toga.

'Ahh, Prefect Perennis,' he said with some surprise, but he quickly recovered and nodded to a Carthaginian officer beside him, the man hastily ordering a gangplank to be extended across the gap. The Roman moved across and the link was quickly severed, the Carthaginian crew visibly relaxing as their charge was given over and the galley moved off a point to re-engage its oars, turning neatly in the sea-lane until its bow was pointing due south.

The *Orcus* continued to drift in the gentle current, the crew, like Atticus, yet to regain their wits.

'Is it true?' the Roman said, taking Atticus by the arm, his fingers digging into his flesh.

'Proconsul?'

'The storm, the losses. You were there. Is it true?'

Atticus shook off his initial surprise. 'Yes, Proconsul, it's true,' he said solemnly.

Regulus's shoulders fell a fraction. He had long ago accepted Hamilcar's version of events, or so he believed; however, upon seeing Atticus his initial hopes and disbelief surfaced, knowing that the prefect had been stationed in Aspis. He looked to Atticus and squared his shoulders, his conviction regaining its dominance over his mood.

'You must give me a full report of everything since our defeat at Tunis,' he ordered. 'Now best speed to Ostia, Prefect. I need to be in Rome before sunset.'

148

'But the Carthaginian galley . . .' Atticus replied, his gaze locked on the retreating enemy ship. 'We should take her.'

'You cannot,' Regulus said. 'I gave them my word that they would be allowed to leave unhindered. They are sailing to Lipara, where they will wait for my return.'

'Your return,' Atticus asked perplexed. 'I don't understand, Proconsul. Why did they bring you back to Rome?'

'Because,' Regulus replied, a measure of pride in his tone, 'I have come to bring an end to this war.'

Septimus dismounted and stretched out his arms, leaning back to tighten the muscles of his shoulders, groaning in relief. He had galloped nearly the whole way from Fiumicino, not wanting to waste a precious minute of his leave and, as he watched Domitian approach across the courtyard, he felt an enormous sense of wellbeing. He handed the reins to the senior servant and slapped him on the shoulder; the older man's smile widened at seeing the youngest son of the family home once more.

'Your parents are in the *triclinium*,' he said, and Septimus strode into the house, making his way quickly to the main dining room.

Salonina leapt up as she saw her son enter and she went to him with open arms. Antoninus rose too, but more slowly, a wry smile on his face. He extended his hand and Septimus took it, matching the iron grip of his father.

'Welcome, Centurion,' he said, and Septimus struggled to conceal his surprise. It was the first time his father had ever addressed him by that rank, and he saw the pride in his father's eyes at his son having attained a rank he once held, centurion of the Ninth Legion. Septimus suddenly felt angered by the overt display of approval, recalling the contempt Antoninus had shown many times for that same rank in the marines, dismissing the position out of hand as a hollow, meaningless title. Septimus found himself re-examining his decision to transfer.

When he had first heard the announcement that the Ninth was to reform he had felt a deep sense of pride, glad that the 'Wolves of Rome' would rise to fight again. It was a valiant unit with a proud history and, as one of its sons, he had always maintained a strong affinity with the legion. His transfer to the navy had afforded him the chance of promotion, and although his decision at the time had been clouded by the loss of his friend Valerius in the Battle of Agrigentum, he had never regretted the choice.

However he had long since recognized and accepted the powerful influence the Ninth had over him, in the strength of his sword arm and through his former comrades, men who knew and respected his father Antoninus. That influence had led him to march into battle with the Ninth at Thermae; but afterwards he had returned to the marines with a clear sense of purpose, confident that he had found a place amongst honourable men in the navy.

That confidence had been shattered with the ending of his friendship with Atticus. With renewed resolve, Septimus had returned to the Ninth, gladly accepting command of the IV maniple. It was a position he seemed fated to occupy, one that his father had once held with distinction, and one that Septimus had served in as *optio* under Marcus Fabius Buteo, a comrade lost in the battle of Tunis.

It was with this mantle on his shoulder that Septimus now stood before Antoninus, outwardly accepting his praise while realizing that, although he had craved this very acceptance in the many years during which he had commanded a maniple of the marines, it now gave him no pleasure. Septimus was disturbed by the realization and, as he accepted the invitation to sit with his parents, he wondered whether he no longer valued his father's acceptance, or no longer valued the command that he had previously held in such high regard.

'How is Hadria?' he asked, wishing to change the subject. 'Is she here?'

Salonina's face fell and she held her hands to stop them trembling. 'She's very ill,' she replied, tears in her voice. 'She is in her room and has not risen since that night when—'

'That Greek whoreson has cursed her,' Antoninus spat, and Septimus felt a renewed surge of anger towards his father. He held his tongue, knowing he could say nothing that would change Antoninus's opinion.

'How is she ill?' Septimus asked, his concern rising.

'She does not speak,' Salonina replied. 'And she barely eats. She just lies in her room. It is worse than when she grieved for Valerius.'

'Do not compare the two, woman,' Antoninus said angrily. 'Valerius was a Roman, this Greek is a *barbarus*.'

Salonina seemed not to hear her husband. 'Time will heal her,' she said without confidence, shaking her head in despair.

On impulse Septimus stood up and left the room, finding his way to the steps that led to the bedrooms overlooking the courtyard. He climbed them slowly, his thoughts on what he could say to Hadria to comfort her, but as he recalled the part he had played in their affair he hesitated. He had always been against it, his motives shifting many times but his conviction never wavering, even after he understood Hadria's level of devotion for Atticus. What mattered was that he had stood squarely against his sister and his friend, and he suddenly felt unsure, shaken by the repercussions; the loss of his friendship with Atticus and Hadria's deep despair.

He reached the door of her room and paused, listening intently, but there was no sound from behind the door and in the stillness he reached out for the handle. He stopped, his confidence giving way under the weight of his guilt, and finally he turned and walked away.

Regulus stood on the threshold of the Curia, listening as the voices of debate rose and fell in a manner all too familiar to his ear. He adjusted the folds of his toga, remembering when he last stood in the hallowed chamber. He had been senior consul then, the most powerful man in Rome, and as he stood to depart on his quest to invade Africa, the Senate had cheered his name. Now he was returning as an ambassador of peace, a harbinger of what he knew would be welcome news. He would be revered as a saviour, a man who showed the city a way through its darkest hour, and the Senate would cheer his name once more.

Regulus was fully committed to the proposed peace treaty, a belief reached after many weeks of discussion and reflection. Rome was beaten; Barca had convinced him of that, and the array of forces he had seen in the harbour of Carthage served to further convince him of the formidable strength yet to be unleashed by the enemy. He would speak to the Senate of peace with honour, of the need to check the advance of the Carthaginian horde, of the opportunity to stabilize the southern frontier of the Republic and gain time to renew their strength.

For a brief moment, Regulus thought of the one aspect he could not have foreseen, the election of Scipio to the post of senior consul, news the Greek prefect had revealed. He had a sworn enemy in Scipio, a man he knew was beyond serpentine in nature, but Regulus believed his cause was honourable, and he trusted the senior consul would recognize that fact for the benefit of Rome, whatever his personal animosity.

Clearing his mind of the inconsequential detail, Regulus straightened his shoulders and stepped over the threshold of the Curia.

The Senate continued to debate as Regulus entered, but the discussion soon gave way to gasps of astonishment as he was recognized. A number of senators got up and walked over to the proconsul, bombarding him with questions, but he ignored them, keeping his expression composed as he looked between them in an effort to ascertain whether Scipio was present in the chamber. He moved towards the podium, the senators giving way before him, and the Senate became quiet as he paused to address them.

'Citizens of Rome,' he began. 'I stand before you this day to bring you glorious news. In our hour of greatest need, the gods of our forefathers have taken a guiding hand in our fate. Carthage desires peace and has offered us terms—'

Shouts of disbelief and protest met his words and Regulus was forced to pause, disquieted by the attitude of his peers. He recalled his own initial abhorrence to the concept of surrender, but that was before he had been persuaded of its merits. He raised his voice, determined to complete his prepared speech, anxious to explain how lenient the Carthaginian terms were, confident that the senators' initial objections would soon dissipate in the face of his logic.

'Senators, Senators,' he shouted. 'The Carthaginians terms merely dictate that we withdraw from Sicily. Given our losses and their strength these are generous terms, worthy of acceptance. We—'

Again he was forced to stop as the level of protest grew, many Senators now on their feet, pointing angrily at him. His confidence began to waver and he re-examined every facet of his argument, finding no flaw. He raised his hands and continued through the hail of protest.

'Our fleet is no more, taken by the gods,' he shouted. 'We have been defeated in open battle. We must accept these terms, if only to give us time—'

'Silence!' a voice roared, and Regulus turned to the source, immediately recognizing Scipio. He had been present the entire time, sitting anonymously amidst the crowd while Regulus spoke. With a rising sense of dread, he watched Scipio stand and make his way across the Senate floor.

'Follow me,' he said disdainfully, and Regulus complied, departing the Senate chamber amidst a renewed barrage of protest.

Scipio led him to the senior consul's chamber at the centre of the Curia. It was a familiar path and Regulus followed without comment, his mind in turmoil. Only when he reached the room did he feel some semblance of calm return. This had once been his chamber and he felt a renewed sense of confidence as he remembered his achievements as senior consul.

The room was a perfect circle, an anomalous shape in the heart of a rectangular building, and the domed ceiling was dominated by an oculus that threw an ever-changing shaft of sunlight on the marble walls. Scipio moved behind the table that dominated the centre of the chamber, watching Regulus intently. Initially, like everyone in the Senate chamber, Scipio had been shocked by the sudden arrival of Regulus. He had watched the proconsul move with a determined stride to the podium but, as Regulus began to speak, that shock had been surpassed by disbelief. He had smiled inwardly as he felt the growing sense of anger among the senators around him.

Scipio had been elected senior consul because he had promised the Senate victory over the Carthaginians and they had believed him. Since that day he had carefully tended that flame of belief, stoking it into a raging fire when he needed their vote to commission a new fleet of quinqueremes, allowing it to recede when he needed to temper their belief with fear, but always ensuring he maintained in them a level of faith in Rome's ultimate victory. His success was confirmed in the immediate reaction of the Senate to Regulus.

Scipio levelled his gaze at the proconsul, feeling nothing but contempt for the man who had once defied him. 'So, you have become the Carthaginians' puppet.'

'I am no puppet, Scipio,' Regulus replied angrily. 'I am on parole, as an ambassador of peace, and I bring with me lenient terms that Rome must accept.'

'You are a fool on a fool's errand, Regulus,' Scipio said mockingly. 'And Rome must accept nothing.'

'Look beyond your pride, Scipio. We are beaten,' Regulus said. 'A peace treaty is our only chance to keep our mainland inviolate. If we continue to fight, we will be driven from Sicily by force and the Carthaginians will not stop at the Straits of Messina.'

'The Carthaginians will be defeated. I have promised the Senate of that. I have given them faith. You just witnessed the strength of that belief in the Senate chamber.'

'That faith is misplaced, Scipio. I have seen the enemy's strength in the harbour of Carthage. We cannot stand against them, not now that we are weak.'

'The fleet is being rebuilt even as we speak,' Scipio said resolutely. 'Soon Rome will be strong again, and when she is I will lead her to victory.'

Regulus noticed the maniacal edge to Scipio's voice, the look of absolute self-belief in his eyes, and he realized that – despite the precariousness of Rome's position – Scipio was determined to continue the war. Perennis had told him of the new fleet, but Regulus had hoped the Greek was misinformed. Now there was no doubt. He was about to continue his argument when he suddenly paused. In the two years since he had cast Scipio aside in this very room, he himself had changed immeasurably, but he realized that Scipio was essentially the same man. He was not seeking to continue the war for the glory of Rome; he was doing so to further his own personal objectives. Despite everything, Scipio still placed his own ambitions above the needs of the state. The realization angered Regulus and he leaned in over the table.

'I once sat in that chair,' he said. 'I remember the power one holds as senior consul and I know how the Senate can be manipulated by words and empty promises. You have led the Senate astray for your own ends.'

'You sat in this chair because I put you there,' Scipio replied viciously. 'And you repaid that debt with treachery.'

'What I did, I did for Rome,' Regulus replied.

'And that is why you fail,' Scipio shouted as he stood up. 'Why you falter now, when Rome's strength falters. Rome is powerful because of men like me, Regulus, men whose strength of will carry the city forward. Rome will not surrender because I will not surrender, and she will be victorious because I will be victorious.'

Regulus stepped back from the table, knowing any further argument was useless, and he returned the full measure of Scipio's malignant gaze as he made to leave.

'I am honour bound by the terms of my parole to return to Lilybaeum in Sicily via Lipara,' he said. 'But know this, Scipio. Your ambition threatens the very survival of Rome, and when the eyes of the senators have been opened to that reality, they will remember men like me – men who place the good of Rome above all else – and they will call for me.'

'No, Regulus,' Scipio said slowly. 'You will be forgotten.' And he turned away as the proconsul left the chamber.

In the silence that followed, Scipio found he could not be still, his temper on edge, and he paced the room, walking aimlessly around the large marble table. He had already decided where his first attack would take place, a stronghold of the Carthaginians that had been a thorn in the Roman campaign's side since the beginning of the war, and a focal point for every attack launched by the enemy on the northern coast of Sicily.

The new fleet was far from ready, and so Scipio would need to call up the remnants of the storm-lashed fleet in Agrigentum to complete his plan. He thought again of his first choice to command the naval arm of his attack and, as before, his reason and his pride were in disagreement. Logically, given the paucity of qualified Roman officers, the Greek was the obvious choice. In his narrow field, he had knowledge that few others possessed. Scipio thought of how the Greek had warned Paullus of the storm, only to have his advice ignored by the idiotic consul. Simultaneously Scipio felt his anger rise that he would even countenance accepting the Greek into his ranks, but again reason prevailed and Scipio thought of the traitor he retained on the prefect's ship. He would keep the Greek at arm's length and use Baro to keep a watchful eye on his enemy, a compromise that sickened him but one he knew was necessary, for now.

The decision made, Scipio turned his thoughts to the other aspects of the campaign. He became engrossed in the minutiae, his sharp mind dealing with each detail in turn while all the while his anticipation rose steadily, the pace of his stride increasing as he moved about the room. He stopped suddenly and looked over to the door, striding towards it with a determined step. He had planned enough, waited enough. Now it was time to put those plans into action, time to fulfil the promise he had made the Senate: time to go to war.

CHAPTER NINE

A single alarm bell was heard across the wide sweep of the bay, followed moments later by a dozen more, the sound rapidly succeeded by the horns of the galleys in the outer harbour, their clamour combining to fuel the panic of the inhabitants inside the walls of the town. Panormus was in turmoil, its streets crammed with people and animals, some fleeing deeper into the town and the docks, others towards the gates, now shut tightly against the advancing Roman legions. The noise was deafening, whipping up the panic of the populace, while above it the shouted commands of officers held sway, sending men racing to the walls, their shields and spears giving them headway in the throng.

Atticus stood on the aft-deck of the *Orcus*, breathing in the atmosphere of the ancient port. Fewer than a dozen Carthaginian galleys were in the bay, their hulls down as they drew deeper into the safety of the inner harbour, the sight of so many Roman galleys hastening their flight. Behind and around the *Orcus* sailed seventy galleys, newly formed from the remnants of the fleet from Agrigentum, which had regained its strength over the previous month. Atticus was in overall command and he nodded to Gaius as he watched the last of his ships round the eastern approaches.

The *Orcus* slowed, coming once more to standard speed. The wings of the formation unfolded as a blockade was formed, a flurry of orders and signals reaching across the length of the fleet until each galley knew its place. Atticus took a moment to look at the trim of his own ship, focusing on the actions of his new crew. Every moment of the long voyage from Rome to Agrigentum and thence to Panormus had been spent in training the raw recruits, and Atticus was satisfied with their progress.

Almost all of the senior sailing crew of the Orcus had been transferred to provide experienced personnel for the new fleet of 220 galleys being built at Fiumicino, and when Atticus had sailed south from Rome some three weeks before, half of those ships were already afloat and undergoing sea trials. It was only a matter of time before they would be unleashed upon the enemy.

Atticus had applied to retain Gaius, a request that was granted because of his rank, but he had been surprised and delighted when Baro also escaped transfer. Many of the experienced seconds-in-command had been chosen to captain new galleys, and the retention of Baro was a stroke of luck that immeasurably speeded up the training of the new crew.

Atticus acknowledged another flood of signals and the *Orcus* came to a stop, her bow swinging neatly to point directly into the inner harbour, her position making her the lynchpin for the entire right flank of the blockade. Atticus moved to the foredeck to get a better view, bringing with him the signalman from aft. Aside from the dozen or so Carthaginian war galleys, there were over fifty trading vessels of all sizes, many of them tethered to the docks, while others milled around the invisible boundary between the inner and outer harbour. Nightfall would bring the first attempts to break out, particularly amongst the smaller trading ships, and Atticus studied their form and disposition, trying to decipher which ones were the more aggressive given their proximity to the blockade.

Blockades were notoriously difficult to maintain given the small range of a galley. They had limited space for supplies, particularly water, a resource quickly devoured by the rowing crew in the late summer heat. It was necessary therefore to set up a system whereby individual ships could disengage from the formation to resupply nearby on land, the ranks thinning around its position until it returned, only to allow another ship to disengage and repeat the process. Any sailor who had witnessed a blockade, and doubtless there were some in Panormus, would know of such limitations and would therefore try to exploit the weakness. Atticus knew of only one solution to this problem, and that was to keep the disengagements random, allowing no advantage to an observant enemy. Even still, in an unfamiliar harbour, there would certainly be some escapees, and Atticus's main concern was that some of those might sail directly to Lilybaeum to warn the enemy there about the blockade.

The high-pitched clarion call of the legions caught Atticus's ear and he turned towards the shore beyond the walls of Panormus. The marching formations of the newly formed Ninth were stark red against the green hills sweeping up from behind town, and even from a distance Atticus could sense their latent energy, a coiled serpent waiting to strike against the walls of Panormus. Atticus turned away from the sight, forestalling the drift of his thoughts to one in particular amongst the legion. He refocused his concentration on the formation of galleys around him, conscious that the battle would soon be joined and the blockade would need to stand firm.

Septimus cursed loudly as he roared at the new recruits in his maniple. In the brief minutes that he had been distracted by observing the walls of Panormus, the strict formation of the unit had once more lost cohesion. The defined gaps between the grades had disappeared and the formerly rigid square was again bowed outwards on both flanks, inviting similar curses from the centurions who commanded the maniples on either side.

The recruits were interspersed with experienced men, but their majority in numbers gave them weight, and the stumbling efforts of one man had an instant ripple effect on the whole. An experienced unit would constantly dress its own ranks, compensating immediately for any uneven terrain underfoot, but the recruits allowed themselves to be shuffled out of position, forgetting even the most basic rules of drill in their heightened state of anticipation. The nervous tension of his men further aggravated Septimus, and the whiplash of his commands brought them once more into formation, a status the centurion knew would not last.

The maniple, indeed the entire legion, was built on the solid premise that experience was essential in maintaining discipline in battle. For that reason the front ranks, the *hastati*, were often the most junior of the soldiers and invariably the lightest. They were backed up by the *principes*, the inner strength of the formation and, to the rear, the *triarii*, the veterans of many battles. These second and third ranks ensured that the legion did not take one step back unless ordered, denying the junior *hastati* the opportunity should they falter under the stress of battle. In the newly formed Ninth, however, the rapid recruitment of its ranks meant that both the *hastati* and *principes* were, in the main, raw recruits, with only the physical size of each man deciding their rank. Only the *triarii* were experienced, drawn from other legions; in the fight to come, they would be the bulwark of the Ninth.

The sound of thundering hooves interrupted Septimus's

invective and he spun around as another squad of cavalry shot past on a headlong dash to the approach road on the far side of the town. That western side had been assigned to the Second Legion and they were already sweeping across the flat tillage fields that separated the landward walls of Panormus from the towering hills that framed the bay. Septimus watched their advance with a studious gaze, noting the ordered ranks of the experienced legion, and he knew it was not by chance that the Second had been assigned the road that led from the enemy stronghold at Lilybaeum.

The command to halt echoed across the Ninth and Septimus instinctively repeated it, an order that triggered a weary sigh from the troops behind him. He frowned at the sound, conscious that his men didn't even possess the basic level of stamina that campaigning required. With Fortuna's blessing, unless the Carthaginians sallied forth from Panormus, there would be no fighting that day, but the day was far from over. Septimus glanced left and right, immediately spotting the men laying out the boundaries for the rectangular encampment that would need to be completed before nightfall. Their marks would delineate the trench to be dug, ten foot wide by five deep, with the earth thrown inwards to form a rampart, on top of which the *sudes*, the six-foot-long pointed oak stakes that travelled with the legion, would be implanted and inter-twined with lighter oak branches. It was a task that a seasoned legion could complete in less than three hours, but one that the Ninth had struggled to complete in five on the previous nights during their march from Brolium. Under the watchful gaze of the enemy, Septimus could only hope that any ineptitude would go unrecognized.

Scipio braced his feet in his stirrups and stood tall in his saddle. The horse shifted beneath him, adjusting its balance, and Scipio instinctively murmured a soothing word, settling his mount once more. She was an Andalusian, a Spanish horse, fifteen hands high, and Scipio had specifically selected her from his own stables, one of three war horses that had accompanied him to Sicily. Specially bred and trained, the horse responded instantly to his shifting body weight and the press of his legs, eliminating the need for reins in battle, allowing the rider to wield weapons in both hands.

Scipio stood motionless as his eyes scanned the width and breadth of the walls of Panormus. They were formidable and, despite the obvious sounds of panic from within the walls, he realized that no military commander would relinquish the town without a fight. Beneath his gaze marched the Second Legion. They moved without command, their only sound a thousand individual rhythms as kit and armour clanged in time with the beat of the march. They were a hardened legion, tried and tested, and would bear the brunt of the assault.

To his right Scipio spied the Ninth deploying to build their encampment. They were legionaries only by virtue of their uniform and were far from being a useful fighting unit. Scipio had ordered them on campaign only as a last resort, wanting their numbers as a show of outward strength, knowing that the Carthaginians on the walls of Panormus would see only the legion and not their fragility.

The march from Brolium had been arduous, over the more difficult inland mountainous terrain, a route taken by necessity to detour around the Carthaginian-held port of Thermae. It was a bold strike, one which had some detractors in the Senate, but Scipio had insisted, wanting to retake the initiative in the war, knowing that a piecemeal, timid approach would rapidly sap the limited time of his consulship without achieving any noteworthy gains. If he could take Panormus, he could begin a campaign to retain proconsul command of the army after his tenure, a prize that could only lead to further possibilities.

He sat back in his saddle and the tribunes around him became immediately alert, waiting anxiously for his command. He looked to the walls again, and to the massive gate that barred the eastern entrance to the town. There was a similar gate no doubt on the western approach, both firmly shut against the Roman legions.

Scipio called a tribune to his side. 'Take a detachment of cavalry and ride to the walls,' he ordered. 'Seek out an enemy commander, someone of rank, and give them this message: "If they surrender without a fight, every man of military age will be enslaved, but their lives will be spared, as will those of the inhabitants. If they resist, when we breach the walls, and we will, there will be no mercy."'

The tribune slammed his fist to his chest in salute and rode off in a cloud of dust, shouting orders as he passed a squad of cavalry. A dozen riders peeled off from the formation and pursued the tribune, catching up with him only as he neared the walls. Scipio watched them with mild disinterest. The offer of mercy was a mere formality, extended on the remote possibility that the military commander was a coward or the inhabitants had somehow overcome the garrison, leaving a civilian in charge. Otherwise these offers were rarely, if ever, accepted.

The minutes drew out and Scipio stood once more in his saddle to get a better view of the cadre of Roman horsemen beneath the walls of the town. Above them he could see a group of Carthaginians on the battlements, the sun glinting off their helmets as they peered down from the heights. Without warning a flight of arrows struck the horsemen from further along the wall, and Scipio watched in anger as the Carthaginians loosed spears directly down on the Roman cavalry. The horsemen broke away instantly, leaving dead and wounded in their wake, and a roar of anger rose up from the previously quiet Second Legion, as those that had witnessed the malicious attack gave vent to their fury. The Carthaginians had given their answer: there would be no surrender.

Scipio's mount became skittish as it sensed the tension of its rider. Scipio spurred his horse to a full gallop, his startled coterie of tribunes reacting more or less quickly in following him as he rode to cut off the retreating detachment of cavalry. He halted their flight and quickly scanned their number. Two of the remaining seven were injured, with arrow shafts protruding from grievous wounds. The tribune was not amongst them, and Scipio looked beyond to the crumpled figures lying in the shadow of the town walls. It was a senseless, wasteful death and Scipio burned the sight into his consciousness. Panormus would fall, of that he had never had any doubt, but now he was determined that the fall would take the town, and all who dwelt within, to the very depths of Hades.

Dawn afforded Atticus his first proper view of the captured trading boat; he rubbed the tiredness from his eyes as he moved to the side rail for a better view. It was a small boat, lateen-rigged for coastal trading, and the trader had tried to slip through the blockade three hours before sunrise. It had been a moonless night, putting the odds firmly in his favour, but Fortuna had taken a hand in his fate and his attempt to slip through a gap in the blockade had coincided with the return of a galley, the *Corus*, to its station.

The trader had been quickly discovered and the skirmish that ensued had been both brief and one-sided. The shouts of alarm and commands had roused Atticus from his sleep; he had rushed on deck to witness the confused encounter that was illuminated only by scattered torches less than a hundred yards away. Orders rang out for the release of grappling hooks, and Atticus judged that at least two other Roman galleys that flanked the *Corus* came to her aid, but it was all over before any other ship could intervene.

In the silence that followed, sporadic cheers rang out, and Atticus quickly shouted orders to be passed down the line of galleys, warning the crews to be vigilant against any other boats that might take advantage of the distraction to make their own attempt at escape. Thereafter the blockade had descended into near silence, but few slept, including Atticus, the nearness of dawn and the brief but intense restlessness brought on by the skirmish combining to keep all alert and awake.

In the dawn light, the crew of the *Corus* had lined the side rail of the trading ship with its own crew, and Atticus watched in silence as he waited to see what fate the victors had decided for their captives. The attitude of the blockade crews had changed over the three weeks since arriving in Panormus. Initially there had been many attempts at escape, particularly amongst the larger trading ships. All had been re-captured and their crews sent to a stockade that straddled the encampment of the Second Legion. From there they would be sent to the slave market and the proceeds would be divided amongst the blockade crews.

As the blockade dragged on, however, and the attempts at escape had become more sporadic and the boats smaller, the Roman crews began to tire of the boring routine of blockading. Their attitude had changed towards any Carthaginian crew that was captured trying to escape. Frustration and tedium had descended into anger, and an unspoken decision was made amongst the men that smaller Carthaginian crews were fair game, not worth the paltry sum they would fetch on the slave market. A precarious balance had begun to emerge between discipline and insubordination, but Atticus had turned a blind eye to the brutal retaliation the men were dealing out to the captured Carthaginian crews, preferring them to vent their frustration at the enemy rather than at their commanders.

Atticus counted fifteen Carthaginians lining the side rail of their captured ship; without warning the crew of the *Corus* pushed them all into the sea. A cheer rang out from the galleys closest to the action and many of the crew of the *Orcus* rushed to the rail to gain a better view. Atticus had witnessed some brutal methods to dispose of Carthaginian crews over the previous days, but this time the method seemed simple: swim or die.

Almost immediately half a dozen men, the non-swimmers, disappeared beneath the water, and the silence that followed their desperate screams was filled with groans of anger and annoyance from those amongst the crew of the *Corus* who had bet on them. The gambling now started in earnest on every galley within sight, and shouts of encouragement and cheers echoed across the deck of the *Orcus*. Atticus watched the scene dispassionately while glancing occasionally to his crew who were bunched on the main deck. Baro stood amongst them, making the book.

Some of the Carthaginians struck out for the shoreline two miles away, but in a panic one man swam directly to a neighbouring galley, calling out to the Roman crew to rescue him. Many of them laughed, but others took to fending off the struggling Carthaginian with the tip of their spears, not wanting to see him survive in favour of the man they had backed. Two other Carthaginians were treading water a dozen yards off the bow of their boat, and it soon became apparent that one of them couldn't swim. He was clinging desperately

168

to the shoulders of his friend, terror etched on his face, and he frantically gulped the air as the swell drenched his face.

Their plight quickly drew the attention of the Romans, and again shouts of anger mixed with those of encouragement as more money changed hands and side bets were taken. Some of the crewmen of the *Corus* on board the trading boat began to hurl objects at the struggling pair, trying to separate them, and the swimmer was accidentally struck on the head with a pulley block. He was knocked unconscious and, as he rolled over in the water, his companion clawed desperately at his back, his frenzied efforts pushing the unconscious man beneath the surface, drowning him. In a panic the non-swimmer lost his grip and he slipped under the waves, leaving behind the body of the man who had tried to save him.

Atticus turned away and looked towards the shore. One hundred yards away another man was struggling, a weak swimmer, and his arm shot up as if clawing at some invisible source of salvation as he slipped beneath the waves. Beyond him only two men remained and all eyes went to them. They were swimming strongly, twenty feet apart, and they had already gone nearly two hundred yards towards the shore. Again the level of noise from the fleet increased as new bets were taken, and Atticus found himself drawn into the intensity of the struggle.

Shouts of anger caught Atticus's attention and he turned to watch a fight break out on the foredeck of the *Corus*. Suddenly a flight of arrows shot forward from the melee to fall with deadly accuracy on the first swimmer, neatly piercing the water around him until one struck his shoulder. His scream could be plainly heard across the galleys, but it was soon forgotten in the brawl that followed. Atticus called his own crew to order and calmed the arguments that had broken out over the settling of bets. The crew moved away quickly but

Atticus could see that on other galleys the captains were struggling to regain control of their men. Atticus cursed the blockade, knowing the situation could only deteriorate if the siege continued, but as he looked to the town he felt his spirits rise.

Over the previous weeks he had watched with interest as four siege towers had taken shape at the eastern side of the town. They had risen slowly from the ground, four hundred yards out from the walls, and on days when the offshore breeze carried sounds towards the ocean, the air would ring with the beat of hammer blows. They had stood immobile as they grew, but today they were no longer stationary, they were moving, inch-by-inch, towards the wall. Over the expanse of open water that separated the *Orcus* from the shore, the progress of the siege towers was almost imperceptible, but soon many others noticed their advance and the last of the angry shouts amongst the fleet gave way to a cheer that could be heard across the bay. The legionaries had finally begun their assault.

'Heave!'

A thousand voices echoed the command, a deep growl that gave strength to their effort. Four men stood behind each bar that passed through the long, blunt-edged poles extending from the back of the siege towers. Thirty yards long, the poles resembled huge stationary battering rams, butted hard against the near intractable weight of the massive siege towers. The lines of pushing men weaved from side to side as they stumbled over the uneven ground, with only their momentum keeping them upright as one hard-fought step was taken after another.

Septimus echoed each shouted command to the men nearest him, his back locked straight as his legs heaved through each step, the bar pressed tight against his chest, the sweat stinging his eyes. He glanced to his right and the ordered ranks of the Second Legion, drawn up two abreast between the pushing poles, directly behind the ladder that led to the top of the siege tower. The Ninth had built the towers, had slaved over them during every daylight hour over the previous weeks, and now, like dray horses, they were heaving them into place, handing their labour and the honour of assaulting the walls over to the Second. It was a bitter trade, and Septimus roared out the order to push, feeding his frustration into the task.

'Incoming, shields up!'

As one, the legionaries on the flanks, protecting the men who were pushing, threw up their shields to accept the first flights of arrows from the walls of Panormus. The Carthaginian archers were stationed further along the walls, loosing their arrows diagonally into the men further back from the tower, those not screened by its bulk, and the legionaries were forced to form an elongated *testudo*.

Septimus looked up. Fifty yards to go and his eyes were drawn to the corpses hanging from the battlements. They were legionaries, captured in a night attack a week before when the Carthaginians had sallied out from the town to try and fire the siege towers. Their attack had been beaten off, but the dawn light had revealed a macabre consequence. The legionaries had been brutally tortured and, as the Roman army looked on, each soldier was hung from the walls, the fall mercilessly breaking the necks of the lucky ones, while the unfortunate were slowly strangled, their desperate struggles drawing cheers from the onlooking Carthaginians.

The blood of each watching legionary ran cold that day but, rather than acting as a deterrent, the brutal act had driven all semblance of humanity from the Romans. Septimus recalled the savage determination that overtook his men after that day as they raced to finish the siege towers.

The order to make ready was heard and the first ranks of the Second moved forward. From the enemy's perspective, the front of the rectangular tower was solid and imposing, a sheer wall of oak reaching above the height of the walls of the town. At the rear, however, hidden from the Carthaginians, a massive inclined ladder, wide enough for four men, reached from the base of the tower to a platform twenty-five feet above the ground, the height of the town's battlements. The leading ranks of the Second jumped up on to the base and climbed up the first rungs of the ladder. Their progress was slow as the tower swayed over the rough ground, but a dozen men reached the top and formed up behind the crude drawbridge at the front of the platform, waiting patiently as each yard of ground was covered.

The rain of arrows intensified and, with it, the calls of encouragement from the centurions and *optiones*. Sporadic cries of pain came from all sides and the men redoubled their efforts as the order to 'heave' became more frequent. Fire arrows soaked in pitch struck the upper works of the tower, striking deep into the timbers, and like tenacious fingers of Vulcan the flames licked the newly cut oak. Sudden cheers rang out from the battlements as fire took hold of one of the siege towers. The legionaries who had stood ready on the upper platform, in jumping to escape the flames, fell to their deaths.

Still the dogged order to advance was heard across the legions and the men of the Ninth looked grimly to the earth beneath their feet as they put their weight behind the attack.

As the gap narrowed, the arrows gave way to spears, the iron-tipped javelins, loosed from the height of the walls, piercing even the strongest shield. The casualties on the ground mounted, the extreme forward flanks of the Ninth bearing the brunt of the assault. Like a wave breaking against jagged rocks, the tight formation of shields formed to protect the men was shattered, leaving the exposed soldiers with nothing to do except pray to Mars as they passed through the killing ground.

Under the lee of the walls, with mere yards to go, the defenders resorted to throwing rocks on the exposed legionaries. Only those men on the siege tower or directly behind it were safe. Further back there was no defence against the missiles, each one the size of a man's head, and they tore bloody swathes through the flanks, killing and maiming as bones were shattered and bodies broken.

The blood ran freely down the side of Septimus's face and he blinked it from his eye as he spat the salty taste from his mouth. It was not his own, and he glanced to the empty space on his right. The rock had hit the legionary on the head, cracking open his skull before driving through into the man behind, shattering his pelvis; his screams echoed in Septimus's ears as he relentlessly pushed forward.

The gap between the siege tower and the wall fell to five yards. Almost without command the men of the Ninth dropped the heavy poles and began to retreat out of arrow range.

That same instant the drawbridge was released and the legionaries of the Second swept across in a savage wave of steel and flesh. The Carthaginians held firm on the narrow battlements, and men fell to their deaths as the struggle descended into a chaotic brawl, the enemies fighting chest to chest, their faces twisted in aggression and rage.

The legionaries streamed up the ladder of the siege tower, creating a crushing momentum that forced the front ranks deeper into the enemy's midst, pushing out the flanks along the battlements, the narrow walkway creating individual battles where strength and will held sway. The Carthaginians fought with demonic resistance, the defenceless inhabitants of Panormus to their backs; within minutes the balance shifted as the Carthaginians first checked, then reversed the tide of battle, pushing the legionaries back towards the towers, striking down any Roman who stood his ground against the maniacal fury of the counter-attack.

Septimus watched the fight from two hundred yards away, his chest heaving from the exertion of the advance and the battle lust flowing in his veins. He had never turned away from the moment of attack before and he cursed the subservient role the Ninth had been given in the assault, the bloody casualties it had endured that would go unreciprocated.

Suddenly he noticed the momentum of the battle turn against the men of the Second on the battlements. The legionaries were no longer ascending the ladder and the platform to the drawbridge was overcrowded as the assault stalled under the weight of the Carthaginian counter-attack. He looked to the other siege towers, trying to judge their situation, but smoke and distance frustrated his attempt.

Septimus looked forward again and, almost intuitively, he decided. 'Men of the IV, to arms,' he shouted.

His maniple reacted instantly, responding to his command without question. They rose up and formed behind their centurion, drawing their swords as one. He signalled the advance and they fell into the wake of the siege tower, their pace increasing as they covered the same ground a second time, this time with the tools of war in their hands.

The sudden headlong rush of the IV maniple caught others in the Ninth by surprise, but they quickly responded. By the time Septimus reached the base of the siege tower, he stood at the head of an unstoppable charge. They pushed past the legionaries of the Second, and like a seventh wave overcoming its lesser predecessors, the IV maniple went on up the slope of the ladder. Septimus pushed through the throng on the upper platform, his head down through the black smoke that was engulfing the space, as Carthaginian fire, loosed from close range, caught hold of the wooden structure.

Through hooded eyes he saw the enemy before him and he bunched his weight behind his shield, his feet instinctively finding purchase on the narrow, blood-soaked drawbridge, the memory of a dozen assaults across a *corvus* guiding his actions. He roared in defiance, his call taken up by a hundred men, and they tore into the Carthaginian front line, shattering it instantly as men were flung backwards from the battlements. He spun on his heel, turning the momentum of the charge along the narrow walkway, and once again the battle was transformed into two narrow fronts as the legionaries tried to sweep the Carthaginians from the walls.

Septimus tasted blood: the remnants of the legionary who had fallen beside him, his own from a shallow sword wound under his helmet, and also the blood of his enemy, a fine spray that covered his face as he twisted and withdrew the blade of his sword from the clinging flesh. The close-quarter combat reached a bloody peak as each side neared the limit of its strength and desperate commands were shouted in disparate languages, driving the men through barriers of pain and exhaustion.

Septimus stabbed his sword forward, his shield arm numb to the shoulder from countless blows but, as he stared into the eyes of his enemy, he began to see seeds of doubt there. Suddenly the tempo of the defence changed from tenacious to desperate. The number of legionaries on the battlements had reached a critical level and an instinctive recognition swept through the Carthaginian line.

The pressure against Septimus's shield fell away and, over the shoulders of the enemy front line, he saw men retreating, fleeing down the steps that led to the street below. The warrior facing him sensed the vacuum to his rear and he stepped back in panic. Septimus stabbed through the Carthaginian's open guard, slicing cleanly into his groin, and he pushed him from the battlements as he led his men onwards, the Carthaginian's dying screams lost amidst the cheers of the Ninth.

They swept down off the battlements and along the narrow street that led to the eastern gate, clearing all before them, dealing quickly with any individual Carthaginian who stood his ground, running at full tilt as blood lust and victory combined to chase all restraint from their minds.

Septimus had led a hundred men from the battlements, but as he neared the eastern gate that number fell to a dozen, the others disappearing into the warren of streets, knowing they were the first, eager to ravage the virginal town before the horde descended. Four Carthaginians stood guard at the eastern gate, the brave remnants of a detachment that had already fled, and they threw themselves against Septimus's men, screaming battle cries of hatred. They were quickly killed, and the legionaries sheathed their swords as they lifted the locking bar clear.

A wave of legionaries swept through the entrance, their cheers laced with a savagery born of a bloody fight. The assaults of the other siege towers had failed and the men of the Second had been badly mauled, a blood-letting that fed their desire for brutal revenge. Like feral animals they threw off all restraint, racing into the deserted streets, their swords drawn against a defenceless foe.

Septimus stood back from the tide, his mind still conditioned to the demands of his command, giving himself pause to still the blood lust in his veins as he took stock. The legionaries were beyond control and, although many of the enemy would stand, individually or in small groups, they were hopelessly outnumbered and the end was inevitable.

Panormus had fallen, and Septimus could hear the screams of terror from the populace, the cries of women and children, of men desperately trying to mount a defence against hardened soldiers who would kill any who stood in their path. Panormus had stood defiant, and for that the inhabitants had sacrificed all claims to mercy. The victors would take their measure of retribution. As the last cries of battle faded, a new, more terrifying sound resonated around the walls: the desperate pleas of a population given over to a cursed fate of rape and death.

'Aspect change on the Carthaginian galleys!'

'Report, Corin,' Atticus shouted, running to the side rail of the aft-deck.

There was a moment's pause as the lookout watched the enemy formation take shape.

'Eleven galleys, looks as though they're making battle speed, heading . . . west, towards the right flank.'

'Baro,' Atticus shouted, 'make ready for battle. Drusus, assemble your men.'

The *Orcus* sprang into action, every man following the dictates of training or experience, the endless hours of drill transforming the galley from an inert state to battle-poised in minutes.

'Signal from shore, the legionaries have breached the walls!'

Atticus looked to Panormus. The siege towers were hard up against the eastern wall, like barbs stuck fast on the hide of an enormous beast, their size dwarfed by the featureless curtain walls and battlements. At least two of them were on fire and, although Atticus had watched their approach to the wall, he was suddenly in awe of the men who had scaled such crude devices to throw themselves against the waiting defenders. He looked to the inner harbour and the tight formation of Carthaginian galleys approaching his command. The town had fallen and soon every ship in Panormus would attempt to break out, many of them in the wake of the galleys, hoping for a breach. Atticus made his decision even as he spoke the command.

'Signal to the left flank: full attack! Tell them to take the inner harbour. We'll take the galleys.'

Gaius immediately called for battle speed and the *Orcus* shot forward from the static formation of the blockade, the galleys on its flank reacting quickly as the signal swept across their decks to be passed down the line.

'Gaius, target the centre of their formation,' Atticus commanded, and the helmsman swung the bow through two points. Their best chance was to overwhelm the Carthaginian galleys quickly and decisively, ending all hope of escape amongst the trading ships. Atticus moved to stand beside the tiller, bracing his feet against the pitch of the deck; he felt the crushing monotony of the past three weeks fall away as a spearhead of galleys formed behind the *Orcus*.

Like the unfolding wings of a hawk preparing to fly, the Carthaginian formation took shape before the Roman attack, the flanks advancing at a faster pace until the enemy galleys were sailing line abreast. They were manoeuvring for sea room, Atticus realized, abandoning any pretence of punching through the Roman formation. They were going to engage. Atticus smiled derisively. Although outnumbered, the Carthaginians were evidently confident they could prevail. After all, the fight would be on their terms, fought on the tip of a ram, but the Carthaginians were underestimating the skill of a trained Roman crew and Atticus vowed they would pay dearly for their imprudence.

He glanced left, watching the opposite flank as it swept in behind the Carthaginian galleys to envelop the struggling mass of trading ships, many of them hopelessly trying to raise sail in the insipid wind, irrationally ignoring the odds. Any chance of a breakout was already being quashed, and with a hard stare he turned once more to the approaching Carthaginian galleys.

The gap fell to four hundred yards and Atticus called for attack speed, the *Orcus* taking on the additional four knots within a ship length. Atticus pointed to the centre galley of the enemy formation, his silent order wordlessly acknowledged by Gaius as he adjusted the tiller a half-point. Hours of training came to the fore and the formation of Roman galleys behind the *Orcus* was forgotten as she cast off the fetters of combined attack to become a lone fighter.

Atticus and Gaius spoke with one voice as the Carthaginian galley neared, the enemy crew having identified and responded to the singular line of attack. The opposing galleys weaved through an invisible line separating the rams, each helmsman subtly countering the feints and ripostes of the other, and the unrelenting drum beat from the rowing deck seemed to increase as Atticus braced for the final thrust.

His mind cleared, the order forming in the back of his throat; he felt Gaius tense beside him, anticipating the command. The Carthaginian galley filled his vision, its dark hull a mirror reflection of the *Orcus*, two creatures born of the same design, forced to fight each other by their warring masters.

'Now,' Atticus said, almost in a whisper, and Gaius nudged the helm, taking the *Orcus* off its true line, a delicate and deliberate error to compel the enemy to commit. The Carthaginians responded instantly in an incredible display of seamanship, and they swept in to strike the *Orcus* on the starboard forequarter. Atticus had anticipated the move, but the enemy's reaction was far faster than he predicted, their skill beggaring belief, and he roared out the final order before he drew breath.

'Hard to starboard, ramming speed!'

The *Orcus* was immediately transported back to the calm coastal waters of Fiumicino and the rowing crew accelerated to ramming speed even as Gaius brought the tiller hard over. A hundred hours' training was realized in the span of a breath, and the *Orcus* cut inside the line of attack, bringing her ram to bear on the starboard flank of the Carthaginian galley.

Atticus was thrown to the deck as the ram struck home, the six-foot bronze fist striking the strake timbers at an acute angle, snapping them cleanly from the bulkheads, the forward momentum of the Carthaginian galley adding to the force of the blow, the galley pushing itself upon the very spear that was slicing into its underbelly. Atticus regained his feet, the shock of attack and the fury of battle heightening his senses. Quickly he took stock. The Carthaginians were thrown by the sudden reversal but they were already recovering; Atticus could hear the angry bark of orders from the enemy decks. They were surging towards the side rails, preparing to board, to trade ship for ship.

'Gaius, full reverse,' Atticus ordered. 'Drusus, prepare to repel boarders.'

The newly promoted centurion commanded his men with crisp, decisive orders and they ran quickly to the foredeck, forming a wall of interlocking shields at the rail, their swords drawn in defiance, daring the Carthaginians to attack.

The rowers of the *Orcus* began to back stroke but, even as they did, grappling hooks were thrown by the enemy, locking the ships together. The timbers of the stricken Carthaginian galley squealed and tore as the ram twisted in the gaping hole. The legionaries drew aside their shields to attack the lines, the ropes parting like bow strings drawn by the strength of two hundred and seventy rowers, but from ten feet the Carthaginians cast spears through the gaps in the shield wall, striking down any legionary who exposed himself. The embrace was sustained as more lines were thrown.

The gap between the foredecks fell to four feet, and the Carthaginians charged the shield wall, jumping fearlessly across, a desperate attack to escape their doomed ship. The legionaries stood firm and a dozen men fell between the grinding hulls of the galleys, their screams of terror lost in the din of battle. The stronger warriors gained the Roman deck but Drusus's men held them fast, checking any breach before it could develop while the increasing momentum of the *Orcus* finally overcame the strength of the tethers and they parted in sequence, the lines whipping back to leave the Carthaginian galley reeling away. The stranded boarders fought to the last, their fate driving them to mindless fury, and many legionaries fell before they were finally overcome.

The *Orcus* swung away under a final hail of arrows and spears from the sinking Carthaginian galley, the enemy's curses reaching across the increasing gap. Gaius brought the galley back up to battle speed, her bloodied ram seeking out further prey.

Atticus watched as the last arrows fell short. He looked to the foredeck and the casualties of the legionaries. The Carthaginians were a fearsome breed and their defiant attempt to board the *Orcus* was a mark of their courage. Nevertheless, they had been beaten on their terms, on the tip of a ram, and Atticus knew his confidence had been justified as he looked once more to the sinking enemy ship.

'By the gods . . .' Gaius began, and Atticus spun around, following the helmsman's gaze.

Eight Roman galleys were sinking fast in the waters behind the *Orcus*, prey of the Carthaginian rams; as Atticus watched in horror, another three ships were struck in rapid succession, second blood for the enemy ships. Only two Carthaginian galleys had been rammed on the first assault.

Atticus had been certain of victory, the sheer weight of odds negating any chance the Carthaginians had. Yet the enemy ships were mauling the thirty-five galleys of the right flank and he realized with sickening dread that his previous confidence had been based solely on the skill and training of his crew. As a commander he had misjudged the situation, believing that all Roman crews possessed the same prowess as his own. But the Carthaginians had neatly exploiting the imbalance of skill, attacking many of the ships with near impunity, with only the more experienced Roman captains able to counter the enemy rams.

With *corvi*, the Romans attacked head-on in line abreast, each galley protecting the flanks of its neighbour, an impenetrable wall against which the Carthaginians had no defence. The skill required of the Roman crew for a frontal attack was minimal compared to a ramming run, and therein lay one of the many strengths of the *corvus*, requiring only that the crew strike the bow of the enemy ship before the boarding ramp was released to hold the galleys together. Now the ram reigned supreme and seamanship was vital, a skill the Carthaginians had honed over generations, using it to deadly effect in the harbour of Panormus.

Atticus roared a course change in anger and frustration and the *Orcus* came up to attack speed. In the waters ahead, a Roman galley was desperately trying to avoid the ram of a pursuing Carthaginian ship, their forlorn attempts to escape neatly countered at every turn. Atticus identified the target to Gaius, the helmsman grimly bringing the ram of the *Orcus* to bear. The Carthaginian crew realized the threat and although, as before, they reacted with lightning speed,

Gaius was their equal and the *Orcus* accelerated to ramming speed.

Atticus instinctively braced himself for the strike but his frustration refused to allow him to focus. A sudden crash of timbers caused him to turn and again he watched with dread as another Roman galley fell victim to the Carthaginians. The sound was repeated twice more in as many seconds and Atticus felt the weight of regret crush him. The *Orcus* would claim a second prize, maybe a third, but all the while other Roman ships would be lost, and Atticus was powerless to defend them all.

Panormus had fallen, the town was theirs, but in the harbour the Carthaginians were exacting a measure of revenge, slowly drawing a blade across the exposed incompetence of the Roman navy, turning the waters red with their blood. The Carthaginians were once more claiming what was rightfully theirs: mastery of the sea.

CHAPTER TEN

Hamilcar watched impatiently as the small bird circled the tower, its wings flapping slowly in the updraught. It dipped suddenly, dropping to the height of the coop, but still it refused to enter and it wheeled away to continue its flight, oblivious to the annoyance of the observer below.

It was only by chance that Hamilcar had seen the bird arrive fifteen minutes before. He had been standing at the window of his room, staring at the distant hills to the east of Lilybaeum, his thoughts focused, as they had been for weeks, on the stronghold of Panormus beyond the natural divide. The carrier pigeon had caught his eye as it flew in close to the ground, a grey-white flash against the verdant background. Hamilcar had immediately raced to the battlements beneath the coop, anxious to receive an update on the siege.

The pigeon flew in close once more, but this time it landed on the protruding ledge of the coop. It stretched out its wings, the tips trembling slightly before they finally came to rest, and then the pigeon gracelessly stumbled through the entrance and out of sight. Hamilcar looked to the door at the base of the tower and a moment later the handler descended with the tiny brass cylinder that had been attached to the pigeon's leg.

He came up short in surprise as he encountered the commander waiting for him; he handed the cylinder over. Hamilcar, resisting the temptation to open it there and then, retraced his steps to his room, rolling the tiny capsule between his thumb and forefinger as he walked.

He entered the quiet of his room and closed the door. It had been more than a week since he had received news and he noticed his hand was trembling slightly as he placed the cylinder on the table. Lilybaeum, on the northwestern coast of Sicily, was only a day's sailing from Panormus, but the Roman siege, on land and sea, had placed a stranglehold on the town. The paucity of news, most of it from ships passing at a distance from the port, made the reports carried by the pigeon all the more important. He opened the cylinder and withdrew the tiny scroll from within. The message was encrypted, an overcautious step considering the Romans were as yet unaware of the unique ability of the carrier pigeons, an ingenious method of communication that the Carthaginians had learned from the Persians a generation before, and one Hamilcar's predecessor had brought to Sicily. He decoded the report and read it through twice, the necessary brevity of the sentence in marked contrast to its weighty content.

'Attack on siege towers failed. Roman assault imminent. Galley captains informed of your last order.'

Hamilcar found that he was holding his breath and he exhaled. Panormus was doomed. The attack on the siege towers was a last desperate gamble that Hamilcar had ordered once he had learned of their existence, knowing the garrison commander did not have enough men for the task, hoping that Tanit, the goddess of fortune, might take a hand; but she had deserted Panormus, leaving it to its fate.

The attack on the town had been a surprise move by the

Romans, in hindsight a typically aggressive and ambitious step, but one Hamilcar had not planned for. The fleet from Gadir had arrived in Sicily, but with his army under Hanno's command in Africa, he had no effective way to lift the siege. He had hoped for more time, to realize a strategy he had already put in motion, but, sensing defeat, he had prepared for its eventuality, and his lips soundlessly mouthed the last words of the report: 'your last order.' He had penned it more than a week before for the galley captains, and it had read: *'If Panormus falls, scuttle or engage, but galleys must not fall into enemy hands.'*

Hamilcar knew three of the captains personally. They would consider it a grave dishonour to scuttle their own ships, but Hamilcar had wanted to give them the option, knowing the odds against them. In his heart he knew they would engage the enemy blockade. It was the course he would take in the same situation. As he reread the report he whispered a silent prayer to Baal to watch over the sons of Carthage.

He stood up and slowly rubbed the thin slip of paper between his calloused fingers, the fibres breaking down quickly. He let the remnants fall to the floor. The Romans had defied him. He had sent them an ambassador with lenient terms and they had dismissed his magnanimity, compounding that insult with an aggressive attack that had taken Hamilcar by surprise. He looked to the scraps of paper at his feet and felt the heat of indignant anger build within him. He would not be made a fool of again. After Panormus, the Romans would surely turn their attention to Lilybaeum and here, Hamilcar vowed, he would break their arrogance against the walls. There would be no more talk of peace, no more benevolent terms, and to make this decision irrevocable, Hamilcar knew there was one symbolic act that needed to be made, one superfluous element that needed to be eradicated. He strode from the room, his decision hardening with each step into cold determination.

The group of horsemen moved slowly through the deserted street, the unnatural silence broken only by the occasional sound of iron-shod hooves hitting random stones beneath the loose straw that was strewn across the hard-packed soil of the road. The horses were skittish and they snorted nervously, sensing the mood of their riders. The group closed ranks, keeping to the centre of the street.

Ahead they spotted the crumpled body of a woman on the road. She was naked below the waist, her legs twisted grotesquely, and she had been savagely beaten, the pool of blackened blood beneath her drawing a swarm of glistening bluebottle flies. Her face was hidden by her matted hair, making her age difficult to guess, but she had the slender lines of a younger woman and the riders looked away as they passed, their own faces pale with shock.

Further on a man was hanging by the neck from an upper storey window, his face blackened from the fire that had consumed his clothes and scorched his flesh. His body twisted slowly in the gentle wind. Beneath him the door of his house stood open and the riders peered in as they passed, unable to resist the animal instinct that compels a man to gaze with morbid fascination upon the very thing that he abhors. The room was mercifully dark, obscuring the fate of the family the man had tried to protect, but the meagre light reflecting off the naked flesh of tiny limbs created a terrible scene in the mind's eye and again the men looked away in horror.

A sudden shriek broke the near silence and the tribune beside Scipio jumped with fright, his mount darting forward ten yards before the young man could bring it under control. Scipio scowled at the officer, a silent admonition, although he too had been startled by the sound. Panormus resembled the far bank of the Styx, a cursed place where the damned lay awaiting their passage to the inner depths of Hades. It had been forty-eight hours since the walls had been breached and the carnage was absolute. No inhabitant had been spared and the outnumbered garrison had been butchered to a man.

Scipio had allowed the men to gorge themselves on the town, wanting to set an example to every other town in Sicily, but even he was shocked by the level of savagery to which the legionaries had descended. In his youth, when he'd served his time as a tribune, Scipio had witnessed the brutality of close-quarter fighting, the fury men displayed in battle when the instinct to survive overrode all others, and where barbarity separated the living from the slain. But never before had he seen that fury unleashed on a civilian population. Although Scipio had long since hardened his heart to the plight of his enemy, he knew that few deserved the fate meted out to the inhabitants of Panormus.

That morning Scipio had ordered in the remainder of the Second Legion to take charge. These men, an unneeded reserve, had not taken part in the assault. They had marched through the open gate in disciplined ranks, tasked with gathering up the scattered legionaries within the walls and ensuring no enemy strong points remained. They had taken to the task with a ruthless efficiency, many of them no doubt angry that they had missed the spoils of victory, and within hours every legionary had been banished from the town, save a garrison force that now occupied a barracks near the docks.

Scipio spurred his horse to a canter and his tribunes came up to match his pace, following the slight downhill slope that led to the docks. They quickly reached the wide expanse of beaten earth that straddled the shoreline and Scipio reined in his mount, his gaze sweeping across the bay. Nearby, a group of legionaries stood guard as Carthaginians, brought ashore from the captured trading ships, gathered up the corpses that lay about the ground, loading them on to carts to be taken outside the town walls, where they would be cremated in an effort to stave off the dreaded pestilence that followed on the heels of every battle.

Scipio ignored them, focusing instead on the galleys anchored fifty yards from the docks. He instinctively searched for the Greek's ship, looking for the prefect's masthead banner; his eyes narrowed as he spotted the *Orcus* in the midst of the fleet. Their losses had been heavy, nineteen galleys in total, although the blockade had been a success and no enemy ships had escaped, vindicating Scipio's decision to leave the Greek in command. He smiled coldly, remembering a story his father had told him as a child of how Dionysius II of Syracuse had demonstrated the precariousness of life by suspending a sword over the head of a retainer, held by a single horse hair. It was an appropriate image, although in this case the Greek was totally unaware of how immediate the threat was.

He turned his back on the fleet and looked again to the town that straddled the shoreline. It was a rich prize, the Carthaginians' main port on the northern coast, and Scipio had already dispatched instructions to his wife in Rome to hire orators to spread the news of his great victory across the entire city. From out of the corner of his eye he saw his tribunes looking at him, their expressions now edged with respect. He was no longer just their consul, he was a victorious commander; triumphantly, Scipio turned to them to reveal the next town that would fall to his sword: Lilybaeum.

*

Regulus paced the floor of his room, stopping occasionally to peer out of his window to the streets of Lilybaeum many storeys below. Each time he looked, his instinct told him that something was wrong. He sensed it in every squad of soldiers he saw moving quickly through the streets of the town, or in the galleys and trading ships entering and leaving the port, all moving with undue speed, their haste signifying some crisis.

He was living in isolation, an enforced seclusion that had begun without warning. It had been five weeks since he had returned to Lilybaeum. He had sailed from Ostia on a Roman military galley to the prearranged rendezvous on the island of Lipara, and from there the Carthaginians had escorted him back to Sicily. He had been taken immediately to see Barca, whereupon he had told the Carthaginian commander of Rome's refusal to make peace. Initially Barca had been furious, but within a few days he had calmed down. Although his demeanour remained cold, he had continued to visit Regulus in his room, questioning him on the reasoning behind Rome's decision.

Three weeks before, however, Barca's visits had stopped, and thereafter Regulus had not seen or spoken to him. In addition, the proconsul's guards had become overtly hostile, refusing to be drawn into any conversation when they delivered his food. Regulus's sense of foreboding had increased with each passing day.

The sound of approaching footsteps alerted Regulus and he turned as the door was thrown open.

'Barca,' he began, but he stopped as he saw the Carthaginian's murderous expression. 'What's happened?' he asked, his apprehension growing.

Hamilcar stood rock still, anger and hatred coursing through him, finding focus in the Roman standing before him, the very enemy he had foolishly thought to parley with. As if for the first time, he saw the arrogant stance of the proconsul, the air of conceit that he had come to associate with – and loathe in – his Roman enemy.

'Seize him,' he said over his shoulder, and two guards rushed in to grab Regulus by the arms.

'What is the meaning of this, Barca?' Regulus said angrily.

'Your usefulness has come to an end, Roman,' Hamilcar said coldly, and he nodded to his soldiers, who jostled Regulus out of the room. Hamilcar followed, watching impassively as Regulus fought against the grip of his captors, shouting over his shoulder, protesting against his treatment.

Regulus turned away from the glare of the noon sun as he was led out into a courtyard. He looked about him, all the while trying to suppress the rising fear he felt in the pit of his stomach.

'Barca,' he shouted, his voice steady, hiding his fear with anger, 'what do you mean? What's happened?'

Hamilcar ignored him and Regulus was led forward. He immediately saw the four spikes in the ground, each one at the corner of an invisible square. He pushed back against his captors, his feet sliding on the loose surface, but they forced him to the ground, pushing him on to his back. Rough hands spread-eagled his limbs, tying each one to a stake.

Regulus kept his eyes shut tightly against the sun, his breath coming in shallow gasps as panic threatened to overcome him. He fought to keep the tone of his voice even, but he heard the tremor in his voice as he called out for Barca, beseeching him to explain what had happened. He sensed someone approach and stand over him, but when he tried to open his eyes to see, the glare of the sun forced them shut.

'I have been blind,' Hamilcar said slowly, 'blind to the true nature of my enemy, into believing there could be a peace.'

'There *can* be peace,' Regulus said, struggling against his bonds, turning his head in Hamilcar's direction. 'The Senate just needs more time. I can get them to see sense—'

'No,' Hamilcar continued. 'My eyes are open, Roman, and now I will open yours.'

Suddenly Regulus felt hands holding his head tightly. He struggled hard, trying to twist away, but they held him fast. Terror swept through him as his eyelid was pinched and held away from his eye and he screamed in pain as the tip of a knife sliced away the thin veil of flesh, his cries reaching a higher pitch as the other eyelid too was cut away.

His vision swirled with the blood but slowly he discerned the shadow of a man standing directly over his face. The pain from his wounds was replaced with another, more terrible agony: the intensity of the blue sky piercing his unguarded eyes.

'Now your eyes are open,' Hamilcar said vehemently, and he moved aside so that his shadow left Regulus's face, exposing him to the full glare of the sun.

Regulus's screams were terrible to hear, his face contorting in a hopeless effort to shield his eyes. The searing pain shattered the last of his self-control. His mind was overwhelmed by the agony, the white light from the brilliant sun like a flame to his eyes. His struggles intensified and he shook his head free, finally turning it away from the light, but the loss of his sight was irreversible and he wailed in blindness and pain.

Hamilcar stood back, hardening his heart to the cries of the Roman. He thought of the man he once was, before the war had taken the better part of his mercy, and knew he could never go back. Ruthlessness was the tool of the Romans, and if Hamilcar was to defeat them he would have to stoop to their level. Regulus would be sent back to his own kind, again as a messenger, only this time to tell the Romans that there would be no more offers of peace. First, however, the proconsul would have to be made ready for the journey.

Regulus surfaced from beneath the torrent of pain, his mind slowly regaining consciousness, his senses returning to the realization of his fate. He was no longer screaming but he called out for release, hearing the voices of the Carthaginians around him.

He felt the first tremor in his back, a dull, rhythmic vibration as if the ground was shifting beneath him. The sensation triggered a hidden memory. Then a sudden bellow cut through the air, a horrifying sound that chased everything else from Regulus's mind.

He began to struggle again, the ropes tearing into his flesh as he pulled against them with all his might and his bowels voided as he screamed in absolute terror, his cries echoed by the enormous elephant. His whipped his head around to face the sound, blindness mocking his efforts to see the beast, but his other senses flooded his mind with detail: an overpowering musky smell, the deep, snorting sound of breathing and the thud of each footfall. The sensations increased and Regulus realized the elephant was standing over him, his defenceless position adding to his terror. He shook his head violently as if to wake himself from his nightmare.

Suddenly he felt a weight on his chest, a solid, immovable burden. The pressure increased, pushing the air from his lungs. He tried to regain his breath but couldn't, his chest unable to expand, and he opened his mouth to scream a stillborn sound. His mind began to fog over and Regulus reached the very depths of his fear, sinking through it as his final reserves of air were spent; as he slipped into unconsciousness on the threshold of death, he heard the sharp crack of his ribs snapping under the weight of the elephant's foot.

Hamilcar nodded to the elephant handler who barked commands at the beast to withdraw, slapping it lightly on its hindquarters with a switch. The elephant moved away ponderously and Hamilcar stepped forward. Although it was an ancient form of execution, Hamilcar had never before witnessed the act, and he was both fascinated and appalled by the result. Regulus's chest was completely staved in, every bone and organ crushed into the ground. Even to the uninitiated there could be no doubt as to how Regulus had died and Hamilcar nodded slowly. Now, the proconsul was ready to deliver his message.

The hollow crack of timber resounded around the main deck of the *Orcus* as the legionaries fought with wooden training swords. They were broken into pairs, each moving independently across the deck, and Atticus's gaze darted from one to the other, assessing their potential with an experienced eye.

A cautionary voice breached his concentration and he looked to the four points of his ship before glancing up at Corin at the masthead. The young man's head was turning continuously through the same circle, his gaze sweeping the horizon, oblivious to the activities on the deck. Atticus nodded in approval. There was a time the youngest member of the crew would often become fixated by what was going on beneath him, a lapse brought on by boredom and one Lucius used to angrily berate him for. Those reprimands, and experience, had quickly taught Corin, and now his keen eyesight was fixed firmly on his task.

Atticus grasped that trust in Corin and kept it in the

forefront of his thoughts, using it to assuage the doubts that had crept into his consciousness since the battle at Panormus, but the relief was fleeting and he looked anxiously to the waters ahead. The *Orcus* was sailing deeper and deeper into enemy waters, a course that was taking them around the north-western tip of Sicily to the next target of Scipio's campaign, Lilybaeum. It was the heart of the Carthaginians' lair and, although victory lay in the Romans' wake, Atticus had little confidence in the task ahead.

Ten galleys had been left in Panormus as a garrison force, although four of those were heavily damaged and would require weeks of repair. The remainder sailed behind the *Orcus*. Atticus knew if his command were to be caught in open waters by a comparable Carthaginian force, his fleet would be annihilated. For the Romans, safety lay only in numbers, and Atticus eagerly anticipated his contact with the first half of the new fleet that he was scheduled to meet in the lee of the Aegates Islands, west of Lilybaeum.

An angry shout caught Atticus's attention and he looked to Baro, the second-in-command's expression twisted with frustration as he manhandled a legionary aside to demonstrate once more the sequence of sword thrusts he was trying to teach the soldiers. Despite the seriousness of the task, Atticus smiled in sympathy. Baro's patience had worn through after only an hour's training, long after Atticus felt his would have lasted, and he noticed the stubborn, almost hostile, expression of the legionary that Baro was instructing.

Atticus knew from experience that it would be a near impossible task to persuade the legionary commanders of the need to train the men in one-to-one combat, vital for a force that was going to board an enemy ship. His only hope, he believed, was to train the legionaries on the *Orcus* and thereafter use them to demonstrate the possibilities and effect of such training, but even this limited objective was going to be difficult to achieve.

The younger legionaries, Atticus had observed, were eager enough to adapt, however much they hid that enthusiasm behind indifference. They were relatively new to the army and had not forgotten some of the skills of swordplay they had learned before joining the legion. The older soldiers, however, were intractable, their abilities with a *gladius* forged in countless battles into a smooth obelisk of instinctive manoeuvres that was near unbreakable. They had fought the same way for years, had bested many foes with the technique, and saw no reason to change, particularly to a style that mocked one of the fundamental tenets of legionary combat: the protection of closed ranks.

Fundamental to that protection was the *scutum*, the long, broad shield of the legions, and the second obstacle to any transformation. Too cumbersome for boarding, the legionaries had been ordered to stack their *scuta* on the foredeck and take up the rounded Greek *hoplon* shields used by the sailing crews of the fleet. It was an exchange offensive to the legionaries, and added to the difficulties of training, as the men wielded the smaller shields as they would the larger, a fault that would be instantly exploited by a skilled Carthaginian fighter.

As Baro spoke, Atticus glanced at Drusus, the centurion standing quietly to one side, his sword and *hoplon* held as Baro demonstrated, mimicking the second-in-command's every move. As a legionary centurion, there were few better. A strict disciplinarian, he was a man of singular conviction and one of the most determined fighters Atticus had ever met. He followed orders to the letter and expected his men to do the same, the embodiment of every rigid component that was the backbone of the legions, and therein lay the essence of the problem. In single combat, rigid adherence to rules led to predictability and death, but to teach the legionaries the necessary fluidity of style meant reversing years of ingrained training.

Looking at Drusus, Atticus felt overwhelmed by the enormity of the problems facing him. The sailing crews were outmatched and would need months of training in ramming techniques, and the legions were no longer able to call on their inherent indomitable strength; they would need to adapt quickly to a new style of fighting. Before the *corvus* had been invented, these had been exactly the problems that Atticus had faced, but back then he had not been alone in trying to solve the problem.

With Gaius's help, he could train the sailing crews. Together they had honed the skills of the crew of the *Orcus*, and perhaps he could draw on the trust that Duilius assured him he had amongst the fleet captains. Maybe he could pass on to them his own belief that the only way to defeat the Carthaginians was by matching their prowess with the ram. Atticus, however, knew he had no such relationship with the legions. His link, and any trust he gained, had always been through Septimus, and although the centurion was a strong advocate of one-to-one combat training for all marines, he no longer stood at Atticus's side, or at the head of the legionaries on board the *Orcus*.

Baro was a good teacher but he was not a legionary, and it was obvious the soldiers had no faith in the new techniques. They followed his instructions because they were ordered to do so. Atticus was suddenly doubtful that even his limited approach would be successful. If he couldn't persuade the legionaries of his own ship, how could he possibly convince others? Not for the first time, Atticus wished Septimus was on board.

He looked to the four points of his ship again, trying to find comfort in the routine tasks of sailing, and his thoughts strayed to the *Aquila* and his life before he was drawn into the war with Carthage. He focused on the memory, refusing to let it go as the *Orcus* sped onwards.

CHAPTER ELEVEN

Calix glanced at the wind-driven ripples across the surface of the water, estimating their speed, and looked to the northeastern horizon beyond the reaches of the headland, turning his face directly into the oncoming wind. It was laden with moisture, the remnants of a distant storm, and he rubbed the sheen of soft water from his face and his shaven pate.

The course of the wind had not changed in the two days since Calix's galley, the *Ares*, had arrived on station in the Aegates Islands and, as he looked to the sun, he calculated that if it remained steady for another two hours, this day would also be wasted. The realization did not bother him. He was a patient man. Although he had been told his task was urgent, he was apathetic. A lifetime at his trade had given him an intimate knowledge of the winds and tides around this part of the Mediterranean, and he knew above all else that they could not be changed by any man's desire or supplication. He would wait, at ease in the knowledge that if he did not depart today, then there was always tomorrow. Either way he would reach his destination.

He was known as 'the Rhodian', a label he had not created himself, but one he had nonetheless allowed to spread. Normally, in his business, it was unwise to become recognizable.

Anonymity was a significant ally, but he had discovered that notoriety also had its benefits, and chief amongst them was that his clients had become increasingly important, men with considerable resources who were uncompromising in their demands and therefore only hired those that they perceived to be the best.

It was true that Calix was from Rhodes, as were his ancestors, although he had spent the better part of his early life on Ithaca. There, from the age of seven, he had been apprenticed to the captain of a bireme, a trader who had quickly discovered that his Greek protégé had innate sailing skills that surpassed any he had ever known. At seventeen, Calix was a seasoned boatswain, and he had moved to Syracuse to work for one of the larger trading houses. Again his skills had singled him out, and within three years he had been promoted to captain, a rank he held over the many years he spent sailing the coastal waters of Sicily and beyond to the outer shores of the Mediterranean.

Syracuse was a trading hub for the entire Mediterranean and, in a city where there were few secrets, Calix's skills were widely known and respected. This simple fame led to his first contract, some years before, an unsolicited offer by a man to take him to the then Carthaginian-held city of Agrigentum at night. The gathering clouds of war were on the horizon, and Calix suspected the man was Roman, for why else the subterfuge? He had been poised to refuse him when the Roman produced the gold he was willing to pay for the simple task. For one night's work, it was more money than Calix earned in six months working for the trading house, and his refusal died in the twinkling light of gold coins.

He was scheduled to take cargo to Agrigentum, a fact he suspected the Roman already knew, and so he sailed as planned with his passenger on board. He had lingered on the journey, laying off Camarina until nightfall and entering the port under the cover of darkness. It was a difficult task, but Calix knew the approaches intimately and his skills were equal to the challenge. He had dropped off his passenger after midnight and then patiently awaited the dawn to unload his cargo, his presence unnoticed on the busy docks, another vaguely familiar bireme that had been seen in Agrigentum many times.

Over the following years, the escalating conflict between Rome and Carthage had increased the opportunities for profit, and Calix had become adept at exploiting them. He soon outgrew the need for the cover provided by the trading house and purchased his own bireme, changing his usual cargo of cloth and grain for weapons and agents. All his initial contracts had come from the Romans, unfamiliar as they were with Sicilian waters and lacking any skilled crews of their own, but Calix had soon found work with the Carthaginians too, the Punici recognizing the unique advantage of stealth that an anonymous trading galley possessed.

He was loyal only to his profit, and smuggling cargo rapidly gave way to skirmishing and even piracy as each side in the conflict became more embittered against their enemy. His reputation as a mercenary grew and he commissioned his own ship, the *Ares*, specially designed and built by the finest shipwrights of Greece and manned by a select crew. With his new ship, stealth was no longer his weapon, but speed and agility.

He pursued only the most lucrative of contracts, and so, a week before, when he was approached by a member of the Council of Carthage, he had quickly accepted the task, ensuring that the price was commensurate with the risk.

Just then Calix sensed a slackening of the wind and ordered his crew to stand ready. They moved quickly and within minutes the *Ares* was poised to sail. The galley became still again, each man turning their faces to the wind, trying to judge the eddy and flow, the steadfast breeze teetering on the edge of change. The wind shifted suddenly, swinging wildly to the west before reverting back to its original course, and then again to the new heading, stubbornly hanging on until it became steady once more. Calix smiled. He could not have asked for better timing and he looked to the falling sun behind him. He nodded to the helmsman and his gesture was seen by every officer on board, who issued their orders almost as one, the fluidity of command bringing the *Ares* up to standard speed within a ship length, its course now firmly fixed for the besieged city of Lilybaeum.

Septimus wiped the sweat from his face as he looked to the fading sun. The glare stung his eyes but he continued to stare, savouring the sight of its slow demise, knowing his day was almost complete. He turned back to his men and barked an order, his voice as hard as it had been at dawn, neatly hiding the weariness he felt, seeing that same exhaustion in the faces of his men.

They had arrived at Lilybaeum two weeks before and again their task was almost complete, with four new siege towers standing resolute before the walls of Lilybaeum, silently observing their prey. They had been constructed at a faster pace, utilizing the remnants of the towers at Panormus, but again the work had been carried out by the Ninth. The Second had been awarded a battle honour for their assault on Panormus, with the Ninth mentioned only in dispatches, an injustice Septimus had brushed aside, persuading his newer recruits to do the same. It was not the first time, nor would it be the last, that the deeds of men in battle were overlooked.

The speed of construction had also been augmented by the men's eagerness to complete the siege. Panormus had been surrounded by pasture land and tillage, solid ground with good drainage, ideal for siege lines and the necessary congregation of so many men in semi-permanent camps. At Lilybaeum, however, the confluence of two streams behind the town walls had created a marshy swamp that girdled the walls and, although it was late summer and weeks before the arrival of the autumn rains, the ground was soggy underfoot and at dusk huge swarms of mosquitoes rose up to torment the legionaries.

The men of Septimus's maniple complained bitterly under their breath each evening as they slapped the exposed flesh of their bodies, waging a constant battle against the tiny insects. Septimus let them moan, knowing it was better that they should vent their frustration, but all the while his own worries mounted. He knew nothing of the mysteries of pestilence, why some men escaped while others were fated to be struck down, and, of those, how Pluto decided which men would succumb to death and which would recover. But Septimus was well aware, as were many others, of the deadly plagues that dwelled in the toxic vapours of marshes. Years before he had fought in the battle of Agrigentum, a Roman-led siege where the legions themselves had been besieged by a relief army, and for weeks they had been imprisoned on marshy ground between the outer walls of the town and a line of contravallation. Casualties quickly mounted, not from blades and arrows but from pestilence, and Septimus remembered how roll call each morning quickly became a butcher's bill of men who had breathed their last during the dark hours of night.

The memory caused Septimus unconsciously to hold his own breath, and he coughed as he finally inhaled the warm, fetid air into his lungs. It tasted of the deep muskiness of earth, and he suddenly craved the clean, salt-laden air that swept over the deck of the *Orcus*. He had not thought of that life in days, and he was surprised, as before, what triggered his memories. He recalled how he had at first hated that raw sea air, the cool wind that blew perpetually across the exposed galley, but now, as he filled his lungs with the humid air of the marsh, he missed the unsullied air of the sea.

He brushed the memory aside, suddenly angry at himself. That life was behind him now and to think of it fondly was a weakness that undermined his loyalty to the Ninth. His future lay with the IV maniple, not with the marines, and he forced his mind to focus on his command.

He looked to the siege towers, their wheels buried to the axle in the soft ground. They would be ready in less than three days and Septimus muttered a prayer to Mars that Scipio would grant the Ninth the honour of leading the assault. He knew, however, that it was a forlorn hope. The Ninth was a newly formed legion. The Second was the veteran formation. They had taken Panormus, even if in reality the ragged charge of the Ninth had pushed them over the battlements, and they would lead the assault again. The Ninth would watch from a distance and, as Septimus kneaded the hilt of his sword, he wondered if he would get a chance to draw his blade in the battle for Lilybaeum.

Hamilcar looked over the shoulder of the engineer seated in front of him, trying to read the tiny script of the annotations, but he could not, and so he concentrated on the sketch itself. He glanced out over the battlements to the Roman siege towers four hundred yards away, beyond effective arrow range. The engineer's sketches were impressive, considering the distance, and Hamilcar questioned him on some of the details, knowing the engineer was using his judgement to draw what he could not see. He nodded slowly as the explanation was given, looking again to the siege towers, wondering when they would be ready.

The Romans' ability to build effective siege engines was one of their military strengths, and to have siege towers constructed within sight was an opportunity Hamilcar could not allow to pass. The Carthaginian army had little knowledge of such modern technology and normally relied solely on time to force a besieged town to capitulate. The Romans had appropriated the design of the Carthaginian quinquereme. Perhaps Hamilcar could return the gesture by constructing siege engines of Roman design for his army. Panormus had fallen to such devices, and although Lilybaeum had more complex and stronger defences, Hamilcar knew that – should the infernal towers be brought to bear against the city walls – the outcome could not be predicted with any certainty. That was why Hamilcar had already put his plan of defence in motion and why the sketch of the towers was important.

Hamilcar looked at the sea beyond the harbour of Lilybaeum. He could see the blockade fleet of the Romans, their galleys moving slowly across his view. The width of the bay, and its unique approaches, had removed both the ability and the need for the enemy to form an unbroken blockade line, and so they were concentrated on the flanks, with smaller squadrons sailing continuously back and forth across the bay. Their numbers had been estimated at one hundred and fifty, a figure that had surprised and troubled Hamilcar, as he had thought their fleet to be a fraction of that number. Reports from Panormus spoke of a blockade fleet of seventy ships. He had surmised that some of them were destroyed in the ensuing battle in the harbour, and so expected only the remnants to arrive at Lilybaeum.

At first he had thought that many more Roman galleys had survived the storm after the battle of Cape Hermaeum, but then he began to hear disturbing rumours, second-hand reports from traders, that the Romans had constructed a massive new fleet north of Rome. He had dismissed the rumours out of hand, but then he had received confirmed reports that the bulk of the ships blockading Lilybaeum were part of a Roman fleet, over a hundred strong, that had been seen sailing southwest past Lipara towards the Aegates Islands weeks before.

The report had staggered him. What manner of men were these Romans that they possessed such self-belief, that they could endure the loss of so many ships and men and rebuild again so quickly. Their confidence and commitment to the war seemed indomitable and Hamilcar wondered if the Romans stood in awe of any men or gods. He thought of Carthage, how its forces were divided across two fronts, fully committed to neither, its political leaders split into competing factions, while the Romans stood squarely behind a single purpose.

Hamilcar had resolutely brushed his doubts aside. Others might believe that Carthage's destiny lay elsewhere, but he was fully committed to the war against Rome, and to that end he was determined that Lilybaeum would not fall. With the arrival of a larger Roman fleet the odds had changed, but the foundation of Hamilcar's defensive plan remained solid.

Weeks before, when the first reports confirmed the Roman encirclement of Panormus, Hamilcar had quickly dispatched a galley to Carthage carrying two requests to his father. The first of these was for men, land forces, to strengthen the garrison, preferably Carthaginians if he could procure them from Hanno's army or, failing that, the mercenaries they had discussed. Hasdrubal had reacted quickly and, within three weeks, as the walls of Panormus were falling, a fleet of twenty transport ships arrived in Lilybaeum carrying two thousand Greek mercenaries and a message from Hasdrubal that he was pursuing the second request.

Hamilcar had then turned his attention to the sea; before the Roman fleet had arrived, he had ordered his own Gadir fleet north to the port of Drepana to avoid the stranglehold of the blockade. There they remained, over one hundred and twenty galleys, poised in readiness and awaiting his arrival. He had wanted to sail with them, but he had remained in Lilybaeum to finalize the city's defences and oversee the operation he had devised for the Greek mercenaries, an attack that would buy him time and allow him to complete his plan.

He looked to the setting sun, cursing the one missing piece that was vital if he was to overturn the blockade of the harbour and lift the siege. Eventually he would have to escape the encirclement of Lilybaeum to link up with his fleet in Drepana, and his escape depended on the second request he had made of his father. He had no way of knowing if Hasdrubal had been successful, if he had managed to contact the one man Hamilcar knew was capable of effecting his escape, who possessed the skills and local knowledge that none of the commanders in the Gadir fleet had, the one man who could carry him past the Roman blockade.

The *Orcus* moved slowly under a smooth press of canvas with the southwesterly wind off its port aft-quarter. The breeze had shifted hours before, allowing the squadron of ten galleys to ship their oars, and they sailed in near silence, with the noise of the water against the hull and the occasional shouted order being the only sounds heard in the absence of drums.

Atticus stood motionless and looked out over the side rail of the aft-deck, his thoughts given free rein in the silence, quickly becoming aimless after two monotonous weeks of manning the blockade. The sea around the *Orcus* was as smooth as polished marble but, only two hundred yards away, towards the harbour, the telltale ripples of troubled water were evidence of the treacherous shoals that bedevilled the inner approaches to Lilybaeum. Only a narrow channel on the northern end of the bay guaranteed safe access to the harbour, and it was here that the bulk of the Roman fleet lay under the command of a newly arrived Roman prefect, Ovidius. He had insisted on commanding this touch point, eager to attack any ship that dared to run the blockade, and Atticus had readily conceded the position, knowing that, unlike Panormus, there would be few who would try to escape such a tight noose.

Instead Atticus had ordered his ships to patrol the lagoon that ran the full width of the harbour between the inner and outer shoals of the bay. There were numerous other small channels that ran through both sets of shoals, known only to Poseidon and the locals, and if any Carthaginian were to attempt escape it would surely be through these straits. In the end, however, the efforts of both Atticus and the Roman prefect had counted for naught. No Carthaginian ship had run the blockade and the two weeks had passed slowly and without incident.

Atticus stared at the distant town of Lilybaeum, its white-washed walls stained pink by the dying sun, the docks seemingly devoid of any activity. The sight sparked a memory of a similar scene and his forehead creased as he sought to capture it. Then, to his surprise, he realized that he was remembering his home city.

It was many years since he had last seen Locri, a place where he had grown up in squalor and poverty, a city on which he had turned his back at the age of fourteen to join the Roman coastal fleet. His only fond memories of Locri involved his grandfather, who took him fishing and enthralled him with stories of the ancient Greeks and their triumphs over the Persian Empire. For Atticus, that time had come to represent the old world, a world in which his grandfather had dwelt, when the Greeks were masters of Magna Graecia, Greater Greece, a network of colonized cities and states that included southern Italy, a period that the Romans had ended when they conquered the lands and imposed upon the people their own culture and laws.

That old world now existed only in memory, and to his shame Atticus could not remember the last time he had thought of Locri or his grandfather; when he had last re-kindled the links within him to his ancestors. When he had captained the *Aquila* and hunted pirates in the Ionian Sea along the Calabrian coast, he had existed only on the fringes of the Roman Republic. Now he was immersed in it. Rome affected everything he did and everything he was, and Atticus realized he was glad his grandfather had not lived long enough to see how separated he had become from his own people.

'Galley, off the port aft-quarter. One mile out, passing through the outer shoals!'

Atticus shot around to follow the call but he instantly shied away, the setting sun still too bright, although he did discern a darkened shape in the water. He looked instead to the mast-head.

'Identify,' he called up, and Corin leaned forward slightly at the waist, his hand up to his eyes.

'I can't, Prefect. He's approaching directly out of the sun,' Corin replied in frustration. 'Definitely a galley under sail though.'

Atticus didn't hesitate.

'Baro, take in the mainsail. Ready the oars. Gaius, come about, battle speed.'

The *Orcus* spun neatly at the head of the squadron and the other galleys followed her course, reacting quickly to the signals sent from the aft-deck of the command ship, their oars extending as the sails were furled.

'She's sailing under canvas and oars,' Corin called out, and Atticus cursed as he confirmed the lookout's call, the changing aspect of his own ship affording him a better view. It took a highly skilled crew to sail a galley under a full press of sail with the oars engaged. The advantage was additional speed without taxing the rowers, but it relied heavily on tight helm control and a disciplined rowing crew. She was a bireme, a galley with two rows of oars; whoever the captain was, he was a clever whoreson and he knew the approaches intimately. He had avoided detection until he was a mile out, using the glare of the sun as a cover and the trailing wind to give him speed and the advantage. The galley was sailing apace, on an oblique line to the centre of the harbour and, as Atticus calculated the angle of attack, his brow furrowed. Even taking the combination of sail and oars into account, the bireme was moving way too fast for a ship of its class.

'Gaius, attack speed,' Atticus ordered, already sensing that he was too late, his simple calculations confirming it.

The *Orcus* was beating across the wind under oar power only, and the unidentified galley was already halfway across the lagoon, her bow aimed at some invisible channel. Atticus slammed his fist on the side rail, his mind racing to find some way to reverse the inevitable.

'She's a quadrireme,' Gaius realized.

Atticus studied the hull more closely, knowing now how it was able to achieve such speed. On a bireme, with two rows of oars, each oar was manned by one rower. On a quadrireme that number was doubled, with each oar manned by two men. The two galleys were similar in height and draught but the quadrireme was broader in the beam, a necessary increase to accommodate the additional rowers. It was a rare breed of galley, slower than a quinquereme but more manoeuvrable, quick to turn with a very shallow draught.

This realization did not assuage Atticus's frustration, however, and he watched in silence as the quadrireme passed a half-mile ahead of the bow of the *Orcus*, her course changing slightly as she negotiated the inner shoals. The *Orcus* was as close as it was going to get, and Atticus turned to issue the order to withdraw when he noticed Gaius's troubled expression.

'What is it?' he asked.

'The captain had all the cards in his favour and his approach was flawless. There was no luck involved, none,' Gaius replied intently. 'And he sails a quadrireme.'

The helmsman let his thoughts hang in the air, his gaze still locked on the galley, and Atticus considered the implied question, one he had not considered in his frustration. The captain of the galley was highly skilled, knew the approaches intimately and his ship was a quadrireme. He looked to Gaius and nodded, agreeing with his deduction. It was the Rhodian.

CHAPTER TWELVE

The sentry pulled the rim of his helmet lower as he peered into the darkness, his head turned slightly to pick up any sounds of approach. Huge torches burned high on the walls of the city four hundred yards away, playing havoc with his night vision, but he kept his eyes to the ground and the black space that separated the enemy from the Roman lines.

He was an *optio* of the II maniple, the unit whose turn it was to post the *vigilae*, the night guard, and although the sentry could take consolation in knowing this would be his only night watch all week, he was weary after working the entire day on the siege towers and his eyes were heavy with exhaustion. He sought to keep his mind active, knowing that any lapse in concentration would invite the mortal danger of falling asleep on duty, an offence punishable by summary execution. He felt an ache in his lower back and he suddenly noticed his shoulders had slumped. He quickly straightened and cursed under his breath, drawing his dagger from its scabbard.

He placed the ball of his thumb on the blade, pressing down slightly until the blade pierced his skin. He winced against the pain, but he felt his mind react sharply and he kept his thumb in place, shifting it slightly from time to time to keep his senses alert. It was an old trick, and the legionary's thumb was laced with ancient scars that bore testament to his years in other legions. He scowled in the darkness. It was going to be a long night.

The commander of the Greek mercenaries heard the grating noise of a blade against a scabbard and he froze. In the darkness around him he sensed his men react, the tiniest rustle of disturbed grass giving way to total silence. He held his breath. Had the Roman sentry heard them? He remained still, opening his mouth slightly to improve his hearing and he began breathing again – short, shallow breaths that sounded no louder than the warm wind. In his mind's eye he pictured the Roman sentry, perhaps poised as he was, and he waited for the inevitable challenge, knowing any sentry, however experienced, would feel compelled to call out. A minute of complete silence passed, however, and the mercenary commander felt confident they had not been discovered.

He moved forward again and smiled, his mouth closed. The Roman sentry was no more than twenty yards away and the mercenary commander moved his head from side to side to try to locate him, using the random torch-lights of the distant Roman stockade to silhouette the standing sentry. He had advanced with a hundred men in a spaced row towards the Roman sentry line, while fifty yards behind, a further five hundred men moved equally silently. Now he was poised to attack and he nodded to himself in the darkness. He had achieved surprise.

The mercenary commander advanced a further five yards and then stopped again, allowing time for his men to get into position. The main force would continue to move forward, unaware of their leader's position, so he could not linger. His hand felt to his side and the hilt of his sword, the ivory handle familiar in his grip. He angled his body towards where he had heard the metallic sound and then slowly came out of his crouch, his legs tensed with coiled energy. He paused for a further heartbeat and then whistled. A sharp, short blast that signalled the charge. He shot forward, drawing his sword as he did, coming up to a full run as he sought out his prey.

He spotted the sentry to his right, a shadow within a shadow, the legionary standing beneath one of the massive siege towers. The mercenary commander leaned into the turn, bringing his sword up high as the Roman reacted, the beginnings of a call of alarm escaping his lips as he tried to draw his weapon. The Greek struck him down with a single blow, his sword striking the legionary in the neck, and he fell instantly. The mercenary commander continued on, running directly to the siege tower; as he reached it he heard the first cries of alarm from sentries who had reacted faster.

Their calls were quickly silenced but, like a spark to tinder, the Roman soldiers guarding the towers exploded into action. A figure surged out of the darkness towards the mercenary commander, a misshapen beast with shield and sword held outwards in attack. The commander crouched low and slashed his sword across the legs of the oncoming legionary. The Roman screamed out in pain and fell to the ground. The Greek spun around and stabbed his sword down into the legionary's exposed back, the blade glancing off the spine before plunging into the kidneys.

The mercenary commander stood up quickly and charged his sword once more. The main body of his men were rushing past him and the darkness hid a growing maelstrom of sound as they struck the centre of the Roman night guard behind the towers. The enemy had reacted fast, as the mercenary commander knew a disciplined army like the Romans would, but within seconds they were hopelessly outnumbered. The commander stayed out of the desperate fray, his eyes on the growing lights of the nearby legion encampment; and, as the last of the valiant night guard were put to the sword, a momentary semblance of calm descended around the towers, at odds with the growing cacophony of shouted orders from the encampment.

The Greek mercenary commander knew they had to act fast before the full force of the legion arrived to counter-attack. He could not stand against such numbers, but with luck his task would be complete before then. He stepped back from the tower as the first of his men bearing buckets of pitch arrived. They threw the pitch at the base of the tower while others ran around to ascend the ladder to the platform above, spreading the viscous liquid over as many of the timbers as they could. Once lit, the pitch would give the flames purchase on the newly cut timbers that were still heavy with sap, but it would take several minutes for the fire to take hold and become an unquenchable inferno. Vital minutes that the Greek mercenaries would pay for with blood.

Septimus was jolted from his sleep by the first calls. He jumped up, his mind fogged by fatigue as he shrugged on his armour and grabbed his weapons. By the time he emerged from his tent, the cries of alarm had given way to a general call-to-arms. He automatically repeated the order, shouting at individual men of his command as they emerged from their tents, ordering them to form up and make ready.

He looked to the ramparts of the encampment, trying to discern the point of attack from the rush of men responding to the strident orders. It was difficult to see in the half-light, but a dozen torches quickly became fifty and then a hundred and uncertainty suddenly gave way to realization. His mind became fully alert following the first rush of action, and he ran towards the main gate, a feeling of dread rising from the pit of his stomach.

His maniple ran after him in a confused rush, his *optio* shouting orders for the men to form up on the run, understanding sweeping through the ranks as the whole encampment became aware of the enemy's target and the legionaries of the IV maniple increased their pace. Septimus barged into the bottleneck at the main gate, his size and rank giving him the advantage as he pushed through into the open ground beyond the gate. The darkness outside the ramparts was almost total and he stumbled on the uneven ground, his eyes locked on the siege towers two hundred yards away. They were silhouetted against the torches mounted on the distant town walls, four massive shadows, and Septimus could intermittently see figures surging around their bases, indistinguishable as friend or foe.

He glanced to his right and the Second Legion's encampment half a mile away. It too was coming to life, reacting to the din coming from the Ninth. The ramparts bristled with torch-lights, the soldiers wary of the surrounding darkness, not knowing if they were witnessing the main attack or a diversion. Septimus had no such doubts and he drew his sword as ran on, his ears filled with the sounds of hundreds of men snarling and panting, of swords rasping against scabbards, of heavy footfalls as they charged towards the towers.

When the Carthaginians had attacked the siege towers at Panormus the arrival of reinforcements from the main encampment had quickly routed the enemy and saved the beleaguered maniple on guard duty. Now the enemy had repeated that action and, as Septimus ran, there were legionaries on all sides, with only those who had reacted more quickly in front of him, the soldiers advancing to defend the towers without orders, and all semblance of manipular order lost in the head-long charge.

Two hundred yards became fifty and Septimus shouted out the first commands, the men responding immediately to the centurion amongst their ranks; but only a ragged line was formed, distorted by the darkness and the rush of attack. Septimus tightened the grip on his sword, tensing his arm behind the bulk of his shield. He peered ahead into the darkness, searching for prey, expecting them to be already in flight in the face of the Roman charge.

Suddenly an orange plume appeared on the nearest tower, a dancing light that pierced the skin of legionary discipline, and the Romans roared in anger, their shouts becoming a terrifying battle cry as they saw the flames whip up the height of the tower. Septimus saw a host of men suddenly appear as if from nowhere, exposed by the light from the fire, twenty yards away, their ranks steady, their swords charged against the oncoming counter-attack, and Septimus yelled a desperate order for the line to coalesce, alarmed by the apparent discipline of the enemy force, their coordination in marked contrast to the night attack at Panormus. His command came too late, though, and the Romans charged into the enemy line as a multitude of individual fighters.

Septimus thrust his sword forward in anger and frustration, alarm still ringing in his mind as he sensed the chaos around him. The fight was already a desperate brawl where enemies and weapons were veiled in the half-light of the fires consuming the siege towers, a confusion of thrashing limbs where sword and shield were used with equal force, the men whipping around to face the enemy that was suddenly on all sides, the lines becoming completely enmeshed.

*

The clash of swords resounded in the shadows and men shouted angrily in attack and defence. The Greek mercenaries added to the noise, hammering their shields and shouting out conflicting commands, raising the level of confusion, calling out orders to advance while their lines remained steady. The mercenary commander stood back from the fight, his eyes locked on the fires that were on the cusp of becoming un-controllable infernos.

He cursed the Romans' swiftness, their unholy charge from the encampment that had brought them sweeping into his ranks long before he thought it possible. Any other enemy would have been wary of the darkness, advancing only in numbers, but the Romans had counterattacked at the pace of the quickest man, a ragged charge that would not defeat his men but would increase his casualties. He dared not withdraw too soon for that would give the Romans the opportunity to douse the fires; however, every passing second brought the risk that the ever-increasing enemy numbers would overwhelm and trap his forces.

He drew in a deep breath, a blast of warm air from the surging fire drying his throat, and he reached for the horn at his side, bringing it slowly to his lips, his eyes ever locked on the fires. He paused, waiting for the right moment. 'Now,' he decided, and he spat to wet his throat before sounding the order to disengage, a command that was normally tantamount to suicide in close combat, but the Greek mercenaries were well drilled and prepared for the order and the commander was counting on the Romans ignoring their flight as they rushed to save their siege towers.

The air was filled with the lowing sound of a horn, a continu-ous, steady note. The attackers swiftly disengaged from the fight, many of them surging forward one last time, only to turn and run through the guiding light of the flaming towers into the darkness beyond. Septimus instinctively shouted at his men to continue the fight, to exploit the moment of maximum weakness when an enemy turned his back; but in the darkness and confusion of the tangled skirmish his order was meaningless, and the attackers swept from the fight like a wave receding over a pebble beach, carrying some Romans in their initial wake but ultimately escaping unencumbered.

Septimus quickly forgot the enemy's withdrawal at the dread sight of the fires consuming the siege towers. He slammed his sword into his scabbard. He swept around and shouted at the bloodied, winded legionaries to run for water, but his command was unnecessary as hundreds of men emerged in ordered ranks from the encampment bearing buckets and amphorae of water. Going as close as they dared to the raging fires, they attacked the flames, throwing the meagre contents of each container at them.

Septimus stood back, the skin on his face burning with the intensity of the fire. He leaned against his shield, allowing the other centurions to command their own maniples in the fight to save the towers. It was hopeless, and Septimus mourned the loss of so much hard work. He looked at the ground surrounding the towers, littered with the slain who had fought to defend the hollow wooden prizes.

The II maniple had been all but wiped out, along with dozens more legionaries who had charged fearlessly from the encampment into the chaotic vortex where the enemy had stood resolute and disciplined. The attackers had antici- pated the counterattack, had fought hard and withdrew only when the fires had taken hold, their staunch defence dissi- pating at the sound of a horn.

Septimus searched for their slain and saw they were but a fraction of the total, barely visible in a sea of red-cloaked soldiers. He walked over to one and kicked over the body, noticing, even in the half-light of the fires, that his uniform and armour were unlike any he had ever seen on a Carthaginian. His anger flared unbidden as he realized the attackers had been mercenaries, hired swords, their loyalty extending only to money and plunder. To a legionary they were the lowest form of vermin, and to have been bested by them was a bitter insult that compounded the dishonour of defeat.

Septimus was distracted by a scuffle nearby and he watched as a group of legionaries beat a captured mercenary. He was badly wounded, but the legionaries, enraged by their loss, showed little mercy. A centurion struggled to call them off, needing to keep the mercenary alive for interrogation. The legionaries refused to back down, wanting the mercenary dead, and the centurion drew his sword to enforce his will. Septimus watched apathetically. What did it matter if the mercenary had any information? The defeat was irreversible. He turned again to the pyres that had once been the siege towers, the men no longer trying to douse the flames but standing back, breathing heavily, their blackened faces twisted in anger and frustration.

Even from four hundred yards away, Hamilcar imagined he could feel the heat off the smouldering piles of debris, although he knew it was the warmth of the dawn sun, its light perfectly framing the triumph that was the mercenaries' night attack. The Greeks had more than proved their worth, and Hamilcar wished his father had been there to see the harvest of his choice.

Apart from the destruction of the siege towers, the attack served one other important purpose: putting to rest a doubt that had plagued Hamilcar ever since the hired Greeks had arrived. He had long used mercenaries as part of his forces, but never had he allowed them to outnumber his own native troops, a necessity at Lilybaeum forced upon him by Hanno's possession of the Carthaginian army and the spectre of betrayal that had hung over Hamilcar and the garrison. That fear was now vanquished by the Greeks' successful attack on the siege towers and the death of so many Romans at the hands of the mercenaries.

Hamilcar had little doubt that the Romans would build again, but at a slower pace, hindered perhaps by the need for greater security or an underlying fear that their labour would be for naught. The Romans were wilful to the point of arrogance, but even they must feel the uncertainty that follows on the heels of defeat.

Whatever the enemy's course, Hamilcar's plan was now firmly in motion. The destruction of the siege towers had bought him valuable time. Lilybaeum was safe from a land assault for the immediate future and Hamilcar could now turn his attention to other side of the battle. For this he needed to leave the city, to escape the siege. He turned towards the sea and the quadrireme waiting for him at the quayside.

Atticus strode impatiently across the aft-deck of the *Orcus*, his mood foul after a sleepless night. The arrival of the Rhodian in Lilybaeum was an ill omen, a subtle but vital shift of the odds in the Carthaginians' favour. Their easy approach and evasion had made a mockery of the blockade; Atticus had sent one of his galleys to Ovidius, the Roman prefect at the northern end of the bay, to warn him of the quadrireme's arrival.

To add to his disquiet, Atticus had heard the sound of battle from behind the town during the dark hours of the night, the noise travelling easily across the still waters of the bay. Trapped out in the lagoon, it was impossible to tell what was occurring but, as the noise abated, the orange glow of fires could be seen. It was evident that the siege towers had been attacked and Atticus's thoughts were with Septimus and the Ninth Legion, his concern keeping him awake until dawn.

He held his hand up to his face to shield his eyes, the rising sun behind the town illuminating the inner harbour, and he saw a number of boats sailing aimlessly across the docks, while others pulled gently at their anchor lines in the shoal-weakened swell. In light of the Rhodian's arrival, Atticus was tempted to abandon the blockade and immediately sail the fleet into the inner harbour via the northern channel, to force the issue and end the torturous waiting, but he dismissed the idea, knowing that the Carthaginians had not attacked him in the enclosed harbour of Aspis for the same reasons he could not here, and in Lilybaeum there would be the added danger of needing to land men on a hostile dock with a precarious line of retreat. The town would have to be taken from the landward side by the legions or, failing that, the inhabitants would need to be forced to surrender through starvation and deprivation, a tactic that would only work if the bay were sealed and the town cut off from resupply.

As a blockade runner, the Rhodian was the blade that could slash the entire fabric of the siege. Atticus turned abruptly from the town to continue pacing the deck, his mind revisiting every thought he had had during the night on how he could capture the Rhodian when he inevitably tried to run the blockade again. The heat of the day was building, the sun beating down from a clear blue sky, and the sweat prickled on Atticus's back, sharpening the fine edge of his dark mood.

Hamilcar nodded as permission to come aboard was granted. He walked quickly up the gangplank, jumping down on to the main deck, followed by twenty of his own men. He looked to the aft-deck, searching for the Rhodian, his shaved head a distinguishing feature that singled him out. He saw the Greek standing by the helm, his expression one of anger. Hamilcar strode towards him, his men fanning out across the deck behind him, and the Rhodian approached to close the gap, meeting him on the main deck.

'The agreement was for you alone, Hamilcar,' the Rhodian said. 'There was never any mention of these additional men.'

'They are here for my protection, Calix,' Hamilcar replied evenly. 'You have worked with the Romans before and I wanted to be sure you would not be tempted to hand me over to the blockade. So, at the first sign of treachery, my men have orders to strike *you* down.'

Calix bristled at the insult against his honour, and Hamilcar sensed the Greek crewmen around him react with similar anger, but he kept his eyes on the Rhodian.

'There will be no treachery, Hamilcar,' Calix replied with suppressed resentment. 'I have also worked with your people in the past and my reputation is without stain.'

'Nevertheless,' Hamilcar said firmly, 'my men stay.'

Calix stared at the Carthaginian commander for a moment longer. 'Very well,' he said. 'We will discuss the price of their passage after we escape the blockade.'

Hamilcar smiled. 'Agreed,' he said. He had known Calix would ultimately comply – how could he not, given he was yet to be paid? – but to have him back down so quickly and swallow the slight against his honour was a mark of his professionalism. For many men whose allegiance was for sale, loyalty could easily be secured by a higher bidder; but with the Rhodian, Hamilcar was now confident his loyalty was also bound by his word and his reputation.

Calix ordered his crew to cast off and shouted down the

open hatchway to the rowing deck to make ready. Hamilcar glanced down and was immediately surprised to see the rowers moving freely around the deck, many of them running to their oars in answer to Calix's command.

'They're freedmen,' he said almost to himself, and Calix turned.

'The strongest rowing crew in the Mediterranean,' he said with unassuming confidence, and he began calling orders at his crew again as the *Ares* moved sedately away from the dock.

Hamilcar watched the rowing crew at work, their stroke even and clean. He had heard the Greeks used freedmen as rowers, but he had never encountered them before. For a fleet the size of Carthage's, apart from the difficulties of procuring such manpower, the cost of using freedmen as rowers would be enormous, although Hamilcar could see the advantages.

As the order was given for standard speed, the *Ares* jerked forward under their combined strength. He was poised to turn away when one other realization struck him, his ear so attuned to the sound that he did not notice its absence; there was no drum beat. Just as he wondered how the rowers kept time, they suddenly began to sing, a deep sonorous tune that matched the pace of their stroke. They bent their backs to the task with the enthusiasm of professional labourers who took pride in their work.

The *Ares* swung her bow through ninety degrees and Calix called for battle speed. Beyond the inner shoals, two squadrons of ships were sailing slowly across the lagoon while the bulk still straddled the northern channel. As Hamilcar moved to the helm, Calix adjusted the course of the *Ares* once more, deciding on an inner channel that would take the *Ares* between the two squadrons but closer to the southernmost one, a calculated risk to lower any pursuit to a minimum.

Hamilcar looked to the Roman ships less than a mile away

and, with a sailor's heart, he shrugged off the concerns of command to concentrate on the contest about to unfold. He was committed; his fate was in the hands of the gods and the skilled crew of a Greek mercenary.

'Enemy galley, four points off the starboard bow.'

It took mere seconds for Atticus to spot the approaching ship and discern its course and intent.

'Battle speed, steady the helm,' he shouted, running to the side rail. It was the Rhodian, there was no doubt. Making battle speed and heading for a channel in the inner shoals about half a mile away. Atticus looked to his other squadron nearer the northern end of the bay. They too were responding, coming about to close the vice, but Atticus could immediately see they were too far away. Only his squadron was in a position to intercept the Rhodian.

'Gaius, your assessment,' Atticus asked over his shoulder.

'He's making battle speed,' Gaius replied, his hand steady on the tiller. 'And if his channel through the inner shoals is straight, he's going to reach the lagoon before we can intercept him. Recommend we go to attack speed and head for the outer rim of the lagoon.'

Atticus nodded without turning. 'Make it so,' he said, and the *Orcus* accelerated, the staggered response of the rest of the squadron creating a slight gap behind the command ship.

Gaius turned the helm through two points to port and the *Orcus* leaned into the turn, her ram slicing across the gentle swell, creating curved waves that marked her course.

'Baro,' Atticus shouted, and the second-in-command ran to the aft-deck.

'Have Drusus ready the legionaries. It's time they put their new skills to the test.'

Baro nodded with a conspiratorial smile. He had trained

the legionaries relentlessly over the previous weeks and was anxious for them to cut their new teeth in battle. He ran back to the main deck and began speaking with Drusus, occasionally pointing to the quadrireme off the starboard beam.

Atticus watched them for a moment longer and then turned his attention to the Rhodian. The quadrireme was approaching the inner shoals, still sailing at battle speed, an incredible pace considering the obstacle he was about to negotiate; but his committed course allowed Atticus to recalculate the angles, his confidence rising slowly as he drew his conclusions.

Hamilcar instinctively leaned forward as the ram of the *Ares* approached the shoals, the speed of the quadrireme raising the hairs on his arms. He glanced at Calix, the Rhodian's gaze locked on the Roman squadron on the far side of the lagoon. Hamilcar looked over his shoulder to Lilybaeum, wondering which landmark the helmsman was using to align the galley to the hidden channel, impressed by the confidence shown by all on board but, as he looked again to Calix, he saw his brow was wrinkled in puzzlement.

'What is it?' he asked.

'The Romans,' Calix replied slowly. 'I had expected them to come straight at us as we emerged from the inner shoals and then give chase, but they have sailed to the far side of the lagoon. It is a clever move, one to their advantage . . .'

He turned away abruptly and began talking to the helmsman, as if Hamilcar were no longer there, and both Greeks looked towards the Roman squadron. Hamilcar watched their discussion. Greek was the trading language of the entire Mediterranean and Hamilcar possessed a reasonable grasp of the language, but the dialect and speed of their conversation frustrated his efforts to listen. He saw them nod in unison as they reached a decision.

He looked to the waters around the *Ares* and noticed they were almost through the shoals. Beneath the crystal-clear green waters he could see the shadows of the rocks, some of them reaching up to the surface not twenty feet from the bow of the *Ares*, jagged spires that would pierce even the strongest timbers, and again he marvelled at the skill and confidence of the Rhodian, knowing that any mistake would be punishable by utter ruin.

The deck tilted suddenly beneath Hamilcar, and he centred his balance as the *Ares* accelerated to attack speed, her bow coming around to a point further ahead of the Roman squadron. The Rhodian had obviously abandoned his original course and was now striking for a more distant channel, forced to do so by the Romans' initial perceptive reaction. Hamilcar felt a stirring of doubt but he shrugged it off. Despite the slight deviation in plan, he trusted the Rhodian.

'Aspect change,' Corin shouted. 'The Rhodian is coming about two points to starboard. Moving to attack speed.'

'I make it more like three,' Baro said, but Atticus and Gaius remained silent, their concentration riveted on the quadrireme's every move.

'Helm, one point to starboard,' Atticus said. 'Give me a hundred yards off the port beam between us and the outer shoals.'

Gaius nodded and made the change. The quadrireme was almost directly off their starboard beam on the far side of the lagoon, but their course was convergent, the Rhodian striking for a channel in the shoals somewhere ahead of the *Orcus*. Atticus was looking to close that apex, to intercept the quadrireme just short of its target, knowing that if the Rhodian reached the shoals the race would be over. The quadrireme's draught was at least four or five feet less than that of a quinquereme's, and

Atticus knew, if the roles were reversed, he would choose a channel that only a lighter boat could traverse.

'We should accelerate to ramming speed,' Baro said, but Atticus ignored him. It was too soon for such a last-ditch move. The rowers could only maintain ramming speed for five minutes maximum and, given that the Rhodian might change course again, Atticus might need that reserve of strength. He looked to his other squadron, approaching on their position, but again, even with the convergent courses, they would still not intercept the Rhodian before he crossed the lagoon. The *Orcus* was leading the charge and only they could thwart the enemy.

'Ramming speed,' Calix ordered, and the *Ares* was transformed into the very creature its namesake watched over, the galley taking flight across the smooth waters of the lagoon, its sleek, shallow draught offering minimal drag. The ram surged clear of the water with each pull of the oars.

Hamilcar listened to the rowers sing, their tune changing to match the increased tempo, their words sung on the exhalation of each pull of the oar. The Roman squadron was closing off the port beam, perhaps three hundred yards away, while ahead Hamilcar could not yet see the telltale signs that marked the beginnings of the outer shoals. He looked to the Rhodian, unnerved by his confidence. For Hamilcar the order to increase to ramming speed had come too soon, and he wondered if Calix was perhaps blinded by his own self-belief. He had thrown the final die and committed the *Ares* to its top speed. The Romans were sure to respond in kind and he tried to calculate the result, deducing only that it would be close. He was tempted to challenge the Rhodian but he held his tongue, and his nerve.

*

'They've gone to ramming speed,' Baro shouted. 'I told you—'

'Quiet,' Atticus barked, thrown by the unexpected move. 'Gaius?' he said.

'It's got to be a mistake,' the helmsman said. 'He's shown his hand too soon.'

Atticus nodded but, regardless of any perceived mistake, the Rhodian's move had to be countered.

'Ramming speed,' he shouted, and Baro needlessly ran to the hatch on the main deck to repeat the order, the drum master already responding to Atticus's voice.

The *Orcus* charged forward with the strength of two hundred and seventy rowers, making its ramming speed a shade faster than a quadrireme's, and Atticus saw Baro nod to Drusus on the main deck, a final salutation of comrades before the fight.

Atticus glanced to the four points of his ship, the waters ahead clear, the shoals off his port beam, his squadron taking up the rear, and the enemy galley sailing desperately to get ahead of the *Orcus*, their slight lead being eroded with every stroke of the quinquereme's oars.

'It's the Greek,' Hamilcar said venomously as he recognized the command ship of the Roman squadron.

'Who?' Calix asked, perplexed.

'Perennis, the Greek prefect.'

'Perennis,' Calix repeated slowly, taking a greater interest in the lead galley. She had gained over a ship length on the boats behind, a testament to a more skilled crew. He had heard of Perennis, and had remembered his name: a Greek who had risen in the Roman navy, a testament to his abilities in itself. He nodded, feeling a slight tinge of regret that he would best one of his own people.

Hamilcar kept his gaze locked on the Roman galley, less

than two hundred yards away, its course locked on a point ahead of both converging ships, and he realized with sickening dread that the Roman galley would reach that point first and block the *Ares*'s access to the shoals. There was no escape. Even if they turned inside they would be turning into the entire Roman squadron. There was no choice but to retreat; even then their chances were slim, given that the rowers could not maintain ramming speed for the time it would take to re-cross the lagoon to the inner shoals. The Rhodian had misjudged his run and Hamilcar turned to him with a murderous expression.

'We can't make it,' he said angrily. 'You pushed them to ramming speed too soon.'

Calix did not respond but held up a hand to silence Hamilcar as he spoke rapidly to the helmsman, both men glancing over their shoulders to some distant point on the land behind. Calix nodded in agreement and then turned to Hamilcar.

'Forgive me, Hamilcar, but our approach to the channel must be exact,' he said calmly.

'We'll never reach that far. Perennis will cut us off. We must withdraw.'

'We will yet outrun them,' Calix replied, and shouted out an order for the rowing deck to make ready.

'We are already at ramming speed and Perennis's quinquereme is faster,' Hamilcar said exasperatedly.

'His rowers are slaves,' Calix replied, never taking his eyes off the Roman galley. 'As are yours, Hamilcar. Therefore you think like a master of slaves. They respond only to the beat of the drum; however well trained they are, they are bound by its beat. Ramming speed is merely the limit of the drum. Any faster and the beats overlap, causing the rowers to lose coordination. But my rowers are freedmen. They were not trained by the rhythm of a drum and for a crew such as mine, coordination is almost instinctive. Strength alone is their only limitation, and I know they have not yet reached that threshold.'

He turned to Hamilcar.

'Now you and Perennis will witness the true speed of a galley,' and he ordered the rowers to increase their pace, leaving Hamilcar to watch in awe as the *Ares* accelerated to an incredible sixteen knots.

'By the gods, they're increasing speed,' Gaius whispered, and Atticus ran to the side rail to confirm what he could not believe. The gap between the two ships continued to fall as their courses converged, but now the pace of the quadrireme was outstripping the *Orcus*. Atticus's mind raced to try to devise some way to stop the Rhodian, exploring every conceivable course change and discounting it in the same moment. Speed alone would decide the contest and the Rhodian had somehow reversed the outcome.

The quadrireme passed within a ship length of the bow of the *Orcus* and Gaius swung the galley into its wake, knowing there was little else he could do. Atticus stared at the aft-deck of the enemy ship. There were Carthaginians amongst the mercenary crew, their faces indistinguishable across the distance, and Atticus felt overwhelmed by his frustration.

'He'll have to reduce speed once they hit the channel,' Baro said. 'We still have a chance.' And he shouted forward to Drusus to make ready.

'It's over,' Atticus said. 'We can't enter the channel. It's too shallow for us.'

'You can't know that,' Baro argued angrily. 'We have to stop them.'

'The Rhodian knew he would be pursued,' Atticus replied. 'And he would have picked a channel that he alone could traverse.'

Baro looked to Gaius, but the helmsman remained silent, in tacit agreement with Atticus.

'How do you know?' Baro said, turning once more to Atticus. 'Because he's Greek, like you? Is that it? You all think alike?'

Atticus's expression became murderous and he stared into Baro's face, causing the second-in-command to step back instinctively.

'It's over, Baro,' he snarled. 'Now get off my aft-deck.'

Baro straightened up and stalked away. Atticus turned to Gaius, the helmsman nodding, and he ordered 'all stop', the *Orcus* drifting to a halt as the quadrireme reached the outer limits of the shoals, when it too reduced speed to navigate the channel. The squadron of galleys behind the *Orcus* responded to the command ship's order, fanning out to allow themselves sea room to stop safely. All were given leave to watch the Rhodian complete his passage of the outer shoals, the quadrireme raising sail with impunity to strike away into the west.

Gaius requested further orders, ready to bear away, but Atticus did not hear him, his entire being focused on the escaping galley. He recalled every detail of the chase, every manoeuvre the quadrireme had made, and stored it away beneath his anger, determined that he should use it to find a way to seal the loophole the Rhodian had exposed in the blockade and forge a new defence that would not break so easily.

Scipio watched with a slight smile at the edge of his mouth as the legionaries flogged the trader with the flat edges of their swords, whipping their blades away after each strike with a slight twist of their wrists, causing the leading edge of the blade to cut neatly through the trader's clothes and score his skin, shallow flesh wounds that would leave scars as a reminder of his crime. He was bent over almost double as he ran, his cries for mercy unheard by the jeering crowd, and the legionaries pursued him all the way to the main gate, stopping only when they reached the threshold to spit and curse at the fleeing trader, shouting unnecessary warnings that he should never return.

In the charged atmosphere of the legionary encampment, the trader's crime was simple. He was Greek. He was a camp follower, one of more than a hundred who had flocked to the stationary camps offering all manner of wares, from replacement kit to wines and exotic foods, and a taste of the local women. For some it was a full-time profession: they had travelled from Rome on foot for the profits that could be made over an entire campaign season. The Greek was one of these men, a trader who had shadowed the legions in Sicily for years and was well known amongst the quartermasters. He, like the other camp followers, had been tolerated – even liked, Scipio suspected – but that had all changed with the discovery that the surprise attack on the siege towers had been carried out by Greek mercenaries.

Legionaries were conditioned to hate the Carthaginians by the hardships of the campaign and the loss of comrades in previous battles, but the discovery that it was the Greeks who were responsible for the destruction of the siege towers seemed tantamount to treason, given that the Republic encompassed former Greek territories that had always been treated magnanimously.

For Scipio it was evidence of the beliefs he had always held about the treacherous nature of non-Romans: that their disloyalty was simply a mark of their innate inferiority. In watching the trader being beaten from camp, Scipio had pictured Perennis beneath those same swords, spat at and told never to return, as the Romans who had tolerated him for years finally

233

became aware of the true nature of the outsider in their midst. For now, the Greek prefect still served a purpose, but Scipio was finding it increasingly hard to stick to his original conviction, and it was with difficulty that he suppressed the urge to summon Perennis to the camp under some pretext in order to expose him to the wrath of the legionaries. He calmed himself, conceding once more that time was on his side and that eventually he would dispose of the Greek as thoroughly as the legionaries had his compatriot.

Scipio was distracted by the approach of a *contubernia* of soldiers led by a centurion, and his eyes narrowed in curiosity as he looked at the long timber box they carried on their shoulders. The centurion stopped before Scipio and saluted. His expression was fearful and his forehead beaded with sweat.

'Beg to report, Consul,' he said haltingly. 'We found this box inside our lines this morning. It must have been placed there during the attack.'

'What is it?' Scipio asked impatiently.

'It's . . .' the centurion stammered and he looked to the box, unable to answer.

'Set it down,' Scipio ordered irritably.

The soldiers quickly complied and then backed away. The box had already been opened, Scipio presumed by the centurion, but the lid had been reaffixed. Scipio could hear a faint buzzing sound emanating from within and his brow furrowed in puzzlement.

'Open it,' he commanded, and the centurion stepped forward, drawing his sword as he did. He crouched down and slid the blade under the lid and then turned his face away, before abruptly twisting and lifting the blade with one sweep of his arm.

The lid flew off and a cloud of flies erupted from the box, causing Scipio to lean back and look away as the swarm

234

dissipated. He waved his hand angrily in front of his face and stepped forward to peer down. His stomach heaved, a violent spasm from the depths of his bowels, and he turned away before looking back upon the rotting corpse laid out in the box. Regulus stared up at him sightlessly; his eyes long since devoured by the voracious flies that had nested there, the swarm resettling once more on his flesh.

Scipio looked down to the butchery that was Regulus's chest, unable to comprehend what would cause such a horrendous wound. It was as if . . . and Scipio suddenly realized what he was seeing, the shape of the elephant's pad-like foot clearly visible around the lower edge of the wound. He fought against the wave of nausea that swept over him.

'Cover him up,' he ordered the centurion harshly, and he turned to enter his tent, anxious to be alone.

Once inside he stumbled over to a basin and splashed water on his face, closing his eyes as he did so. The image of Regulus flashed before him and he opened his eyes wide again, his nausea suddenly coupled with a primal fear of retribution. Regulus had been his enemy and Scipio had wanted him destroyed, but he realized that the terrible fate the proconsul had suffered had affected him deeply. He had sent Regulus to that end, and again the image of his hollow stare flashed before him.

Scipio brushed the vision aside, suddenly angry at his own weakness, that he should feel remorse for Regulus. The proconsul had brought his fate upon himself with his foolish attempt to broker a peace treaty, and the Carthaginians had carried out the barbaric execution, not Scipio. Yet a shred of culpability remained on his conscience. He poured a goblet of wine from an amphora and drank deeply, allowing the sharp taste to cleanse the last of the nausea from his throat.

The return of Regulus's body was no doubt meant as a

personal warning to the Roman commander of the fate that awaited him, but for Scipio it merely hardened his heart. The Carthaginians had rid him of his enemy and, however merciless they perceived their method of execution to be, Scipio had witnessed the legionaries descend to the same level of savagery in their sack of Panormus. If Carthage believed that Rome had not the stomach for the fight, they were sorely mistaken. Scipio would open their eyes to that error. He would go back on the offensive, and wipe the stain of Regulus's demise from his conscience by inflicting a terrible reprisal on the Carthaginian foe.

CHAPTER THIRTEEN

Hamilcar looked out along the length of the city of Drepana to the harbour as the *Ares* rounded the small islands at the head of the bay. The Gadir fleet was anchored in neat lines, the ships tethered by their sterns, their bows facing out, ready to slip their moorings at a moment's notice. He heard warning cries carried on the offshore breeze, and from out of the inner harbour two quinqueremes approached, turning neatly together to intercept the unusual ship that had sailed brazenly into the jaws of the fleet.

Hamilcar smiled and moved to the foredeck to identify himself as the gap narrowed, impressed but not surprised by the alertness of the fleet's commanders. Gadir was on the very fringes of the empire, and the fleet based there was one of the best: independent and resilient, it existed outside of the realm of the relative protection of Carthage and was often cut off for months during the winter. The crews were renowned for their strict sailing discipline and the fleet possessed the agility and reaction times of a force half its size.

The *Ares* passed through the guardsmen and into the long neck of the harbour, while Hamilcar returned to the aft-deck to instruct Calix to sail past the fleet and tie up at the docks beneath the walls of the town.

'An impressive fleet, Hamilcar,' Calix said as the *Ares* moved slowly past the serried ranks.

'There are few finer,' Hamilcar replied, with the same unassuming confidence that Calix had shown when he spoke of his crew.

Calix nodded, realizing the depth of pride the Carthaginian had in the men he commanded. They were indeed a race of skilled mariners, their expansive empire a fitting testament to that skill, but Calix believed they could not claim the mantle of the finest seafarers. That rested solidly on the shoulders of the Greeks, an ancient claim that was reasserted with each new generation.

'You are right, Hamilcar,' Calix said, looking proudly around at his crew. 'There are few finer, and they are here.'

Hamilcar smiled with amusement. 'You must continue to prove that, Calix,' he said. 'I need to keep a line of communication open with the besieged garrison. You must return to Lilybaeum immediately.'

Calix nodded. He had expected as much, given that only he could run the blockade.

'Pay me for the passage for you and your men first, then we will negotiate a fee for running the blockade with dispatches,' he said.

'I will pay you what we agreed,' Hamilcar replied. 'And the same amount again each time you return here from Lilybaeum.'

Calix's eyes shone with avarice. It was more than he'd hoped for and Hamilcar had offered it without hesitation. The potential purse was enormous and, given that he had already bested the Romans, even the notable Greek prefect, it would be an easy task.

Hamilcar saw the self-assurance in Calix's face and felt his doubts ease somewhat. It was a risk sending the Rhodian back to Lilybaeum, given that – if he was caught – he would certainly reveal the strength and location of the Carthaginian fleet; but Hamilcar knew he had to keep in contact with the garrison, albeit only until he had readied the Gadir fleet for battle.

Continuing to use the Rhodian also sorted out one other potential problem. If Hamilcar ended his contract, the Rhodian would be free to sell his information to the Romans. The alternative was to seize the Rhodian's ship but, considering how dependent Hamilcar was on mercenaries, any such blatant persecution of one of their own kind would surely cause the others to question his loyalty to their agreements.

'Then we are agreed,' Hamilcar said to Calix's silence. 'When you reach Lilybaeum, submit yourself to the garrison commander.'

Again Calix nodded and, as the gangplank was lowered on to the dock, Hamilcar beckoned to his men to depart.

Calix followed with men of his own, anxious to receive the money he was due and depart the bottleneck of the port. He felt hemmed in, an unfamiliar feeling for a creature of the open sea, and he looked around him furtively, taking solace in knowing that he would soon be away, his bow turned to the southwest and the Aegates Islands, there to await a favourable wind that would carry him once more through the blockade at Lilybaeum.

Atticus watched with interest as the trireme made its way slowly towards the *Orcus*, its familiar lines bringing a smile to his face. He glanced at Gaius, seeing the same satisfaction in the expression of the normally stern-faced helmsman. She was the *Virtus*, almost an exact replica of the *Aquila*, and both men looked past the differences to see the galley on which they had once sailed with pride.

The *Virtus* pulled alongside and Atticus jumped across the gap on to the lower main deck, followed by Gaius and ten other men. He looked over his shoulder and nodded curtly to Baro on the aft-deck of the *Orcus*, signalling the beginning of his nominal command of the quinquereme, and the *Orcus* pulled neatly away from the smaller galley. Gaius went immediately to the helm while Atticus took a moment to look about the ship and its assembled crew.

They were a picked crew, the best from every ship in his entire squadron, ninety men in all, three times the normal sailing complement of a trireme, but the *Virtus* carried no legionaries as each sailor was a skilled boarder, a vital attribute given they were planning to take a larger galley.

Atticus knew many of the men by name; others had been recommended by their captains, trusted men who knew what was at stake and would give their best to the task. He called the captain of the *Virtus* to his side and ordered him to organize the men into watches while he went below to the rowing deck.

The space was overly crowded, with men squatting silently on the walkway that ran the length of the deck, while others filled the cabins of the trireme. It was a cumbersome arrangement, but Atticus had managed to increase the relief from forty to one hundred rowers, an additional weight that increased the draught of the trireme by a foot but still kept it under that of a quadrireme. Again the men had been hand-picked from amongst the entire squadron, seasoned rowers who had lived through many battles and whose nerve could be trusted. By necessity they would be unchained to allow for a frequent and fluid system of replacement, so, to ensure the rowers would remain at their oars, Atticus had promised them all their freedom should their assault be successful, a loss he planned to make up from his prey.

Atticus nodded to himself, content that all was in order, and he went back on deck. He had no idea what cargo or personnel the Rhodian had ferried into or out of Lilybaeum, but he was convinced the Rhodian would return, for without his abilities the siege remained intact and the city cut off from supply and communication. He re-examined his plan, trying to anticipate every possible variant, relying the most on the skill of the crew he had assembled.

He had concluded that he had beaten the previous time because he had blindly followed convention, forgetting the skills he and many of the other men had gained through years of skirmishing with individual pirate ships. His manoeuvres had been those of a fleet commander, not an individual captain, and the Rhodian had exploited that predictability.

Atticus had forgotten the power of one ship, of one crew, believing instead in the strength of numbers, and he had dismissed the Rhodian's first evasion as a fluke, the product of a surprise approach, confident that a ship so vastly out-numbered would be easily caught if they were vigilant. But the Rhodian had escaped him a second time.

Now Atticus possessed, as nearly as he could, an equivalent ship; and although he did not know the exact location of the channels the Rhodian had used to escape, he had formed a reasonable approximation. He had positioned other ships of his squadron to tempt the Rhodian to use the same or nearby channels in his next attempt.

Baro had asked if he believed he knew the Rhodian's mind because he was Greek, but Atticus had realized it was because he had once been like him, relying solely on one ship and its crew, skilfully seeking out and exploiting an enemy's weaknesses, fighting each battle from a chosen position of strength, stacking the odds in advance to ensure victory. It was the way of a lone wolf, a creature who shrugged off the safeguards but also the burden of a hunting pack to become a more efficient killer. With the *Virtus*, Atticus had become that creature once more and, as he looked to the western horizon, he sensed his prey was near at hand.

Calix held up his hand as the distant features of Lilybaeum became more distinct and the helmsman immediately shouted orders for the running rigging to be released. The mainsail lost its shape, the corners of the canvas sheet flapping in the westerly wind coming in over the starboard aft-quarter, and the *Ares* slowed, the helmsman just managing to keep her bow steady in the swell. Calix moved to the side rail, his gaze sweeping across the width of the bay, and the altered disposition of the Roman blockade.

The *Ares* had lain off the Aegates Islands for three days awaiting a favourable wind, and had set sail only hours ago. They had approached, as before, under canvas, keeping the strength of the rowers in reserve; but Calix was about to order them lowered when he noticed the revised Roman formation. The enemy galleys were now deployed in a blockade line that reached across the breadth of the lagoon, a tactical change to cover the hidden channels and deny their use to a blockade runner. It was a misguided approach, Calix thought, for the channels were not so numerous and the Romans were now too thinly spread to form any sort of protective barrier. Even in the centre, the location of the channels last used by Calix for his escape, the line was no stronger, with the Roman galleys separated by at least four hundred yards in the calm of the lagoon.

He moved once more to the tiller, conscious of the fact that, if he could see the Romans, so they could see the *Ares*, and they might rush to group around his line of approach. He shouted for full ahead and the mainsail was made taut once more, the wind taking the lion's share of the load as the rowers engaged their oars at battle speed. He ordered the helmsman to make for the same outer channel as before, one of only three available to him and the only one in the centre, and he locked his gaze on the Roman galleys directly opposite that point, confident that he could easily shred such a thin veil. The channel was a dogleg and so could only be negotiated safely under oars but, once in the lagoon, Calix would have a choice of three channels through the inner shoals, each one too shallow for a quinquereme. For the Rhodian the pieces had moved but the game, and the inevitable outcome, remained the same.

'Galley approaching.'

'Identify,' Atticus shouted animatedly.

'It's him, Prefect,' Corin replied from the masthead of the *Virtus*. 'He's heading is on a line bearing two points off our starboard quarter, between us and the *Copia*.'

It must be the same channel as before, Atticus thought with a smile, but aloud he cursed, unable to see the approaching ship from behind the hull of the *Orcus*. He looked to Gaius.

'Shadow her every move,' he said, and the helmsman nodded, holding the *Virtus* steady on station behind the *Orcus*, keeping her hidden from the open sea.

The order for battle speed was shouted from the aft-deck of the *Orcus* by Baro and the quinquereme moved off, the *Virtus* sailing in her shadow, Gaius handling the tiller with gentle, deft strokes, trusting Baro to keep a steady line.

Atticus looked to the other ships of the blockade, the nearest ones already converging on points inside the outer shoals where it was estimated the Rhodian might emerge, a natural reaction to his approach. He cursed his line of sight again and on an impulse he ran to the rigging and climbed hand-over-hand up to the masthead, keeping his grip firm on the rough-hewn ropes until he reached the top, and he lifted himself up on to the mainsail lifting yard. Corin smiled beside him and moved over to allow Atticus to stand tall and find his balance.

At the head of the mainmast the gentle roll of the deck was multiplied, and Atticus was suddenly conscious that he had not been aloft in many years. His grip tightened on the mast and his movements were exaggerated in contrast with Corin's almost innate sense of balance, but he steadied his breathing and looked out over the deck of the *Orcus* sailing alongside the *Virtus* to the horizon.

The Rhodian was approaching as before, under sail and oars, but Atticus knew he would need to slow as he passed through the channel. Despite this, the converging Roman galleys would still not be in a position to challenge him as he emerged into the lagoon, and again Atticus begrudgingly admired the Rhodian's utmost use of the prevailing elements to his advantage. His grip remained firm on the mainmast, only now it was an outward sign of his inner determination and, as the Rhodian furled his sail to begin his run, Atticus shouted down the order for battle stations.

Calix's head darted from side to side as he tracked the approach of the four Roman quinqueremes. As he suspected, they had left their positions in the blockade line to converge on his approach but, with the *Ares* already halfway through the outer shoals, he would reach the lagoon before they had a chance to close the neck of the channel.

The *Ares* swung neatly through the turn in the dogleg and Calix called for attack speed, turning briefly to nod at the helmsman in silent commendation for a perfect approach. The quadrireme moved quickly over the surface of the water and the crew worked with silent efficiency as they readied the ship for the run across the lagoon, securing the mainsail, its broad canvas too easy a target for a fire arrow; while below the rowers shouted encouragement to each other over the sound of their own singing.

The *Ares* tore out of the channel at twelve knots, Calix standing firmly beside the helmsman, his eyes darting from the approaching Roman galleys to seemingly random points on the inner shoals a mile away. The helmsman began a series of evasive manoeuvres in an effort to keep the Romans guessing; but, before they had covered two hundred yards, Calix had made his decision.

'The centre channel,' he ordered, and the helmsman confirmed the course, shifting his rudder a half-point, already looking to the landmarks that would allow him to make the final adjustments as he neared the shoals.

Calix watched the Roman galleys turn as they realized they could not cut him off, their bows slowly coming about to a convergent point a half-mile ahead of the *Ares*. The nearest galley was less than one hundred and fifty yards off his starboard forequarter and Calix recognized it as the quinquereme Hamilcar had identified, the Greek prefect's boat. The beginnings of a smile creased his mouth as he relished the chase to come, but it quickly evaporated as he noticed an anomaly: the slender shaft of an additional mast, hidden until now by distance and the sailing skills of an unseen opponent. He was about to shout out a warning to his crew when the Roman galley shot out from hiding. It was a trireme, a small, sleek ship, and it sped neatly from beneath the shadow of the quinquereme.

Calix lost vital seconds as he stared at the trireme, completely thrown by its sudden appearance. It was a smaller, slower boat than the *Ares*, and should logically be no threat, but the Romans had obviously devised some plan with the trireme as its crux. His helmsman shouted for further orders, apprehension in his voice.

Calix spun around. 'Two points to port,' he ordered. 'Keep us out of range of that trireme.'

The helmsman nodded and the *Ares* leaned into the turn. Calix looked to the approaching Roman ships again, his confidence shaken. He tried again to understand the Romans' plan when a realization struck him. The trireme had been hiding behind the prefect's quinquereme. He was the master of this plan, and Calix looked to the trireme again, suspecting that Perennis was the commander.

His fists clenched instinctively, the realization steeling his nerves once more. His contract with the Carthaginians made the Romans the enemy, but now two sons of Greece would lead the fray for each side, and Calix knew his every skill would be tested.

The drum hammered out the rhythm of attack speed, but to Atticus the *Virtus* seemed to move at a faster pace, its nimble hull turning neatly at every touch of Gaius's hand on the tiller. The *Orcus* was swinging around behind him, its turn wider and slower, but its attack speed was a knot faster and it shadowed the *Virtus*, bearing down upon her.

The Rhodian was less than one hundred yards away off the port forequarter of the *Virtus*, aiming to sweep past the bow of the *Copia*, which was approaching rapidly on its port side. It would be a tight run but Atticus could see the Rhodian had chosen his angle perfectly, allowing himself sufficient sea room to adjust his course and still break through.

'Signal the *Fulgora* and *Honos*,' Atticus ordered, referring to the two quinqueremes on the outer extremes of the chase. 'Tell them to break off and block the channel the Rhodian just used.'

The quinqueremes broke away in succession, leaving only three Roman galleys in the chase.

The Rhodian's galley passed the *Copia*, her course changing slightly again as she lined up for an invisible channel in the inner shoals. Gaius brought the *Virtus* into her wake but the trireme was already falling behind the larger, faster galley, the gap increasing beyond a hundred yards. Atticus waited patiently, the *Copia* sweeping past his left flank to continue the chase, while over his right shoulder he could hear the drum beat of the *Orcus* from inside its hull at it too began to overtake the *Virtus*, the spearhead formation of the three Roman galleys becoming inverted as the trireme tip was overtaken.

Every galley was moving at attack speed, looking to conserve their energy, waiting for the right moment to commit to a ramming-speed attack run or, in the Rhodian's case, an escape run, each captain knowing that the strength of their rowing crew was finite and there was no room for error in the enclosed lagoon. Atticus knew from their previous encounter that the Rhodian believed he had the advantage of both speed and manoeuvrability over the quinqueremes, but the *Virtus* had brought one other factor into play, one where Atticus alone had the advantage: stamina.

'Ramming speed,' he shouted, and the *Virtus* surged forward, her ram rearing out of the waters at the first pull of the oars at thirteen knots.

She quickly began to retake the lead from the quinqueremes, re-establishing the spearhead until she was sailing neatly in the wake of the Rhodian, the *Orcus* and *Copia* falling away, following orders to conserve their strength until the battle was joined.

The shoals were still half a mile away, the Rhodian less than a hundred yards ahead, and the *Virtus* was committed.

'Ramming speed,' Calix shouted, his eyes locked on the approaching trireme. 'Archers to the aft-deck.'

He spun around and looked to the shoals ahead. The deck of the *Ares* shifted beneath him, a minor course adjustment as the helmsman brought the bow of the quadrireme to bear on the mouth of the channel, still a half-mile away.

He looked to the trireme again, the gap between the boats becoming steady and then increasing as the quadrireme's greater speed came to bear once more. The *Ares* would reach the channel first, but what then, Calix thought? The trireme would follow, its shallow draught allowing it access. Would it maintain a higher speed, risking all to catch the quadrireme as it slowed through the channel? Would it follow the *Ares* into the inner harbour? Calix could not be sure, his mind trying to place himself on the aft-deck of the Roman galley, to see as Perennis saw, to plan as he would. His conclusions all reached the same point. He must not allow the trireme to catch up and somehow cripple his ship.

'Helmsman,' he shouted. 'Come about six points to port. Take us through the left channel.'

'But Captain,' the helmsman replied, 'that's over a mile away. The rowers—'

'Do it now!' Calix shouted, his eyes locked on the trireme. 'There's only one way to stop that trireme: we must bleed its rowers white.'

The *Ares* heeled over into the turn, the helmsman straining through the effort of turning the rudder at ramming speed. The Roman galleys matched the course change, the trireme's sleeker lines allowing it to respond faster, and within two ship lengths the formation of the chase was re-established, although the quinqueremes, continuing at attack speed, were falling further away from the smaller lead ship.

Calix could hear the slow creak of drawn bows to his side and a flight of arrows whooshed away from the aft-deck to the pursuing trireme. He watched the arrows fall, a sporadic hail of death, but as the archers prepared to loose again, Calix suddenly became aware of a silence behind him. He turned and strode to the aft-hatch on the main deck that led to the rowers. They had been rowing at ramming speed for three minutes. Six, maybe seven minutes was their absolute maximum, and Calix glanced back over his shoulder to the trireme. Perennis was subject to the same restrictions and the gap was still increasing. Calix still held the advantage, but as he looked down to the rowers he felt the seeds of doubt taking root within him.

They were sweating stoically at their oars, their faces twisted in grotesque masks of exertion, their laboured breathing like that of a blown elephant. They were strong men, not easily given to exhaustion, but it was the lack of a customary sound that had drawn Calix's attention – for the rowers had stopped singing.

Atticus took one last look at the stern of the quadrireme before ducking his head below deck. The rowing deck seemed in chaos, the central walkway crowded with the fallen, while fresh rowers ran to take abandoned oars in hand. They had passed the five-minute mark and still the drum hammered out eighty beats a minute, a gruelling, punishing pace that only the strongest could maintain. Atticus counted at least two dozen men near him who had not yet fallen. Rarely had he seen such determination, like indomitable legionaries in the face of an enemy charge, the rowers' backs straight through each pull of the oars, their very freedom at stake. They laboured with a savage-like trance on their faces, betraying the deep-seated hatred for the very task into which they poured every ounce of their strength.

Another man fell, then another, and another, their cries pitiful in the hollowed-out carapace of the trireme, the screams of men broken on the yoke, their will driving them beyond the endurance of their bodies until muscles cramped in excruciating pain and they fell, their twisted, near lifeless bodies thrust aside by relief rowers whose strength roused the men around them to greater exertion, the air filled with voices calling out in half a dozen languages in encouragement and anger, in frustration and pain as another man fell, and another, and another.

The drum master roared at the top of his lungs, shouting out the beat even as his hammer fell, viciously calling on the rowers to bend their backs through the slide, to take the strain of the catch and pull through the draw, telling them the enemy was at hand, the fight almost upon them, the end but minutes away, and the rowers responded to his words with renewed determination.

Atticus went back on deck, his nerve steeled to a fine point by the rowers' display of raw courage. He strode back to the aft-deck, ignoring the arrows that slammed into the timbers around him and the sporadic cries of crewmen struck by the pitiless missiles. He turned and stared along the length of the *Virtus* to the quadrireme ahead.

The gap had increased to two hundred yards but the five-minute threshold had been passed. Ramming speed on the *Virtus* was being maintained by the determination of the strongest and the massive influx of relief rowers. They could not last indefinitely, but Atticus was confident that, without relief, the Rhodian's crew had to be suffering more.

His plan was simple. Run the quadrireme down. Not to

cripple it for the quinqueremes, but to take it himself, the trireme's shallow draught ensuring there would be no withdrawal this time. The Rhodian had yet to turn and commit to a channel, the quadrireme still running parallel to the inner shoals not one hundred yards away off the starboard beam, but the turn was close, Atticus could sense it, could feel it through the desperation of his rowers, a palpable anguish that he knew must be drawing the heart out of the Rhodian's own crew.

'By the gods,' the helmsman shouted, glancing fearfully over his shoulder. 'She's still coming on.'

The Rhodian felt the same panic rise within him and he struggled to push it aside. What had it been: seven, eight minutes? What kind of men were powering the trireme?

'One hundred and fifty yards,' one of the archers called beside him, shouting out the range for their next flight.

The gap was falling. The *Ares* was losing speed, fast; her rowers were past exhaustion, past the limits of will and determination, of pride in their strength, with only the dread fear of capture keeping them pulling, knowing that if they were to fall into Roman hands they would become slaves to the very task they performed as freedmen.

'Distance to the channel,' Calix shouted angrily at the helmsman, refocusing his attention. His looked ahead, his gaze darting from the sea to the land.

'Two hundred yards, Captain,' he replied.

'Prepare to make your run,' Calix said, and he looked to the trireme again. The gap was still falling; a gap he had believed would be four or five hundred yards by now, with the trireme drifting aimlessly in the wake of the *Ares*, her rowers blown, her strength gone. But still it came on, and Calix let his hand fall to the hilt of his sword as his options fell away to one. He had seen the two Roman quinqueremes take station on the channel through the outer shoals. His route there was blocked, even if his crew had the strength to re-cross the hostile lagoon, which they had not. The channel ahead was his only escape, and there the trireme would catch him, in the narrows of the channel, where the lack of sea room would make evasive manoeuvres impossible.

The sudden clarity of purpose gave Calix new confidence, and he slowly drew his sword, the muscles of his arm welcoming the familiar weight. The chase would end soon, on Perennis's terms, but in the shallows of the channel it would be a duel between mismatched ships, with the Roman quinqueremes unable to assist. The *Ares* could yet escape to the inner harbour. But first Calix and his crew would have to draw the blood of the Roman crew and their Greek leader.

'Aspect change,' Corin called, pre-empting the turn by a heart-beat as he saw the helmsman put his weight behind the tiller.

The Rhodian's galley swung hard to starboard, finally reaching the channel.

'All hands, prepare for boarding,' Atticus shouted, and the men cheered, eager to get in the fight, the minutes spent under the rain of arrows sharpening their aggression.

Gaius brought the *Virtus* through the turn, keeping the ram on a line to the rudder of the quadrireme, now only fifty yards ahead. The quadrireme began to slow further, the breaking waves of the shoals enveloping her bow as she entered the channel, and Gaius called for battle speed, keeping his pace above that of the Rhodian's, not needing to antici-pate the turns in the channel in the wake of the quadrireme pathfinder.

Atticus looked over the side to the waters below. Only half

the oars of the *Virtus* were still engaged, the others having been withdrawn, the rowers collapsed upon them. The sea seemed to boil on all sides and Atticus could see the deadly fangs of the shoals piercing the surface of the water not twenty yards from the hull.

'Best guess,' he said to Gaius. 'Get us alongside the aft-deck.'

The helmsman nodded, his eyes never leaving his prey. The chase was over but the mortal stroke had yet to be delivered. It was impossible to guess what sea room was available in the channel and Gaius knew he would have to judge which side to attack from the manoeuvres of the quadrireme. It was a difficult task, but as he saw the prefect hesitate at his side, ready to offer help, he broke eye contact with the quadrireme for the first time.

'Go,' he said vehemently. 'I have her.'

Atticus nodded and ran from the aft-deck, the crew responding to his flight by gathering in a wave behind him. He drew his sword, a commitment that was echoed by his men and, as he reached the foredeck, he grabbed a discarded *hoplon* shield.

The crews roared at each other across the gap, battle cries and challenges, while arrows were loosed at near point-blank range, the barbs striking deeply into shield and flesh, fuelling the belligerence of each crew. Atticus stood silent amongst his men, his shield held tightly against his shoulder as he looked to the waters around the stern of the quadrireme, trying to discern the sea room, to give Gaius some advantage.

The two galleys sped through a turn in the channel but, as the quadrireme straightened out, Gaius continued the turn for a second longer, the nimbler hull of the trireme cutting inside the line of the bend. Atticus felt the hull buck beneath him as Gaius called for attack speed, a final push from the exhausted rowers to bring the port bow quarter in line with the starboard aft of the quadrireme.

'Grappling hooks,' Atticus shouted without conscious thought, and a line was thrown but instantly parted under the strain of the uneven stroke of the galleys. A dozen more followed, the majority finding purchase, to be attacked by the Rhodian's crew with axes and swords.

The Romans drew the remaining lines in, heaving them hand over hand until the hulls slammed against each other, the timbers grating, the galleys reluctantly giving way to each other's pitch. Atticus led the men over the rails with a roar that unleashed their savagery, and they jumped across the treacherous maw of the clashing hulls to slam into the first rank of the defenders, their momentum checked then revived as they gained a foothold on the enemy deck.

Atticus kept his shield at chest height, slashing forward with his sword, his eyes locked on those of the defender before him, the man's eyes wide with anger, but they suddenly dropped low, signalling the strike of the sword. Atticus dropped his shield to counter the blow before driving his blade to the flank, the defender reacting with incredible speed to parry the strike. He came on again and Atticus reversed his block to push the sword away, exposing the defender's torso and, risking all, he threw his body off balance to bring his sword to bear, the defender trying to react as he sensed the unexpected strike, his reflexes too slow to avoid the blade. Atticus punched the sword through, twisting the blade as it sank into the defender's stomach, and he whipped it back to free it, a gush of warm blood and viscera spilling out over his hand. He pushed forward against the dying man with his shield, knocking him underfoot to the deck.

The aft-deck was in chaos but slowly the Romans made headway, their numbers twice those of the Rhodian. The helmsman never left the tiller as the battle raged, his eyes ever locked on the shoals and the narrow line of the channel; but, as the battle line advanced beyond him, he fell under the slash of a Roman sword. Released from the control of the rudder, the bow of the *Ares* skewed sideways, the pressure of the *Virtus*'s bow against its stern hastening the turn, and the strake timbers of the bow struck the shoals that clawed out from the edge of the channel.

The battle descended into a ferocious brawl as the Rhodian's men felt their ship shudder beneath them. They roared in anger and hatred, stopping the Roman advance on the fringes of the main deck. The Romans rebuked the challenge, giving no quarter, and the line of battle steadied as each side fed more men into the fray, the opposing ranks becoming increasingly intertwined as anarchy reigned.

Atticus surged forward in frustration, the din of war filling the air around him, his ears ringing with the sound of his own blood rush, the numbness of his sword arm ignored as he thrust it forward into the groin of a defender, slicing the flesh cleanly, taking no respite as he withdrew his blade to attack again. His chest ached from an old wound, the tightness squeezing the vice of his anger, and he shoved a man back with his shield to expose him to the blade. He looked around him, searching the faces of the defenders for some sign of submission, that they were nearing the end of their resolve, but each face was twisted in courageous defiance.

He spotted a man in the centre of the mêlée, his sword charged but not engaged, shouting orders to men around him, his shaven head splattered with the blood of the slain and injured, his reddened blade testament to his skill. It was the captain, Atticus realized in a moment of clarity, the Rhodian. He roared a challenge across the fight in gutter Greek, the language of a native, and the Rhodian turned to the voice, seeing the scarred face of his challenger amidst the ranks of the Romans. Perennis, he cursed, and he surged forward through the fights around him to charge the precipitator of his doom.

Atticus came on against the Rhodian's charge, keeping his body low to maintain his balance on the blood-soaked and body-strewn deck. He shoved a man aside, keeping his line straight, and bunched his weight behind his shield, his battle lust pouring out of him in a guttural roar of challenge that the Rhodian answered with his own cry. They reached each other amidst the heaving fight. Atticus slammed his shield into the Rhodian to unbalance him, jabbing his sword forward; but his blade was immediately knocked down with a force that jarred the muscles of his arm and Atticus realized he was well matched. He dropped his shield an inch and stared into his opponent's face, seeing past the fearsome mask of hostility to the eyes, readying himself for the assault.

Calix broke away to put the strength of his shoulder behind his strike. He brought his sword around like a scythe, the blade whistling through the air. Atticus reacted instinctively, a lifetime's training guiding his arm, and he dropped his shield to accept the strike, the hammer blow knocking him off balance. He recovered with a counter-stroke, but with incredible dexterity the Rhodian reversed the strike and Atticus, acting on sheer reflex, parried the killing thrust with his sword, twisting his wrist to expel the Rhodian's blade from inside his guard.

The steel swords rasped together and Atticus took a step back, regaining his balance as he drew breath before renewing his attack. Calix met him head on, both men unable to sidestep on the crowded deck, and again they were locked chest to chest, their faces inches from each other and the sweat and breath of the Rhodian mingled with Atticus's own in his nostrils. He shifted his weight to his right foot, using his left to propel him forward and swung his sword around, but in the crowded fight his blade caught on an unseen soldier, and the Rhodian's eyes flashed with triumph, his opponent exposed. He lunged forward inside the attack and Atticus, unable to give ground on the perilously slippery deck, was forced into a desperate defence.

He hooked his arm around to parry with his sword but the Rhodian pushed forward relentlessly, switching his attack from left to right and back, breaking his own rhythm with unexpected twists that kept Atticus on the back foot. The tortured muscles of his sword arm conspired with his laboured breathing to feed the creeping panic that clouded his mind as each strike of the ceaseless attack came within a hair's-breadth of penetrating his frantic defence. He fought on, the battle surrounding him blurring into insignificance, his reactions to the Rhodian's blade predetermined by reflexes and innate skill.

Atticus could see nothing beyond his opponent and the flash of steel between them. He was close to defeat and the realization stirred the fury within him. He had brought this fight to the Rhodian. This was his battle, fought on his terms, and suddenly his panic ceased, replaced with a cold determination.

The Rhodian brought his blade in low and Atticus swept it aside, reversing the parry, forcing the other to bring his shield down to stifle the blade. In the same instant, Atticus swung his own *hoplon* around, slamming it in the Rhodian's exposed shoulder. He staggered backwards to regain his balance.

Atticus followed through, keeping the Rhodian off balance, and the roles were neatly reversed, Atticus tapping every reserve of his strength, knowing he needed to end the fight, that he was close to reaching his limits. He swung his blade through a series of strokes, a recurring sequence of cut and thrust, purposefully allowing a deadly predictability to creep into his attack while he watched the Rhodian's face intently, waiting to see the first signs of recognition that the attack had become rhythmic.

Calix could not give ground on the crowded deck and he stood firm, his mind numb to the searing pain in his chest as he parried blow after blow. The attack was unceasing, Perennis's strength seemingly limitless, and Calix started to search desperately for a way out. He had information the Romans could use – it was his only advantage; but as he made to utter a call for surrender, his warrior's instincts registered a fatal flaw in Perennis's attack, and he readied himself for what he knew would be the final strike.

Atticus saw it, the tiny light of triumph in the Rhodian's eyes, and he suddenly broke the rhythm that had lulled the Rhodian, reversing his blade at the arc of his stroke to swipe inside the Rhodian's defence. The Rhodian was completely unprepared and Atticus's sword sliced cleanly into the under-side of his opponent's outstretched arm, cutting through muscle and flesh until the blade met the smooth edge of the bone. The Rhodian cried out in pain and his sword fell from lifeless fingers. Atticus pulled his own blade clear to deliver the killing stroke, arching back, his eyes still locked on the Rhodian's, seeing there the desperation of defeat. The Rhodian's shield fell, his hand clasping his wound, trying to staunch the flow of blood, and his eyes came level with his executioner's.

'Quarter, Perennis,' the Rhodian shouted, the shock of hearing his name causing Atticus to hesitate. He twisted his blade aside, staying his attack to bring the tip of his sword up to the Rhodian's neck.

'Your fleet,' the Rhodian gasped, knowing death was still at hand. 'Your fleet is in danger . . .'

Atticus remained poised to strike the Rhodian down, his sword hand trembling with suppressed battle rage, but the Rhodian's words forced his hand.

'Order your men to stand down,' he shouted through parched lips.

The Rhodian quickly complied, calling on his crew to lower their weapons, and the outnumbered mercenaries followed his order, stepping back from their attackers, their arms held out as they looked about the ruin that was the deck of the *Ares*.

Atticus lowered his sword from the Rhodian's neck, although he kept it charged, knowing the conflict that rages within the mind of a defeated foe, the sudden shame that can sweep a man who has surrendered his arms, a shame that can compel him to restart the fight. His crew did likewise and they moved forward quickly to distance the mercenaries from their fallen weapons, ordering them to relinquish their remaining blades.

Atticus stepped back and stared at the Greek mercenary. His face was drawn in a grimace of pain, but his eyes remained defiant and he held Atticus's gaze.

'I have information that can save your fleet from defeat,' he said, his words coming slowly through ragged breaths.

'What information?' Atticus asked impatiently.

'The location and size of the Carthaginian fleet,' Calix replied.

'Where are they?' Atticus asked.

'I will speak only with the consul,' Calix said, knowing he had to regain some measure of control over his own fate if he was to survive. His contract, and therefore his loyalty to Hamilcar, was severed the moment he surrendered, rendered void by his inability to complete the task. Now his loyalty extended only to the task of securing his own freedom.

Atticus stepped forward once more, angered by the Rhodian's evasion. 'You will tell me now, Rhodian,' he spat, 'or I will have my men torture you until you do.'

'You are no fool, Perennis,' Calix replied evenly, straightening his back to stand tall, his face twitching slightly from the incessant pain in his arm. 'You know my information will be more valuable if I give it willingly.'

Atticus knew the Rhodian was right, that a man would confess anything under torture, even untruths. He relented and brusquely ordered his men to take the Rhodian back to the *Virtus*.

He watched them leave and then looked down to the deck and the carnage that the few minutes of fighting had wrought. The quadrireme was taken, the blockade once more secure, but the cost had been high and Atticus counted a score of fallen men, Roman sailors who had charged fearlessly into the fight. He stepped through their ranks slowly, and then crossed once more to the *Virtus*, quickly making arrangements for a prize crew to take command of the Rhodian's galley.

Within minutes Gaius had the *Virtus* under way, turning its course to the northern end of the bay as it cleared the channel, the *Orcus* falling into its wake. Atticus stood on the aft-deck, watching quietly as a sailor bandaged the wound on the Rhodian's arm. The fight was won but the Rhodian had increased the prize. Capturing the quadrireme had become only a part. The Rhodian's knowledge was the balance and Atticus was determined to take his full measure of its worth.

Atticus coughed violently as the dust thrown up by the horse's hooves coated the back of his parched throat. The effort to breathe hurt his chest and he gazed through exhausted eyes to the main gate of the legion encampment ahead. The rush of battle that had possessed him only an hour before had fled, and he looked grimly to the charred remains of the siege towers two hundred yards away. They were being picked over by a dozen soot-stained soldiers, searching for salvageable remains of iron, like ants scavenging a carcass after a larger predator has eaten its fill.

Atticus looked to his own blood- and sweat-stained tunic, blacked by the fires of battle. Then he glanced at Ovidius, the Roman prefect, riding by his side, at his immaculate tribune's uniform. He felt no inferiority, though; he was glad he had been able to locate his fellow fleet commander as he landed on the northern shore of the bay, knowing he too needed to hear the Rhodian's information first hand. He saw Ovidius glance at the cavalry troop in their wake and the prisoner in their midst, noting with satisfaction that the Roman prefect had taken Atticus at his word and was conscious of the importance of the Rhodian.

The horsemen rode through the gates unchallenged, many of the legionaries looking with undisguised curiosity at the ragged sailor riding shoulder to shoulder with the tribune. They made their way directly to the command tent in the middle of the encampment, dismounting even as their horses slowed, and Atticus felt a renewed surge of energy flood his reserves as he watched two cavalrymen manhandle the wounded Rhodian from his mount. An *optio* approached Ovidius and, following a terse request, withdrew into the tent, reappearing after a minute to summon the men forward. Ovidius led Atticus and the Rhodian inside.

The interior was bathed in canvas-filtered sunlight, subdued by the dark rugs underfoot. After a brief pause inside the threshold, the men stepped forward. Scipio was seated at the far end of the tent, behind a dark stained desk, a solid piece built for the rigours of a campaign; but closer inspection revealed the intricacies of its elaborate carvings, the work of master craftsmen. His face was drawn with irritation and he barely acknowledged the salutes of his two prefects, his eyes darting to each in turn but lingering a second longer on Atticus.

'Speak,' he said to Ovidius.

'Prefect Perennis,' Ovidius began, glancing at Atticus, 'captured this man and his crew as they tried to run the blockade earlier this morning. He is the mercenary known as the Rhodian.'

Scipio shrugged his shoulders imperceptibly, looking to the wounded man behind Ovidius.

'And . . .?' he said impatiently.

'He claims the fleet is in danger from a Carthaginian attack,' Atticus interjected, hiding his own impatience, wary as always of Scipio's hostility.

'Claims?' Scipio said.

'He knows the location of the enemy fleet, Consul,' Atticus continued.

'Where is it?' Scipio asked.

'He will not say. He demanded to speak only to you, Consul,' Atticus explained. 'And, given the importance of the information, I judged it best that it was given willingly.'

'You are a fool, Perennis,' Scipio said dismissively. 'He is bargaining for his life. He would say anything.'

Atticus bristled at the insult.

'I believe him, Consul,' he said through gritted teeth. 'He escaped this harbour days ago carrying Carthaginian officers, and when captured today those men were not on board. With the wind shift in the past twenty-four hours, I believe they must have disembarked at some location not a day's sailing from here.'

'They could have transshipped to another galley,' Scipio said mockingly, 'or simply landed somewhere along the coast.'

'I brought them to their fleet,' Calix said, speaking for the first time, noting the open hostility the consul displayed towards the Greek prefect. The identity of his passenger entered his mind, but Calix chose to retain that information, knowing he needed to keep something in reserve to strengthen his bargaining position.

Scipio grunted in reply but he tempered his scornful remarks, the seeds of fortune and opportunity combining in his mind. Perhaps this was his chance to go on the offensive. He beckoned the Rhodian forward with a wave of his hand.

'You are who Perennis claims you are?' he asked.

'My name is Calix.'

'But men call you the Rhodian?' Scipio said, smiling coldly at the confident tone of the captured captain.

'I am of that island,' Calix replied.

'So you too are Greek,' he said slowly, the smile falling from his face. 'Like the mercenaries who attacked the siege towers.' And he glanced unconsciously at Atticus.

Calix saw the sideward glance. 'I know nothing of them,' he said. 'I was hired by the Carthaginians for a specific task, as I was hired by the Romans in the past.'

Scipio's eyebrows rose in surprise and he leaned forward, his interest piqued by the revelation. 'When were you hired by the Romans?' he asked, and Calix listed the operations he had carried out at the beginning of the war.

Scipio sat back again, intrigued by the mercenary's obvious indifference to both sides in the conflict, his adherence to any cause purchased only for the length of a single contract. Scipio had known and manipulated men of this sort his entire career, and he knew the measure of their loyalty, and how easily it could be bought.

'So now you will reveal the location of the Carthaginian fleet in exchange for your life?' Scipio asked and Calix nodded.

'Where is it?' Scipio asked.

'You will release me?' Calix said.

Scipio nodded.

'The Carthaginian fleet is anchored at Drepana.'

'How many?' Atticus asked.

'Over one hundred galleys,' Calix replied over his shoulder. He turned back to Scipio. 'They are planning an attack. I do not know when.'

Again Scipio nodded.

'Guards,' he called, and four legionaries entered.

'Take this man to the guardhouse and hold him there,' he said.

'But our agreement,' Calix said angrily.

'Will be honoured when we have confirmed your information,' Scipio said dismissively, and he returned the Rhodian's hostile gaze as he was escorted out.

Calix followed the legionaries across the beaten earth in the centre of the encampment, the acid bile of anger in his throat. He swallowed his fury, knowing he needed to remain calm. The consul's actions were not wholly unexpected and Calix focused on the remaining information he held. The Romans would have confirmation of his report when they reached Drepana and, whether they attacked or remained in defence, the identity of the Carthaginian commander was salient information.

Calix suddenly recalled the hostility he had witnessed towards Perennis. The Greek prefect had been victorious, had taken a valuable ship as a prize, and yet the Roman consul had offered no praise. He had even looked at Perennis when he spoke of the attacks perpetrated by Greek mercenaries. Such an open schism was an obvious weakness and Calix kept it at the forefront of his thoughts, knowing that if he were to escape with his life, he would need every advantage he could gain.

Scipio looked to Atticus and Ovidius in the silence that followed the Rhodian's departure, his mind already formulating a plan, a mortal blow to the Carthaginian fleet.

'How far is Drepana?' he asked of the two men before him.

'No more than four hours,' Atticus replied. 'We must plan our defence so we can be ready at a moment's notice.'

'Our defence?' Scipio said incredulously. 'By the gods, Perennis, you Greeks are a timid race. We will attack, immediately.'

'We cannot, Consul,' Atticus said, struggling to contain his anger against Scipio's hostility and denigration. 'The men of the new fleet aren't ready for an open, offensive battle.'

'We have surprise and numbers on our side, Perennis,' Scipio said, a cold edge to his voice. 'If you have not the courage to fight on even these advantageous terms, then I shall remove you from your command.'

Atticus took a half-step forward to retort, but Ovidius spoke first.

'We can be ready to sail by nightfall, Consul,' he said, looking to break the conversation between the other two men. He did not know the source of the consul's antagonism towards the prefect, but he was eager to deflect it, confident in the opinion he had formed of the Greek since arriving in Lilybaeum.

This was Ovidius's first naval command, granted to him weeks before in Rome when he was tasked with sailing the first contingent of the new fleet south to the Aegates Islands in preparation for the siege of Lilybaeum. Unfamiliar with naval warfare, he relied heavily on the experienced captains of his squadron, and had spoken to each exhaustively over the course of the monotonous weeks of the blockade. The Greek prefect's name had been mentioned many times, and Ovidius had quickly become aware of the high regard in which the men held him.

He did not understand the Greek's hesitation and agreed with the consul's assertion, but he also knew it was in the fleet's best interest for Perennis to retain command of his squadron.

'By nightfall,' Scipio said, looking to Ovidius, the distraction causing his mind to focus once more on the incredible opportunity the Rhodian's information had unlocked. He pushed his anger aside.

'Yes, Consul,' Ovidius replied. 'We can sail up the coast during the night and attack at dawn, and a night approach will ensure the Carthaginians are not forewarned by land.'

Scipio stood up in anticipation. 'Ready the fleet, Ovidius,' he said, striding around the table. 'We sail at dusk.'

Ovidius saluted and as he made to turn he saw the Greek ready himself to argue once more. He grabbed him by the arm, staying Atticus's words, and led him from the tent.

Once outside, Atticus shrugged off Ovidius's hand angrily.

'This is madness, Ovidius,' he said. 'We cannot fight the Carthaginians on their terms, not yet.'

Ovidius held Atticus's hostile gaze. 'The battle will not be on their terms, Perennis,' Ovidius replied. 'We have surprise on our side.'

'It will not be enough,' Atticus said, not even convinced the Roman fleet could carry off a night approach. He looked once more to Scipio's tent, the frustration of knowing his opinion counted for naught consuming him, seeing in Scipio the arrogant figure of Paullus before the storm.

Ovidius watched Atticus closely and stepped forward once more.

'You do not know me, Perennis,' he said evenly. 'But I know of you. Take command of the vanguard. The honour is yours.'

Atticus turned to Ovidius, noticing the same unwavering

confidence he had witnessed so many times before in other Roman officers, the indomitable self-assurance that could not be shaken. Ovidius slapped him on the shoulder and mounted his horse once more, the stallion wheeling in a tight circle before the Roman spurred it towards the gate. Atticus watched him leave and then mounted himself. He looked to the sun, its zenith already passed, and he spurred his horse in pursuit of the Roman prefect.

CHAPTER FOURTEEN

The day dawned under a leaden sky, prolonging the long dark hours of the night. The sea was troubled, the swell erratic and grey, like twisted cold metal long since cast aside from the furnace. The southwesterly wind had tormented the Roman fleet throughout the night, further complicating the already difficult task of maintaining the cohesion of the attack formation, and the dawn light revealed a seascape littered with individual galleys.

Scipio stood alone on the foredeck of his flagship, the *Poena*, his anticipation honed to a keen edge after long hours of waiting, his mind playing out his future. He breathed in the moist air, expanding his chest until the straps of his armour restrained him. He had spent his youth in the legions, pursuing the path that all ambitious men in Rome must tread, his legitimacy in the Senate as a military leader founded on the bedrock of legionary service. Now the armour felt light across his chest, a second skin he had long since grown accustomed to.

Those years in the legions had embedded many traits within his character, particularly patience, a skill he had developed during his time in the Senate into an almost impenetrable armour of self-discipline. Only hatred for his enemies pierced that armour, and not for the first time since sailing from

268

Lilybaeum four hours before, Scipio felt the white heat of his temper overwhelm him, his mind swimming with the vision of one man whom he had sought to destroy at his ease but whose very existence was becoming too vexing to bear.

He turned and strode from the foredeck, the alert crew of the *Poena* stepping aside to allow him passage, wary of unwittingly colliding with the consul, an accident that would undoubtedly result in summary punishment. Scipio watched the crew as he stood on the main deck, looking beyond them to the ragged formation of the Roman fleet in surrounding waters. He felt his previous confidence ebb, and he cursed the creeping doubts with which the Greek had infected him. Battle was imminent, the enemy lying just beyond the horizon, outnumbered and unaware, and yet Scipio could not shake the warning uttered by Perennis.

He reached the aft-deck and beckoned the priest to his side, the older man moving deferentially towards the consul. Scipio glanced over his shoulder and immediately saw that many of the crew were watching surreptitiously. He nodded to himself. They would bear witness to the simple ceremony, its outcome putting mettle into their resolve, and Scipio would get the signalmen to spread the word across the fleet.

It was an arcane and ancient ritual, one Scipio had seen many times but had never held in any esteem, believing his fate to be controlled by a higher power than the creatures the priest carried in his hand. Today, however, on the eve of what would be his greatest victory, Scipio needed to dispel the curse of uncertainty, that slight shift in his confidence that he barely acknowledged even to himself. This ritual would cleanse him and, as Scipio watched the priest prepare for the almost farcical ceremony, he silently vowed that Perennis would never again stand tall in his presence. After today, he would finally break him. Whether he put him to the sword or to a galley oar in chains, Scipio would be rid of the Greek.

The priest began a slowly incantation, calling on the god Mars to rise up from his slumber and stand astride the battlefield over the ranks of the Roman forces, to look down upon the enemy over the shoulder of every legionary, to put his strength into the sword arm of every son of Rome so he might strike down the foe who would dare to defy him. Scipio listened to the droning voice, seeing past the words to the subtle essence of the invocation, allowing it to fill his heart while, behind him, the entire crew of the *Poena* ceased their tasks to gaze upon the ceremony.

The priest held out his left hand and scattered the grain on the timber deck, his voice becoming stronger as he crouched down to release the three chickens in his right hand, the birds squawking loudly as they flapped their clipped wings and found their feet. These birds were sacred, bred to perform in this one simple ceremony and complete a basic task that would signify that the gods favoured the Romans in the battle to come: eat the proffered grain.

Scipio stood silently watching the chickens circle the scattered seeds, his doubts already dispelled by the formality and reverence of the ceremony. He felt his confidence rise, and he held his breath in anticipation of the first peck of the chickens' beaks, ready to use that moment of fulfilment of the ceremony to rouse the crew of the *Poena* and the fleet.

A minute passed, followed by another, and still the chickens would not eat, their seemingly aimless steps across the grain scattered beneath them breaking the previous spell of the ritual. Scipio looked to the priest, his expression twisting into furious anger, and the priest immediately crouched to shepherd the birds to the centre of the grain. Scipio felt a groundswell of superstitious fear sweep the crew behind, their muttered concerns rising to a cacophony of open alarm.

He rounded on them, glaring at those nearest, but they looked past him to the birds. He spun around again and charged at the priest, pushing him aside as his temper slipped its bounds. He picked up a chicken, squeezing its neck in his hands, the bird's squawking increasing. He held the bird aloft and turned to the crew.

'If they refuse to eat, then let them drink,' he shouted, and he cast the bird over the side of the galley, reaching around to gather up the other two quickly and throwing them over with equal fury.

The crew stood aghast at the sacrilege. Scipio again lost control as he shouted at them to continue their preparations for battle, his voice and raw fury breaking the spell of their shock, but each man turned away with fear in his heart. The gods had spoken. If the Romans joined battle, they would do so alone, without the favour of Mars.

Scipio watched through the mists of his own anger as the last of the disillusioned crew went back to work. He strode to the side rail, past the cowering priest who was trying to avoid the consul's wrath. The birds were lost from sight some- where in the wake of the *Poena* and Scipio felt the cold hand of doubt close over him once more. He crushed it mercilessly, banishing the ill omen of the ceremony from his mind, dismissing it for what he had always believed it to be, a super- stition from an ancient, unenlightened time. He redirected his anger, letting it fill the void caused by his lost confidence, using it to steel his will. Perennis had precipitated this weak- ness, the Greek whoreson whom Scipio now realized he should have disposed of months before, despite his usefulness.

He looked to the brightening horizon, and the long line of Roman galleys sailing northward towards the enemy at Drepana. The battle was at hand, the odds unchanged, and victory was within Scipio's grasp. He would triumph this day and, after the last Roman blade had been drawn across Carthaginian flesh, Scipio vowed he would turn that steel against Perennis.

Drepana slumbered unawares, with much of the city still enveloped in the fading darkness of early dawn, the shadows giving way slowly under a dawn light struggling to overcome the heavy cloud cover. The city was built on a peninsula that stretched westward out to sea, and Atticus looked slowly along its entire length, his eyes moving upwards to the lines of trailing smoke that marked the first cooking fires of the day, and the dying torches on the battlements of the city walls. All was quiet and Atticus nodded grimly with satisfaction. The night approach had succeeded, no warning had been received in Drepana by land; but as Atticus turned to look behind him, he conceded that the price of that success had been significant.

The Roman fleet was strung out in a loose formation that reached to the southern horizon and, although the individual captains of Atticus's squadron were already closing ranks, beyond this vanguard the fleet was in complete disorder. Drepana's inner harbour was but three miles away; if the Carthaginians were to be blockaded in the narrow inlet at the base of the peninsula, the Romans would need to strike with the force of a clenched fist, not with an open-handed cuff. He looked to the four points of his galley. The choice was clear. Slow his advance to allow the fleet to coalesce and concentrate its strength and run the risk of the element of surprise being lost, or strike now with the vanguard alone, a force that might be inadequate to the task.

'Enemy galleys off the port bow. Two miles.'

Atticus followed Corin's call and immediately spotted the darkened hulls of the two patrol galleys. They were sailing in the lee of the two elongated islands beyond the tip of the peninsula. As Atticus watched, they turned their bows eastwards in the direction of the inner harbour, the galleys becoming almost invisible as they sailed under the shadows of the city walls.

Atticus cursed. Fortuna had usurped his choice and forced his hand. 'Battle speed,' he shouted.

The crew rushed to secure the mainsail for battle. Drusus ordered the legionaries to form ranks. The restlessness of a night's sailing was thrown off. The squadron was signalled and, before a mile was covered, the *Orcus* was sailing at the tip of a slowly forming spearhead.

Atticus stepped to the side rail and leaned out over the water. The wind had fallen away but the speed of the galley swept the cold morning air over his face. He looked down the length of the hull to the bronze ram slicing through the lead-coloured waves and studied the swell, judging the strength of the tide. It was on the turn, offering no advantage to either side. He looked beyond. The patrol galleys were entering the inner harbour at what was at least attack speed, a perilous pace given the narrow approach.

Atticus realized that everything now depended on the calibre of the Carthaginian commander. If he was competent, the enemy fleet would stand ready to slip their anchors at a moment's notice; if not, then Atticus had a reasonable chance of ending the battle before it could begin. He glanced over his shoulder. The vanguard was still not fully formed, the fleet beyond too far out of position to assist. His squadron would meet the enemy alone. He smiled grimly as he turned to the helm. He had known worse odds.

'Patrol ships returning at attack speed,' the lookout called, and Hamilcar ran the length of the *Alissar* to the foredeck, leaning out over the rail to look to the entrance of the inner harbour.

'All commands, battle stations,' he shouted without hesitation, his gaze locked on the approaching galleys, their reckless pace alerting him to the unseen danger.

The Carthaginian crews reacted quickly, the general order sweeping down the length of the anchored fleet. The *Alissar* slipped its stern line and shoved off, her oars finding firm purchase in the deep-water inlet. Her bow swung out of the anchored formation, the patrol ships adjusting their course as they saw the flagship emerge from the ranks.

Hamilcar watched the fleet come alive with a critical eye, looking to each galley in turn. The Gadir fleet had been poised to sail for the past two days, awaiting only a favourable wind to carry them to the Aegates Islands, where they would make their final preparations before sailing to Lilybaeum, there to be unleashed upon the unsuspecting Roman blockade. The men were prepared for a battle in a distant port, not in the narrows of Drepana, but they were responding to the unexpected order without panic, their urgency tightly controlled as each galley became a drawn bow, ready to be loosed upon the enemy.

The *Alissar* sailed down the length of the fleet, many of the men cheering as the flagship swept past their bow, but Hamilcar ignored their calls, his eyes locked on the approaching patrol ships. He moved to the foredeck as the order for 'all stop' was given on all three converging ships, and he listened intently to the captains' reports, making his decisions even as they finished, ignoring the inner voice in his mind that cursed the vicissitude of Tanit, the fickle goddess of fate who had somehow reversed his plans to surprise attack the Romans.

He looked to the entrance of the inlet. Escape was the first priority and he ordered the *Alissar* to restart at battle speed, the order flashing down the length of the fleet, the report of enemy sighted and the flagship's lead pressing the men to greater speed.

The *Alissar* neared the entrance and Hamilcar anxiously counted the yards left to cover, glancing over his shoulder at the fleet rapidly forming in the wake of the flagship. The inlet was no more than two hundred yards across at its widest point, a safe anchorage in foul weather but a deathtrap in battle, and he whispered a silent prayer to Anath to grant him the time he needed to extract his fleet from the jaws of captivity.

Hamilcar ran to the portside rail as the *Alissar* breached the mouth of the inlet, his gaze taking in the entire vista of the southern approaches to Drepana before he could draw a single breath. A spearhead of Roman galleys was but half a mile away, approaching at attack speed, the galleys rigged for battle, and Hamilcar cursed the sight, slamming his hand on the side rail. The fleet would escape the inlet but the initiative was lost, and with its loss, the fate of Drepana hung in the balance. He searched his mind for a strategy to reverse the Romans' ascendancy, but the sight of the Roman fleet behind the spearhead stopped him short, the advance of the *Alissar* affording him a better view with each passing oar stroke.

The enemy ships were scattered across the southern approaches, an inexplicable arrangement that for many seconds eluded Hamilcar's comprehension, until he realized that it was accidental, caused by the Romans' inability to maintain shape during their night approach. He smiled savagely and looked back to the tight formation of the Gadir fleet, the galleys sailing with only yards between them, even though they were advancing at attack speed, the incredible skill of each helmsman matched by those fore and aft of his position.

He turned to the Roman spearhead, now less than a hundred yards from the entrance of the inner harbour. No more than forty ships, too few to stop the escape of the Gadir fleet, and Hamilcar repentantly withdrew his censure of Tanit, knowing that had the entire Roman fleet kept pace with the vanguard, his ships would have been annihilated in the bottleneck of the inlet. He glanced once more at the spearhead, ready to dismiss it, when he suddenly recognized the lead ship, his immediate fury sending his hand instinctively to the hilt of his sword. It was Perennis's ship. The cursed Greek was leading the vanguard, and Hamilcar spun around to face the helmsman, tempted to turn the *Alissar* into the path of the spearhead.

He cursed loudly and turned to stare at the enemy once more. To attack the Roman vanguard would be to abandon the chance granted to him by the chaos of the enemy fleet. Its destruction was his priority, and for that he needed to extract his entire fleet from the inner harbour. The battle would be joined, the Gadir fleet unleashed, but Hamilcar now had a further objective. As the *Alissar* continued west under the shadow of Drepana, his eyes remained locked on his sworn enemy.

Atticus strode across the deck to the helm as the *Orcus* reached the southern edge of the inner harbour, his hand kneading the handle of his sword, his frustration of only minutes before – at seeing the leading galleys of the Carthaginian fleet emerge from the inlet – being slowly replaced with a sense of relief. The enemy seemed intent on escaping, sailing in a line astern formation a mere two hundred yards away at the other side of the inlet. Already over forty galleys were outside the bounds of the inner harbour, and although Atticus was in a position to strike at the enemy's flank, he knew the lead galleys of the Carthaginian fleet would immediately turn back into the fight and trap him.

Even as a coherent force, Atticus had little doubt in the Romans' chances against a determined Carthaginian fleet. A surprise blockade had been their only chance and, given that Scipio's ill-conceived plan of attack had been further weakened by the lack of coordination in the Roman fleet, the enemy's withdrawal was a godsend. He looked to the lead ship of the enemy fleet, remembering his previous thoughts on the calibre of the Carthaginian commander. His hand fell away from his sword in shock, his feet taking him unerringly to the side rail. He leaned against it, his gaze locked on the distant galley, the unmistakable masthead banners. Barca's ship.

He spun around, dread clawing at his stomach as he stared at the scattered Roman fleet. He knew Barca too well, knew he would not retreat in the face of such a disorganized and exposed foe. The Carthaginian fleet was not escaping. It was gaining sea room in order to regroup.

'Prefect . . .' Gaius said, alarmed by the look he saw on his commander's face.

The helmsman's voice snapped Atticus back.

'Full about,' he shouted, and Gaius reacted without hesitation, bringing the *Orcus* and the vanguard about at the entrance to the inner harbour.

The crews of the opposing fleets looked across at each other over two hundred yards of iron-grey sea, many of them in silence, while others shouted sporadic curses and threats, eager to engage with the enemy. They did not know the intentions of their commanders, the experienced crewmen knowing they were powerless to control their destiny, subject as they were to the commands of their officers, slaves to their judgement, never realizing that those men were subject to the same tempestuous fate.

*

'Confirm,' Scipio shouted impatiently to the masthead, striding across the width of the aft-deck, pausing at each rail in turn to look ahead. His command was followed by a moment's silence, prompting the captain to order a further two sailors aloft, eager to assuage the consul's impatience. The *Poena* was still two miles short of Drepana; from his position, Scipio was unable to see what was happening, his frustration quickly boiling over to compound his anger.

The lookout had reported the concentration of the vanguard and its advance towards the inner harbour, only to report minutes later that the Carthaginian fleet was escaping the confines of the inlet and sailing west in the lee of the city. The opportunity for a surprise attack had been lost and Scipio was immediately overcome by a sense of desperation, of helplessness, unable in his position at the rear of the fleet to bring the Carthaginians to battle.

'Confirmed, Consul,' one of the new lookouts called. 'The Carthaginian fleet is escaping. The vanguard did not reach the inner harbour in time.'

Scipio halted his incessant striding at the portside rail and watched the long line of Carthaginian galleys extend to the limits of the peninsula, the unmolested enemy ships in a tight formation that mocked the chaotic disposition of the Roman fleet.

'Shall I order battle stations, Consul?' the captain asked, wary of the proximity of so many enemy ships.

Scipio seemed not to hear him, his attention turning to the city.

'Consul?'

Scipio turned around irritably, his mind slowly absorbing the captain's original question. He waved his hand dismissively.

'No, it's hopeless,' he said. 'We are too far out of position to stop the Carthaginians escaping. We will advance to the inner harbour and take control of the city.'

The captain hesitated but thought better of challenging the consul, and he nodded his ascent, ordering the minor course change.

Scipio nodded to himself. Drepana was a small consolation given his original plans and he knew he would need to embellish his account of its capture if he was to gain any credit for such an insignificant victory. The Carthaginian fleet had escaped, the surprise attack had failed, and Scipio cursed the deities for robbing him of his victory.

'Hard to port, standard speed,' Hamilcar ordered, and the *Alissar* turned tightly around the seaward end of the narrow island, the vista to the fore of the flagship changing from the empty western horizon to the teeming waters of the southern approaches to Drepana. The galleys behind the *Alissar* began their turn as they reached the same location, each one dropping off a fraction of a point to sail beyond the flagship, maintaining battle speed until they came up on its starboard beam before dropping to standard speed, the formation rapidly extending into line abreast, the Carthaginians bringing their rams to bear on the Roman foe.

The low cloud cover and feeble sunlight reduced visibility to less than five miles but Hamilcar could see the entire Roman fleet was encapsulated within that sphere. His gaze swept over them, counting them quickly with a practised eye. He was outnumbered by at least thirty galleys, but the Romans were woefully out of position and Hamilcar now had the advantage of superior sea room.

He walked over to the helmsman and pointed out the cluster of galleys that made up the Roman vanguard under the command of Perennis, issuing the helmsman with a terse order. The Greek had extracted his galleys from the inner harbour in the time Hamilcar's ships had taken to sail the length of Drepana, and was now engaged in forming a defensive line. He nodded grimly. Perennis had anticipated his turn. It was not unexpected. He knew the Greek to be a skilful opponent. But he was the only one who had predicted the counter attack, and Hamilcar smiled as he looked upon the centre and southern flank of the Roman fleet, still advancing towards Drepana in a scattered screen of galleys.

Hamilcar felt the *Alissar* shift slightly beneath him; he looked along its length and onwards to the enemy formation a mile away. The helmsman was following his orders to the letter, keeping the *Alissar* fixed on the command ship of the vanguard, and he slapped him on the shoulder before striding away to check the unfolding formation of the Gadir fleet. The battle line was almost formed, the galleys still moving at standard speed, poised to accelerate to battle, attack and then ramming speed.

Hamilcar turned his focus to the Greek's ship. He would get only one chance, one opportunity to attack before having to withdraw to take command of the entire battle. He would not be able to order his men to board. There was no time; the overall battle was too important for him not to command personally. One ramming run would get him close enough. Then he would strike.

'Damn it, Baro,' Atticus shouted. 'Signal them to tighten the formation.'

Baro nodded and ran to the signalmen on the foredeck, skirting around the formation of legionaries on the main deck. Atticus looked to the western approaches and the rapidly forming Carthaginian battle line.

'Corin, report,' he shouted and looked up to the masthead. The lookout turned around and looked down to the aft-deck.

'Thirty galleys still sailing behind the line,' he shouted. 'No more than five more minutes.'

Atticus waved to acknowledge the report and looked anxiously to the remainder of the Roman fleet to the south of the vanguard. The line of his ships was being extended along the coastline by the galleys of Ovidius and, beyond, Scipio, the haphazard defence only slowly taking shape, the Roman captains taking their lead from the vanguard, while only a mile away the Carthaginian battle line was forming with deadly efficiency. Atticus turned to his helmsman.

'Gaius?' he asked, requesting his steady assessment.

The helmsman looked to the four points of the ship as his hand continued to move on the tiller, making minor adjustments to his own charge. He looked to Atticus.

'Our only chance is a tight defensive line,' he said. 'The Carthaginians will try to ram and they have the sea room to back water if we try to grapple them and board.'

Atticus nodded. He could see no other way, and his first command to form up on the coast remained sound.

He met Gaius's steady gaze. It was a testament to the helmsman's loyalty that Gaius had not questioned the overall strategy of the attack, or Atticus's part in its planning. Atticus had not discussed his reservations with any of the crew, but he knew Gaius would be of the same mind. The Roman fleet simply wasn't ready, and that disparity in skill would be compounded by an unfavourable position in the battle ahead.

Atticus took strength from Gaius's faith, using it to suppress his growing fear. The storm off the southern coast of Sicily had cost the fleet many ships and countless lives. Now a new storm was on the horizon less than a mile away, a tempest of steel and men, with a squall line of bronze rams that would overwhelm the exposed and vulnerable Roman fleet.

'They're advancing,' Corin called from the masthead. 'Estimate battle speed.'

'All hands, make ready,' Atticus shouted and the crew roared a defiant war cry, many of them looking to their commander standing firm on the aft-deck before focusing all of their attention on the oncoming enemy. Atticus spotted Baro on the main deck and called him to his side, wanting to bury their recent enmity in the face of a shared danger.

'They're moving to attack speed,' Corin called. 'Close formation.'

'Close formation . . .' Baro repeated to himself. 'To make sure we don't break through.'

Atticus nodded and turned to his second-in-command. 'Who says we want to escape?' he said with a wry smile.

Baro did not reply, the prefect's glib remark irking him, and he kept his gaze locked on the approaching enemy ships.

The sun broke through the low clouds with spears of light that reached down to the sea, turning great swathes of the surface from grey to blue. The *Alissar* sailed into one of the shafts at attack speed, her spear-like hull making a shade over twelve knots in the tideless waters. Hamilcar looked up to bathe his face in the heat of the sunlight. It was a good omen, the light of Shapash, the sun goddess, was upon them, and Hamilcar muttered a brief prayer of gratitude.

He looked to the main deck and the tight knot of men taking instructions from Himilco, the captain. Many were nodding grimly, glancing over their shoulders to the Roman line, and with a final command they broke to take up their assigned positions. Himilco returned to the aft-deck and saluted his commander.

'I have given them your instructions,' he said, and Hamilcar nodded in reply.

He looked to the bow and watched a solid line of shadow sweep along the length of the *Alissar* towards him as the quinquereme breached the outer edge of the shaft of sunlight. Shapash had bestowed her blessing, and Hamilcar looked to the Roman line less than three hundred yards away, wallowing in grey seas, their formation still not exact, even amongst the galleys of the Greek's command.

Hamilcar examined his decision one last time, knowing he was risking a great deal to strike this one blow against Perennis, concerned that his personal vendetta was clouding his judgement, but he quickly rationalized his choice, conceding that the Greek was one of the most skilled commanders in the Roman navy and his loss would be significant. His attack would be swift and brutal, specifically targeted to kill the Greek, and Hamilcar could trust Himilco to have the *Alissar* back in a command position before the battle was fully engaged. He nodded to himself, his remaining doubts dispelled, and he looked to the captain to issue the order of commitment.

'Ramming speed.'

Atticus looked along the length of the approaching Carthaginian battle line, the bows of the galleys dipping and rising out of sequence, like the heads of cavalry horses charging in line. He knew the Roman fleet should have advanced to meet the Carthaginians in the centre of the bay in order to gain some sea room, but that command had remained impossible. With many of the galleys still not in position, a ragged charge would have led to utter chaos. However disadvantageous, their only chance now was a defensive battle plan, with the Roman galleys remaining in close proximity to each other.

'Enemy galley on ramming course!'

'Battle speed, full ahead,' Atticus shouted, reacting instinctively to Corin's warning.

The rowers were holding the *Orcus* on station, the majority of them with their oars dipped in the water, but they moved with lightning speed to Atticus's command, all of them having heard Corin's call from the masthead, knowing that if the *Orcus* was holed they would share its doom.

Atticus ran to the side rail to look past his own main deck to the approaching galley. He recognized it instantly.

'Barca,' he uttered, knowing that the focused attack could not be mere coincidence, that the enemy commander had identified the *Orcus* as he had the Carthaginian's flagship. His hand fell to the hilt of his sword. The odds against the Roman fleet were staggering, but now there was a chance to sever the head of the serpent. The realization steeled his determination to strike down the Carthaginian commander whom he had fought too many times.

The one hundred-ton hull of the *Orcus* moved forward at a torturously slow pace, its previous inertia fighting the strength of the rowers.

'Your helm, Gaius,' Atticus said over his shoulder. 'Wait for the turn.'

Gaius nodded and lightened his touch on the tiller, his hand moving slightly from side to side, waiting for the moment when the speed of the hull would allow him sufficient rudder control to turn quickly. The *Orcus* might gain only a ship length in the time it took for the Carthaginian galley to cover the final gap, and in that limited sea room Gaius knew he would have only one chance to thwart the Carthaginian's ramming run, to foul the angle of attack and prevent the enemy's ram from penetrating the hull.

'One hundred yards,' Corin called.

'Steady . . .' Atticus said almost to himself as he returned to the helm, his trust in Gaius absolute.

'Prepare to repel boarders,' Baro shouted, and the sailing crew drew their swords, the legionaries following suit at the command of Drusus.

'Fifty yards . . .'

The *hastati* raised their *pila* spears, ready to loose them.

'Aspect change, turning to starboard,' Corin shouted frantically. Gaius reacted before Atticus could utter the command, the helmsman throwing the tiller hard over, the *Orcus* turning to port to counter the attack. Atticus nodded. Gaius had done it. The Carthaginians would not be able to cut back inside to ram. They would have to board over the bow rail and take the ship along its entire length, giving the defenders a greater chance. He drew his sword and braced his legs for the impact, Baro drawing his own blade beside him, while Gaius kept both hands on the tiller, the gap falling to thirty yards, twenty . . .

'They're withdrawing oars,' Corin shouted suddenly, panic in his voice. 'Starboard side . . .'

'They're going to sweep the oars!'

Again Gaius reacted without hesitation, but travelling at battle speed he could not turn quicker than a galley approaching at ramming speed, and the Carthaginian ship gained a yard on the starboard side as it covered the last ten.

Time slowed for Atticus as he watched the turn. His heart seemed to stop beating, overwhelmed by a surge of dread and anger, Barca's perfect ruse bringing a roar of utter defiance to his lips which he twisted into a forlorn command.

'Starboard oars, withdraw! All hands, brace for impact.'

The Carthaginian ram slammed into the starboard bow of the *Orcus*, striking the forward strake timbers with a force that heeled the *Orcus* over into the strike. The entire crew was thrown to the deck, the mainmast tilting over thirty degrees as the *Orcus* absorbed the blow, and Corin was thrown from the masthead, his cry cut short as he struck the water over the starboard side.

Atticus regained his feet and ran to the side rail. Corin had resurfaced, along with two other men who had fallen over the rail, and Atticus looked with horror at the approaching Carthaginian galley, the three men directly in its path. The deck beneath shuddered again, this time under the impact of the cutwater of the enemy galley striking the starboard oars, the sound of the fifteen-foot-long oars snapping was overwhelmed by the screams of the dying on the rowing deck, the remnants of the oars scything through the chained men on their mountings, killing any within their reach.

Atticus ran back to the helm, desperate to try and save Corin, to somehow turn his devastated galley into the sweep and gain a precious yard of distance on the starboard side. Gaius already had the tiller hard over, the portside oars hastening the turn, but at ramming speed the Carthaginian galley was moving too fast and Atticus looked again to the side rail, hearing the desperate cries of Corin and the others. He turned to Gaius, desperation in his eyes, helplessness overcoming him, his entire focus concentrated on saving his ship and crew, never seeing the approaching danger on the foredeck of the Carthaginian galley.

Hamilcar staggered as he ran the length of the main deck, the *Alissar* bucking wildly beneath him as it smashed through the oars of the Roman galley. The noise was overwhelming, the screams of dying men, the crack of oars snapping, the sporadic boom of the hulls slamming against each other as they reeled from the initial strike. He reached the foredeck within seconds and glanced over his shoulder to Himilco standing at the helm, his eyes locked on his commander, waiting for the order that would trigger his command to turn away from the stricken Roman galley and rejoin the battle at large.

The deck beneath Hamilcar was littered with the splinters of the shattered oars, while yet more rained down upon him as he came up behind the group of men he had stationed on the foredeck. They stood unmoving, their weapons poised in their hands. Hamilcar looked beyond them to the Roman galley, the mainmast now directly opposite him, now behind. He turned to the enemy aft-deck. Three men stood there and Hamilcar immediately recognized Perennis amongst them, issuing orders to his helmsman while frantically looking to the starboard rail. Hamilcar smiled coldly.

'Make ready,' he shouted above the cacophony of noise. His men raised their weapons.

Drusus stood stoically on the main deck of the *Orcus* at the head of his demi-maniple, his legs braced against the shudder of the deck beneath him, his expression murderous behind his raised shield, his eyes locked on the passing Carthaginian galley. As a soldier trained and forged in close combat, where you could smell the breath of your enemy, where the shadow of death was cast over all, the concept of attacking an enemy with impunity was abhorrent.

There was no honour in the naval tactics of ramming or sweeping oars, striking your foe with a crippling or even mortal blow, only to sail away without ever having faced down your enemy. That was not the way of the legions, and Drusus craved the chance to take the fight to the Carthaginians, hoping that they might yet board the *Orcus* and taste the steel of the men to his back.

A shattered piece of oar slammed into his shield. The bow of the Carthaginian galley passed, moving at the speed of a running man, and Drusus's eye was immediately drawn to the knot of men on the enemy foredeck, their attention fixed on the aft-deck of the *Orcus*, their intention clear. Drusus did not hesitate. He ran, shouting for his men to follow, the more alert reacting instantly, the Carthaginian galley outpacing them all as they raced to the aft-deck.

Atticus heard his name being called through the deafening noise and turned to the main deck. Drusus was running towards him with a half-dozen men, while behind him the rest of the maniple seemed in confusion, with many others turning to join the flight towards the aft-deck. The *optio* was screaming his name, pointing frantically to a point somewhere to Atticus's right, and he spun around.

The foredeck of the Carthaginian galley was all but level with his position and Atticus immediately saw the danger, the tight knot of archers with their bows drawn, their arrows pointing directly at him, Baro and Gaius. Behind them he saw Hamilcar, his gaze already locked on Atticus. Across the maelstrom of shattered oars and the wall of screams from the rowers below, Atticus saw the hatred pouring from Hamilcar's eyes and the triumphant, twisted smile on his face.

Atticus reacted without conscious thought, striking out with his left hand to shove Baro to the deck, dropping the sword from his right as he made to turn towards Gaius, his eyes still locked on Hamilcar, his mind registering the open mouth of his enemy, forming a single shouted command: loose.

The Carthaginians released their drawn bows as one, the trajectory of the arrows almost flat across the narrow gap, and Atticus immediately felt a solid deadening punch in his right shoulder and leg, the realization of the dual strikes flooding his mind with alarm, numbing his senses as the deck fell away from beneath him and his gaze swept across the iron-grey sky.

The air was blown from his lungs as he struck the deck. Sensations assailed him like waves crashing endlessly against a stricken hull; the struggle to breathe, the numbness in his shoulder and leg giving way to searing pain that built like heat in a furnace, his ears filled with cries of alarm as unseen bodies clamoured around him, the thud of arrows striking raised shields punctuating the endless noise.

He rolled on to his side, crying out in pain as the shaft of the arrow in his shoulder broke under the weight of his body. His hand shot to the wound, the blood gushing through his fingers, and his vision began to swim, a darkness creeping in on all sides. He roared a guttural cry of defiance, pushing back the darkness, knowing he needed to stay alive, that his ship was in danger, his crew.

He slammed his bloodstained hand on to the deck and pushed himself up, immediately seeing Baro taking cover behind the shield wall of Drusus's men while the *optio* shouted for his *hastati* to let fly on the escaping galley with their spears, a furious, hopeless order to exact some measure of vengeance.

Atticus turned his head, a wave of nausea sweeping over him; again he repressed it savagely. He looked to the helm, the tiller swinging steadily against the grey backdrop of the sky, and then he dropped his gaze to the deck, his heart breaking as he spotted Gaius not five feet away, the helmsman's eyes wide in fear, his bloodied hands clutching the shaft of an arrow that was protruding from his neck.

Atticus crawled across the deck, his own pain forgotten, his vision filled with the sight of Gaius. He reached out and grabbed Gaius's tunic with his left hand just as the helmsman began to fall, and he eased him on to the deck. Gaius's eyes locked on Atticus. He opened his mouth, blood gushing out to run down his cheeks. He tried to speak, his eyes opening wider in a silent plea as the words died on his lips, choked by blood and the terrible wound. Atticus put his hand to Gaius's cheek, quieting him, nodding slightly as if in under-standing, and the helmsman calmed, the pleading in his eyes turning to gratitude before death robbed them of their sight.

Hamilcar continued to look over his shoulder as the *Alissar* made its turn through the empty waters beyond the Romans' northernmost flank. The Greek's ship was drifting aimlessly, its starboard side a tangle of broken oars, the rail lined with men waving wildly at the *Alissar* to return and fight. The taunts were lost over the increasing distance, but Hamilcar still felt their sting, a part of him wanting to strike again and board Perennis's ship, to take it as a prize, to be the captain he once had been.

He turned and made his way back along the main deck, his thoughts on the frantic seconds of the attack, the moment of clarity before the order to loose, when Perennis had looked him in the eye. He recalled the arrows striking the Greek, knocking him to the deck, and the sudden arrival of the legionaries, their wall of shields blocking Hamilcar's chance to confirm the kill. He replayed the moment again and again in his mind, each time becoming more convinced that his attack had been successful, and with satisfaction he put the matter beyond doubt in his mind, knowing he needed to focus his energy on the greater battle.

The *Alissar* came about behind the Carthaginian battle line, affording Hamilcar an uninterrupted view of the fight. No Roman ship had yet broken through, the disciplined ranks of the Gadir fleet preventing any escape. The southern flank was more exposed; the disparity in numbers allowed for some Roman galleys to fall outside the net, but Hamilcar dismissed the loss as inconsequential, knowing the Roman centre was ensnared, its doom already sealed.

He would further concentrate his forces, squeezing the centre until it buckled under the strain, forcing a surrender that would give him a bounty of captured galleys, each one a replica of his own, save the calibre of the crew. At Drepana the sons of Carthage would prove their worth and write their claim upon the sea with Roman blood.

CHAPTER FIFTEEN

Baro looked anxiously beyond the wake of the *Orcus* as the dawn sun illuminated the seascape. The northern horizon seemed clear, devoid of any Carthaginian pursuit, the clouds dissipating over an empty sea. Nevertheless his fear remained, the endless tension of the previous twenty-four hours having shredded his nerves to breaking point, and his grip tightened involuntarily on the tiller, irritated by the slow rhythm of the drum beat below decks, wishing he could increase the tempo, despite the exhaustion of the remaining rowers.

He recalled the desperate hour after the Carthaginian galley had swept the starboard oars of the *Orcus*. The prefect was grievously injured, the helmsman dead, and so he had taken command, redistributing the rowers and oars below decks, getting the *Orcus* back under way with only one purpose in mind: escape. He had broken away from the northern flank, his flight followed by three other Roman galleys, one of which had been rammed and was taking water. He had cursed their company, believing where one galley might slip away, a group would be followed, but the Carthaginians were concentrating their attacks on the centre and the small flotilla had sailed west unmolested, away from the carnage of battle.

Now that flotilla was finally nearing Lilybaeum, and Baro looked again to the other ships. The damaged galley was off his starboard beam. The crew had strapped a canvas sail over the hull, lessening the inflow of water, but she was still listing badly, and the crew continued to fight a running battle against the ocean, with two lines of men baling out the lower hold. The others were undamaged but they maintained the same speed as their wounded sister ships, holding position on the outer flanks. A protective shield against an enemy that would overwhelm them in minutes, Baro thought sardonically.

He looked over his shoulder again, his growing confidence causing him to unconsciously glance down at the deck under the tiller, and the fate that might have been his. The blood there was turning black, staining the deck timbers with an indelible mark, as if the *Orcus* wanted to remember its helmsman. Baro had cast Gaius's body overboard during the night, the danger of pursuit – still existent at the time – forcing him to grant the helmsman only a perfunctory funeral. He looked away from the bloodstained deck, remembering the attack, a deep anger swelling within him.

The Greek had saved his life, had pushed him to the deck as the first flight of arrows struck, and the thought stirred his anger further. Baro believed that Perennis, as commander of the ship, was the obvious target, while he and Gaius had been unfortunate bystanders, the helmsman paying for that misfortune with his life.

'Lilybaeum ahead,' the lookout called, and the crew cheered, the shout taken up by the men on the other galleys.

Baro's mind remained enraged, however, his eyes fixed firmly on the waters ahead, his grip still tight on the tiller. The Greek was still his enemy, but now he was beholden to that whoreson for his life, a debt that was abhorrent to him. As the *Orcus* sailed ever closer to Lilybaeum, Baro began to hope that one other man had survived the slaughter at Drepana.

Scipio drew his sword with a fluid sweep of his arm and slashed the blade down with all his fury, striking the bulk-head timber with a force that embedded the blade two inches into the seasoned timber. He wrenched it aside, trying to free the weapon, shouting angrily as his temper slipped beyond control. Suddenly the blade snapped and he fell backwards. Regaining his balance in the middle of the cabin, he stared at the broken haft, his anger unbounded, and threw it away with all his might, the metal resounding off the timber bulkhead before falling to the deck.

He stormed out of the cabin and on to the main deck of the *Poena*, the crew moving quickly away, none daring to look at the enraged consul. Scipio looked to the sun, its arrival mocking him, as it illuminated the pitiful remnants of the Roman fleet that had escaped Drepana. Twenty-three ships surrounded the *Poena*, twenty-three from the southern flank that had fled behind their consul as the battle at Drepana descended into utter disaster.

The *Poena* had been one of the last to take its place in the defensive line. The Carthaginians were already engaged, and Scipio had quickly realized that the situation was hope-less: the centre enveloped, Ovidius's galley lost from sight, the Roman prefect trapped between the shoreline and the impenetrable wall of timber and iron that was the Cartha-ginian battle line. Time would have placed Scipio's flank in the same net, and so he had ordered a retreat, turning his back on the lost to save what he could, beginning a head-long flight that had ended in the darkness of night in Lilybaeum. Only then did Scipio pause to examine his defeat. In the quiet pre-dawn gloom of his cabin, his plans for the future, his thoughts of glory and fame, had slowly unravelled.

He moved to the foredeck and looked out over the remaining galleys, the cold onshore wind clearing the surface of his anger, allowing him to think. He would sail for Rome. It was his only choice if he was going to limit the repercussions of Drepana. He began to think of how he would formulate his argument to retain his consulship, knowing that, given time, he might yet salvage some semblance of dignity.

Scipio knew from long experience that the crux of that argument would need to be the apportionment of blame. With defeat came retribution, and if Scipio could redirect the responsibility for the loss, he might be spared the full wrath of the Senate. He would begin by interrogating the Rhodian further. The mercenary had been in the paid service of Rome many times. He had said the Carthaginians were preparing for an attack. That testimony would justify Scipio's decision to make a pre-emptive strike.

But what of the battle? His fleet had outnumbered the Carthaginians'. How had he failed? He could blame Ovidius for the loss of the centre, or Perennis for not sealing the Carthaginian fleet in the inner harbour, but either way he would be blaming a dead man and Scipio knew that such an approach would be seen as cowardly: putting responsibility on a man who could not defend himself, who had given his life for Rome. He needed to put something or someone between him and culpability.

A call from the masthead distracted Scipio and he looked to the northern approaches to the bay. Galleys were rounding the headland and many of the crew shouted warnings of a Carthaginian attack, their frantic voices tearing the thin veil of calm to reveal the panic hidden just beneath. Scipio moved to the rail, apprehension rising within him, until he saw they were but four ships, his anxiety turning to shame as the lookout identified the galleys as Roman.

Scipio watched them slowly approach. They were a forlorn sight. Four ships, and only two of them undamaged. Of the others, one was listing heavily to port and the last . . . Scipio's hands tightened on the rail, recognizing the masthead banners. He smiled coldly, nurturing the first seeds of confidence after many hours of despair. The Greek was alive, and with him Scipio's chances of saving his political fortune.

Septimus looked up at the familiar profile of the *Orcus* as the skiff approached the quinquereme. The starboard side of the galley was heavily scored, with many of the oar-holes damaged, the raw, exposed timber stark against the darker, sea-stained hull. He glanced into the open wounds, catching glimpses of shadows, and the lighter tone of the rowers' naked flesh, the men moving slowly, still in obvious shock from the devastating attack.

Septimus shook his head and turned away. The sun was beginning its descent to the western horizon, taking with it the heat of the day; he savoured the light breeze sweeping over the wave tops. He looked to Drusus sitting in the bow of the small boat. As befitting his usual reserved manner, the centurion was staring impassively at the shoreline over Septimus's shoulder, and Septimus was forced to stay his impatient questions, knowing Drusus's terse answers would only increase his frustration.

Drusus had arrived in the legion's encampment an hour before, formally reporting to Septimus that Atticus had been injured in battle. He had come personally, of his own volition, and yet, save to repeat his brief report, he had refused to be drawn in detail on any of Septimus's immediate questions, prompting Septimus to forgo the attempt and go with all haste to the *Orcus*.

The skiff nudged against the hull and Septimus clambered up on to the main deck. The galley was quiet, overlaid with a silence that seemed unnatural given the hour of the day and the number of men on deck. He went quickly to the main cabin, accepting the salutes of the legionaries he passed, nodding in silent greeting at those he recognized.

Septimus entered the dark, airless cabin and immediately felt a wave of relief as he spotted Atticus lying on his cot. His shoulder and leg were heavily bandaged and his skin was pale under a sheen of sweat, but his eyes were alert and he smiled as he saw Septimus. He shifted slightly to sit up but a stab of pain caused him to wince and pause, prompting Septimus to cross the cabin to help him.

'Take it easy,' Septimus said with a smile as he helped Atticus prop himself up further on the cot.

'How did you . . .?' Atticus began.

'Drusus told me,' Septimus replied, and he stepped back to sit down on the only chair in the cabin. A silence drew out between them, both men suddenly uneasy in each other's company, their previous conflict foremost in their minds. Atticus was first to speak, his face crestfallen.

'Gaius and Corin are dead,' he said.

'How?' Septimus asked, and Atticus used the prompt to relay the events of the entire battle, the recollection causing him to shift restlessly on the cot, his breathing becoming laboured as he dominated the pain of his wounds.

'Barca . . .' Septimus said maliciously as Atticus finished his account.

'We just weren't ready,' Atticus said, and again he began to speak at length, telling Septimus of his warning to Scipio.

Septimus's brow furrowed at the mention of the consul's name.

'Scipio's campaign against Lilybaeum has been a complete

failure – on land, and now at sea. He is sure to be recalled to Rome to answer for that failure.'

'He has already given the order,' Atticus replied. 'What's left of the fleet sails for Rome on tomorrow's tide.'

Septimus thought for a moment. 'He wants to defend his defeat on his own terms,' he said. 'Why else would he face the Senate voluntarily?'

Atticus nodded, having already reached the same conclusion after receiving Scipio's pre-emptive order to return to Rome. Septimus stood up and began to pace the cabin. He stopped and turned to Atticus. 'You must look to your back,' he said, and Atticus raised his eyebrows in question.

'The attack on the siege towers . . .' Septimus began.

'I saw the fires from the bay,' Atticus said, sitting straighter on the cot.

Septimus nodded. 'But what you might not have heard is that the Carthaginians used Greek mercenaries for the attack.'

'Greeks?' Atticus said in shock.

Again Septimus nodded, and he told Atticus of the skirmish in detail; in particular how the II maniple had been wiped out to a man by the skilled Greek fighters. He then went on to describe the anger amongst the legionaries of the Ninth and how they had driven a Greek trader from the camp.

Anger coursed through Atticus as Septimus relayed the story, and he watched the centurion closely for any indication that he agreed with the actions of his fellow Romans. There was none, and Atticus suddenly felt ashamed for having thought so little of him.

'You and I both know Scipio for the man he is,' Septimus said. 'He will not accept blame for his failure. He is sure to look elsewhere; as you were one of the commanders at Drepana, he might try to implicate you.'

Atticus nodded thoughtfully, and the two began to talk

through the defeat at Drepana in detail, concluding at length that Atticus had nothing to answer for.

'But just be wary,' Septimus said finally. 'Scipio will not concede without a fight.'

'We've known worse odds,' Atticus said with a wry smile, and again they settled into a protracted conversation, this time recalling the battles they had fought over the years, the enemies they had faced and vanquished together. The slivers of light entering the cabin slowly turned from white to red as they spoke, and it was near dark when Septimus rose once more.

'I have to return to the encampment,' he said, and he reached out with his hand and clasped Atticus's uninjured shoulder, glad once more that he was not seriously wounded.

'Will the legions continue the siege?' Atticus asked.

'Doubtful, given the blockade has been lifted. The land behind the city is putrid and already we have had men fall ill with soldier's fever. I suspect we'll pull back to higher ground.'

Atticus nodded, and again a silence descended, both men remembering when last they had spoken and the irresolvable fight that had prompted Septimus's transfer to the Ninth. Atticus thought of how Septimus had come immediately to see him when he'd heard he was injured, of the battles and trials they had faced together in the past, and of the comradeship the centurion had shared with Gaius and Corin, with all the crew of the *Orcus*, and with Atticus himself.

He held out his hand and Septimus took it without hesitation, his grip firm. He nodded slightly to Atticus in silent acknowledgement before turning to leave the cabin.

Hamilcar felt the thrill of victory at hand surge through his veins as the *Alissar* rounded the headland, the drum beat hammering out attack speed, the flagship sailing at the head of a seventy-strong fleet. He shouted out the order to deploy, the signalmen relaying the command, the fleet responding swiftly and the flanks advanced to cover the width of the bay at Panormus, trapping the pitiful Roman force that was moored within.

He had captured ninety-three galleys the day before at Drepana, with only a few escaping south as the battle raged, but Hamilcar had been content to let them go, knowing their destination. After the battle he had moved quickly to secure the remnants of the Roman fleet before assembling a reduced fleet of galleys, drawing additional soldiers from the remainder of his ships at Drepana to supplement the crews of those chosen to sail, anxious to continue the fight, to maintain the momentum his victory had granted him. He had put to sea, taking two Roman captains from the captured enemy fleet at Drepana with him, and had steered his fleet north, rounding the northwestern tip of Sicily in the still hours of the night, confident that no landward warning would reach his destination before him.

That confidence had been well founded. As Hamilcar gazed across the width of the entire harbour he knew he had taken the Romans at Panormus by surprise, the ten Roman galleys sallying out to meet his fleet hopelessly outmatched and outmanoeuvred. He ordered his left flank to turn into the Roman defence and overwhelm it, leaving his centre and right flank free to advance to the shoreline beyond the walls of Panormus. Once there he would deploy his troops to besiege the town and his ships to blockade the port. He would release the two Roman captains and hand them over to the garrison, ensuring that news of Rome's utter defeat at Drepana would be given first-hand to the defenders, knowing it would sap their resolve to resist.

The *Alissar* sped on as the left flank met the Roman defenders. Hamilcar watched the skirmish with a growing sense of justice. He had stayed awake during the night voyage, preferring the open aft-deck to the confines of his cabin, searching the stars for the constellations that signified the gods of Carthage. He had whispered a prayer of thanks to each in turn, believing he could sense their satisfaction at Carthage's triumph over the Roman foe, that it was their hand that had given him such a flawless and complete victory, divine retribution for Rome's arrogant dismissal of his proposal for peace.

The first galleys of Hamilcar's fleet reached the shore and the soldiers began to disembark. Hamilcar watched them form orderly ranks, expecting he would be able to return to Drepana within two days, leaving the siege in the hands of one of his commanders. Some of the Roman fleet had escaped to Lilybaeum, and might already be sailing onwards to more secure Roman waters, but Hamilcar felt it was of little consequence. Whether the Roman fleet was there to be taken or already gone, they were too weak to be a threat, and so Lilybaeum was once more an open city and could be continually supplied from Drepana until Hamilcar had the means to attack the landward besiegers.

To that end, and to deliver the news of his victory in person to the One Hundred and Four and the Supreme Council, he would return to Carthage. The war in Sicily had taken a significant turn in his favour. Lilybaeum was saved, Panormus would soon be retaken, and the Roman fleet had been annihilated. Now was the time to finally retake Agrigentum and sweep the Romans from western Sicily.

CHAPTER SIXTEEN

The crowd surged forward, straining against the line of legionaries at the base of the steps, the soldiers holding their *pila* spears level to form a solid barrier, the centurions shouting for the people to draw back as a group of senators walked across the top of the steps, moving towards the entrance to the Curia. A roar went up from the crowd, a conflagration of abuse and anger.

The remnants of the fleet had arrived back in Ostia over a week before, bringing with them news that had thrown the city into lamentation, the defeat at Drepana coming so soon after the loss of so many to a storm. That grief had quickly turned to anger towards the Carthaginians who had wrought such carnage, but then a more insidious fury took hold of the people, towards the leaders of Rome who had allowed defeat to follow disaster. The Senate had sensed the mood of the people and, fearful of their wrath, they had acted: Scipio, the senior consul and commander of the fleet, would be tried for the crime of *perduellio*, treason.

It was a trial that drew thousands to the Forum at the foot of the Senate house and again a roar went up as more senators entered the chamber. The crowd was restless and angry. Rome did not suffer defeat; she did not fail or lose heart in the face of an enemy. She was flawless. Only men were flawed, and one of them had brought Rome under the shadow of danger. For that, the people demanded justice and retribution. In the silence that followed their roar, a man came out from the Senate chamber, shouting a message to the crowd below that could be heard across the Forum. The trial had begun.

Scipio reached to the depths of his self-control to keep his expression impassive, the indignity of the trial surpassing the limits of shame. He had stood before the Senate less than a week before to announce the defeat at Drepana, his prepared speech never proceeding beyond that opening report as the entire Senate had turned on him in fury and shock. He had left the Senate chamber under a wave of shouted abuse, only to receive notice the following day that he was to be tried for the crime of *perduellio*, for 'injuring the power of Rome'. So now he sat in a chair alone by the speaker's podium, a central position that placed him under the baleful view of all three hundred senators.

To add insult to this charge, Aulus Atilius Caiatinus, the junior consul, had been temporarily granted Scipio's power. He had appointed his patron, Duilius, as the lead prosecutor, pitting Scipio against his arch enemy. The ancients had put men convicted of treason to death, but Scipio, if found guilty, would face exile, a punishment of living-death that would end his every ambition and destroy his political life. The Senate was baying for blood, for retribution, and Scipio could trust no other to speak for him. He would defend himself, putting his faith in his oratorical skills, his stature as a member of an ancient line of patricians, and the one defence that might save him: the revelation of a traitor.

'Senators of Rome,' a voice called out, and Scipio turned to see Duilius walk out from his seat in the front row of senators.

'Today I am tasked with a grave duty, one demanded of me by my consul,' Duilius turned and nodded to Caiatinus, 'and my city, whose power and safety has been irrevocably injured by one man, Gnaeus Cornelius Scipio *Asina*.'

A murmur of anger swept across the Senate and the speaker hammered his gavel to restore silence.

Duilius turned to Scipio, meeting his hostile stare, wary of him despite the overwhelming evidence. The importance of his prosecutorial task caused him to pause. Here was a chance to finally rid himself – and Rome – of a man who never saw beyond the limits of his own ambition, who forfeited the safety of Rome many times for his own ends, whose offences were so well hidden that even Duilius did not know of their full extent, much less of any evidence that he could ever expose. Only Scipio's reckless attack at Drepana stood against him and, in prosecuting him for that crime, Duilius would expunge all the consul's previous wrongs, wiping them forever from the heart of Rome.

Duilius first called the captain of the *Poena* to testify. He was a man who fearlessly commanded a flagship but he stammered through his testimony under the glare of the most powerful men in Rome. He spoke of Scipio's desecration of the ancient ritual to confirm divine approval and many of the elder senators gasped in disbelief at Scipio's blatant effrontery to the will of the gods, in itself a crime that demanded dire punishment.

Duilius then called other captains to speak of the decision to withdraw the southern flank and retreat to Lilybaeum as the battle raged, but Scipio neatly cross-examined them, forcing each to admit that the situation was beyond hopeless when he had issued the order. Duilius nodded to Scipio to concede the point, wanting to lull him slightly, and the consul smiled coldly at the gesture. Only then did Duilius call his last witness.

Atticus limped forward. He ignored the gazes and whispers of the entire chamber, keeping his eyes and attention locked on Scipio, knowing him to be the most dangerous viper in the nest. He vividly recalled their last encounter on this very floor, and how Scipio had bested him, and he glanced at Duilius out of the corner of his eye, taking strength from his presence. He and Duilius had prepared in detail, predicting every counter-argument that Scipio might make, every defence he might employ. All that was needed now was for Atticus to deliver the final, fatal strike, and he brushed his doubts aside as the Senate came to order.

Duilius began with a detailed account of Atticus's career in the war against Carthage, his command of the flagship at Mylae, his promotion to prefect for his valour at Cape Ecnomus, his part in the victory at Cape Hermaeum. The senators listened in silence, many of them only sitting forward with attention as Duilius ended his introduction and began his questioning.

'Prefect Perennis,' Duilius said. 'Can you recount your conversation with the consul on the evening before the battle?'

'I warned him that the fleet was not yet ready for an open, offensive battle.'

'Not ready?' Duilius asked, raising his voice above the murmur of surprise.

'With the loss of the *corvus*, the enemy holds the advantage over us in seamanship. Our only chance is to drill our sailing crews in how to ram and our legionaries in how to board.'

'And our fleet is not yet trained in these tactics?' Duilius asked, looking to Scipio, wondering why he was not interrupting to challenge Atticus's view on fleet tactics, a view that was not universally held, and the only weak point in their attack.

'No,' Atticus responded evenly, also perplexed, his carefully prepared response to Scipio's expected rebuttal no longer needed. 'The fleet was not ready and I made this fact clear to the consul.'

'Thank you, Prefect,' Duilius said, and he turned to the senators, his gaze level in silent but obvious criticism of Scipio's foolhardy dismissal of Atticus's warning. Many of them nodded in agreement, looking to the consul with censorious expressions, their decision on Scipio's guilt already made.

Scipio stood up amidst the growing sound of disorder and looked to the speaker. The older man hammered his gavel and silence descended once more, albeit with an undertone of whispered conversations as senators debated the evidence privately.

'Prefect Perennis,' Scipio began, his tone offhand, 'who do you claim was present when you say you made this warning?'

As Duilius had advised him, Atticus ignored the sceptical subtext of Scipio's question and he turned to the consul.

'You and Prefect Ovidius,' he replied.

'And with Ovidius dead,' Scipio said, 'the Senate only has your word that you ever spoke such a warning to me.'

A number of angry voices were raised at Scipio's accusation of perjury and Duilius stepped forward. 'The prefect's word is beyond question,' he said.

Scipio smiled coldly. 'Really . . .?' he replied, and he turned his back on Atticus. 'Where were you born, Perennis?' he asked.

'Locri.'

'So your ancestors are not of Rome,' Scipio said, his tone mildly accusatory.

'They are Greek,' Atticus said proudly, refusing to be baited by Scipio's attempt to blacken his word, again perplexed by the insubstantiality of the consul's attack.

Duilius stepped forward again. 'The prefect's loyalty to Rome is also beyond question, and I put to you, Senators, that the consul is engaged in a futile attempt to somehow besmirch the prefect's honour in the hope it will lessen the impact of his damning testimony.'

The chamber rang with murmurs of agreement, but Scipio ignored them. He was ready to make his decisive strike, to call his own witnesses: two men whom he had questioned in depth since Drepana and who, by the grace of Fortuna, had revealed auspicious information that could yet save him.

'You say the prefect's loyalty is beyond question?' he asked the Senate, before nodding towards the entrance to the chamber.

Calix and Baro entered and stood where all could see them. Scipio introduced Baro and then spoke of Calix, referring to him as the Rhodian, a mercenary in the paid service of Carthage at Lilybaeum, but a man who had also served Rome honourably in the past. Atticus looked only to Baro, his initial shock turning quickly to suspicion and then resentment that his second-in-command should stand before him.

'Baro,' Scipio began, the entire Senate now poised to listen with interest. 'Tell us how this man, the Rhodian, escaped the blockade at Lilybaeum.'

Baro described the event in detail, mentioning how the Rhodian had first slipped through the blockade and how they had expected his eventual attempt to escape. He spoke of the final chase, with the *Orcus* leading the Roman pursuit, the Rhodian's galley only a ship-length ahead, before ending with a carefully scripted condemnation.

'We were in full pursuit and were about to catch his ship when the prefect ordered us to break off,' he concluded.

'Because we could not pursue him through the shallows,' Atticus protested angrily, never taking his eyes off Baro.

'At least, that is what you told your crew at the time,' Scipio interjected.

307

'He's standing here now,' Duilius said, indicating the Rhodian, trying to avoid a trap he could not have foreseen. 'We can ask him if Perennis was correct.'

'I have only two questions to ask of this man,' Scipio said, and he turned to Calix. 'Who was on board your ship when you escaped?'

'Hamilcar Barca,' Calix replied. 'The overall commander of the Carthaginians.'

'And where did you take him?'

'Drepana.'

There was an audible gasp from the Senate and Scipio quickly turned to address them. 'And this not hours before our siege towers were attacked by a Greek force, causing many casualties amongst our valiant legionaries – moreover, a Greek force in the paid service of the Carthaginians.'

Many of the senators automatically looked to Atticus, the Greek in their midst.

'Then the overall commander of the Carthaginians, the man who subsequently led their fleet at Drepana, slips through our blockade,' Scipio continued. 'His escape orchestrated with the help of other Greeks who had enemy gold in their hands. Perennis's own second-in-command confirms that Hamilcar Barca could have been captured had Perennis pressed home his supposed pursuit.'

'No one knew Barca was on that ship,' Atticus shouted, looking to Duilius, who seemed transfixed by Scipio's evidence.

'And when in command of the vanguard at Drepana,' Scipio said, more loudly, as if Atticus had not spoken, 'Perennis failed to confine the Carthaginian fleet in the inner harbour, allowing them to escape and overwhelm us.'

'The attack was doomed from the start,' Atticus shouted, stepping forward to confront Scipio, unable to control his anger.

'Because you were in league with the enemy,' Scipio shouted back, and again the Senate descended into cacophony of angry voices, this time not all of them directed at Scipio.

Atticus turned to the senators, overwhelmed with disgust; not only because of Scipio's baseless accusations, but also at the fact that he had found a complicit audience amongst the senators.

'Enough,' Duilius shouted, regaining his wits. 'These accusations are completely unfounded and unsubstantiated.'

'We have the word of Baro,' Scipio countered.

'The word of a subordinate over that of his commander,' Duilius said.

'The word of a Roman over that of a *barbarus*, a foreigner, a Greek, whose people Rome defeated only a generation ago. Are we now to believe those same people are loyal to their conquerors?'

'And what of the prefect's valour at Ecnomus, or his injuries at Drepana at the hands of Barca himself?' Duilius asked.

'A valorous act at Ecnomus from which he escaped unscathed,' Scipio retorted. 'And Perennis had outlived his usefulness when Barca attacked him at Drepana. Carthaginian victory was already assured. They are a dishonourable race: why would Barca not kill Perennis and save the blood money he had agreed to pay him?'

Duilius made to respond but he stopped himself. Scipio had an answer to every question he posed, each one veiled in half-truth and innuendo, each one more damning than the last. He looked to the senators and saw that they were wavering and, worse, that many were looking at Atticus with open hostility. His only chance was to attack, to bring the focus back to Scipio and end the trial.

'Senators,' he shouted, glancing at Atticus, 'what you are witnessing here is a dishonourable attack on a man who has served this city with distinction, a man whose loyalty, before today, was not only unquestioned, but was rewarded many times by his commanders. He may not be of Rome, but he is surely more Roman than Scipio *Asina*, a man who has brought defeat upon this city, not once, but twice. To listen further to his vile accusations is to draw shame upon us all, and I call upon the Senate to vote now on the consul's guilt before we are all tainted with his treason.'

An uproar followed Duilius's words, the senators continuing to argue amongst themselves, with many shouting at the protagonists on the floor of the chamber. The speaker hammered his gavel and slowly a semblance of order was restored. He quickly called a vote, asking for a show of hands for a guilty verdict. Of the three hundred senators, two-thirds raised their hands, condemning Scipio by majority, the uproar beginning anew as the speaker made to announce the result.

Atticus stood as if in the centre of a maelstrom, his eyes moving across the crowd, picking out the numerous hostile expressions directed towards him. Scipio had been condemned, but not by a unanimous vote, and Atticus knew that each vote in Scipio's defence represented a senator who believed the consul's accusations. The thought sickened him and a fierce hatred rose unbidden within him – not for Scipio, not for the senators, nor for the prejudices of the society that surrounded him, but for the all-enveloping evil that was Rome itself.

He stepped forward, passing Duilius without a word, the senator lost in his own thoughts, his victory soured by the split vote. He looked to Baro, who stared at him with a hatred finally unleashed into the open, seeing past him to the seemingly countless Romans who had looked upon him the same way, before he finally turned to the man he was approaching, Scipio.

The consul, like Duilius, was also staring at the audience of senators, his near expressionless face showing only a hint of some other emotion that Atticus hoped was despair. He stood beside him, unnoticed in the turmoil, his hatred for Rome finding a focus in its progeny standing before him. Scipio became aware of Atticus and he turned, his expression changing immediately, no longer controlled.

'If you ever question my honour again, I will end you,' Atticus said, holding Scipio's hostile stare for a moment before turning to leave.

'This fight is not over, *Greek*,' Scipio said, spitting the last word in disgust.

Atticus rounded on Scipio and grabbed him by the throat, throttling him slowly as he stared into Scipio's eyes, the consul's face turning red under Atticus's iron grip. Rough hands grabbed Atticus from behind, breaking his hold, and Scipio stumbled back as Atticus spun around to face Baro. Atticus struck him in the face with his forearm, the strike jarring the wound in his chest but knocking Baro to the floor, and he turned again to find Scipio standing with his hand to his throat, his faced mottled with anger.

'You dare to strike a consul of Rome?' he said, his voice ragged.

'You are no longer a consul,' Atticus said, stepping forward, causing Scipio to step back instinctively. 'You are nothing, an exile . . . and you are beaten.'

He turned away again and moved towards the exit, his hand clutching the wound on his chest, ignoring the continuous uproar in the Senate chamber.

'And what are you, Perennis?' Scipio shouted mockingly, keeping the spectre of his total loss at bay with his frantic taunts. 'Where do you call home? What are you but an exile?'

Atticus tried to ignore Scipio, weary to the very depths of

his soul, but as he stepped out through the colonnaded exit of the Curia, the questions began to burrow into his thoughts, their answers all too evident in the shadow of his growing contempt for Rome.

Duilius walked quickly from the chamber after Atticus. He had seen the scuffle in the corner of his eye, turning to see Atticus strike Baro and confront Scipio before leaving. Duilius had reacted quickly, knowing the furious debate would rage on. The fact that the vote had already been cast and was inviolate would do little to assuage the anger on both sides of the argument. Scipio was condemned. He was finished, and Duilius barely glanced at him as he passed, or at Baro, sitting on the floor of the chamber, his hand cupped over a bloody and broken nose.

He paused outside and looked around, quickly spying Atticus limping down the steps. The gathered crowd was cheering the verdict, their faces upturned in laughter, and Duilius looked upon them with derision. They were a mob, an undisciplined horde whose fickle anger was easily dissipated by the illusion of justice. However much it pleased Duilius, Scipio's conviction did not reverse the enormous loss of so many galleys and men at Drepana. For Duilius, justice would have seen Scipio irrevocably destroyed after his defeat at Lipara, never to rise again to take command of a fleet as a consul of Rome. Now it was too late, the loss irreversible, and Duilius turned from the crowd to pursue Atticus to the foot of the steps.

Atticus would have to leave Rome, Duilius thought, for a few months at least, until the edge of Scipio's accusations had dulled. Too many senators had been swayed by his argument, and Duilius was forced to admit that even he had experienced doubt for a moment, that Scipio's sudden evidence, however false, had been compelling. Atticus was in danger, the involvement of the Greek mercenaries in the attack at Lilybaeum a damning connection that tainted Atticus and could lead to a separate trial for treason, and while Duilius was sure of Atticus's innocence, he knew well that his faith was not shared by all.

Only outside of Rome, out of the immediate reach of the Senate and the minds of the senators could Duilius ensure Atticus's safety from prosecution. He would persuade Caiatinus, now the senior consul, to repress all debate on the subject, knowing that, with time, the senators would forget and move on. The war still raged and victory was now further away than ever. All he needed was Atticus's compliance and he pushed through the outer fringes of the crowd, his eyes on Atticus only yards away. He called his name and Atticus turned.

Duilius was immediately taken aback by Atticus's murderous expression. His anger was understandable, but Duilius discerned something else, something deeper, a look in his eyes that seemed to suggest that all he saw was abhorrent to him.

'Atticus,' he said, his words coming slowly, distracted by the prefect's expression. 'I know you're angry, but we could not have foreseen Scipio's attack on you.'

'It is not his attack that angers me,' Atticus replied vehemently. 'It's how quickly and easily his words persuaded many of the senators that I was a traitor.'

'The defeat at Drepana unnerved them,' Duilius said. 'They were easy prey for Scipio's lies. They will soon forget, but in the meantime you should leave Rome. I'll send word when it is safe to return.'

'I'm sailing with the tide for Brolium,' Atticus said coldly. 'But . . .'

He stopped short of saying he would not return, not wanting to listen to any words Duilius might speak in Rome's defence.

They would be hollow arguments that would do nothing to assuage his hatred. He looked to Duilius, the senator's face showing mild surprise, as if he had expected Atticus to resist his request to leave the city. Duilius held out his hand and Atticus shook it perfunctorily, not hearing the senator's final words of farewell. He turned and walked away, his thoughts already on his ship and the open seascape to the south, determined that, if the Fates allowed, he would never set foot in Rome again.

Hamilcar paced across the small antechamber outside the Supreme Council's meeting room, his impatience bidding him to turn to the door continually. He had been summoned unexpectedly an hour before, only to be ordered to wait, the undeclared reason for his summons only adding to his anxiety. He paused and listened again, holding his breath in the quiet of the antechamber. He could hear voices raised in anger but they were muffled by the heavy oak door and he was unable to identify the words or the speakers.

He had arrived back in Carthage five days before, announcing his victory – amidst rapturous applause – to the One Hundred and Four, and to fractured elation from the Supreme Council. Hanno, the newly elected suffet, and his faction remained subdued while his father, and his supporters, sent heralds out into the street to proclaim the victory, to ensure that every voice in Carthage would speak Hamilcar's name with pride and jubilation.

A louder voice suddenly rang out within the meeting room and a silence descended, causing Hamilcar to stare transfixed at the door. It opened and Hasdrubal, his father, beckoned him in, his face crestfallen, unable to meet his son's gaze. Hamilcar stepped in and stood in the centre of the room, facing the council. Hanno was directly before him in the centre, seated in the suffet's chair.

'The Council has decided,' Hanno began, without the formality of a greeting, 'that the Gadir fleet will return to Iberia forthwith and that the Greek mercenaries will be withdrawn and their contract ended.'

Hamilcar was speechless. He looked to his father, but Hasdrubal could only stare back impassively, his own arguments having already fallen on deaf ears.

'But what of the campaign?' Hamilcar asked, turning to Hanno. 'Are those forces to be replaced?'

'No,' Hanno scoffed. 'The campaign is over. The Romans are beaten; the seaways around Sicily are secure. There is no reason to commit any more resources to that godforsaken island.'

'But we have a chance to retake lost territory, to retake Agrigentum,' Hamilcar protested. 'If you give me the men and galleys—'

Hanno held up his hand to quiet Hamilcar, his expression suddenly hostile. 'The council has made its decision, Barca,' he said. 'That is an end to the matter, and this meeting is adjourned.'

Many of the councillors rose up immediately, some going to Hanno who was still seated while others walked straight from the room, brushing past Hamilcar without a glance. Hasdrubal approached his son and, taking him by the arm, led him to the side of the room.

'It's over, Hamilcar,' he said. 'We knew this day would come.'

'But what of the other councillors?' Hamilcar asked. 'What of their support for the Sicilian campaign?'

'The vote was nine to three against continuing the war with the Romans. I am isolated, and those who would be swayed are cowed by Hanno. As suffet his power is too great to challenge.'

Hasdrubal glanced over his shoulder at Hanno. 'Come,' he said to Hamilcar. 'We must go.'

Hamilcar shrugged off his father's hand. 'I will speak with Hanno myself,' he said, looking past his father to the suffet. The room was all but empty, the last of the councillors leaving, with only one remaining at Hanno's side, speaking to him in whispered tones.

'No,' Hasdrubal said, 'you cannot confront him.'

'I must,' Hamilcar hissed, and he stepped away from his father, moving once more to the centre of the room to stand before the suffet's chair.

Hanno saw him and waved the last supplicant away, the councillor leaving quickly. Hasdrubal paused for a moment longer, looking to his son's back. He could not drag him away, Hamilcar was his own man, and he too left, closing the door to leave his son alone with the most powerful man in Carthage.

'Why?' Hamilcar asked.

'Because it is within my power,' Hanno said simply, enjoying the realization of a long-held desire.

'But if we strike now we can end Rome's plans of dominating Sicily forever,' Hamilcar protested.

'I have told you before, Barca,' Hanno said. 'I care nothing for Sicily. I concede that Lilybaeum is an important trading hub for Carthage, and for its defence I agreed to the use of the Gadir fleet, but I want nothing more of that island. The war against Rome has been a drain on our resources for too long, and to what end?' He paused and hardened his stare. 'So you can write your name in the annals of history?' he asked with a sneer.

'You think I want Sicily for personal glory?' Hamilcar asked incredulously, anger in his voice. 'And you would end the campaign simply to thwart that ambition?'

Hanno laughed mockingly. 'This was not personal, you young fool,' he said. 'I may despise you for your reckless ambition and mindless obstinacy, but that is not why I end the campaign on

Sicily. Lilybaeum is safe and Panormus will soon be in our hands. Seaports are what count on that island, and with those in our control the trading route around the northwest of the island is secure. There is nothing more to be achieved.'

He stood up, walking over to stand before Hamilcar, his expression grave once more. 'My loyalty to Carthage runs as deep as yours, Barca. Perhaps even deeper, despite what you think, and I believe this city's future lies in Africa, not on some island to the north. We are not vile conquerors like the Romans, we are traders, and Africa is where we will expand our empire and our wealth, by extending our reach from the sacred soil of this city; something we cannot achieve if we are fighting a war on two fronts.'

'Then let me finish our war against the Romans decisively,' Hamilcar said, fearful of allowing Rome to recover. 'You must give me the forces I need to do this.'

'I do not answer to you, young Barca,' Hanno said, angry again.

'Then you will answer to the children of Carthage,' Hamilcar said vehemently. 'Rome will rise again. They are relentless in their quest to expand. If we do not contain them on their peninsula they will threaten Carthage again. With control of Sicily we can achieve that. Otherwise our children will have to fight them as we have.'

'You overestimate the Romans, Barca,' Hanno scoffed. 'With their losses in the storm and Drepana, their ambitions to control the sea-lanes are finished.'

Hamilcar made to retort but, as before, Hanno held up his hand to stay his words. He had not intended on explaining himself to the young commander, his dislike for Barca running as deeply as before, but he had felt a sense of magnanimity in the wake of his victory. He forced his temper to cool, focusing on what Barca had achieved at Drepana.

'I will allow you to retain the galleys you captured at Drepana and Panormus,' he said evenly. 'Use them to keep Lilybaeum supplied by sea until the Romans abandon their futile siege, as they surely will in time. Now go, I grow weary of this argument. My decision is made and the council has voted. From this day, the armies of Carthage will fight only on African soil.'

Hamilcar stared at Hanno for a moment longer and then turned and walked from the room. To argue further was pointless, and while every futile word he spoke pricked his honour, Hamilcar knew in his heart that Hanno was wrong. The Romans were a ruthless foe, far more dangerous than the Numidians to the south of Carthage. They were not beaten, they would rise again; and as Hamilcar made his way through the corridors leading from the centre of power in Carthage, the black bile of utter frustration consumed his every fibre.

CHAPTER SEVENTEEN

The trading ship moved steadily over the dark sea, its wake barely troubling the surface of the gentle swell. The bow kicked up sporadic waves that reflected the sallow light of the crescent moon. A muted command broke the silence and the sharp edges of the triangular lateen sail collapsed, giving the captain an uninterrupted view of the solitary running light of the galley ahead. He moved to the rail, wary despite the pre-planned meeting off the north coast of Sicily, and he looked to the four points of his ship as it came to a steady stop.

The galley ahead advanced under the power of half its oars, the drum beat punctuating the night air. It was a standard quinquereme, indistinguishable from the dozens the trading captain had observed over the previous weeks, and he peered into the gloom in a vain attempt to identify the banners fluttering from the masthead. He moved to the foredeck of his ship, passing through the ranks of his crew as he did, their eyes locked on the approaching galley.

The two ships came bow to bow and a line was thrown from out of the darkness and made secure. Two men came to the forerail of the quinquereme and the captain smiled as he recognized them, his apprehension lifting.

'Well met, Atticus,' he said.

'It is good to see you, Darius,' Atticus replied.

The trading captain nodded and briefly acknowledged the other man standing opposite him, the taciturn centurion who, as usual, showed no sign of response.

'What news?' Atticus asked, drawing Darius's attention.

'The same as before,' Darius replied. 'The Carthaginian fleet has disappeared. Only the Roman galleys that were captured at Drepana remain. They have been moved to the inner harbour of Lilybaeum.'

Atticus's brow furrowed in puzzlement. 'And Panormus?' he asked.

'From what I could see from the sea-lane, there are perhaps twenty galleys in the harbour, no more than that, although I cannot tell of their origin. The Carthaginians have closed the port.'

Atticus nodded and looked beyond Darius into the darkness, his eyes narrowing as he thought. 'Have you heard any rumours as to the enemy's intent?' he asked after a pause.

Darius smiled slightly. He was a citizen of the Roman Republic, but as a native of Siderno on the Calabrian coast he considered himself to be Greek first. The Carthaginians were no enemy of his. He was a trader, and as such he recognized few boundaries. The risks he took in spying for Rome were not engaged in because Carthage was the enemy. They were taken because Atticus had asked him.

He had known Atticus for many years, from a time when the captain from Locri commanded a trireme in the Ionian Sea. As a pirate hunter, Atticus had kept the sea-lanes open for traders like Darius, and he felt deeply indebted to his fellow Greek.

'I have heard nothing beyond what I have observed myself,' he replied sincerely, seeing the frustration on Atticus's face. 'But I will continue to keep my ears open, my friend.'

Again Atticus nodded. 'Thank you, Darius,' he said, disappointed at the paucity of Darius's report. 'Can you meet me here again when Arcturus reaches its zenith?'

Darius nodded and called over his shoulder for the mainsail to be raised. The line between the two ships was released and the trader slipped away from the bow of the *Orcus*, the offshore wind bringing it about quickly, and within minutes it was lost to the darkness.

Atticus turned away from the rail and made his way back to the aft-deck. Drusus followed, stopping briefly on the main deck to order his men to stand down for the night.

'I don't like it, Drusus,' Atticus said quietly. 'It's been nearly four months since Drepana, and still the Carthaginians have not advanced. Our defences in Sicily are wide open. The enemy must know that. Surely they are shadowing our ports as we are theirs?'

Drusus shook his head in puzzlement and the two men lapsed into silence, the mystery of the Carthaginians' unwillingness to pursue the fight defying reason.

Atticus looked once more in the direction taken by Darius. The Greek trader was one of four that he was using to spy on the Carthaginians, an intricate net he had constructed in the three months since returning to Sicily. Aulus, the harbour master at Brolium, was at the centre of that net, a fixed point that allowed Atticus to coordinate his intelligence gathering, but thus far the four Greek captains had shed little light on the Carthaginians' inexplicable motives.

Atticus had known each captain for years, the confines of the Ionian Sea ensuring that all had crossed his path on many occasions during the time he commanded the *Aquila*. They were amongst the finest and ablest of sailors, each one a shrewd trader, and Atticus knew that nothing would escape their notice. If they believed the Carthaginians had withdrawn their fleet from Sicily then there could be no doubt.

Panormus was lost, and with it the supply lines to the legions encamped across the approaches to Lilybaeum. This further setback after Drepana had already forced Rome to recall the Ninth Legion from Sicily, leaving the Second to maintain the landward siege and rely solely on a precarious supply line to Agrigentum to the south.

Lilybaeum was no longer threatened. Drepana and Panormus were safe. The enemy were secure on all fronts, while the Roman-held ports of Brolium and Agrigentum were ripe to fall. Atticus felt the knot of frustration tighten further in his stomach. He had done all he could do in Sicily to divine the enemy's plans. Only one other possible source of information remained, one man who might yet know what the enemy planned.

'Your orders, Prefect,' Drusus said, causing Atticus to spin around to face the centurion.

'First we sail east to Brolium,' he said without hesitation, his mind made up. 'I will inform Aulus to keep me apprised should the trading captains report any enemy activity, but there is nothing more we can do here. We will sail for Ostia at noon.'

Drusus nodded and left the aft-deck. Atticus moved to the tiller and ordered the helmsman to get under way and the *Orcus* turned neatly towards the strip of light that ran the length of the eastern horizon. Brolium was no more than an hour away; the *Orcus* would be there to see the sun rise. Atticus cast his thoughts to the days and weeks beyond. Rome still had a fleet, a hundred quinqueremes, the second half of the *Classis Romanus*, now anchored in the shallows of Fiumicino. The Carthaginians were granting him time and Atticus knew he would have to put it to good use.

The morale of the Roman fleet had been mauled beyond redemption. A new spirit would need to be born, one forged in a belief that the Roman navy could match the prowess of the Carthaginians. Even after the ravages of Drepana and the storm off Camarina, there was still a core group of experienced captains in the fleet. They could be used to train the others.

As the *Orcus* came up to standard speed, Atticus turned his back on the western horizon and the Carthaginian-held territory of Sicily. The threat remained, it could not be ignored; but, while the enemy slumbered, Atticus would prepare for the inevitable fight to come.

Septimus stepped back from the contest, his chest heaving with exertion, the sweat running freely down his face, the wooden training sword still charged before him. His opponent was bunched over, his hand massaging his bruised ribs, and Septimus walked over to place a hand on the legionary's shoulder, helping him to stand upright and retake his place in the ranks. It had been a hard-fought contest, a testament to the distance the legionaries had come in the months since they had arrived at Fiumicino.

Septimus stood before his men and demonstrated the sword stroke he had used to end the fight before ordering them to break up into pairs to practise the technique. They moved quickly and the air was soon filled with the hollow, staccato sound of wooden swords. He watched them for a moment with a critical eye before moving off, wiping the sweat from his brow with his forearm as he went, the wooden sword swinging loosely in his hand as he subconsciously rehearsed a sequence of thrusts.

He was pleased with the progress of his men. The training schedule was relentless, the techniques and shield foreign to them but, as new recruits of the Ninth, they had taken to the task without complaint, eager to avenge their loss at Lilybaeum and to take to the seas against the Carthaginian foe.

That same sense of purpose had pervaded each maniple of the legion; as Septimus passed through the camp he recognized other former marines training the men in boarding techniques and one-to-one combat. Every soldier of the Ninth was conscious of the fact that the *corvus* was gone, and with it the advantage a traditional legion had in close-quarter fighting; the powerful shield wall that was built on mutual support. In the battle ahead there would be no opportunity to deploy into ranks. It would be man against man and speed, more than strength, would determine the outcome.

Septimus reached the edge of the encampment and crested the sand dunes that led to the beach, pausing at the top. The galleys encased in scaffolding were all but finished, with workmen clambering over the decks and rigging. They had worked ceaselessly during the hours of daylight and the remaining galleys were the last of the new fleet, a consignment that would bring the strength of the *Classis Romanus* to two hundred quinqueremes.

The consular elections had taken place a month before and the two new consuls, Aulus Postumius Albinus and Caius Lutatius Catulus, had issued a declaration to the citizens of Rome. After the losses of Drepana the navy would have to be rebuilt; however, the Treasury of the Republic was empty and the consuls called on its wealthy citizens to advance the city a loan that would be repaid when the Carthaginians were defeated. The response had been overwhelming, and within days of the announcement the keels of the new fleet were being laid down in the hard sand of Fiumicino, each one a symbol of the allegiance and determination of the citizens of Rome.

Septimus looked beyond the beach to the sea. It was alive with galleys, their number pushing out the malleable boundary of the north–south trading lane that ran past Fiumicino.

The crews were in training, following a schedule as gruelling as that of the Ninth. They were moving in small squadrons, each group changing course as one, like a flock of birds evading a predator, or at ramming speed, like a pack of wolves chasing down their prey.

Septimus turned and headed back towards his men, his thoughts on the days ahead. As a legionary he had learned never to see beyond that immediate future, his destiny in the hands of his commanders and the Senate of Rome. The soldiery did not know what lay ahead in the war against Carthage, no more than the sailing crews did, but all were aware that precious time had been granted to them. They would continue to train and, as Septimus reached his maniple, he kneaded the hilt of his wooden sword, determined that the IV would be ready.

Atticus stood for a moment at the foot of the steps to the Curia, the heat of the sun raising the sweat on his back. He narrowed his eyes against the reflected glare off the flagstones and looked up to the colonnaded entrance, conscious of how easily his self-imposed exile from Rome had been broken. He had arrived in the city the day before and, after brief enquiries, he had learned of the fate of the man he wished to question. He turned to sweep his gaze across the Forum, the central square all but empty under the noonday sun, and he strode away towards his destination, anxious to complete his task and leave the city once more.

The prison stood to the side of the Curia. It was a low building, with an unadorned and imposing façade, while behind it the Capitoline Hill swept up to the temples of Jupiter, Mars and Quirinus. A single legionary stood guard at the door, his *pila* spear held out at an angle, his expression inscrutable under the brim of his helmet. Atticus approached slowly, marshalling his thoughts, conscious that the man he was about to see would have little reason to cooperate with him. He stood before the guard.

'I am Atticus Milonius Perennis, Prefect of the *Classis Romanus*, and I wish to see the prisoner, Calix.'

'Yes, Prefect,' the legionary responded, standing to attention before hammering the butt of his spear against the door. A hatch opened at eye level and the legionary motioned for Atticus to step forward. He repeated his request and, as the hatch closed, Atticus heard a series of bolts being opened. The door swung outward and he stepped in over the threshold.

The glaring sunlight gave way to an almost impenetrable darkness and Atticus closed his eyes to help them adjust as the door was shut behind him. He opened them and looked about the candlelit interior. The room was small and windowless. There was only one door, the one that led to the outside, and Atticus's gaze was quickly drawn to the circular hole in the middle of the floor. It was flanked by an *optio* and four legionaries.

The officer stepped forward. 'You wish to see the Rhodian, Prefect?' he said.

Atticus nodded, his eyes never leaving the hole, and he heard the legionaries move about as they prepared to lower a ladder into the hole.

'You weapons, Prefect,' the *optio* said, holding out his hand, and Atticus surrendered his sword and dagger without comment.

He stepped forward and prepared to descend. 'Are there many others?' he asked of the *optio*.

'He is alone,' the officer replied, and Atticus nodded again.

The Romans had little use for prisons. Any nobleman suspected of a crime was kept under house arrest and, if found guilty, they were either fined, exiled or put to death. For lesser citizens of the Republic, justice was swifter and the sentences summarily carried out. Imprisonment was used only for enemy commanders captured in battle, a brief incarceration while their fate was decided.

Atticus swung his feet on to the rungs of the ladder and started down. He slowed as his head fell below the level of the floor and he looked about the near pitch-blackness of the lower room. A single candle was alight in a far corner and he kept his gaze locked on it as he descended further. An over-powering stench permeated the air, a combination of human waste and stale sweat, a smell of despair and decay. Atticus was reminded of the bilges of a galley, beneath the rowing deck, where the slaves slept while on relief; but here, in the bowels of the prison, the stale air had no escape and Atticus had to reach for each breath.

He stopped at the end of the ladder and tried to find the Rhodian, expecting to see him in the halo of light surrounding the candle.

'Perennis,' a voice spoke, and Atticus spun around.

'Calix,' he replied to the darkness.

'Why are you here?' the voice asked.

'I have come to seek your help,' Atticus replied.

Calix snorted in derision and stepped forward out of the darkness to brush past Atticus, his body hiding the flame of the candle until he reached the light and he spun around to sit down beside it. Atticus followed, glancing over his shoulder as the ladder was withdrawn once more through the hole in the ceiling.

Atticus sat down and studied the Rhodian's haggard face. His pallor was grey but his eyes had lost none of their intensity, and he returned Atticus's gaze over the candle flame. His expression was defiant but Atticus thought he could also see desperation behind his eyes.

'I have just returned to Rome from Sicily,' Atticus began,

and he described to Calix the Carthaginians' inexplicable hesitation in advancing the war.

'And how can I help?' Calix asked warily as Atticus concluded.

'You smuggled Barca out of Lilybaeum,' Atticus said. 'I thought you might know something of his plans, that maybe he confided in you or that you might have overheard something that would explain his strategy.'

Calix nodded, his eyes never leaving Atticus. 'Why should I help *you*?' he asked disdainfully.

'Because, if you do, I will speak to one of the senators on your behalf. He is a powerful man and can ensure the Senate will be lenient when they decide your sentence.'

'The last deal I made with a *Roman* was with that whoreson, Scipio,' Calix replied. 'My testimony for my freedom – and yet I am here.'

'I'm not Roman, I am Greek,' Atticus said, 'and I am true to my word.'

'You are no Greek, Perennis,' Calix spat. 'If you were, you would have no loyalty to Rome, the very city that enslaved our people.'

'My loyalty is not to Rome,' Atticus said defiantly, and he stood up and paced out of the candlelight, suddenly consumed with anger, the Rhodian's words stirring the conflict within him.

'But it is, Perennis. You fight for Rome, and for a people who despise you,' Calix continued, remembering the contempt Scipio had shown towards Atticus and how he had used Perennis's Greek origins to attack his loyalty during the trial. To Calix, Perennis was a blind fool, and he smiled contemptuously as he saw the effect of his words on his enemy.

Atticus paced around in the darkness, stumbling over the waste beneath his feet. He had said he had no loyalty to Rome without thinking but, as he examined his words, he knew them to be true.

'So what do I fight for?' he thought, and he looked to the Rhodian. Calix was a fellow Greek, but his loyalty was to money, not to his homeland. For Atticus, Locri had ceased to be his home from the day he had sailed away at the age of fourteen. The Magna Graecia of his grandfather's time was gone – it no longer existed.

As a pirate hunter, Atticus had fought in the Roman navy to protect his people, the fisherman and traders of the Calabrian coast whom he had known all his life. It was they who commanded his loyalty. But in the war against Carthage he was fighting for a city where he was often treated as an inferior outsider. And yet he had fought on, never shirking from the fight, always conscious of the men who stood beside him in battle, and in that moment Atticus suddenly realized where his loyalty stood. He stopped pacing and remained still for a full minute, repeating his conclusion in his mind, taking strength from it. He walked over to the Rhodian once more.

'Will you help me?' he asked brusquely.

'I cannot,' Calix said with a sneer. 'Barca never spoke to me of his plans. Your journey here has been wasted, Perennis.'

Atticus nodded and turned away. He called for the ladder to be lowered.

'So what now, Perennis?' Calix asked, eager to strike a final blow. 'You will fight on for this cursed city?'

Atticus paused and turned to the Rhodian, 'I do not fight for this city, Calix,' he said. 'I fight for the men who stand beside me in battle. It is they who command my loyalty, not Rome.'

The ladder touched the ground beside Atticus and he ascended, leaving the Rhodian to the solitude of his prison.

In the upper room, Atticus was handed back his weapons.

He left the prison and retraced his steps to the foot of the Curia. He looked up at the Senate house, the very symbol of Rome. The building had spawned many of his enemies, some of whom had taken that fight to the field of battle. But for each of these, there were other Romans who had stood beside Atticus in the fray. Duilius, his advocate in the Senate; Gaius, whose first duty was always to his ship and fellow crewmen, his loyalty above question; Marcus of the Ninth Legion, killed at the battle of Tunis, a grizzled centurion who had trusted Atticus to guard the back of every Roman legionary fighting on land; and Lucius, who had given his life to save his Greek captain.

Atticus lowered his head as one other name came to the fore of his thoughts, a man who had given his hand freely in friendship when they had last met. He, above all other Romans, had stood shoulder to shoulder with Atticus against every enemy.

He glanced one last time at the Curia before setting off across the Forum, eager to return to Fiumicino. For now, the Carthaginians' plans would remain a mystery, but one thing was certain. The war was not over. There were still battles to be fought, and in these Atticus vowed to stand with his Roman comrades and fight for the honourable dead who commanded his loyalty.

Hamilcar paced the study in his house, impatiently waiting for his father to return, his anxiety causing him to mutter curses under his breath. The sound of boisterous playing in the courtyard below distracted him and he moved to the window, peering out to look down upon his three sons. Hannibal, the eldest at seven, was fighting Hasdrubal, the five year old, in a game of mock swordplay, while Mago, the youngest at two, clambered around them, shouting their names in encouragement as they lunged at each other, their youthful aggression held in check by Mago's mispronunciation of their names, causing the older boys to laugh uncontrollably.

Hamilcar was about to shout at them to silence the uproar, but he paused, realizing that the distraction had allowed a couple of minutes to pass when his mind was not consumed by his thoughts of the campaign in Sicily, so he continued to watch them surreptitiously, knowing that if any of them saw him, particularly Hannibal, they would escalate the ferocity of their fight to impress him, a ferocity that always led to injury and tears.

He had arrived back in Carthage only two days before, following a summons from his father, leaving Himilco in charge at Lilybaeum. After many months of frustrating inaction, the message, which spoke of a Roman build-up of forces, had had an unusual effect on Hamilcar: what should have been a disquieting report actually gave him a moment of exhilaration, for the Romans' activities, if true, would escalate the war once more.

He had spoken exhaustively of the unconfirmed reports over the previous two nights with his father, their conversations eventually becoming cyclical, their conclusions the same each time. Hanno had said that only a direct threat against Lilybaeum would make him consider allocating additional forces to Sicily. Now it was possible that threat was about to materialize and, for the first time since Drepana, Hamilcar and his father had grounds to force the Council's hand to commit additional forces to Sicily and push the war to a conclusion.

The sound of his sons' excited voices distracted him again, and he looked out to see his father, Hasdrubal, cross the courtyard, the boys gathered around their grandfather, each shouting to be heard above the others. Hasdrubal had gone to the Council chamber in answer to a summons, and his purposeful stride told Hamilcar his father was returning with news.

He turned from the window and went to the door of his study, opening it as Hasdrubal entered the hall below, the boys' shouts becoming louder in the confines of the house until Hasdrubal shooed them away. He climbed the steps and saw his son looking at him from the study door.

'Well?' Hamilcar said.

Hasdrubal nodded as he approached. 'The reports are confirmed,' he said. 'The Romans are assembling a fleet of some two hundred galleys just north of Ostia. We have it from three different sources, traders who have seen the galleys with their own eyes.'

'But they have yet to sail?' Hamilcar said, pacing the room once more, his mind racing.

'As of four days ago they were still in port,' Hasdrubal said.

'And we know nothing of their plans?' Hamilcar asked.

Hasdrubal shook his head. 'We do not,' he said. 'But I put forward your argument to the Supreme Council that Lilybaeum is the most obvious choice, given the Romans still have a legion encamped nearby.'

'And . . .?' Hamilcar said expectantly,

'The Council has agreed to your proposal,' Hasdrubal said with a smile. 'A fleet is to be assembled here in Carthage in anticipation of responding to whatever advance the Romans make.'

Hamilcar slammed his fist into his open palm in triumph. Time had passed but nothing had changed and Hamilcar thanked Anath, the goddess of war, that the Romans had lost none of their arrogance. They would certainly put to sea once the storms of winter had passed, perhaps believing because of his forces' inertia that Lilybaeum was vulnerable once more. He smiled coldly. That belief, or whatever conceit possessed them, would be their undoing. The forces of Carthage in Sicily might have slumbered but they were far from inert. They could be battle-ready by his command within days, while an additional fleet would soon assemble in the harbour of Carthage, ready for his hand to lead them into battle.

Drepana was merely a prelude. His next victory would be nothing short of annihilation. Beyond that, Hamilcar was determined not to repeat his previous naiveté. He would not return to Carthage to trumpet his victory, nor would he relinquish his forces. He would retain them and, after the Romans had been defeated in pitched battle, he would pursue them relentlessly, even to the very shores of Rome, a punitive voyage to destroy every last galley they possessed and forever crush their ambition to conquer the island of Sicily.

Septimus sat in the bow of the skiff, his rounded *hoplon* shield across his lap, his gaze on the quinquereme ahead. The *Orcus* had been in port for over three weeks, although Septimus had been unable to call on the galley until now, the demands of his rank keeping him in camp. He called for permission to board and quickly climbed up the ladder from the skiff to the main deck, the familiarity of the galley bringing a rough smile to his face.

He went towards the aft-deck and saw Atticus approach to meet him, his hand extended in friendship. Septimus took it. 'It's good to see you, Atticus.'

'And you,' Atticus replied, maintaining the grip.

'What news from Sicily?' Septimus asked, and Atticus told the centurion of his progress over the previous months, the two men lapsing into a conversation as Atticus tried once more to fathom the Carthaginians' plans. They walked to the side rail together.

'I heard about Scipio,' Septimus said, a wry smile on his face.

Atticus nodded, his satisfaction at the demise of his enemy still tainted by the support Scipio's accusations had found amongst the senators, and he told Septimus the details of the trial.

'And where is Baro now?' Septimus asked.

'I don't know,' Atticus replied, 'I only know he hasn't been seen since.'

Septimus tightened his grip on the hilt of his sword as he thought of Baro and Scipio, regretting that he had not been there to stand beside Atticus as he had done when his friend had first faced the senator in the Curia, his command of the IV of the Ninth keeping him in Sicily.

He looked at Atticus's scarred face. So much had happened between them since he had first been assigned to the *Aquila* years before. They had fought together many times, against each other over Hadria, but on the same side against every enemy. He thought of the absolute trust they had always placed in each other in battle and their mutual conviction to stay and fight, side by side, against any foe. The war had yet to be won, the fight was not over, and Septimus knew he should honour the friendship that had been forged in the fires of battle.

He turned to Atticus, his decision made. 'When the fleet sails, the Ninth will sail with them, and I will ask to be assigned to the *Orcus*. As a prefect you could overrule that request, given my previous resignation . . .'

Atticus never hesitated, a smile breaking out on his face once more. 'The command is yours,' he said, and in that simple acceptance the last vestiges of their previous conflict were swept away.

'Duilius has told me of the Ninth's training,' Atticus said, breaking the silence that followed. 'What's your assessment?'

334

'Given time they'll be ready, Atticus,' he said with total conviction. 'Fully trained to the standard of any marine on the *Aquila* before the war.'

Atticus nodded. 'I've already seen how the fleet performs. The remaining experienced captains and I still have a lot of work to do, but by the time the winter storms pass the new crews will be ready to sail south.'

'Then we'll go back to war,' Septimus said, looking forward to the time when the Ninth would once more become a front-line legion.

'We'll go back,' Atticus said. 'Only this time, we'll face the Carthaginians as equals, on their terms.'

'Rome victorious,' Septimus said.

'Rome victorious,' Atticus responded, the phrase taking on a new meaning for him, one that spoke of the loyalty to his comrades that he now knew could never be broken.

CHAPTER EIGHTEEN

Hamilcar looked up at the verdant slopes of the mountain soaring up from the shore of the 'sacred island' to the clouds racing overhead. The sky was a reflection of the sea, the heavy swell following the course of the clouds, racing to keep up under the force of a strong westerly wind. He placed his hand on the side rail, gripping it tightly as the *Alissar* rolled beneath him, and he gazed about him at the Carthaginian fleet holding station in the lee of the island.

Over the winter months, Hamilcar had slowly assembled a fleet of one hundred and sixty galleys in Carthage. Hanno had refused to re-release the Gadir fleet and so Hamilcar had been forced to draw his forces from the minor fleets guarding the African coastline and trading routes. They were skilled sailing crews but he had been forced to admit that they lacked the battle-hardiness of the Gadir fleet, and the cold months had had to be spent reinforcing their training, while waiting for news from Rome that the enemy fleet had sailed.

Reports had arrived four days before, not from Rome but from Lilybaeum – disastrous news that the Romans, with a fleet of two hundred ships, had taken the undefended port of Drepana in a surprise attack from the north. Hamilcar had hastily set sail with his fleet, his course taking him directly to

Hiera, the sacred island of the Aegates, to find Himilco already waiting there for him with the ninety galleys of the Lilybaeum fleet, the very ships they had captured from the Romans at the battle of Drepana over a year before.

Himilco had abandoned the port, fearful of being blockaded and, knowing that a battle with the Romans was inevitable, he had taken with him the entire garrison of a thousand men. It was a bold and decisive move that Hamilcar approved of, although he knew Lilybaeum was now ripe to fall. If the Romans were to attack from the landward side, the population might well panic, and without a garrison to control them they would throw open the gates to save themselves. It was imperative, therefore, that his fleet reach Lilybaeum with all haste, but Hamilcar had nevertheless waited for a favourable wind to give his approach an additional advantage in what were now enemy-infested waters.

With a combined fleet of two hundred and fifty galleys, Hamilcar was confident that he could challenge any blockade of Lilybaeum; but, given the Roman's boldness in bypassing Panormus and taking Drepana, he knew that blockade would never materialize. The Romans were seeking battle. It was surely why they had attacked Drepana without warning, for they had expected to find a Carthaginian fleet there.

Hamilcar had always known the Romans to be arrogant, but given their defeat over a year before in these very waters, their return and audacious attack displayed a level of arrogance that was staggering to behold. Hamilcar's fleet was inexperienced but nonetheless they were Carthaginian, and he outnumbered the Romans by at least fifty ships.

After Drepana he had wanted to push the war to a final conclusion. Now the Romans were handing him that chance, confronting him like a dying warrior reaching for his last weapon, marshalling his final strength for one last great effort.

They would not succeed, Hamilcar thought triumphantly; he would end them, here, in the cold grey waters off the Aegates Islands, and with a shouted command that carried on the wind, he called his fleet to battle stations, knowing that between the sacred island and Lilybaeum he would meet and finally destroy the greatest foe he had every known.

Atticus stood on the foredeck of the *Orcus*, his tunic soaked through from the sea water crashing over the bow rail, the cutwater of the quinquereme slicing through the endless rows of wind-driven waves. The drum master was hammering out standard speed, but the quinquereme was only barely making headway, while Atticus squinted into the wind to the grey horizon and the distant island of Hiera.

He glanced over his shoulder to the rest of the fleet taking shelter around the southernmost headland of Aegusa, the largest of the Aegates Islands and the closest to Lilybaeum, five miles away to the east. He wiped the sea spray from his eyes, searching again for some flash of movement, some sign of colour, anything that would betray the exact position of the Carthaginian fleet in the shadow of Hiera.

He turned and looked back along the length of the *Orcus*. Catulus, the junior consul, was on the aft-deck, standing by the helm, his personal guard close at hand. He stood with his legs apart, braced against the pitch of the deck, his gaze reaching past Atticus to the western horizon, his bearing one of total confidence. The senior consul, Aulus Postumius Albinus, was also the *flamen martialis*, a member of the priesthood, and was forbidden by religious taboo from leaving the city. The position of overall commander had therefore fallen to Catulus.

The junior consul had quickly chosen the *Orcus* as his flagship, wishing to sail with his most experienced prefect, and from the outset he had consulted with Atticus at each stage, reminding Atticus of another junior consul years before on the eve of the battle of Mylae. Catulus knew the limits of his experience, and was content to allow Atticus to make front-line decisions, giving him effective command of the fleet.

Atticus looked to the heavens, knowing that Fortuna was continuing to toy with him. His approach from Rome had been flawless; his tactic of keeping the bulk of the fleet out of the normal trading lanes and away from the sight of land, coupled with avoiding Panormus, had allowed him to take Drepana completely by surprise. But only then did Fortuna reveal her presence. Drepana had been abandoned by the Carthaginian fleet, and although Atticus had been gifted a secure harbour, his ultimate goal to bring the enemy fleet to battle had been thwarted.

He had sent out patrol ships, through which he'd received reports that the only ships the Carthaginians had in the area had fled Lilybaeum and sailed west, another stroke of bad luck that was neatly reversed when the enemy fleet was seen approaching from the south to take up position at Hiera, a staging post for a run at the port of Lilybaeum. Atticus had immediately ordered his fleet to Aegusa, knowing the Carthaginians would have to sail past, but again Fortuna had spun her wheel, stirring up a strong westerly wind that churned the sea into a heavy swell.

Atticus had continued the training of the fleet during the winter, and his confidence had increased during the voyage south from Rome, the disciplined formations of the fleet holding even during the hours of darkness. Individually the seamanship of the Romans would never be of the standard the Carthaginians possessed, a skill learned over a lifetime, but in a massed battle the finer subtleties of seamanship mattered little, and Atticus was confident that his men were trained to a high enough standard to match the enemy.

But now the gods were conspiring to foul those odds, giving the Carthaginians the advantage of a tail wind and the Romans the potentially ruinous disadvantage of facing into a heavy swell. The Roman rowers would have to work twice as hard to take up position against the Carthaginians, and if any of the crews misaligned their hulls, the swell would turn them out of position, leading to collisions and exposing their broadsides to the enemy rams.

Atticus glanced at the new helmsman. He was a master of his craft, a skilled navigator and pilot, but although Atticus had shared the aft-deck with him since Drepana, he had yet to establish the level of trust that he had had in Gaius. The sailing crews were untested in battle and, with the elements against them, any battle fought on this day would be a challenge beyond any he had envisaged. He wished Lucius and Gaius were by his side, two steadfast advisors from whom he could draw counsel, and he looked once more to the western horizon, the wind robbing him of his breath at the moment he spotted the line of dark hulls in the distance.

'Enemy galleys approaching, dead ahead,' the lookout called, and without command the *Orcus* came to battle stations.

Atticus stood silent. The time for deliberation had passed. Now he had to commit one way or the other: withdraw to the safety of Drepana and wait for a better opportunity, or take the fight to the Carthaginians and trust in the men he commanded. He suddenly realized that Septimus had come up to the foredeck and was standing beside him, the centurion looking out beyond the bow rail to the enemy ranks, his expression as hard as iron.

'The final battle,' he said, and Atticus looked to the enemy. If we dare, he thought.

Septimus glanced over his shoulder, looking to his own men on the main deck, Drusus at their head. He was too unskilled in boarding to be given a command in the navy, and so he had accepted a demotion to *optio* in order to remain on board, gladly taking his place beside his former commander.

'They're ready,' Septimus said, referring to his legionaries, the men drawn up in tight ranks, their rounded shields held firmly by their sides.

Atticus nodded. 'They are,' he said, thinking of his own command, the sailing crews – and the simple admission ended his doubts. They were ready and the enemy was at hand. He looked past Septimus and called a runner to his side.

'Signal the fleet. All hands prepare for battle.'

'Enemy galleys ahead!'

'Battle speed. Secure the mainsail,' Hamilcar shouted, and the actions of the crew of the *Alissar* were repeated on the galleys flanking the flagship, the preparations for battle rippling down the length of the fleet. Hamilcar stared at the waters ahead, watching as the Roman battle line extended, the enemy galleys beating directly into the wind, the spray thrown up by their bows as they sliced through the heavy swell visible even from his distant vantage point. Whether through stubborn arrogance or mindless courage, the Romans were obviously determined to precipitate a battle, and Hamilcar sneered disdainfully at their folly.

From the *Alissar*'s position in the centre, Hamilcar looked to his flanks and the expanding line of his own fleet, their deployment hastened by the wind-driven waves. A sliver of annoyance rose within him as he noticed that many of the galleys were not gaining their position with the alacrity he would expect, the less experienced coastal galley crews being unused to large fleet manoeuvres, but he ignored the feeling,

341

vowing instead that after the battle he would ensure that every crew was trained to the level of the Gadir fleet, an exemplar for the entire empire.

The battle line coalesced and hardened into a solid wave of timber, steel and men. Hamilcar moved to the foredeck, glancing left and right down the line, acknowledging the signals relayed from Himilco on the right flank that the Carthaginian line extended beyond that of the Romans, an implicit assurance from the experienced captain that he would allow none to escape to the south.

Hamilcar was captivated once again as he watched the bows of the galleys surge forward with the sweep of each oar stroke, the rams overtaking the swell, catching each wave and slicing through its crest, the hull bearing down through the trough in an unstoppable charge. He let the sight fill his heart and he thought back to the battles he had fought, on the sacred land of Carthage and the cursed earth of Sicily, on the all-encompassing sea, the domain of his ancestors. He thought of his foes, the invidious Romans and the Greek whoreson who had risen in their ranks, and the misguided leaders of his own beloved city who sought to confound his every move. It would all end in the waters ahead, decided on the blunt-nosed tip of a bronze ram or the steel tip of a sword, and Hamilcar ran his gaze across the length of their battle line before focusing dead ahead on the centre of the line and the heart of his foe.

The gap fell to a mile, the final boundary of commitment, the last chance for the combatants to disengage, but the fleets continued to converge without check or alteration. Hamilcar let his hand fall to the hilt of his sword. He drew it slightly and looked to the shard of exposed steel. It was polished, sharpened to a fine edge, and he tilted the blade to catch the sunlight, imprinting the image on his mind, knowing that by the end of the day it would be stained with Roman blood.

'Six hundred yards,' the masthead lookout called, and Hamilcar strode from the foredeck, nodding to his men on the main deck as he passed them, their eyes determined and hostile, locked on the approaching enemy, silently goading them on, waiting for the order to strike. Drepana had steeled the nerve of every man, even those who had not fought that day, the crushing defeat inflicted on the enemy navy exposing the Romans as mortal men, vulnerable to the blade of a sword and the power of a ram. They returned their commander's nod, ready to follow him against the enemy, and Hamilcar felt the awe-inspiring faith of Carthage on his shoulders as he took up his command position beside the helm.

'Four hundred yards,' the lookout called.

'Attack speed,' Hamilcar ordered without hesitation, the entire fleet responding within a ship length. He closed his eyes and whispered a final prayer to Anath, to guide his hand and watch over his men, and when he opened them again, he raised his voice and led his men in a war cry, calling down death upon the enemies of Carthage.

Atticus heard a war cry on the back of the wind, a surging wave of sound that swept over the advancing Roman fleet. It was met with silence by the legionaries, discipline holding them firm. Only the order to attack would unleash their fury; until then, each man would hold that fire within him. Septimus moved among his men, speaking slowly of the battle to come, of how he expected each man to attack without hesitation, without mercy, reminding them of Drepana and the measure of vengeance that their fallen comrades called for from beyond the Styx.

The legionaries stood in silent ranks, rocking slowly with the pitch of the deck, their gaze locked on the enemy, seemingly oblivious to Septimus's words, but each one was heard clearly and, as the order for attack speed was called from the aft-deck, a deep growl came from the men of the IV maniple – a reactive, momentary sound that revealed their readiness for the fight.

Atticus looked to the flanks and the neat formation of the line. The fleet had accelerated to battle speed almost as one, months of training dictating their approach. It was a fine display of seamanship, but one given in open water surrounded by their own galleys. He looked to the enemy, now only two hundred yards away. Once engaged and the battle joined, the lines would become fully entwined, and only then would the true strength of the Roman fleet be revealed.

He glanced at Catulus, the junior consul, standing on the other side of the tiller. No more orders could be given, no more preparations made. Once the gap between the fleets fell to one hundred yards, all would increase to ramming speed and every galley would become a lone fighter. Atticus, as fleet commander, would lose control for those first chaotic minutes, and only after they had passed would he be able to ascertain the level of parity between the crews. If both sides were evenly matched the battle would descend into a determined fight; if one or other crew were much stronger, the battle would become a slaughter. With an acceptance of fate that comes from a lifetime at war, Atticus placed the first assault in the hands of Mars.

One hundred yards.

'Ramming speed,' Atticus shouted, and he indicated a target ship to the helmsman, the *Orcus* shifting slightly beneath him as the attack line was set.

He swept his gaze across the centre of the Carthaginian line, picking out individual ships, the foredecks crammed with men, their faces grotesquely twisted as they roared defiance and hatred. The gap fell to fifty yards, the helmsman adjusting the course of the *Orcus*, countering the galley opposing him, gaining the advantage, bringing the ram to bear.

Atticus glanced to his left and right, at the extended line of the enemy. Suddenly he froze, his mind reacting to a moment of brief recognition, and he looked again, focusing on the masthead banners of a galley a hundred yards further down the line. He stepped forward instinctively, his mind transporting him back over a year to Drepana and a vision of a blood-soaked aft-deck, of Gaius's head cradled in his arms, of Corin, crushed beneath the hull of a galley. It was Barca's flagship.

Atticus looked to the front and the anonymous Carthaginian galley bearing down on the *Orcus*. The lines were now thirty yards apart. It was too late to change course and target another ship. The *Orcus* was committed, but Atticus now knew where the heart of the enemy lay. 'Helmsman, forget the ramming run. Prepare to sweep the starboard oars,' he shouted, and the order was carried forward to the rowing deck as the gap fell to twenty yards. The *Orcus* had gained the angle to ram but Atticus was sacrificing it to avoid the entanglement, needing to get beyond the battle line so he could seek out Barca's galley. Catulus looked on without a word, not understanding the sudden change, putting his trust in the Greek commander.

'Centurion Capito to the aft-deck,' Atticus called, and he saw Septimus respond immediately.

Ten yards.

'Withdraw!' Atticus roared, and the helmsman leaned into the tiller, decreasing the angle of attack to stop the ram from penetrating.

The *Orcus* struck the bow quarter of the enemy galley as Septimus reached the aft-deck, the shuddering blow knocking him off balance, and Atticus shot out his arm to grab him. The ram glanced cleanly off the strake timbers, swinging the stern of the *Orcus* around. The momentum of her charge carried her down the length of the Carthaginian galley, her cutwater snapping off its starboard oars, the unexpected change of attack throwing the enemy crew into confusion.

'All oars, re-engage,' Atticus shouted as the stern emerged into open water and the *Orcus* continued on, the sea clear all the way to the fringes of the western horizon.

Catulus looked over his shoulder to the crippled Carthaginian galley, its crew shouting challenges to return, their individual voices lost amidst the deafening noise of battle – the sound of galleys striking deadly blows against each other, the crack of timbers and the screams of men. He spun around to Atticus, baffled by the decision to alter their attack at the last moment.

'Why did we not ram?' he asked. 'The marines were ready to board. Now that ship will escape under canvas.'

'Let them,' Atticus replied. 'They are minnows, and I have seen the heart of the enemy.'

He turned to Septimus

'Barca's galley is there,' he said in explanation, pointing to a nearby mêlée of ships. 'And we're going to take her.'

Septimus nodded, agreeing without question, though he knew the flagship would be the most heavily manned galley, remembering the enemy command ship at Mylae.

Atticus ordered the helmsman to bring the ship around and the *Orcus* turned broadside to the swell before neatly coming about, giving Atticus an uninterrupted view of the battle. It was chaotic, as he knew it would be, but for an instant he thought the Roman fleet looked to have the upper hand, a judgement he knew was fraught with hope. He focused on the confusion of galleys off the port bow quarter, searching for his prey. He thought again of Corin, whose sharp eyes would have seen Barca's galley by now, and Gaius, whose deft touch on the tiller would have sent the *Orcus*, like the arrow that slew him, into the heart of the enemy.

Within seconds he saw it again, Barca's ship, withdrawing its ram from a stricken Roman galley. He shouted the course change to the helmsman, calling once more for ramming speed. The *Orcus* bore down into the attack, its ram smashing through each rushing wave.

'You have the aft-deck,' Atticus said to the helmsman, and he brought his hand to the hilt of his sword as he strode to the main deck, gathering up a *hoplon* shield as he came up to stand by Septimus's side. The centurion glanced at his friend and nodded, understanding Atticus's need to see this fight through to the end.

Septimus looked to the waters ahead and Barca's galley, the enemy as yet unaware of the *Orcus*, since its attack run was coming from the reverse side of the battle line. He drew his sword, an action followed by Drusus, his prompt order bringing the legionaries to the cusp of battle, their swords singing out as they swept the blades from their scabbards.

Septimus turned to his men, holding his sword aloft. 'For Rome!' he shouted, and the men cheered as one, hammering the back of their shields with their swords, the noise coming to a deafening roar that put steel in each man's heart for the brutal fight ahead.

'And for her fallen,' Atticus said to himself as he drew his own sword amidst the cheering of the legionaries.

The *Alissar* re-engaged her oars at attack speed, the helmsman swinging the bow away from the flagship's first blood and Hamilcar cheered in triumph with his crew, memories of Drepana flooding his mind, and the incredible prize that was once more there for the taking, an entire Roman fleet ripe for capture. He looked to the battle beyond the *Alissar*, already forming in his mind the signal he would send to his ships to ensure that most of the Roman galleys be spared from sinking; but, as he looked out over the portside rail, the smile died on his face.

Not thirty yards away, one of his ships was being overwhelmed by a Roman boarding party, the attack being repeated on a dozen other galleys within his range of view, while others had fallen victim to Roman ramming runs. His own galleys had scored only a handful of hits. Even where they had boarded, the Roman legionaries were pushing back the assault and reversing the attack.

Hamilcar put his hands on the rail for support, a terrible dread overwhelming him. He had believed his understrength crews would still outmatch the hapless Romans, his faith based on his crushing victory at Drepana, but the enemy had come out fighting, somehow overcoming their previous inadequacies in seamanship and naval combat. The doubts that had consumed him after Ecnomus flooded back, deriding him for his blind faith in Carthage's naval superiority. He felt helpless. How could he defeat such a foe? He had crushed their army at Tunis and their fleet at Drepana. The gods had commanded a tempest to shatter their galleys, and yet each time the Romans had returned, each time eager to fight on, rebuffing any talk of peace, their navy ever renewed, ever undaunted, relentlessly sailing out against every fleet Hamilcar could muster, their strength of will an unconquerable force that knew no bounds.

In the past the Romans had succeeded using their cursed boarding ramps, or at Hermaeum using sheer weight of numbers, but at Drepana Carthage had finally been able to use the one advantage they had always possessed, seamanship, and the result was complete victory. Now it seemed that their one advantage had been surpassed. How had the Romans channelled their resources and strength of will to create a fleet that could outmatch one from the home waters of Carthage, and who amongst them could command such a force?

'Galley on a ramming course off the starboard beam,' the lookout called frantically and Hamilcar spun around.

A lone galley sailed stark against the empty seascape, approaching on an unanticipated angle of attack that only the vigilant lookout had spotted, the entire crew sharing their commander's interest in events on the port side. Hamilcar was stunned and he lost vital seconds as the Roman galley came to within a hundred yards of the *Alissar*.

'Hard to starboard, turn into her,' Hamilcar roared, his wits returning, and he ran to the tiller, putting his weight behind the helmsman's turn. 'Ramming speed!'

The Alissar came about swiftly, the sweep of the battle line passing before her bow. Hamilcar kept his eyes on the ram of the lone galley, watching it as it turned inside the *Alissar*'s turn, its course ever locked amidships of his galley. His gaze swept up and suddenly his hand fell from the tiller, the sight of the masthead banners triggering an automatic grab for the hilt of his sword.

The Greek's ship. Perennis.

He was alive, and in an instant Hamilcar's questions were answered, his doubts falling away to be replaced by cold determination. Here was the enemy: not the forces of Rome, but the demon who had honed their strength.

The gap fell to fifty yards and Hamilcar ran to the main deck, his sword clearing his scabbard as he ran.

'All hands, brace for impact,' he shouted. 'Prepare to repel boarders.'

He moved to the starboard rail, his men bunching behind him, ready for the assault. The oncoming galley filled his field of vision and he threw up his shield as a black rain of spears

349

erupted from the bow of the Greek's ship, falling heavily on his crew, the barbs finding prey in the massed ranks. His crew yelled in pain and anger, defiance steeling their nerves, and they called on the inexorable fight, eager to repay every injury, every drop of blood.

Hamilcar let them roar, his own mouth clamped shut in a thin line of hatred. The fate of his fleet might be beyond his control. The *Alissar* was moments from damnation and he could not save her. But Hamilcar vowed that if on this day he should pass under the hand of Mot, the god of death, he would not go alone. The Greek would go before him.

Atticus stood with every muscle tensed, the impact seconds away. His sword felt light in his hand, his shield was held tight against his shoulder and he breathed deeply as the final yards were covered. His mind was filled with the din of battle, and the utter conviction that comes on the cusp of mortal danger, when the spirit has overruled the instinct and committed the warrior to battle, when the enemy's numbers become inconsequential, their strength irrelevant. Only the man who stands defiant before the warrior matters; in the midst of a greater battle, he fights not for victory but for survival.

Atticus was propelled forward as the *Orcus* struck home, the deck bucking wildly beneath him, the six-foot bronze ram of the quinquereme driving deeply into the hull of the Carthaginian galley, the air rent with the sound of timbers snapping under the hammer blow and the terrified cries of men who could foresee their death in the cold water that rushed past the ram into the lower decks.

Atticus used the impact to begin his dash to the fore rail, Septimus running at his right shoulder, the legionaries coming on behind like the scourge of Nemesis, bearing retribution for the loss at Drepana. Atticus jumped up on to the rail, never hesitating as he cleared the four foot gap to the main deck of the enemy galley, his shield and sword charged against the Carthaginians who were re-forming after the shock of impact. He slammed into an enemy soldier, his momentum throwing the man back against the throng behind, the Carthaginian ranks attempting to expel the invaders before they could gain a foothold.

Atticus lashed out with all his fury, knowing the first seconds were vital, that the enemy defence had to be checked until the legionaries could board in force. The attackers were few, heavily outnumbered, constricted by the narrow sliver of deck they controlled. The *corvus* put forty men on an enemy deck in twenty seconds, but now they crossed in twos and threes, and the momentum of their attack stalled as many took the place of fallen legionaries in the front line.

Atticus fought on, ever conscious of the hollow sensation at the base of his spine, the treacherous space behind him, a thin rail separating him from the oblivion of a pitiless sea trapped between two opposing hulls. He struck out low with his sword, concentrating on the enemy in front of him, constantly fighting the temptation to check his exposed flank, knowing he had to trust the legionary at his side, to put his faith in the skill of the man fighting next to him.

The Carthaginian line hardened as the initial strength of the Roman charge was absorbed and Atticus bunched his weight behind his shield as he felt the first counter-surge from deep within the enemy ranks. The pendulum had swung back in the Carthaginians' favour, their numbers and command of a wider front allowing them to push their ranks forward from the back, giving their front line no choice but to step deeper into the Roman assault in an attempt to push the attack line back in turn.

Atticus heard a roar of command from his side, and out of

the corner of his eye he noticed that Septimus stood beside him, the centurion's voice carrying clearly above the clash of steel and the cries of death and fury. Behind he could hear the deeper tone of Drusus's voice, urging the men forward against the crush, harnessing the stamina of soldiers bred on the march, their strength halting the Carthaginian surge.

The battle line became compressed, forcing Atticus to shorten his sword thrusts, each riposte and recovery of his blade testing the strength of his sword arm as he drove his weapon back into the fray, a defender not inches from his chest, the man's eyes locked on Atticus's, his roar of defiance lost in the noise of battle, the spittle from the Carthaginian's war cry mingling with the sweat on Atticus's face as he fought on and on.

The front line was a shambles, a place of butchery, where men's lives were sacrificed for inches of deck space and the slain fell only where the crush allowed. The deck underfoot was coated with the blood of both sides, the battle line becoming static as the pressure equalized on all sides. The pendulum of advantage had swung back from the Carthaginians, but only to the nadir of its arc. It dangled over the capricious battle line, waiting to see which side would break first.

Hamilcar stood in the midst of his men, calling to them to push ever onwards, to sweep the enemy from the deck of the *Alissar*, to fight as if the Romans were threatening the very walls of sacred Carthage. His senses picked up the slight tilt in the deck beneath him, his galley already dying, its final demise stayed only by the Roman ram deep within its bowels, keeping the *Alissar* afloat. It was a realization that put further steel in his heart and he heaved forward with his men, robbing those fighting at the front of the room to wield their swords, sacrificing them in an effort to reverse the Roman attack.

The pressure increased and again Hamilcar called for his

line to advance, his breath catching in the crush of men, the grunts and gasps of the heaving mass overcoming the sound of clashing steel in the battle line. Hamilcar looked to the row of Roman helmets not six feet away, his eyes drawn to the tallest man in the centre. He was the centurion who had stood beside the Greek before the battle of Cape Hermaeum.

The sight caused Hamilcar to redouble his efforts and the men around him took heart from the determination of their commander, their war cries reaching a ferocity that emboldened the Carthaginian ranks. The line seemed to tremble, like a bow drawn to its furthest limits, a shuddering tension that threatened release, and Hamilcar felt his blood lust intensify as he suddenly took a full step forward, the pressure abating in front of him, his men responding with a savage cheer as the Carthaginian line advanced.

Septimus stared coldly over the leading edge of his shield at the Carthaginian soldier inches from his face, the man screaming a curse in guttural Punic, his face twisted in exertion as he tried to push the Roman line back. Septimus struck out with his sword, blindly judging the angle of attack, and the Carthaginian's scream turned to one of agony, blood erupting from his mouth as Septimus twisted his blade to savage the flesh and free his sword. The man slumped, unable to fall freely, and Septimus turned his shoulder slightly to clear his sword, ready for the next attack.

The fight seemed unrelenting but, while his legs ached from the effort of holding back the flood of Carthaginian warriors, his sword arm felt tireless, the close-quarter fighting a natural environment for the *gladius* in his hand, the simple thrust and withdrawal of the blade an almost reflex movement.

His men around him fought without check or mercy, the bodies of the enemy slain laid thick before them, and Septimus judged the Carthaginians were losing two or even three men to every Roman lost. Again the pressure increased and Septimus tensed the muscles on his lower legs, pushing the hobnails on his sandals into the timber deck to give him purchase under the surface of viscous blood and viscera. He was staggered by the intensity of the Carthaginian defence, the sheer blind fury of an enemy that would use the leading edge of their ranks as a ram to break through the Roman line.

A Carthaginian soldier heaved over his fallen comrade and Septimus struck out again, stabbing low, the crush turning his blade off true. He sliced through the edge of his opponent's inner thigh, a brutal injury that was a death sentence in a fight where rotation out of the battle line was impossible, and Septimus stared into the terrified, pain-twisted face of the Carthaginian before striking out again with impunity, his opponent unable to defend himself in the agony of his injury.

Septimus withdrew his sword, ready to strike again, when he was arrested by a blood-chilling sensation down the left side of his body. An incredible surge swept through his shield arm and down his leg, a force that surmounted all that had come before, and he felt his body give way under the strain, his mind registering the cheer of the Carthaginians as the entire Roman line was driven back a pace.

A sudden panic overwhelmed him and he shouted to his men to hold fast, the call taken up by Atticus by his side and Drusus to his rear. It was a forlorn command, and within seconds another foot of deck space was lost. Septimus lashed out with his sword, the blade finding exposed flesh, but the pressure never slackened. Cries of alarm to his rear rang out and he looked over his shoulder through the crush of legionaries that filled the six-foot deep sliver of Roman-held deck. The side rail was giving way and Septimus stared in horror as three men disappeared over the side, their fall to the sea lost in the rising chaos, their deaths sealed by their heavy armour.

He spun around, his conscious thoughts receding under a terrible fury, and the knuckles of his bloodstained sword hand turned white under the strength of his grip. If his men were to die, they would die fighting the enemy, not like vermin cast overboard. He summoned up the full measure of his will, knowing he had to reverse the momentum of the enemy's charge.

'Men of the Ninth!' he yelled, and the legionaries around him looked to their centurion. 'Prepare to redeploy!'

They roared in reply, a ferocious affirmation to a commander they had followed into the maw of death.

'Wedge formation!' Septimus roared, and he immediately twisted his body to the side and shoved forward with all his strength, his shield angled to drive between two Carthaginians to his front in a desperate attempt to negate the enormous strength of the Carthaginian line, to force a breach and give his men a fighting chance.

Atticus followed Septimus without hesitation, pushing against the Carthaginian to the centurion's left, his body angled to guard Septimus's flank. The strength of the Carthaginian line was concentrated in the advance forward while sideways their cohesion was weaker, and the sudden lunge of the wedge formation drove the leading edge deep into the enemy ranks. The legionaries fought with brute aggression, punching their swords into the Carthaginian ranks, and they fed into the back end of the wedge, completely changing the aspect of their attack within seconds.

The Carthaginians responded, absorbing the initial momentum of the Roman counter-charge, but the respite had been gained; the Romans were no longer threatened with being pushed into the sea. Now the fight was on two wings, their backs to fellow legionaries, but in escaping the fate ordained by the Carthaginians, Septimus had gambled all. If they could not force a breach and split the Carthaginian front, they would be surrounded, and slaughtered like the men who stood their ground at Tunis.

Atticus grunted as he wrenched his sword free from the flesh of a Carthaginian soldier. His throat was dry, his breathing laboured, and he had a vile taste of blood and sweat in his mouth. His shield arm was numb, with only the straps to his forearm holding the *hoplon* in place, and his shoulder registered the strike of yet another blade while his body screamed for rest. He retched bile into the back of his throat as his battle lust demanded greater effort.

He sensed Septimus beside him, the centurion cleaving a path through the enemy ranks, and Atticus fought to keep pace, knowing that if any man were to become isolated he would be overwhelmed in seconds. The tip of the wedge was halfway across the deck and the amorphous Carthaginian formation continued to adapt, concentrating their numbers ahead of the wedge, trying to blunt the head of the attack. But it was a forlorn hope; the Romans would not be stopped and they pressed further on, while overhead the pendulum of battle followed their course.

Hamilcar shouted to his men to stand fast, his call lost in the din of battle, heard only by those closest to him; their scant numbers could do little to stem the momentum of the Roman advance. He had been moments from victory, but the disciplined Roman soldiers had broken out of his vice and Hamilcar realized that the fate that was befalling his fleet would soon meet his crew. Split in two, Hamilcar knew his men would founder, unable to stand against a wall of Roman legionaries who no longer feared an enemy to their rear. That moment of collapse was but moments away and Hamilcar accepted the inevitable, turning his fury to the fight within a fight he was honour bound to seek.

He looked to the head of the Roman formation, seeing again the towering stature of the centurion and, at his side, through the crush of men, he saw the Greek's scarred face. He went to press his way forward but just then he sensed the first ripples of retreat in the men around them, the temper of their war cries changing, many of them glancing over their shoulders, no longer looking to the enemy at hand. He shouted one last time at his men, calling on them to take heart for Carthage and the *Alissar*, but they were beyond hearing, the instinct to survive resurfacing through the fog of battle lust.

The Romans reached the far rail and almost as one the Carthaginians stepped back, as if a command had been issued, the seasoned warriors knowing the Romans could no longer be defeated in formation fighting, knowing that from now, each man would stand alone, and that Mot already walked amongst them, selecting those who would be spared and those who would follow him through the gates of the underworld.

Hamilcar alone stood steady, his eyes locked on the Greek, the separating mass of his men giving him a clear line of vision. Perennis was but ten yards away, his sword charged outward, the Romans already in a line that would sweep the length of the deck. One of Hamilcar's men bumped against him as he stepped back but Hamilcar ignored him, the command of his men no longer important. He was a warrior of Carthage and his enemy stood before him: nothing else mattered. He drew in a breath, steeling his will for the fight and he roared out a single word of challenge: 'Perennis!'

*

Atticus heard his name clearly and he darted around, seeing Hamilcar standing square while those around him backed away. He reacted without thinking, surging forward from the Roman line, his sword held high as he roared Barca's name in answer. Behind him he heard the command for the lines to advance, one facing forward and the other aft, but Atticus ignored them. He was unfettered, and the enemy who had taken much from him stood to his fore.

The Carthaginians were retreating but one turned to challenge Atticus. Without check, he bunched his weight behind his shield and shoved him aside, never taking his eyes off Barca. His brought his sword down and, as he covered the final yards, he saw Barca drop into a defensive crouch, his face a belligerent mask of hatred, his mouth opened wide as he bellowed a war cry.

Atticus slashed his sword around, using all the force of his momentum to land a strike on Hamilcar's flank. Hamilcar dropped his shield, accepting the blade, but the force of the blow knocked Hamilcar off balance and he sidestepped before bringing his own sword around, looking to strike the Greek in the flank as he turned into the fight. Atticus parried the blade, circling his sword in a wide arc to expose Hamilcar's centre, but the Carthaginian sensed the danger and he whipped his sword back to break the contact.

The two men stepped in to close the distance between them, neither man fighting for space or looking to circle his enemy. Their blind hatred drove them deeper into close combat, their eyes locked on each other, silently repeating the curses and vows of retribution for losses suffered through years of warfare. Hamilcar slammed the edge of his shield into Atticus's shoulder and stabbed forward with his sword. Atticus reacted reflexively, swiping down with his own weapon, and although he parried the strike, the tip of Hamilcar's blade sliced across his thigh, drawing first blood.

Atticus backed off but Hamilcar followed through, never allowing him to regroup, and the Carthaginian used his momentum to begin a series of sequenced strikes, his sword becoming a blur of steel that Atticus could only avoid by giving in to his instincts, his sword arm reacting faster than conscious thought. Again Atticus felt the weight of fatigue but he refused to relent, knowing that a second's respite would cost him his life and leave the deaths of Gaius and Corin unavenged.

The thought steeled his determination and he stood fast, drawing on Hamilcar's attack, not willing to give one further step to his enemy. He matched Hamilcar's ferocity, his strength finding reserves in his will to finally end the fight. He looked for the chance to counter-attack but Hamilcar's assault never abated, his sword strikes constantly pushing Atticus to defend with ever-increasing desperation. A cold panic crept into his thoughts, a dread terror that Hamilcar was but seconds away from penetrating his defence. He furiously suppressed the growing fear in his mind, searching for a way through, and suddenly he saw a weakness in the Carthaginian's attack.

Hamilcar's blade hammered off his shield and Atticus pushed out against the strike, knocking the Carthaginian's sword away, exposing his centre. Hamilcar reacted to the threat, bringing his shield in close for the expected sword strike, but instead Atticus suddenly whipped his own shield back around, the heavy iron edging striking Hamilcar in the side of the face, and the Carthaginian wheeled away, stunned by the blow. Atticus seized the chance and stabbed forward with his sword, the tip finding Hamilcar's exposed right shoulder. The blade punched through his defences, the sword driving deeply into his flesh before Atticus whipped it back, twisting the blade as he did. Hamilcar screamed in pain as he fell to the deck, landing at the foot of the Roman line, which had already advanced halfway across the main deck.

A legionary made to finish the Carthaginian foe at his feet, but Atticus shot forward, his sword staying the fatal strike as the line advanced beyond the fallen Carthaginian commander.

'Finish it,' Hamilcar cursed as he looked up at Atticus, his hand clasped over his wound.

Atticus stared down at his enemy, his thoughts still reeling from the fight, wondering why he had lunged forward to save Hamilcar from the legionary's blade. Hamilcar saw Atticus's hesitation and he tried to raise his sword, but Atticus swiped it away with a force that knocked the weapon from his hand and it clattered across the deck. Atticus brought the tip of his sword over Hamilcar's chest but again he paused. The sounds of cheering and Roman trumpets signalling victory rang through the air.

'What are you waiting for?' Hamilcar demanded angrily.

Atticus searched his mind for the answer. Hamilcar was beaten, the fight was won, and although his battle lust called for the final strike, he could not deliver it. He thought of Gaius and Corin, of Lucius, and how they had always fought with honour. His enemy lay at his feet, unarmed, and for all the retribution his sword demanded, Atticus knew that if he killed Hamilcar now, the dishonour of slaying a defenceless foe would blacken the memory of the very men he had fought for. He lowered his sword.

'It's finished,' he said and he stepped back.

Hamilcar tried to struggle up, his face etched in pain and anger.

'You would spare me?' he asked, the dishonour of absolute defeat robbing him of the will to survive the fight.

Atticus nodded, thinking once more of his fallen crew. 'I will not kill an unarmed man,' he said.

Hamilcar scoffed. 'Is this Greek honour?' he asked scornfully.

'No,' Atticus replied. 'Roman.'

And he turned away, sheathing his sword as he did so, the base of the hilt slamming home against the locket of the scabbard, a solid strike that marked the end of the fight. He walked over to the side rail, stepping over the slain as he did, Roman and Carthaginian, their lives given in the final act of a bloody war. Beyond was the restless sea, its surface churned by a wind that swept the stench of battle from the air, its black depths oblivious to the fate of men who had fought to call themselves masters of its domain.

EPILOGUE

The chariots moved slowly through the petal-filled air, the horses nodding their heads skittishly as the deafening roar of the crowd washed over the triumphal march. The narrow streets were festooned with decorations and the spear tips of the legionaries brushed against the low hanging garlands, their ranks compressed by the cheering masses that lined the route to the Forum Magnum.

Caius Lutatius Catulus, the junior consul, rode in the van, his chariot succeeded by a hundred slaves, carrying aloft a single Carthaginian bronze ram as a symbol of his victory, a prize that would take a place of honour at the foot of the column raised by Duilius after his victory at Mylae. He wore a purple toga, a symbol of victory, and he raised his hand to the sound of trumpets as he emerged from the street into the Forum.

Behind the consul's entourage, Atticus stood tall in his chariot with Septimus by his side, the IV of Ninth marching as a guard of honour in their wake, Drusus at the head of the maniple, his stern face at odds with the ecstatic expressions of the crowd. Both men were silent, any conversation impossible in the tumult, and they looked in awe upon the incredible outpouring of joy from the citizenry of Rome.

Carthage had been defeated and made subject to an unequal peace; the island of Sicily had been gained and the enemy forced to pay an indemnity of 2,200 Euboean talents each year for the next twenty years, a staggering sum that would fill the coffers of the city and end the taxes levied for the war.

The Roman prisoners taken at Tunis and Drepana had been returned, reuniting men thought dead with their families, while the Carthaginians had paid extortionate ransoms for the return of their own. Though many of them had already been returned to Africa, Catulus had insisted on delaying the departure of a select few so they could be paraded in his triumphal march.

Hamilcar marched at the head of this group, followed by the senior commanders and noble-born captains of his fleet. His head was held high, an outward display of pride that he could not marshal, and his gaze bored into the back of the Greek, Perennis, and the Roman centurion by his side. His father had paid a crippling sum for his release, a shame that went unfelt in a heart cauterized by defeat and ignominy. What remained was utter hatred, and Hamilcar felt his lungs burn with every breath he took of the cursed air of Rome.

The torment was pitiless, the crowds around him jeering and spitting curses in a language that had become abhorrent to his ear. His thoughts turned to home and his sons and how he would have to stand before them. Hasdrubal and Mago were too young to understand, but Hannibal was astute beyond his years and he would understand his father's humiliation. It was a realization that fed Hamilcar's hatred and he had already decided he would not shield his boys from the truth. In time they would all know of his hatred for Rome; it would become central to their characters, their ambitions and their loyalty. Carthage would always have enemies, in Africa, Iberia or beyond, but for Hamilcar, the Barcid clan would bay only for the blood of one people, the Romans, and he held close the hope that one day the sons of Hamilcar Barca would exact a terrifying measure of revenge in the name of Carthage.

Atticus stepped off the back of his chariot at the foot of the Curia steps. He began to ascend with Septimus by his side, the cheers of the crowd increasing as they recognized the commander of the fleet and his centurion. Their names were known throughout Rome, endlessly proclaimed by the orators hired by Duilius to stand at the corners of every Forum, and the crowd surged forward against the cordon of legionaries.

Atticus walked with his eyes upturned to the top of the steps and towards the assembled leaders of Rome: Aulus Postumius Albinus, the senior consul in the centre, Catulus by his side and, behind them both, Duilius, who nodded with a smile as he caught Atticus's eye. Atticus had trod this path before, after the battle of Mylae, but so much had changed since then. On that day, Duilius had offered him a place by his side in the heart of the city, but Atticus had declined, believing he would never call Rome his home, that his destiny lay elsewhere. Now he was about to confound that belief and forever bind his fate to Rome's. He turned at the top of the steps and looked out over the crowd, hearing his name amongst those shouted in celebration, the sound filling his heart with pride.

The senior consul stretched out his arms and the noise abated to a clamorous din. Albinus began his speech, his words reaching only those at the front of the crowd. He spoke of Catulus and the defeat of the Carthaginian fleet, of the strength of Rome and how none could stand against her, and how Sicily was merely the beginning of a new and incredible opportunity for the Republic to expand its borders across the sea that had once marked the boundary of their ambitions.

The crowd roared in support, their cheers rippling across

the breath of the Forum, an infectious celebration that touched even those who could not hear the consul's words. Albinus called for quiet once more and he ordered Atticus to stand before him.

'Citizens of Rome, people of the Republic,' he announced. 'Today we honour one man who stands shoulder to shoulder with Consul Catulus, a man who commanded the fleet to victory and made safe the future of this city. For this deed and all others, I hereby declare Atticus Milonius Perennis to be a citizen of Rome of the equestrian class.'

Again the crowd roared in approval, their cheers reaching a crescendo as the senior consul took Atticus's hand. Amidst the tumult, the senators nearest to Atticus offered their congratulations. Atticus smiled as Duilius stepped forward, knowing that the senator had orchestrated the endowment of citizenship, and they shook hands as they had many times before, as allies and friends. Atticus turned and sought out Septimus, the centurion shouldering his way through a knot of senators to reach his friend and they stood before each other.

'Welcome to Rome, citizen,' Septimus said with a smile, and Atticus laughed as he took his friend's hand.

Septimus stretched out his other hand and turned Atticus towards the crowd.

'Down there,' he said, and he indicated the front row of the crowd at the foot of the steps.

Atticus looked and he immediately saw Hadria staring up at him. She looked as she had done the first night he met her, and in an instant his heart relived the sensations of that first encounter. She was smiling, her face lit with an ecstatic glow that spoke of every feeling she had ever shared with him. To her side was Antoninus, her father. He too was smiling; as Atticus caught his eye, the former centurion nodded slightly.

Atticus looked to Hadria again and he realized that the most precious thread that had once bound him to Rome was re-forming within him, that the social barriers that had once severed that bond had fallen, never to be rebuilt, and he returned her smile.

He looked out over the crowd to the temples and build-ings surrounding the Forum, and beyond to the Servian Wall that encompassed the city. He could see the verdant haze that marked the southern horizon, and in his mind's eye he travel-led over two hundred leagues to the city of Locri. There, the bones of his ancestors lay in arid soil, generations deep. They had been proud people, as was their son, and Atticus thought once more on the city that was now his home and the fellow Romans who stood about him. He would always be of Locri and Magna Graecia, his ancestors deserved no less, but from this day he would also be of Rome, and in his heart he was proud that, one day, his sons would be as he had become: Roman.

HISTORICAL NOTE

Master of Rome opens with a brief account of the Battle of Tunis in 255 BC. The Carthaginians led their attack on the Roman infantry line with elephants, while the Roman cavalry, who were outnumbered by four to one, were quickly routed. Thereafter the Carthaginian cavalry attacked the flanks of the hard-pressed legionaries and only two thousand Romans on the left escaped, while Marcus Atilius Regulus led a brief but ultimately unsuccessful breakout at the head of five hundred men. The Carthaginian army was led by a Spartan, Xanthippus, who, according to Polybius, the Greek historian, left Carthage after the victory.

Upon hearing news of the defeat, the two consuls for that year, Marcus Aemilius Paullus and Servius Fulvius Paetinus Nobilior led three hundred and fifty ships to Aspis to evacuate the survivors. They were challenged by two hundred Carthaginian ships and a brief battle ensued off Cape Hermaeum, one that ended in defeat for the Carthaginians with the loss of one hundred and fourteen ships captured. Polybius tells us that the consuls were eager to build on this defeat by attacking cities on the southwestern coast of Sicily. They were advised against this by the experienced seamen of the fleet, due to the likelihood of adverse weather; however, they ultimately ignored this advice and the Roman fleet, enlarged with captured Carthaginian galleys, was caught in a storm off Camarina. All but eighty ships were destroyed. Estimates of the dead vary, but certainly run into the tens of thousands.

Gnaeus Cornelius Scipio *Asina* was elected consul in 254 BC, a significant political achievement given his defeat at Lipara six years earlier, and with Aulus Atilius Caiatinus they captured Panormus after a successful siege.

The fate of Marcus Atilius Regulus after the Battle of Tunis is shrouded in myth. Polybius does not record his fate; however, other historians writing of the events hundreds of years later claim that he travelled to Rome as a Carthaginian ambassador, only to advise the Romans to reject any agreement. Bound by honour, he then returned to Carthage where he was tortured and killed.

The siege of Lilybaeum began in 250 BC. From the outset the Romans had difficulties imposing a blockade and the Carthaginians' local knowledge of the shoals allowed them to breach the siege line several times. The most notable of these blockade runners was a man known as 'The Rhodian'. He was Carthaginian, although in *Master of Rome* I have changed his nationality for narrative purposes, and he bested the Roman fleet many times before he was eventually caught.

In 249 BC, as the siege progressed at Lilybaeum, the consul for that year, Publius Claudius Pulcher, decided to mount a surprise attack on the Carthaginian fleet anchored at nearby Drepana. Prior to the battle he undertook a ritual to invite the favour of the gods; however, when the sacred chickens refused to eat he is said to have thrown them overboard in a rage, demanding that they drink instead.

The ensuing battle unfolded as described. The Roman fleet arrived in disarray at Drepana after a night-time approach

370

and the Carthaginian fleet slipped out of the inner harbour only to turn and engage the unprepared Roman line, hemming them in against the coastline. The Romans were heavily defeated, with ninety-three ships captured, although Pulcher escaped with some thirty ships. He was subsequently tried for the crime of *perduellio* for his defeat. Drepana is notable as it marked the only large-scale naval battle that the Carthaginians won over the course of the entire war.

Given the defeat at Drepana (and subsequent destruction in a storm of another Roman fleet off Cape Pachynus, near Syracuse, which I did not include in *Master of Rome*), it is possible that the Carthaginians could have pushed the war to a conclusion at this point. However, they did not exploit the opportunity and while the Romans continued to fight on land, the Carthaginians resorted to indecisive raiding of the southern coastline of Italy.

In 243 BC the Romans decided to build a new fleet. Given the scale of their previous losses it is a decision that speaks to their desire to win at all costs, and two hundred quinque-remes were built using funds donated by private citizens. As before, Lilybaeum and Drepana were threatened, and Polybius states that Rome's aim was to force the Carthaginians into a decisive battle.

The Romans crews worked hard to prepare for battle and by 241 BC they were well trained, fed and equipped. In contrast, after Drepana, the Carthaginians had decommissioned many of their ships and it took them some time to muster a fleet of some two hundred and fifty galleys to counter this new threat from Rome.

On the 10 March 241 BC the two fleets clashed in what was to be the final battle of the war. The Roman fleet was com-manded by consul Caius Lutatius Catulus, supported by a senior praetor, Quintus Valerius Falto. The Carthaginians were led by a man named Hanno, while Hamilcar Barca commanded the army on land (as before I placed Barca in command of the naval battle for narrative purposes). The weather was firmly in the favour of the Carthaginian fleet and, with the wind to their backs, they sailed towards Lilybaeum from the Aegates Island of Hiero (present-day Marettimo). Catulus, faced with a heavy swell, gambled on the skill of his crews, and, anxious not to allow the Carthaginian fleet to reach the army besieged at Lilybaeum, sailed out from another of the islands to intercept the Carthaginians. The battle was hard fought but the Romans were victorious, and Polybius states that the Carthaginians lost fifty ships sunk and seventy captured while others escaped after the wind changed during the battle.

Aegates Islands was the decisive victory that the Romans had planned for, and it ended the First Punic War. Hamilcar Barca and Caius Lutatius Catulus negotiated the terms. The central conditions of the peace were: complete evacuation of all Carthaginian forces from Sicily, the return of all Roman prisoners freely while the Carthaginians had to pay a ransom for their own, and the payment of an indemnity of 3,200 Euboean talents over twenty years to the Roman state. The treaty was duly signed, ending twenty-three years of war between the two states.

Rome's victory put an end to Carthaginian naval dominance of the western Mediterranean; however, unlike after previous campaigns against enemies on the Italian peninsula, Rome made no attempt to absorb Carthage into its Republic, either as an ally or a settled colony, primarily because the Roman state, exhausted after a twenty-three year conflict, did not have the resources to fully subdue Carthage.

The Carthaginian power base in Africa and Spain remained intact and within a generation the two cities would once again be at war. It was a war fought by the ancestors of the first conflict, with the son of Hamilcar Barca, Hannibal, leading his army over the Alps into the heart of the Roman Republic, only to be defeated years later, by the most famous son of the Scipio family line: Publius Cornelius Scipio Africanus.